THE GHOSTS OF
THORWALD PLACE

THE GHOSTS OF
THORWALD PLACE

HELEN POWER

CamCat
Books

CamCat Publishing, LLC
Brentwood, Tennessee 37027
camcatpublishing.com

This is a work of fiction. Names, characters, places, and incidents are either products of the author's imagination or are used fictitiously.

Hardcover ISBN 9780744301434
Paperback ISBN 9780744300901
Large-Print Paperback ISBN 9780744300918
eBook ISBN 9780744300925
Audiobook ISBN 9780744300932

Library of Congress Control Number: 2021938212

Cover and book design by Maryann Appel

5   3   1   2   4

For my mother,
who always believed in me.

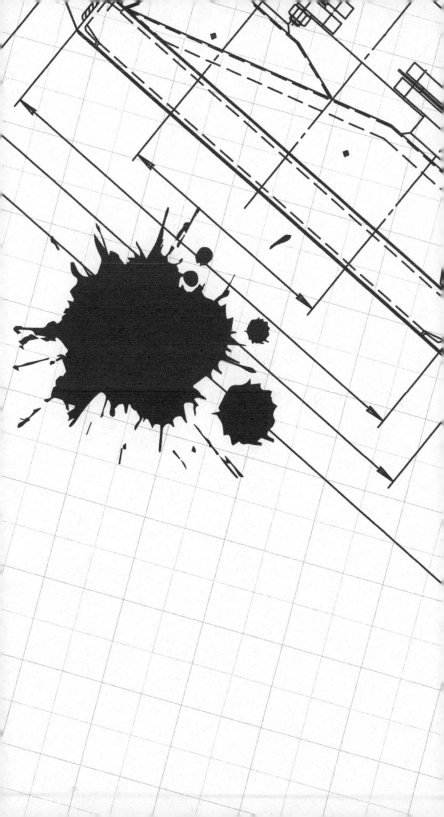

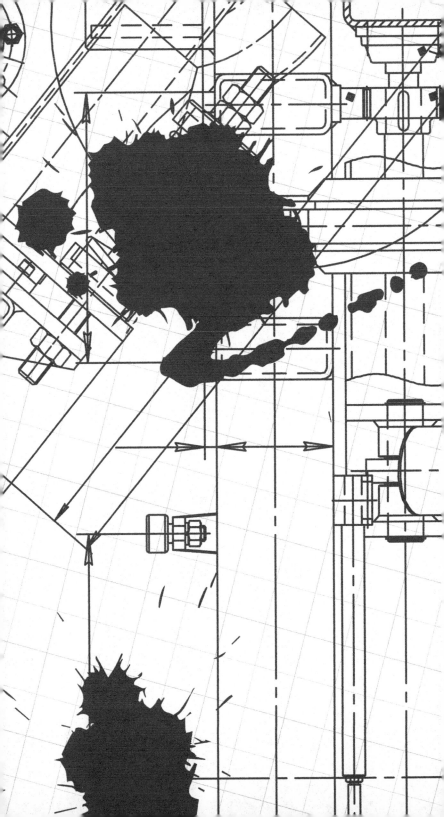

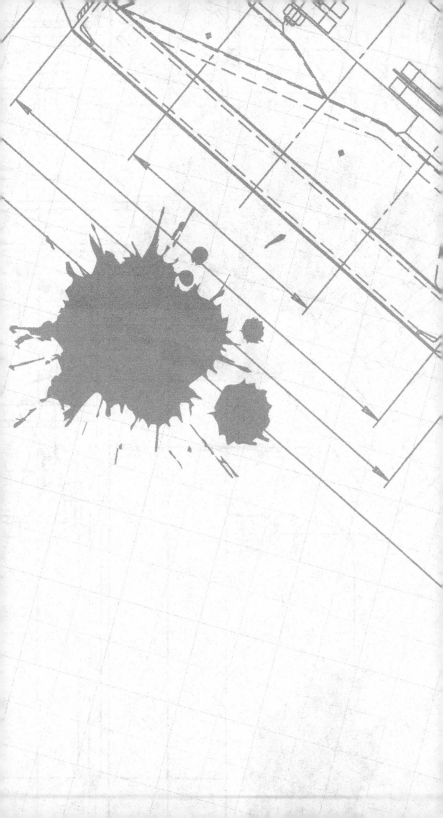

1

"I think he's going to kill me." The voice is barely above a whisper.

I grip the telephone and take a deep breath. My eyes skim across the page in front of me. I know I should use open-ended questions, but I already find myself going off-script.

"If you believe your life is in danger, you need to call the police."

"No! I mean, no. I don't think my life is in danger."

I frown. It's not uncommon for callers to make grand, sweeping statements about murder or conspiracies and then recant moments later. But there's something different about this caller. There's something in her voice that makes me think she might have been telling the truth the first time.

"You can be honest with me," I say. "Tell me about your husband."

She pauses. "Well, he's really sweet. He's handsome. Generous. He buys me everything I could ever want . . ."

"But?"

"He gets horrible mood swings. He gets so . . . *mad* for no reason. I never know when he's going to snap. I think he's been having trouble at work, but he won't talk to me about it."

I bite my lip. "Has he ever hit you?"

The silence stretches like a yawning chasm as I wait for her next words to either topple me over the precipice or guide me safely away from the edge.

"No."

My heart skips a beat. I don't believe her.

"I wouldn't even consider leaving him if it weren't for . . ."

"If it weren't for . . .?"

"If it weren't for Shane."

"Who's Shane?"

She doesn't respond.

"Is Shane your son?"

I worry that she might hang up, but she finally answers.

"Yes."

"Has he ever hurt your son?"

"No."

My frown deepens. Is she lying? "Listen . . ." I falter. Normally I would use a caller's name here, to cement the trust I'm trying to build, but she refused to give it. "I think you should call the police."

"I—can't. I won't."

I want to push her—this might be my only chance to convince her to get help—but instead, I give her a list of places she can go, emphasizing the discretion of the different women's shelters that are strategically located around downtown Toronto, where she has alluded to living.

"You can call any time you need to talk. Ask for Rachel, and they'll connect us if I'm working," I say. "I usually work a little later than this—from twelve to four."

I hear a muffled thump on the other end of the line.

"I have to go. He's awake."

My heart leaps into my throat. I open my mouth, but I'm cut off by the dial tone.

I reluctantly return the phone to its receiver, the springy cord of my vintage, black telephone snapping tightly into place. I take a deep breath and arch my back, stretching my arms to the ceiling. Some—but not all, never all—of the tension releases from my body.

I flip through the pages of the binder back to the first page, ready to start the process over again. I've been volunteering at the distress line for almost fourteen months now, but it never gets easier. The service helps all those in crisis, from teens who just want information about mental health programs to the elderly who are grieving the loss of loved ones. We also get many calls about domestic abuse. Too many. Unless the caller explicitly gives us permission, or if we have reason to believe that someone's safety is in immediate danger, we aren't allowed to contact the police.

Sometimes, I hate this rule. But one of the reasons people feel comfortable enough to reach out to us is because of our discretion. Still, it's hard to hang up and let go of someone who needs my help. I may never hear from this girl again. I may never know the rest of her story.

I make a note on the call log, both online and in my own personal records. I put down my pen and stare at the phone for several minutes, hoping that I can compel the girl into calling back. But it's nearing the end of my four-hour shift, so I likely won't hear from her again tonight.

Housebound, I volunteer for four shifts a week. Usually, I take the most unpopular shift of midnight to four, but tonight I'm working from eight to twelve. Because of my flexible schedule, the hotline has made an exception, and I'm allowed to work from home instead of at the busy call center. Of course, I didn't tell them the real reason why I can't leave my apartment. They think I have mobility issues, which I faked during the company's mandatory therapy sessions. I was given a clean bill of mental health. Ironic.

I head into the kitchen and turn on the kettle. I grab a box of Earl Grey and drop a bag into my favorite mug. The mug is plain and brown and has a tiny chip on its lip, but it reminds me of home, and I always use this one, even though I have a dozen other mugs crammed onto the shelf. I hug my arms across my chest as I wait for the water to boil. My wool sweater does little to warm the chill that has permeated my bones.

Once the tea is ready, I find myself back in my office, cradling the mug in ice cold hands. The wall to my left bears my collection of framed, black and white landscape photos. The only glimpse of nature I've had in over a year. My escape from the reality of being trapped in a city I barely know. To my right are several built-in bookcases, filled with the variety of leisure and professional reading I've amassed over the two years I've lived here. I approach the floor-to-ceiling-length window which fills the wall behind my desk. Toronto's bright city lights wink at me. Down below, the trees whip back and forth in a sharp gust of wind. Heavy rainfall drenches the pavement. Across the street are tall apartment complexes, peppered with the illuminated windows of those who cannot sleep. I sympathize with them. I haven't had a full night's sleep in two years. Instead, I take sporadic naps, giving in only whenever the exhaustion is too great to conquer.

A shrill ring cuts through the silence. The mug slips from my grasp, bounces, and spills, scalding hot liquid ballooning out onto the floor, sinking deep into the rug. I hurry to my desk, leaving the cleanup for later.

"Hello?"

An automated voice greets me. "This is the Toronto Distress Line. You have a caller on the line. If you are able to take this call, press one."

I take a deep breath, then press one.

"Hello, this is Rachel speaking. How can I help you?" I sound surprisingly serene.

"*Rachel?*" The voice is strange. I cannot place my finger on what's wrong, but a sense of dread washes over me. I ignore it.

"Yes. You've reached the Toronto Distress Line. Anything you say is strictly confidential. Tell me why you called here tonight."

"I know where you live . . . *Kae.*"

"What—how do you know that name?" I swallow, my throat suddenly paper dry.

"I'm coming for you."

2

My chest tightens. My heart races. My breath quickens. My vision darkens. The room spins.

I push away from my desk and lower my head between my legs. I take several deep breaths, clenching my fists and relaxing them in time with my inhalation. I exhale through pursed lips. Inhale. Exhale. Inhale. Exhale.

Slowly, the crushing weight on my chest begins to lift, and the fog clears. I sit up slowly and lean back in my chair. I haven't had a panic attack in almost a month. I'd thought I was getting better. I shake my head. *Anyone* would be terrified by a call like that. Although, this isn't the first time it's happened. Predators enjoy making fake calls to the distress line to disturb and upset the volunteers. We always block those numbers to make it more difficult for them to enjoy this twisted pastime. But I've never had a caller who knew my name—my *real* name.

The phone rings, and again, I nearly jump out of my skin. I don't want to answer it, but I'm glad I do. It's Luke.

The words tumble out of me almost faster than I can say them, and I barely remember to breathe. I tell him everything— everything except for the fact that the caller knew my name. Not even Luke knows my *real* name. No one in Toronto does, and I'd hoped to keep it that way.

"Are you okay? Do you need me to come over?" Luke asks in a quiet voice. He knows about my fears, my paranoias, and he pretends to understand them, even though he couldn't possibly. He doesn't know why I am this way. I never told him, and I never plan to.

"No, I'm fine. Really."

"Are you sure? We could binge-watch Netflix like we used to . . . Your choice on the show," he says.

"Tempting," I reply. I find myself actually smiling despite the heavy feeling in the pit of my stomach. Luke is my only friend in the city, the only one that I've made in the two years I've lived here, but I haven't seen him in person for four months. I've been pushing him away. I've been retreating deeper into a prison of my own making.

Luke continues, "I'll bring my mace. To defend you from any potential intruders and that creepy concierge."

At that, I laugh. Luke is six feet tall and heavily muscled, but he carries an illegal hot pink mace with him for self-defense. He's clumsy and has poor balance, and I can't help but imagine he would use it backward if he ever got into a fight.

"Not tonight," I say.

Luke doesn't reply. The silence is deafening.

I bite my lip. I want to know more about the caller, but that information is classified.

Instead, I try a different approach.

"Has this person called before?" I ask, as casually as possible under the circumstances.

Luke is a volunteer like me, but he mostly works behind the scenes, scheduling the volunteers and directing calls based on specific requests. He also takes shifts answering calls from time to time, usually when other volunteers flake on their commitment. Despite having a full-time job as an IT professional, he pours a lot of his free time into the hotline, and I know it's because he feels a responsibility to help others in need. I don't know the details, but he once told me that his mother never would have escaped his abusive stepfather if it hadn't have been for a hotline like this one.

Luke never brought it up again, and I never asked. It's better if we don't talk about our pasts and only look toward the future. Easier said than done.

"I don't think he's called before," Luke says. "I just blocked his number. If he had called before, we would have blacklisted it earlier. Of course, he could be calling from a different phone. Which is unlikely," he adds hastily.

I know I shouldn't ask, but I do anyway.

"Do you have the caller's number?"

There is a pregnant pause. "You know I can't give out that information."

I frown. Without knowing who called me, my options are now limited to one. Run.

"Rach, this is just another prank call. We get them all the time. I've had three in this last week alone. You're perfectly safe, especially in your building. Thorwald Place is practically Fort Knox."

He does have a point.

"Actually . . ." he says.

"What is it?"

"There's something . . . unusual in the log."

"What is it?" I repeat. I grip the armrests of my chair, my nails cutting into the well-worn, brown leather.

He clears his throat. "Rachel, the caller asked for you specifically. But, like I said, I don't think he's called before."

I don't respond. Of course the caller asked for me specifically, but Luke couldn't possibly know that I know, because I hadn't told him that the caller used my real name. The caller's voice had been distorted, as if by some kind of voice transformation app. It's possible that I know him, and I just didn't recognize his voice. A familiar name and face cross my mind, but I shove them away, shutting them behind a locked door in my mind. I can't afford another panic attack.

"I wouldn't worry about it. He's probably the angry boyfriend of one of your regulars, and he wanted to freak you out as revenge or something. He has *no way* of knowing who you are beyond your first name *or* where you are."

He makes a valid point. As a distress line volunteer, you piss off a lot of ex-husbands and boyfriends.

"And my offer for a slumber party still stands. We can paint our nails, and I'll even let you braid my hair," Luke adds.

Caught off guard, I snicker. His hair is so short, I likely wouldn't even manage a single plait.

"Thanks, but maybe another time," I say. "I'm probably being paranoid. I just had a tough domestic abuse call, and I'm still a little shaken up."

Luke is quiet for a moment. "Rach, maybe you should take a few days off."

I don't say anything.

"I mean, you volunteer with us a lot, much more than anyone else, and I don't want you to burn out. Taking calls like these can be really draining."

I don't want to take time off. That would give me time to think about my own problems, which I've become an expert at avoiding. I could always use the extra time for my work, but translation is a lonely business. These four-hour shifts are the only human interaction I get. And it feels good knowing that I'm helping those in crisis. It wasn't too long ago that I was in their shoes.

"Thanks for your concern, Luke, but I'm fine. That prank call scared me, but I know it's just a one-time thing. I'll go down to the gym and work off some of this pent-up energy. Talk to you later." I hang up before he can object.

I begin to pace around the office—ten long strides before I reach the wall, spin around, and repeat the process. I fitfully gnaw at my thumbnail. I still need to know who made that phone call. What Luke said *might* be true. An angry ex-husband could have found out my real name, and he's using it to intimidate me. But what if it's someone who knows about my past? What if it's someone *from* my past?

I imagine a man armed with a high-powered rifle, tracking my movements from a dark apartment across the street. I'm in the crosshairs, and I can almost feel the red laser dot dancing on my forehead. I dart to the window and yank the drapes shut, plunging the room into thick shadows.

I stand there for several minutes, shaking, until I realize I'm standing in the spilled tea, which has gone ice cold, sinking through my socks and soaking my feet. I peel off my soiled socks and drop them in the hamper as I head to the bathroom to grab a towel. I return to the office and mop up the tea without turning on the lights, working by the slice of pale light that slithers through the gap in the curtains.

I've spent so much time being afraid, trying to avoid the dangers of the outside. Whenever I leave my apartment, I'm much more prone to panic attacks, which leave me helpless and exposed. The last time I left the safety of Thorwald Place, something spooked me, and my panic attack was so intense, I passed out. Somebody must have called an ambulance, but fortunately, I woke up before it arrived and was able to get out of there without anyone asking me any questions. But I haven't left this building since. Not for nine months. I cannot afford to be that vulnerable, not when he's still out there.

I'm being ridiculous. I've been so careful; he can't have found me. For all I know, the caller didn't even say my name, Kae, short for Kaela. He could have been saying the letter "K". Like how some people tack on an "eh" to everything they say, maybe this caller shortens the word "okay".

I take several deep breaths, taking solace in the rhythmic movements of scrubbing the floor. After I've finished, I dump the filthy towel in the hamper. I stride across my large living room, past the bookcases that overflow with books and the couch that sits opposite a flatscreen TV that I hardly ever turn on. I hesitate by the front door.

Slowly, I put my eye to the peephole. I see a long expanse of empty hallway. The dim overhead light casts stark shadows on the sloped, maroon wallpapered walls and in the deep depression of the doorways at the end of the corridor. The polished marble floors reflect the faint light back up at me. My apartment is closest to the elevator. I chose this one so I would have the quickest escape route.

On the seventh floor of this ten-story building, I'm too high for someone to climb onto my balcony, but not so high that I can't flee down the stairs if I have to. From my peephole, I can see everyone who comes off the elevator and recognize if it's someone who isn't supposed to be on this floor. If they loiter for too long, I call security. I used to linger in the foyer of my apartment, standing guard at the door any time the elevator ding announced that someone was getting off. I've been getting better, and now, I only check a dozen times a day—usually when the concierge is making a delivery or if a noise in the hall spooks me.

When I realized that I had to run and leave my old life in Ottawa behind, my cop friend, Catalina, helped me set up an airtight, new identity, and it was she who found me this safe haven. Thorwald Place. The condos are spacious, especially for Toronto, with only seven units per floor. The mortgage is high and the condo fees even higher, but it's worth the chunk out of my paycheck and inheritance, if only for the impressive security measures put in place. It is impossible for someone to get in unless they have explicit permission from a resident. There's 24-hour surveillance, and the security guards actually graduated from the police academy but chose this line of work for the higher salary.

Despite my vigilance, I don't know many of the occupants of Thorwald Place. Most of the inhabitants are multimillionaires, which, in my experience, usually leads to snobbishness. I don't mind. I've never had any intention of getting to know my neighbors.

A socialite named Sabryna Hyland attempted to befriend me when I first moved in. She thought a single woman working from home would be the perfect drinking companion. However, I made it abundantly clear that I had no intention of being friendly with *any* of the neighbors, and eventually, she gave up. While I sometimes find myself craving companionship, I can't run the risk of someone getting to know me too well, noticing the gaps in what I've told them about my past, and beginning to suspect that I'm not who I claim to be. Luke began to ask questions, which was one of the reasons why I had to distance myself from our friendship.

The authentic German cuckoo clock over the mantle chimes, informing me that it's already quarter to one. I've spent over forty-five minutes in a frenzy over a phone call that probably means nothing. It's great to note that my mental health is improving. Dr. Favreau would be so pleased.

I need to get out of the apartment. I need to prove to myself that I'm not a frightened child. I stride into the bedroom to change into my gym clothes. I like to work out at night, between midnight and five. The building's fitness center is open twenty-four-seven, but I rarely see anyone down there in the dead of night. Occasionally, I encounter a skinny twenty-year-old, but he sticks with the weights, and I go to the other side of the room for the treadmill. He's very pale, and large, purple bruises circle his sunken eyes. I suspect he uses exercise to deal with his insomnia.

I open my dresser drawer and stare at its contents for so long that I have to shake my head to pry myself away. Whether or not I'm being irrational is beside the point. The caller said a word that sounds like my name. I can't stay in this building a minute longer. I have to run.

I dart into my walk-in closet to grab my duffel bag. I should have prepared a pre-packed getaway bag. Why hadn't I thought of that before this very moment? Working in darkness, too afraid to turn on the light, I load the bag up with the bare essentials. Underwear. Shirts. Pants. I duck into the bathroom and return with my toothbrush. I hesitate, then add more underwear to the bag before zipping it shut.

I head into my office to grab my passport, IDs, and a wad of cash—both Canadian and American. I root around in my desk drawer for my diary. Where is it? I slam the top drawer shut and check the bottom drawer. It isn't there either. It's one of the only things I have left of my past, and I can't bear the thought of leaving it behind. I haven't written an entry since moving to Toronto, and I know I keep it in my desk, where I sometimes retrieve it when I'm feeling masochistic and want to remind myself of the horrors of my past. It isn't here.

Disappointment weighs on my chest as I realize I'll have to leave without it. I haven't any more time to waste. I run to the front door, the bag slung over my shoulder. Once again, I peer through the peephole. Sometimes, I plan what I would do if I see an eyeball staring back at me. Or the barrel of a gun. I would jerk back and flatten myself against the wall. Stick my keys between my knuckles as a weapon.

I unlock the deadbolt, slide the chain, and slowly open the door. The hall is silent, and the dim light reveals both sides of the hallway. I shut the door behind me and lock it. I pull the handle three times to make sure it's locked, not just stuck. I race to the elevator, punching the button several times in quick succession.

I wonder if I'm being irrational, but I've never been able to be objective, not when it comes to my safety. Either way, I'm proud of the action I've taken. Only a month ago, a call like that would have rendered me immobile for weeks. But instead of cowering in the corner of my apartment, waiting for my death, I'm taking charge of my life. I'll get out of the building, find a cheap hotel, and pay cash for the night. Then I'll call Catalina—my closest friend from my past life—and she'll help me find a new place to settle down. Or, at the very least, she'll look into the phone call. She'll figure out if it's a false alarm, or if he's found me.

The elevator arrives, and the doors slide open. Empty. I slip in. I press B. The elevator descends. It moves slow. So slow. Too slow.

I take a deep breath, and my pulse drops back down to the double digits. I continue to breathe deliberately as I watch the numbers gradually change as the elevator passes each floor. A sense of calm washes over me. I'm finally leaving. This is the first time I've taken control of my life since my husband died. I push away all thoughts of him. I can't afford to break down. Not when I'm so vulnerable.

I bite my lip. I'm far from safe. My car has been parked in the basement-level garage for *nine months*. It's been nine months since I last drove it. What if it doesn't start? What if—

Darkness envelops me. A loud grating sound erupts from the cabling above, and the elevator lurches to a stop. Silence. Blinded, I feel my way to the elevator panel and find the call button.

"Hello?" I try to keep my voice calm. "Can anyone hear me? The elevator shut down!"

Nothing.

I push it again, but there's nothing. No dial tone. No soothing voice on the other end. This time, I press the alarm button, but no siren emits. Shouldn't there be a siren? I can't tell if it's working. Has the concierge been notified? Is security on their way? I punch buttons at random. Hysteria bubbles up, threatening to break through the surface.

No. I cannot afford to have a panic attack. I take several deep breaths. In through my nose. Out through my mouth. Again.

My head clears, and I lean my feverish forehead against the cold, gray steel of the elevator wall. There was a weather alert on the news tonight. The power is out because of the storm, that's all this is. But shouldn't the elevator have a backup mechanism for an emergency? I should have researched this myself, before moving into this building. I should have had a packed getaway bag at the ready, and I would have been out of the elevator before the power outage. I should have taken the stairs. I should have prepared for this.

I hold my breath and listen carefully. I definitely don't hear any sirens . . . or anything at all for that matter. The elevator is deathly silent, except for the thumping of my heart.

It was around the third floor when the power went out. I drop my bag against the far wall of the elevator and assess the exit. Slipping my fingers into the crack between the doors, I pull with all my strength. It opens half an inch. I peer through, but I can't see anything. Just a void. A cool breeze slips through the crack, caressing my cheek and carrying the faint smell of something rotten.

I pull again, and the doors slide apart more easily, over a foot this time. The elevator is between floors. I can see the corridor's marble floor barely at chin level. I just need another foot of space, and then I can squeeze through.

Before I can wrench the doors open farther, bright light washes over me. Life returns to the elevator, and the doors calmly slide shut. I cover my eyes, suffering an instant migraine as the light saturates my retinas. The elevator continues its descent as if nothing were out of the ordinary. I shake with relief that I hadn't attempted to climb out of the elevator, or I would have been severed in half, my blood cascading down the doors like in *The Shining*.

A voice in the back of my head chastises me. *What am I doing?* Should I even be leaving the building? The reason I chose this condo was for the high security. If I leave it, I could be walking straight into danger.

The elevator stops. The doors slide open, revealing an empty hall. The basement. I don't know what to do. Should I leave? Should I stay? Should I go to the lobby and find the security guards and demand that they let me stay with them until morning? I shake my head. That's not a long-term solution. I sigh, turning around to pick up my duffel bag.

I never get a chance to grab it.

Strong hands wrap around me, gripping me tight and covering my mouth before I can scream. I bite down hard, but my assailant is wearing thick leather gloves, and I don't even break the skin. I jab an elbow backward, but he dodges it with ease.

I kick with my heel, and it connects with a shin. He exhales sharply and loosens his grip just enough so that his hand is no longer smothering my face.

I open my mouth and gulp down cold air. I'm ready to scream, but something cold and sharp tears across my throat, slicing me open from ear to ear. I don't even manage a whimper. Warmth pours down my chest. Streams of crimson spray the walls, erupting from my throat like a geyser.

The hands release me and shove my body against the wall. I land with a thud. My ice cold fingers claw at my throat, but my hands are too small, too weak to contain the torrents of blood. Footsteps lead away as my killer leaves me to die alone.

But I'm not alone.

I fall to my knees, my vision fading as I struggle to inhale, coughing on the metallic taste of my own blood. Darkness gathers in my peripheral vision, and I turn to face it. The shadows twist and writhe and collect to form the silhouette of a man with no face. He hunches over, his arms outstretched.

I die before he reaches me.

3

It takes forever for someone to find my body. At six, the elevator is called to the fourth floor, and an early riser greets the sight of my body with a shrill scream. He stumbles backward, clutching his briefcase to his chest. I get the impression that he's never discovered a grisly crime scene before. I, on the other hand, am enveloped in the cool indifference that seems to accompany death.

He staggers back to his apartment, shrieking hysterically all the way. Several of his neighbors rush out into the hall. Each person is in various stages of undress. A pregnant woman wearing a silk bathrobe and only one slipper. A man whose face is coated in shaving cream, save for a single bare strip down his left cheek. The look of horror on their faces would have been amusing if I were in the mood for dark humor. The elevator doors slide shut, and I am launched to another floor, where I startle another early commuter. The elevator doors close on the stunned woman's face, lurching toward its next stop. I'm destined for repetition. Perhaps *this* is hell.

The police finally arrive, call the elevator to the ground floor, and put it out of service. I have now informally met a quarter of the building's occupants, which is more than I met in the two years I lived here. A handful of police officers form a perimeter, trying to block the sight of my corpse from the prying eyes of my nosey neighbors. I hover by the elevator door as forensic investigators get to work examining my corpse. I try not to watch—disgusted by the sight of my limp body, which is coated in blood that has begun to cake—but the process is mesmerizing. The flash of cameras, the murmur of voices, and the hypnotic movement of pencils as they scribble in pristine, white notebooks. The forensic experts step gingerly around the scene, careful not to disturb anything, as they scrutinize my body from all angles. As they work, I can't stop staring at my face. My eyes are still open and glazed over with a milky white sheen. My skin is nearly white, a shocking contrast to the deep crimson gash across my neck. My lips are parted in a soundless scream. A forensic investigator in a white bodysuit steps in front of me, cutting off my view. Relief floods through me, and I turn away before the sight of my own corpse enthralls me once again.

I know I gained consciousness only minutes after my death, because blood was still dripping where the arterial spray arched across the walls, looking as if an artist had decided to add a splash of color to the monochromatic gray. I was reluctant to leave my body, but I had no idea what else to do. I had no moment of shock, no moment of revelation where I realized I was dead. I knew it from the instant I opened my eyes and saw the world from the other side. A world which looks different in death. Everything is a little grayer, a little faded. Voices and sounds have a slight echo. It's as though I'm experiencing everything through a thin film—some indescribable substance that separates the world of the living from mine.

But why am I still here? My body has been found; the police are clearly investigating. It won't take long for them to figure out it was he who killed me. I leave the elevator and glance around the lobby. I don't see any obvious doorways or bright lights to follow. How will I know where to go? I bite back the pang of disappointment when I realize that none of my lost loved ones are here to welcome me. No husband. No parents. No Grumpelstiltskin, my childhood dog. Where are they, and how do I find my way to them?

I'm self-aware enough to know that I've always feared the unknown, and it's obvious that this hasn't changed in death. Instead of searching for my escape, I stay locked in place, eyes glued to the crime scene investigators. After what feels like an eternity, the medical examiner deposits my body into a black bag and wheels it out of the building. I begin to follow. Maybe if I slip back into my body, I'll awaken, and everyone will laugh, like this was all just one big misunderstanding.

I'll spend the rest of my days wearing a scarf, elegantly positioned to hide my gaping neck wound, like the girl in that urban legend.

I slam into an invisible wall about a dozen feet from the elevator. Slightly disoriented, I shake my head. I press forward.

Again, I'm stopped by an imperceptible force. I reach out, and my hand flattens midair. I run my hand along this invisible barrier, but it seems to run as high as I can reach and down to the marble floor.

I follow the barrier, tracing my hand along it. It cuts across the entire lobby, but not in a straight line. It's slightly curved. Beyond the wall, I can see the medical examiner exit the building with my body, leaving my soul behind. I slam a hand against the invisible wall once again, but there's no give.

My attention is drawn by the sound of a familiar grating voice. Elias Strickland, the concierge, is speaking with a police officer who looks like he's desperate to leave. The invisible wall can wait. I approach the pair to eavesdrop.

"We have excellent security here," Elias says. His perpetually nasal voice is exacerbated by the tears that stream down his face. "How could this have happened? My residents will want an explanation immediately."

"We have someone reviewing the security footage of the exits. If the killer left the building, we'll have them on film," the police officer says.

"*If* they left the building? Are you saying they might still *be here*?" Elias tugs at his cheap tie.

The killer might still be in the building. I look around and notice for the first time that the residents aren't allowed to simply leave. Police officers guard the front door, questioning each individual before they allow them to go to work or to the spa or to do whatever they think is more important than mourning my death.

"What can you tell me about the victim? Ms. Rachel Anne Drake?" the police officer asks.

"Well . . ." Elias runs a hand through his thinning, brown hair. "She is—was—an odd one. She rarely spoke to anyone. She kept to herself. I think I was her only friend in the building."

I stare at him, just now realizing that the tears streaming down his face are for me. I feel a pang of guilt. I've never considered us "friends." I interact with him once every few weeks—only when I have mail to pick up or complaints about the security guards.

Elias continues, "She even had her groceries delivered. I haven't seen her leave the building in months."

The police officer suddenly looks interested. He pulls a small, wire-bound notebook from his pocket and uncaps his pen.

"Do you think it's possible that she may have been hiding from someone?"

"Possibly . . . She was always really interested in the security in the building. Like that was the main reason why she moved here, not the fabulous party room or the services I provide as *concierge*." I wince in pity as he says the word with a dreadful French accent. He should have picked a line of work that he could pronounce.

"Did she have any visitors?"

"There was a man who used to come around, but I haven't seen him in a few months," Elias says. At the police officer's prompting, he continues on to describe him. I realize he's talking about Luke.

The police officer asks a few follow-up questions, and I'm surprised by just how much Elias knows. He knows the date and time of my weekly grocery deliveries, that once every couple of weeks I'll treat myself to pizza delivered from the greasy place down the street, and that I get a haul of books delivered every time BMV Books has a sale.

"Well, if you think of anything else, please contact us immediately." I peer over the police officer's shoulder to look at the scribbles in his notebook, but he's used a shorthand that I can't decipher.

A nearly identical police officer emerges from the security office holding a flash drive. He glances at the concierge, then turns to his partner and begins speaking rapid French.

"The video doesn't show anybody leaving the building between one and two this morning. But apparently, there was a power outage for about five minutes, and the killer could have left during that window."

"No! That power outage happened *before* I died. The power came back, and *then* he killed me." I blink and glance around. I hadn't thought I'd be able to speak.

It makes no difference. Neither police officer reacts to the sound of my voice. I look at Elias, but he's watching the officers intently. I turn my attention to the rest of the people milling about, but none of them seem to have heard me either. But I'm not yet discouraged.

I approach the pot-bellied man standing the closest to the crime scene tape. He cranes his neck to see into the elevator.

"THERE'S NOTHING TO SEE HERE!" I shout into his face. He doesn't react. I try to shake him, but my hands fall through his fleshy body. I feel nothing—no chill, no warmth—as I slide my hands through him. I examine his face, but it's clear that he doesn't sense me in the slightest.

I strategically progress through the lobby, shouting at each bystander, attempting to reach them through any means.

I try everything I can remember having seen in movies about ghosts—from waving my hands through their heads to shouting obscenities in their ears. No one reacts. No one so much as shivers.

I'm angry, disappointed, and beginning to feel helpless. I brace myself, preparing to do my calming breathing technique, but there are no symptoms of a panic attack. My body is overcome by the numbness of being incorporeal. I could get used to this. I suppose I'll have to.

I glance around, noticing that the police officers have long gone, and they've been replaced by a cleaning crew of four burly men who are crammed into the elevator. They've already bleached the walls in an attempt to remove all trace of my messy execution. The lobby is nearly empty now. Only Elias stands at his station, compulsively wringing his hands in between fielding calls from curious residents and the media.

I survey the expansive, high-ceilinged lobby. Unlike the rest of the building, it was designed with the sole purpose of impressing visitors. The floors are marble, polished to near perfection. The wallpaper is a pale blue with gold foil accents in the shape of falling leaves. A hefty, ornate clock is the only decoration on the stretch of the wall across from the front desk. There are two wing chairs and a sofa positioned underneath it. It serves as a sort of waiting area, though in my two years living in this building, I've never seen a single person sitting out here.

I can only access half of the lobby, so I need to find a way around this invisible barrier. I approach the elevator and look down the hall to the right. I tentatively step through the wall. I'm in the guest suite that's reserved for visitors of building residents. The bed is neatly made, with the corners of the bedspread tucked tightly. There's a lounge area sparsely decorated with cool tones. A gray, leather couch is angled toward an impressively-sized TV.

The room is windowless, but a single painting of a blue sky over a grassy field hangs on the wall opposite the door, creating the illusion of something beyond.

I stride across the plain gray rug and easily pass through this wall as well. I'm in the ground-level parking garage, which is located below the building. I continue to walk until I slam against the barrier. It doesn't hurt, but it's disorienting.

I place my hand on the barrier and follow it around until I reach the wall twenty feet from where I entered. The barrier is clearly circular. Is it meant to keep me contained? I shake my head at that thought, then I continue to follow the barrier through the wall, out of the garage, and into the library.

With gorgeous oak-paneled walls and towering bookshelves, the building's library is quite a sight to behold. The leather couches look comfortable, with antique copper lamps strategically positioned between them. I've been down here several times over the last two years, but I never dawdle. I usually grab a handful of books and hurry back upstairs to the safety of my apartment, where I can actually relax and enjoy my reading.

I walk through the room divider into the "party" area. The dim overhead lights reveal a bar in the corner, which is framed by tall mirrors, making the room seem larger than it actually is. I scan the rest of the room. Circular tables are set up around a polished dance floor. I quickly hit another barrier only a few feet into the room.

I follow this barrier, clockwise, until I've made an entire lap of the enclosure. I was right. It *is* a circle. There are no breaks or gaps in the wall; nothing I can slip through to escape. What is this barrier? Who put it here? I have so many questions and no one to answer them.

Back in the lobby, the cleaning crew has finished their sterilization of the elevator. A starchy-looking woman stands in Elias' face, complaining loudly about the inconvenience of having only one operating elevator. I'm glad that my death is nothing more than a disruption to her "busy" life. Shouldn't she be disturbed that a brutal murder occurred hours ago in that very elevator? That the killer hasn't even been caught? Hell, she should be worried that it's haunted.

She spins on her heel and leaves a bedraggled Elias in her wake. She scowls at the cleaners, who are gathering their supplies and politely averting their eyes from her shrewd gaze. She presses the elevator button and boards the other one, which was already idling on this floor. She didn't even have to wait five seconds. I'd love to see what a *convenient* elevator experience is like for her.

After she's left, Elias tips the cleaners and reactivates the elevator. The doors slide shut, as if sealing my fate.

A man in snug jogging shorts strolls into the building, salutes Elias, and heads to the elevators. Elias nods and returns to his station. I decide to head over toward him to see what exactly he keeps behind the desk. It lies just beyond the invisible wall, so I might be able to see what he always stares at so intently on his computer.

Just as I reach the edge of the invisible barrier, a powerful sensation of vertigo overcomes me. My skin begins to crawl. I stare down at my arms in astonishment. My entire body is vaporizing, shredding into a million pieces, wisps of flesh fading into the world around me. I squeeze my eyes shut tightly, willing the end to come quickly.

4

Just as soon as I think I might actually die—not just my body, but also my soul—numbness engulfs me. I pry open my eyes. I'm back in the elevator, which is climbing so very slowly. The jogger is doing lunges less than two feet from where my body lay this morning. Doesn't he know what happened here? Or maybe he just doesn't care? He had to have been questioned by the police. He must have been told.

The elevator dings, and he steps out onto the eighth floor. The doors drift shut behind him. I wait, but the elevator idles. I float through the door and glance around.

Why didn't my invisible barrier keep me from climbing the floors?

I bite my lip, and I'm surprised to realize that I feel it. Although, it doesn't feel quite the same as when I was alive. There's a dullness to it. I suppose this is a good thing. I still have some sensations, despite being nothing but a walking shadow. But I'd felt extreme pain when my body vaporized and I was torn back to the elevator when it began to move, as if it has some sort of magnetic hold on me. That was the first true sensation I've experienced since I died.

I begin to pace the hall in front of the elevator, and I can't help but notice that my feet don't quite touch the ground. I walk down the hallway, to the edge of my enclosure, about twenty feet from the elevator door. The invisible wall is still there, still containing me, still taunting me with the sight of what lies beyond. What is just out of reach.

The invisible barrier must have traveled with the elevator. The elevator is at the center of my strange, circular prison, and when it moves, so does my personal purgatory.

I wait on the floor for ten, twenty minutes, but the elevator doesn't move again. Across the hall from the elevators there is an oak console table with a bouquet of fake flowers resting on top. There is one just like it on every floor. But it isn't the flowers that catch my attention. It's the gold-framed, oval mirror hanging on the wall above it. I approach it, slowly. I know what my dead body looked like, but I'm not sure I want to know what my spirit looks like.

I stand in front of the mirror, taking a moment to gather the courage to look. My eyes linger on the fake flowers, examining the thin coat of dust that clings to the rose petals. I finally look up. The view of the elevator doors behind me is unobstructed in the mirror. I stand there for a moment, both relieved and disappointed. I don't have a reflection. I look down at my hands, turning them over. They don't even look transparent to me. I study my once gray wool sweater that is soaked with my blood. I can see myself, but I don't have a reflection.

I turn back around and stare at the elevator I'm tethered to. I can't erase the image of my corpse's vacant eyes from my memory. I need to forget.

On a whim, I step through the wall adjacent to the elevator. I'm in a living room that is sparsely decorated with plain, bleached-white furniture. It looks like an advertisement in an Ikea catalogue but without the flash of flavor that lures buyers to their warehouses. There are no decorations, no colors except for a bright red painting of a field of poppies that hangs above the electric fireplace. The splash of red cuts harshly against the bland room, bringing to mind the sight of my bloodied corpse. The bloody gash, my ashen face. My cloudy eyes. Perhaps it's a good thing I can't see my spirit. I don't know if I could bear knowing what I look like.

I quickly tear my gaze away. My eye is caught by the sight of a collection of black picture frames, which are purposefully positioned on the lid of a grand piano, the only hint of personality in the otherwise lackluster room.

Curious, I approach the photographs. The frames are eclectic looking, all black but different styles and made of different materials. I shift my attention to the photographs. One is a graduation photo, depicting a proud father with his arm wrapped around his daughter's shoulders. Another picture shows a young couple kissing on the beach, a golden retriever frolicking in a watery backdrop. A group of friends are having a movie night, eating popcorn and laughing at something off-camera. A pair of twin brothers climb an old oak tree, laughing and smiling as they swing from branch to branch like monkeys. All the pictures are candid, cheerful, and filled with a vivacity that is missing from the rest of the room.

A chill creeps up my spine. These are all pictures of different people. There's no common face peppered across the photos. I step in closer. The photograph dimensions are clearly visible in the corner of every picture. These are not pictures of someone's friends and family. These are the pictures that the frames came with.

A small thud resounds from another room. I jump back guiltily, whipping around. Then I remember that no one can see me. I may be trespassing, but no one will ever know. I try to ignore the heaviness in my chest.

A second thud pulls my thoughts back to the present. Uncertain of what my revelation about the pictures means, I cautiously follow the source of the sound, my old friend Dread back at my side like he never left.

Thud.

I stand in the second doorway off the hall. The room is empty except for a lone figure sitting in the corner of the room. The room bears no adornments, no furniture, nothing other than a battered, brown rocking chair. Nothing but stark white walls and a slender woman, clad in gray.

Thud.

The woman herself has barely moved. The faint sound comes from the rocking chair, which is slowly rocking, thumping against the bare wall. A small impression defaces the wall where the wood connects.

Thud.

The woman stares out the window. Her eyes are empty, dead. I look down at her hands. She wears a modest, gold wedding ring, and her white-knuckled fists clutch something tightly. I can't tell what it is, but I catch a flash of red between her fingers.

I inch forward, but I'm halted by the invisible barrier. I am both relieved and disappointed. I need to get closer. I want to run away. But I can't. I have to understand.

Thud.

But even if I can understand her pain, I can't help her. I can't help anyone. Not anymore.

Thud.

June 14

Dear Diary,

This is my story. My best friend bought me this diary as an early wedding gift, and I promised her I'd use it. I was reluctant at first, but she convinced me that writing in a diary is beneficial, "cheaper than a therapist," and "much more entertaining." Also, she had it engraved with my full name "Kaela D. Archer," so it's not like I can regift it. I have no delusions that I'll write in this every single day, but I'll try to make at least a few entries a month.

Things are pretty hectic at work, and I'm trying to get all my projects tied up before the wedding. Then, after the wedding, I'll likely be busy doing other things . . .

The wedding! Where to begin? Of course the band canceled at (nearly) the last minute, but it was Jay's idea to have a live band, not mine. I always wanted a DJ blasting some hits from the '60s and '70s, which is something his family would love. I pretended to be disappointed for his benefit, but I had already booked a back-up DJ on the off chance that I could change his mind.

Everything else seems to be on schedule. My maid of honor, Cindy, has taken care of everything. She's much more wedding-crazed than me, and she's obsessed with all those reality shows, like Amazing Wedding Cakes *and* Say Yes to the Dress. *Me, I know the names of the shows, but that's about it. When I first asked her to be my maid of honor, she rushed home to get her stacks of wedding planning books and magazines. I seriously think she missed her calling in life and that being a bank teller isn't fulfilling her need for puffy dresses and decadent cakes.*

Anyway, everything is going according to plan. There was a minor setback when the florist called and said she wouldn't be able to get the exact right shade of blue for the flowers for the table centerpieces. I didn't care, because I honestly couldn't tell the difference between the two colors. Cindy went into hysterics, and it took all night and a full pint of mint chocolate chip ice cream to calm her down. I don't know what will happen when it's time for her wedding. She might actually have a mental breakdown, and the ceremony will have to be held in a padded cell. At least straitjackets are white.

I would have been fine without a wedding, just a quick trip to the courthouse followed by a lengthy trip to the Bahamas. But I was naïve, and I decided that a wedding wouldn't be too much of a hassle, and it would make our family and friends happy. It's the honeymoon I'm more excited about. I'm a little embarrassed to admit that I spent more time searching for resorts in tropical climates than I did picking out a wedding dress, cake tasting, or venue hunting combined. Although, my dress is gorgeous, and it's definitely something that I would have missed if we had just signed papers at the courthouse.

I can't admit this to anyone, but I'll be glad when the whole business is over and I'm sinking my toes into the toasty sand on the beach and sipping strong margaritas at the Sandals Resort. I love to travel, and I don't get to do it nearly often enough because of my busy work schedule and the fact that my boss assigns me twice as many projects as the other junior translators. But of course, my boss had to give me time off for my honeymoon for fear that one of his best employees would quit. (Not that I threatened him, but I heavily implied that I had employment options elsewhere.)

Jay and I are getting married on the eight-month anniversary of the day we met. I'm feeling nostalgic, so I'm going to recount the story here.

Let me set the stage for you:

The day was October 20th. It was an overcast autumn day, and there was a gentle drizzle outside the kitchen window. My roommate, Catalina, and I were playing Scrabble at the kitchen table. Of course, I was winning.

Catalina made her word "BIRD," and I was pleased to see that she didn't block my spot. Without even waiting for her to refill her tiles, I put out my word "JERK," which landed on the triple word score.

Catalina didn't look surprised. "Why do I even bother playing with you, Kae?" She rolled her eyes and took a deep sip of her Diet Pepsi.

Lon Chaney, Jr., my brown, domestic longhair, stared at her from his perch on the kitchen counter with a look of disdain mixed with boredom. He barely tolerated Catalina, despite her best attempts to win him over with catnip and crinkly toys.

Catalina started to count up the score as I ate a big spoonful of vanilla yogurt.

"The J is on the double letter tile," I told her.

"Um hmm."

"And since I added the 'K' to 'pin,' that means that word gets tripled too."

"Um hmm." She frowned.

"That's ninety-nine points!" I shouted. I jumped up and began to dance, knocking my yogurt over the board.

Catalina snorted, Diet Pepsi spraying out of her nostrils in a fine mist.

We both erupted into giggles, startling Lon Chaney, Jr., who jumped down from his perch and hid under the kitchen table.

Catalina left to change her shirt, which was soaked. I rummaged around in the kitchen drawer looking for an old hand towel, not wanting to ruin our only good one.

A strange gurgling sound came from the kitchen table. I spun around and saw Lon Chaney, Jr. on the table, licking Scrabble tiles.

"No! Lon Chaney, Jr., get down!" I said in a stern voice. He looked at me, then swallowed.

"NO!" I rushed over to him and pulled him away from the board.

Catalina ran into the room, topless.

I pried open Lon Chaney, Jr.'s mouth, but the tile was gone. I surveyed the board.

"He ate three tiles!"

"Don't panic," Catalina said, her eyes wide with panic. "Let's get him to the vet." She bolted from the room.

I jogged after her. She grabbed the car keys and swung open the front door.

"PUT ON A SHIRT," I screamed.

Astonished, Catalina looked down, then raced out of the room. I always joke with her that it's a good thing that she did put on a shirt before we left or Jay would be marrying her instead of me.

We got to the animal hospital in record time where Lon Chaney, Jr. was immediately rushed into emergency surgery. The veterinary technician said that if he were a bigger cat, they could have possibly induced vomiting, but Lon Chaney, Jr. is no wolf man, and the tiles were wedged in his tiny esophagus.

I paced the waiting room relentlessly until a veterinarian came out to see me.

"Is he okay?" I asked.

The vet was tall with dark wavy hair. A look of polite concern was etched into his handsome features.

"He'll be fine," he said. "We successfully removed the tiles, but he's still unconscious from the anesthesia."

"Are you sure you got all the tiles? There were three missing. A 'J,' a 'K,' and a blank tile," I said, wringing my hands together.

The vet smiled slightly. "There were three tiles, but I didn't check the letters."

I stared at him.

"Your cat—what's his name?" He looked down at the clipboard and raised an eyebrow. "Lon Chaney, Jr. is going to be perfectly fine."

I took in a deep breath and then let it out.

"Now, will you be requiring the Scrabble tiles back?" he said, an impish grin transforming his face. I found I couldn't look away.

"Of course," I replied. "The 'J' and 'K' tiles have high value."

It was a few weeks later, after our fourth dinner date and subsequent sleepover, that we realized the significance of the Scrabble tiles. Lon Chaney, Jr. ate a "J" and a "K," and our couple name immediately became "Jay and Kae." I never told Jay that the word that Lon Chaney, Jr. ate was "jerk." I fear that this might ruin the meet cute story.

I've always wondered about the significance of the blank tile. Clearly Lon Chaney, Jr. is psychic. Assuming, of course, that the tiles he ate have nothing to do with the fact that they bore the brunt of the yogurt spill and were the closest to the edge of the table. Maybe the blank tile represents the future, the endless possibilities of where our life together might lead. Or maybe it represents an unknown element, a person or event that will change our lives forever.

5

R ush hour has an entirely new meaning to me now. I'm pulled up and down by the elevator as residents return home from their productive lives. Up and down. Up and down. I can't help but resent the freedom they have. The ability to come and go as they please. I didn't even have that when I was alive, and I most certainly do not have that now.

I spent the last day and a half exploring my prison. However, during rush hour, I lose even that tiny luxury. Any time I step out onto a floor, I am yanked back into the elevator for another ride. Fortunately, the vertigo is not as terrible as it was the first time. Either that or I'm just getting used to it. During off-peak hours, I run crude calculations, and this morning, I made an afterlife-changing discovery. It appears that my prison is not only round, but it's a sphere. I can drop down to the floor below where the elevator idles, and I can also float upwards to the floor above. My range on these floors is not nearly as great, but it's nice to know that my prison isn't as small as I'd originally thought.

When the elevator is on any given floor, my enclosure has a circumference of approximately one hundred and twenty-five feet. I can travel fifteen feet into the northern and western apartments. But because of the second elevator, I can only go ten feet into the eastern apartment.

I initially avoided going into the condos, especially after observing the hypnotic melancholy of the Woman with No Past. That's what I've started calling her in my mind. But there isn't much entertainment in the hallways of an upper-class condominium. Most of the action happens *inside* the units.

Of course, not everyone within my range is note-worthy, which I have discovered very quickly. I'm currently on the sixth floor, and within my range is Sabryna Hyland—the socialite who attempted to befriend me when I first moved in—a conventional couple with an unconventional son, and a German man who is shouting loudly on the telephone. His face is beet red, and he gestures ineffectually toward the disembodied voice that comes from the speaker.

I don't speak German, so I quickly leave his apartment. I make a mental note. Depending on how long I'm stuck in this limbo, I might enjoy learning another language. Although, from the sound of it, I would likely only learn words that I shouldn't repeat.

Sabryna's husband, Roger, has just gotten home from work. It's late—almost seven. Sabryna is in the dining room, wearing a chic black dress. Her salon-colored, blonde hair is styled in a loose chignon. Her only accessory is a set of tasteful diamond earrings. The cherry oak dining room table is set for dinner, with full place settings for two. A pair of slender, gold candles accentuates the center of the table, and the overhead lights are dimmed for ambiance.

Sabryna follows her husband into the bedroom. "Where are you going?" Her voice is surprisingly placid. Had I made a dinner like that for Jay when he—or I—were still alive, I would have been furious if he'd canceled. Although, I couldn't cook to save my life, so that issue never came up.

"I have dinner with a client," Roger says. He steps out of the bedroom into the hallway, back into my line of sight. He has changed his tie and applied more gel to his already impeccable hair.

Ten years her senior, Sabryna's husband is still handsome. Age has given his face rugged lines that are attractive on men but unfavorable on women. Sabryna is an aging trophy-wife, just past her best-before date.

I look back at the dinner Sabryna has painstakingly pre-pared. I can tell it's been sitting out for a while. Sabryna must not have known when her husband was coming home.

Sabryna pours a tall glass of the Château Pontet-Canet wine and takes a deep sip.

"I made dinner. I slaved over the stove for *hours*, and you couldn't call to say you wouldn't be home on time?" She waves her glass in the air as she speaks. I cringe, expecting wine to slosh onto her husband's fine-tailored suit.

"I mentioned it to you yesterday morning."

"Was I *asleep*?"

"As senior partner, I can't be expected to have consistent work hours. You *know* that, Sabryna."

"Right. Because your hard work is so appreciated. Weren't you overlooked for managing partner?"

Roger's smile becomes strained. He turns to walk away, but he stops by the dining room and takes a sniff. "Boeuf bourguignon. It smells good. Maybe I can heat some up when I get home?"

Sabryna takes the plate from the head of the table, strides to the kitchen, and dumps its contents into the trash. She then proceeds to pour herself another glass of wine. I follow her into the kitchen. In this close proximity, I can see the rage that burns behind her frosty blue eyes.

Roger doesn't move closer, but I can see that darkness has clouded his expression. "I see you're drinking already." He makes a show of checking his Rolex. "Well, I guess it's after five. Might as well get started."

Sabryna's fury drains like flour through a sieve. She gazes down into her glass.

"I never stopped," she says under her breath.

Roger doesn't seem to hear her confession. He storms out the front door and slams it shut behind him.

Sabryna downs the rest of her glass. She goes to refill it, but the bottle is empty. She glares at the bottle for a moment, then she sways from the room to find more.

I remain in the kitchen, staring at the empty bottle. Sabryna had always seemed so friendly and energetic. She'd emanated a nearly irresistible charm that I thought any man would be happy to claim as his own. Even I had had a hard time pushing her away, and that had been about me, not her. I'd assumed she had plenty of friends and other neighbors to spend time with and that she wouldn't miss my company. I frown as guilt slithers its way into my chest. It's clear to me now that her life isn't as idyllic as I'd thought.

The room fades to black as I'm torn back into the elevator. Roger stands beside me, staring straight ahead, a frown marring his handsome features.

The elevator stops at the ground floor. He gets off, but he doesn't head to the exit. Instead, he swerves left and walks down the corridor.

He stops outside the guest suite and glances around the lobby. Satisfied that he's alone, he turns and raps gently on the door. It swings open immediately. A young, red-haired man greets him.

"Are you ready for our *business* dinner?" Roger asks. I frown. There's something off about his tone.

"I thought we'd eat in," the younger man says with a smirk. He grips Roger's tie and pulls him into the room, kicking the door firmly shut behind them.

I stare at the closed door. How could Roger do this to his wife? How could he . . . *in the same building*? No wonder Sabryna seemed so desperate, so angry, so helpless. She's trapped in an impossible situation. I wish I had known when I was alive, then maybe I could have done something. Would I have done something? I suppose I'll never know.

Rage courses through me. I storm away, but I can't go far, not with this wall imprisoning me. I find myself in the library.

I fume for a few minutes before realizing I'm not alone. A pregnant girl is browsing the shelves, her fingers gently tracing the book spines. She's young, barely twenty years old. She has beautifully flawless, creamy white skin and wide-set, Disney princess eyes. She is one of those women who barely gain weight during pregnancy. I genuinely believe she's secretly carrying a watermelon under her conservative green blouse.

I've seen her once before, on my death day, when the elevator door opened to the fourth floor and the shrill cries of the first poor soul who found my body brought her rushing from her apartment to investigate. Her eyes had widened in terror as they beheld my corpse crumpled at the bottom of the elevator.

Now, she's browsing through the shelves, an almost serene expression on her features. She putters around the mystery titles, carefully sliding out books and reading the jacket sleeves. She has good taste. She carefully selects three mystery thrillers that I can personally attest are quite good, though out of date. Sadly, I haven't been able to read books in this genre in the last couple of years. I used to love mysteries before my life became one.

She hums quietly as she heads to the elevator bay. I'm pleased when it is my elevator that greets her. There is something about this girl that I like. I think we could have been friends. If I hadn't been so afraid of the unknown. Maybe in another lifetime.

The elevator begins its gradual voyage to the fourth floor. I continue to study the girl. Her green blouse is buttoned all the way to the base of her neck, and she wears a pair of ugly—but comfortable-looking—stretch pants. I can't help but feel that she and Sabryna should become friends. She would help the socialite overcome her loneliness, and Sabryna would, in turn, help her with her crimes against fashion. Not that I'm one to talk. I will spend the rest of eternity in a plain gray, wool sweater and jeans that I chose for comfort over style.

On the fourth floor, the girl skips to her apartment door, surprisingly agile for someone who must be at least seven months pregnant. This only supports my suspicion that she's not pregnant but carrying a large fruit strapped to her belly.

Her husband is waiting in the living room when she enters. He mutes the television which is playing the hockey game. The Maple Leafs are down by two goals, and it's only the first period. There are some things that never change.

"Hi, Oliver," the girl says.

"Where have you been?" Oliver asks, prying his eyes from the screen.

"I went downstairs to find some books."

"Don't you have enough books already?" he laughs and gestures toward the bookcase.

There are a measly two shelves, with less than seven books in total.

Oliver follows his wife's gaze to the bookshelf and shrugs. "Did you find anything good?"

She nods. "Yup. A mystery by Mary Higgins Clark."

Oliver frowns. "You know I don't like it when you read that kind of book."

"I know. But they didn't have anything else," she lies.

Oliver's eyes narrow ever so slightly. He gets off the couch and steps toward her. He snatches the book from her hand and flips through it. She flinches when he slams it shut.

Oliver raises his eyebrows and laughs. "What is it, Melody? Why are you so nervous? It's just a book."

He shoots her a charming smile. But there's something missing in his hollow eyes. A look of warmth or a spark of compassion. Love. A familiar chill creeps down my spine.

"You're right. It's just a book," she says, but her feigned indifference sounds forced, even to me, a complete stranger.

Oliver closes the distance between them and gives her a hug. He lets go abruptly, then returns to his spot on the couch. He turns the volume back on and continues to watch the game.

Melody places her books on the shelf. She casts a glance back at her husband before slipping into the kitchen. Out of his line of sight, she slouches against the wall, cradling her stomach between delicate hands.

I follow, but not before glancing back into the living room. There's something off about Oliver. Both the way he reacted to Melody's reading selection and her fearful reaction seem strange. But maybe I'm wrong. Maybe he's just aggravated by the Leafs losing.

I begin to pace the length of the kitchen. There must be something I can do to help. I may be dead but I'm still here. If only I can figure out how to interact with the world. There must be a trick to it. I put my hands on either side of the kettle, and I get ready to put all my energy into moving it.

"It's going to be okay," Melody whispers to her baby. "We're going to be okay, Shane."

I freeze. That whisper. I recognize it.

Melody was the girl on the phone. The one who called the hotline. My last client.

I worried that I'd never hear from her again, that I'd never have the chance to help her.

I reach out to pat her shoulder, but my hand falls straight through. Melody doesn't react. She can't sense me. A heaviness settles into the pit of my stomach. I can't help her. I can't do anything. I am nothing but a ghost.

6

The moon has already staked her claim in the midnight sky when a strange man returns home to his second floor apartment. According to the tags on his suitcase, he just got off a flight from Las Vegas. He looks vaguely familiar, but I can't quite put a finger on where I've seen him before. I've never spotted him around the building, or I would remember, since I'd always taken care to record and scrutinize my interactions with fellow residents . . . especially the peculiar-looking ones. And this one is *definitely* peculiar looking.

He is tall, well over six feet, and reed thin. He looks to be in his late fifties, but his face bears no lines. His skin is loose and transparent. He reminds me of one of Madame Tussauds' wax-work creations, one that was left in the heat for so long, it has begun to melt. A tiny, silver skull pierces the top of his right ear. His left arm is tattooed from wrist to elbow with whirling designs, Celtic knots interwoven with Russian characters. The tattoo looks like a loose silk sleeve gently clinging to bone. He is bald, without a single hair on his head or arms. Despite the late hour, there's no stubble shadowing his chin.

His height and extreme emaciation make him all sharp angles; every movement slices through the air around him. By contrast, Elias appears short and round, though he is of average height and build. Elias trails behind this bizarre man, trying not to appear out of breath while dragging the large suitcase.

They arrive at apartment 204, which is directly across the hall from my elevator. Elias produces a key and holds open the door. A bony finger flips the light switch, but the room remains cloaked in darkness. The walls are painted a matte black, and the furniture seems to have been carefully selected so not even a smidgen of color appears anywhere in the room. It's all black.

I follow them into the belly of the beast.

"Where would you like your suitcase, Mr. Utkov?" Elias asks. He doesn't seem to be at all perturbed by the apartment's interior design. Perhaps he's used to Mr. Utkov's idiosyncrasies, or perhaps he's paid too much to care.

"On the bed." Mr. Utkov waves a hand.

Elias hurries to the bedroom and deposits the luggage on the bed. Mr. Utkov tips him handsomely on his way out, which only seems fair because it is well after midnight, and I know Elias is up and at his station by six in the morning. Elias, who is ordinarily impeccably groomed, is wearing wrinkled slacks, and the buttons on his shirt are mismatched. I've noticed that he has been less presentable lately, and I begin to wonder about his personal life. It seems that everyone in this building has a persona that they reveal to the public, but their true selves only surface when they are alone—when they do not know they are being watched.

When I was alive, I must have come across as aloof and unfriendly, when in reality, I was in hiding and terrified. I never realized until now that there are so many others hiding their own truths.

Mr. Utkov heads into his office, which is also entirely black. All this darkness can't be good for his eyesight. This might explain the thin, red rims that circle his sunken eyes.

He sits in his plush leather chair and pulls out a cell phone. He puts it on speakerphone, rapidly dialing his voicemail, and listens to his messages.

"Alexei! It's Carlos. Let me know how your pitch went in Vegas. I know they're going to love you, but give me a call when you get a chance."

So . . . "Alexei" made a pitch in Vegas. I study him. He does look like he could have some kind of novelty show. I can easily picture him swallowing a sword or slicing a scantily clad woman into pieces in front of a hushed crowd.

The second message plays. "Is this Mr. Rasputin? I was hoping to reach you . . . a colleague of yours gave me your number. I couldn't make it onto your finale show, and I was really disappointed. I would like to make an appointment for a séance? My wife died a few months ago, and I would give anything to contact her. The price is a little steep though, but I'm hoping that we can negotia—" Alexei presses delete, muttering under his breath about idiots getting his personal number.

Rasputin! Now I remember how I know him. He's the cable television medium who contacts lost loved ones—for a fee. Luke is obsessed with his show. He watches it every night, and he would call me at least twice a week to rant about how mysterious Rasputin is and to tell me about the people he's helped to move on from their grief. It was amusing how Luke was torn between believing in the supernatural and thinking that Rasputin was some kind of an eccentric genius. Despite how adamant Luke was about how it's the best show on television, I've never caught an episode.

Rasputin's show was canceled last month. To say that Luke was upset would be putting it mildly. I'd almost caved and invited him over. Almost.

I'd had no idea that Rasputin lived in my building. A medium. Right here within my reach. I embrace the first glimmer of hope I've felt since long before my death.

I open my mouth to speak, but I am torn back into the elevator.

"No!" I punch my fist against the wall, but my hand simply slides through without a sound or the slightest bit of resistance. I feel nothing but the helplessness that threatens to overwhelm me.

Just as I was about to communicate with someone for the first time since my death, I am pulled away. What did I ever do in my life to deserve this torment in death?

The elevator doors glide open to reveal the basement corridor, but nobody is there. There is *nothing* more irritating than someone who presses the button for the elevator, then decides to take the stairs. While this was just a mild inconvenience when

I was alive, now, it is *much* more than a nuisance. I need to get up to the second floor. I *have* to try to communicate with Alexei or Rasputin or whatever his name is. If I can talk to him, maybe he can help me figure out what I'm supposed to be doing with my afterlife. There has to be more to death than just riding an elevator up and down, up and down for all eternity.

I turn to the elevator panel. I gather all my energy and focus on pressing the "2" button. It doesn't light up.

I try again.

Nothing.

Frustration bubbles up inside me. This is not my first attempt at moving the elevator, but the disappointment cuts through me as strongly as if it were. If I could move the elevator, my life—well, death—would be so much easier.

The elevator doors open again.

I'm still on the basement level, but no one is waiting. No one is there to push the button.

The elevator doors don't close. They stay open well past the time they should have defaulted to shut. This isn't normal. With a shiver, I realize that I haven't been down to the basement since my death. The elevator rarely idles down here. I poke my head out the yawning doorway, but no one is in sight.

I laugh at the absurdity of it all. I have nothing to fear. I'm dead. Even if the man who killed me returns to the scene of the crime, he can't hurt me anymore. The worst has already happened.

I step off the elevator and into the narrow hallway. The doors creep shut behind me.

There is nothing in the basement but storage units, the fitness center, and the basement-level parking garage. I dip my head through the wall to peer into the garage. There isn't a soul in sight. Before I turn away, I catch a glimpse of my battered and dusty Toyota, unused and neglected for so long that I almost feel sorry for whoever has to deal with it. I return inside and float across the hall to peek through the glass window of the fitness center's door. It's empty.

I almost enter the fitness center, but something keeps me from leaving the narrow hallway. I turn back. It seems... different somehow. The glamour and vitality that is prevalent in the rest of the building is noticeably lacking down here. The dim overhead light casts dark, angular shadows in the corners. I don't remember the basement being this shabby when I was alive. The carpet is a faded rust color; the busy paisley wallpaper is yellowing in the corners. The ornate bronze wall sconces are dull. The nearest lightbulb flickers. A faint scent of stale air tickles my nose. With a start, I realize this is the first time I've smelled anything since my death. Where is the scent coming from?

Everything looks faded from the other side, hazy and surreal. But this looks *different*. Rundown. Frayed. Uncared for. My eyes are drawn to the door at the end of the hall. I don't know why. I don't hear anything. I don't see anything. But I know that someone is in there.

I drift down the hall, not even conscious of the decision to move. I plunge into the room beyond the metal door. The storage room is dark, with only the red-tinged glow of the exit sign illuminating the space. I stand in an even narrower corridor, lined with large chicken-wire enforced enclosures. The smell is stronger here, like mold with a sour, metallic scent.

The shadowy outlines of the contents of each storage unit border the path before me. I move deeper into the center, following the path, traveling its twists and bends. Most of the storage units are full, stuffed haphazardly with boxes, oversized Christmas decorations, and the occasional set of winter tires. A bald and naked store mannequin with a painted face leans toward me on my left.

Who would even keep that? I shake my head and continue to scan the shadows until my eyes settle on a dark form huddled in the corner against the furthest wall. It looks like a small child standing in the corner as punishment. I take a tentative step forward. The scent grows stronger.

As I edge closer, the figure's details come into focus. It's a little girl wearing a red and white gingham dress. Her long, brown hair is tied back into two messy braids. She still faces the corner, swaying slightly in her petite Mary Jane shoes.

There is something different about her. She isn't blurred and indistinct like the rest of the world. She is crystal clear. I inch closer still until there is less than two feet separating us.

She doesn't seem to sense me, not like I sense her.

What am I doing? I should leave. I should get out of here. Instead, I say, "Hello?"

Inhumanly fast, she spins around, but her feet never move. Just now, I notice she is floating several inches above the ground. Like me.

She looks up. I lurch backward, gagging at the sight coupled with the realization that the overwhelming stench was rotting flesh. She has no eyes. Her face has two empty sockets where her eyes should be. Two large, gaping holes, carved deep into her skull.

Not a moment too soon, I feel the tug of the elevator. For once, I welcome it.

7

have avoided returning to my apartment since my death. This
has been difficult, considering the number of police officers
who have been traipsing in and out during the three days
following my murder. Now, I stand by the idling elevator, willing
for someone to call it away. I need to return to the second floor
to see the medium, especially now that I know I'm not the only
spirit haunting this building. Most of the second-floor residents
prefer to take the single flight of stairs over the elevator, so I
only had a twenty-second window this morning, during which I
barely made it to Alexei's bedside before I was torn away.

I need to be patient, but patience has never been one of my
virtues. When I was alive, I was always on the move, seamlessly

flowing between activities, never idling, never stopping. Never allowing myself time to think. To remember. Now, I have nothing to do. There's nothing I *can* do but watch as others live their lives at a snail's pace, not appreciating how little time they have left. With all this free time on my hands, my mind often wanders to dark places. It takes all my focus not to remember my life before, my husband, his death. How it was all my fault.

The numbness that overcame me when I died has finally worn off. I'm beginning to think it was just shock. If ghosts can even feel shock. After my *encounter* in the basement last night, my nerves are frayed, and I feel a familiar weight on my chest along with the fear that a panic attack could be waiting for me right around the corner. I feel almost human again, except for the maddening fact that I cannot interact with anyone or anything.

My strongest feeling is regret. I regret having holed myself up for nine months. I regret not making friends in this city. I regret pushing Luke away. I regret not letting him come over that night, because then, I wouldn't be here now . . . dead. I regret spending most of my waking hours working, building a fat savings account that's useless to me now and will likely just finance my brother-in-law's addictions. I regret staying trapped in a prison of my own making, and now that I am truly imprisoned, there is nothing I want more than freedom.

Yesterday, the police finally finished their investigation of my apartment. They found nothing of consequence; however, they did get ludicrously excited when they discovered my registered gun. It was tucked away in my bedside table, nestled between anti-aging cream and a book of poetry. A lot of good it did me there.

At least they were able to identify my body and notify my in-laws. I changed my name when I moved to Toronto, but it didn't take the police too long to figure out who I was. The police had found the legal document I left in my desk drawer, stating that in the event of my death, everything would go to Jay's parents. I had hoped that my in-laws would come, and they still might. They were the closest I've had to family in a long time. My parents died in a car crash when I was seventeen. A horrible accident caused by a drunk driver who left me orphaned.

I push aside these memories. Instead, I focus on the present. I am dead and trapped, but there must be something I can do, something to ease the tedium of the afterlife.

There must be a reason I'm stuck in this purgatory. According to nearly every movie or book about ghosts, I must have "unfinished business."

But what could that be?

The most obvious possibility is that I must identify my killer and somehow avenge my brutal murder. I already know who killed me, so it cannot be that difficult. *He* must have found me. He called the crisis hotline to mock me and terrify me before he finally killed me.

I feel stupid for having left my apartment that night. I made myself vulnerable, and I deserved to die for it. However, he is patient. He would have eventually caught up with me.

The door to my apartment is propped open. I wonder if the police aren't quite finished yet. I sigh. What more could they possibly expect to find? I push forward to investigate. A large, black duffel bag holds the door open. I can tell it isn't a police issue because it has no TPS logo on it. There are a couple of cardboard boxes stacked in the foyer. Confused, I frown down at them. It looks like someone is moving in, not packing my belongings to move me out.

The other elevator door dings, and a man steps out carrying a large cardboard box that hides his face. He stumbles over the duffel bag. I reach out to help him before I remember. I hesitate. There is something about him that looks very familiar. His hair color, the contour of his shoulders . . .

He turns around, surveying my apartment. His strong jawbone, soft blue eyes, Grecian nose. I am overcome with an unsteadiness that has nothing to do with the elevator.

I recognize this man. I *know* him.

But this is impossible.

He's my dead husband.

August 26

Dear Diary,

Ghosts don't exist.

At least, that's what I told Jay when he was making an argument for going on a haunted walk downtown. He was convinced that it was a perfect date opportunity. I was convinced that it was a perfect waste of time. However, I felt guilty because we hadn't had time for a date night since our wedding. I've been working overtime, trying to make up for taking a week off for my honeymoon and to remind my control-freak boss that I'm an invaluable asset to the company. Jay and I have just finished the move into our newly purchased house, and we've been spending most of our free time unpacking. Well, Jay unpacked while

I sat on the couch, snacking on pretzels and giving him contradictory instructions.

So, we ended up going on the haunted walk. It was a little embarrassing because we were surrounded by goth teenagers and ogling tourists. We didn't quite fit in. But I knew I had to tough it out, for Jay. The walk was actually kind of interesting at first. The guide told us spooky stories about people who threw themselves into the Rideau Canal for no apparent reason. We learned that Château Laurier is extremely haunted, and I'm glad none of those spirits showed up for our wedding reception. What do you even serve a ghost? Bloody Marys? Deviled eggs?

By the time the tour progressed to the Bytown Museum, it was fully dark, and I was starting to get a little antsy. Any time something moved in my peripheral vision, my skin began to crawl, and I would spin around, fists at the ready. (Because fists can protect you from an evil ghost.) It usually ended up being one of the other people on the tour or a feisty squirrel soaring out of a garbage can.

Long story short, by the time we got home to our newly purchased, two-story house, I was absolutely freaked out. I usually avoid watching horror movies or anything remotely creepy. I claim it's because I don't believe in the supernatural, but it's actually because that stuff freaks me the hell out. I spent the rest of the night in the office, fact-checking and shrieking when discovering the ghost stories were "true." Jay eventually gave up on trying to seduce me. He went to the bedroom and watched an episode of Game of Thrones. I'm still peeved that he didn't wait to watch it with me.

I finally got around to finishing the thank you cards for the wedding gifts last night. So, not sleeping after the ghost walk had its advantages. Apparently, it's classy to write them by hand, which is an archaic way of thinking, but I didn't want to offend anyone. So my hand is still cramped from using muscles I haven't exercised that vigorously since elementary school. I apologize, Dear Diary, if my writing becomes illegible at any point.

Jay and I received a lot of Scrabble themed gifts.

I guess that's the problem when you have an epic meet cute and you insist on telling and retelling it to anyone who'll listen (my bad). We got a Scrabble blanket, K and J mugs and assorted dishware, towels, and little throw pillows for our couch. I don't know why we bothered to register when it's clear that nobody intended to even look at the gift list. I honestly don't know what we're going to do without a gravy boat. I guess our gravy will have to sail the high seas on a raft. (Seriously, what is a gravy boat? Cindy insisted we needed one, and I just agreed so we could get out of the store as quickly as possible. I had a hankering for froyo, and there was a Menchie's next door.)

Well, I have digressed from the true reason why I am writing in this journal. As I mentioned before, Jay and I just moved into a new house we bought downtown, just a few blocks from the ByWard Market. It's an old house with a lot of character—gorgeous original crown moldings, hardwood floors, and only a few renovations required. (It even has a claw foot bathtub which was the major selling point for me. Don't tell Jay.)

So anyway, last night I discovered that the house is haunted.

8

The Woman with No Past stands at the window, her breath condensing against the cold, hard glass. The room is dark. The only illumination comes from the city lights, which filter through the grimy window. Her eyes remain vacant and impassive despite the bustle of cars below and the sound of sirens in the distance.

She wears an oversized gray, knit shirt and a pair of darker gray pants. I can't be certain, but I think they are the same clothes she wore the last time I saw her. Without warning, she turns and goes to her bedroom, which is furnished with bleached white furniture matching that from the living room. Colorless and utilitarian.

She swings open the door to the walk-in closet. My barrier doesn't allow me to follow her into the bedroom, but I can see from my position just outside the bedroom door that her closet is filled with clothes, many made with bright, vibrant fabrics. I cannot imagine her wearing them.

She sheds the gray, letting her shirt and pants fall to the floor. I can count her ribs from across the room. She is too thin, almost emaciated. She enters the closet and selects a dress without much deliberation. It is a floor-length gown, formerly midnight blue but faded from age. She slips it over her head, the silk embracing her skeletal figure. The hem has frayed along the base of the dress, and tiny tendrils of thread escape the fabric in little wisps, giving her an ethereal appearance.

She stands at the vanity and twists her dull, dark hair into a bun, which she fastens with a tarnished silver clip. She applies a thick coat of red lipstick, which only serves to accentuate her skin's grayish hue. She fails to color within the lines, and the result is a clownish grin—macabre and unsettling. She applies a single swipe of thick blue eyeshadow to the whole of her lids. She looks like a child playing with her mother's makeup, pretending to be something she is not.

The woman turns and walks through me, leaving a chill in her wake. I gasp. I haven't felt anything or anyone from the other side before. *What does this mean?*

I hurry to catch up to her. I find her standing in the dark living room. Watching. Waiting. But for what?

Music begins to play.

An old song from another time, an era with ballroom dancing and romantic courting. I look around, but I cannot identify the source of the music.

The Woman with No Past starts to move, swaying gently to the music. Her limp arms extend, and she reaches out to an imaginary dance partner. She begins a waltz, spinning around the room in perfect time to the music. Somehow, she manages to avoid every piece of furniture without looking down or removing her empty gaze from the point right in front of her.

It is only now that I realize that the music, while haunting in quality, doesn't have the typical echoic resonance of sounds from the other side. It plays smooth and unhindered. Every chord reaches my eardrums unimpeded by the thin veil that separates our worlds. This music is spiritual in origin. But the woman, with her hazy appearance, is most definitely alive, not a ghost like the little girl with no eyes.

If she can hear the music, maybe she can hear me. I open my mouth, but fear engulfs me. Not a word comes out. This woman is mad. She waltzes around the room, limp arms extended like those of a marionette, her expressionless, painted face glowing in the faint light.

I leave.

My husband never spoke much of his twin brother. Jay was kind-hearted, but he didn't suffer fools or swindlers, and according to him, his brother was both.

The elevator has finally returned to the seventh floor, and I'm surprised to discover that Jay's twin is still here. Will stands in my living room, perusing my bookshelves, likely looking for anything he can sell. Well, I don't have any designer shoes, silverware, or first edition books, and the sooner he realizes this, the sooner he can leave. The sooner I can stop being reminded of my dead husband.

After the initial shock of seeing him had worn off, I began to notice the little differences between Will and my husband. His face is thinner, slightly drawn, which is likely a result of the heavy drug use. I cannot believe that his parents allowed him to come here, to rifle through my things like it's a Sunday afternoon at the flea market. They're aging, but they could have sent someone to pack up my things, like an estate agency or a friend from my past. Anyone but him.

I drift toward the three cardboard boxes Will brought into my apartment. I worry that he plans to fill them with the spoils of my death. Right now, he's focused intently on my shelves, taking each book down and carefully leafing through.

"Looking for a little light reading?" I ask. "Get out of my house!"

Of course, he doesn't react. He continues to methodically examine each book.

Once he finishes, he goes into my office and begins to rummage through my desk drawers. I'm reminded of the night I died. I'd searched these desk drawers for my diary to take with me on the run, but in my hysteria, I couldn't find it. It looks like it really isn't in here. But where could it be? I can't help but feel a tinge of relief that it's missing. I don't want Will to read about the darkest time in my life—when his brother's light was snuffed out. They may not have been close but I wouldn't want him to have to endure the heartbreak of reading about his brother's death. I shove these thoughts aside as Will moves toward the filing cabinets. I watch as he proceeds to read each file on clients from cover to cover. He takes a battered notebook from his back pocket and scrawls illegible notes. My curiosity is peaked. What's he doing?

He groans when he realizes that I have a lot of files. I meticulously recorded all my client interactions—whether they be salary negotiations, instructions, or payments. In my previous life, I was a translator working for an Ottawa-based company that handled medical contracts from across Canada. After I escaped to Toronto to get away from my husband's murderer, I went freelance. Cooped up in my apartment with nothing else to do, I spent most of my waking hours working and built quite a nest egg for myself. I sincerely hope that Will won't get to see any of it.

He bites the end of his pencil, a mannerism that is startlingly familiar. The sight of this rips open old wounds. Memories flood back.

Jay, sitting at the kitchen table, working on a *New York Times* crossword puzzle. The crinkle in his brow as he chews the pencil, struggling to solve the final clue. I watch him while eating dry cereal. I toss pieces at him to get his attention. He doesn't even notice. His focus is resolute. His face breaks out into a huge grin when he fills in the last letters. He looks at me, then tosses a piece of cereal back at my face. He had noticed after all. I dodge, giggling as it barely misses.

No. I construct a mental dam to hold back the flood. I cannot remember. It's too painful.

I embrace the call of the elevator and the sensation of being pulled away. Away from the painful reminder of lives lost.

All hope is gone.

Alexei sits on his black leather couch, browsing the Internet on his phone with the TV turned low. I have tried everything imaginable, but I cannot reach him. I haven't even been able to make him glance up from his cell phone screen. I screamed insults at the top of my lungs. I waved my hands in front of his face. I even played punching bag with his silky bald head, but nothing has worked.

I wish I'd listened to Luke more closely when he'd talked about the show. I do remember that he'd told me that Rasputin required certain tools to communicate with the dead. Rasputin couldn't just conjure up and chat with ghosts, not like other television mediums. He needed to hold actual séances, which, I suppose, added to the atmosphere and perceived authenticity of his show.

I hover by the couch where Alexei is now watching the news. I catch part of a story about my murder investigation. Apparently the police are following leads, but they won't reveal much else to the public.

Alexei quickly changes the channel, apparently disinterested in valuable information about a murder in his building. Instead, he puts on a local TV medium's late night show. From the look of it, this woman is the reason why Alexei's show was canceled. She's warm and charismatic. She comforts the grieving and encourages them to move on. Alexei is cold and uncaring, and I understand the loss of appeal and the subsequent drop in numbers once this woman's show premiered last fall. People go to mediums for more than just to communicate with the dead. They want to be comforted. They want to be assured that their brother or mother or husband is in a better place. I cannot picture Alexei fulfilling this need.

I wonder if Luke is watching this new show right now. Does he like it? Will he be as obsessed with this woman as he was with Alexei? I sigh. I suppose I'll never know.

The phone rings and Alexei jumps to his feet.

"Hello?" he says, excitement making his accent thicker.

He's silent for a moment. His face falls.

"I have plans to give the show 'pizzazz' as you call it—"

He is interrupted. His face develops crimson splotches as he listens.

"All right. Goodbye then."

Alexei throws the phone across the room. It bounces off the couch and clatters to the floor. Hands clenched in fists, he paces the large living room, his spindly legs only requiring four strides for each lap. His eyes are alight with fury.

After several minutes, he stops abruptly. He retrieves his phone and speed dials someone.

"It is Alexei. Find that man who wanted to commune with his wife. Give him my address and make an appointment for Friday at midnight. I am doing the séance."

9

This morning, the elevator is summoned to the ninth floor, where it idles patiently. One of the only residents I willingly interacted with when I was alive lives on this floor. A fellow widow, Dr. Sylvie Favreau is a cardiac surgeon at the Toronto General Hospital. When I explained my predicament to her, she instantly became my personal physician, for a *small* fee. She was relatively understanding of my condition, although she frequently suggested I see a psychologist.

She thought I needed desensitizing to release my fears of the outside. I never told her the true reason for my phobia, so she believed that I was a born agoraphobic. But I wasn't born this way. I was made.

Dr. Favreau is standing at the kitchen stove, cooking bacon and an omelet for herself and her son, Etienne, to share. Her son has always been quiet, which I assumed was because he is shy and soft-spoken. But I'm surprised to see that he is still quiet in the privacy of his own home, with no one but his mother to hear him. He's sitting at the table, staring at his empty plate as his mother hovers by the stove. She prattles away in French about work, her plans for the day, and the incompetent anesthesiologist who recently transferred from Saskatchewan. A patient began to rouse mid-surgery, and the hospital is possibly facing a lawsuit because of it.

I imagine what it would be like to slowly regain consciousness on the operating table. Feeling the slice of a knife through the flesh of my stomach. Hearing the nurses chatter away about their boyfriends and manicures as they hand the doctor more instruments of torture. Seeing a gaggle of probing eyes from the viewing gallery, as Toronto General Hospital is a medical school, and there would be many interns and residents observing the operation. Watching the doctor's bloodied hands plunge deep into your abdomen, feeling the shifting organs and hearing the sloshing and snipping. The slick feel of gloved hands caressing your organs. The scent of your bowels permeating the air.

I shake away these thoughts as Sylvie plops sizzling bacon onto her son's plate.

The boy mumbles a *"merci, maman,"* and starts to eat. He cannot be more than nine years old, but I am impressed by his dexterity with a knife and a fork. He cuts open the Western omelet with precision. He doesn't drop any of the slippery egg onto his lap. He is clearly his mother's son, and he might consider surgery as a future profession.

If he can overcome his staggering shyness, of course.

I watch as they eat their eggs in stilted silence. Sylvie is no longer talking. After she finishes eating, she gets up from the table and leaves the room, and Etienne quietly loads the dishwasher and wipes down the kitchen table.

I trail after Sylvie. I find her in the spare bedroom, which is windowless and dark. A large medical cabinet sits against the far wall, with a wheelchair folded up beside it. My eye is drawn to the center of the room where a hospital bed is set up. A heart monitor beeps quietly from the corner, the faint glow of a jagged line cutting across the screen.

A man lies in the bed. His eyes are closed, and he looks to be in a peaceful dreamland, far away from the horrors of this world. He has an intubation tube protruding from his thin, pale lips.

Sylvie replaces his IV bag, moving quickly and efficiently. She has clearly become well-versed in this routine.

As she is about to leave, she hesitates. She returns to his bedside and strokes the top of his head with the back of her hand.

"Raymond . . ." she murmurs before planting a tender kiss on his cheek. She whispers something in his ear that I cannot make out.

Raymond? The husband who died five months ago? I stare at the man on the hospital bed. Sylvie had told me that her husband had had a heart attack, but she didn't elaborate, and I hadn't pressed for details. But she had heavily implied that he was dead. This doesn't look like dead to me. Believe me, I know what dead looks like.

Sylvie eventually exits the room, shutting off the lights behind her. The room is immersed in darkness.

But Mr. Favreau and I are not alone. There is a figure in the corner of the room. Squinting in the dark, I see that it faces away from me, toward the wall. It is a man gazing upward, staring at a large, brown stain that has blemished the ceiling.

This man is not clear. He doesn't have a crisp outline like the Girl with No Eyes. He appears slightly faded, as if he is trapped between this world and the next. Every inch of me screams that I should run away, but instead, I creep closer. I discover the cause of his indistinct appearance. He is vibrating, shaking at an inhuman speed. He stands perfectly still, save for his incessant shuddering. He continues to stare at the stain. He doesn't know I'm here, and I'm not sure if I want to attract his attention.

I follow his gaze upward. The stain is not stagnant; it seems to shift and grow, churn and writhe as I watch it. It is mesmerizing. A strange sensation overcomes me, and I begin to shudder.

"No!" I tear my gaze away from the hypnotic discoloration in the ceiling. I don't understand it, but I know that it must be making this man this way. I step closer and place my hand on his shoulder, but his violent vibration shakes me off, and I fly across the room. But not before I catch a glimpse of his face.

It's Raymond Favreau, Sylvie's husband.

10

ate that evening, I haunt the lobby, resting on one of the wing chairs that I've yet to see being used by a living soul. I wonder if that is why they look so pristine. Is there is an unwritten rule that they should be looked at, but not touched? I've spent the better part of the last hour counting the gold leaves in the wallpaper, but I keep losing count or losing my spot. The highest I've been able to reach was three hundred and fifty.

A man wearing a tweed suit enters the building. He's quite unremarkable looking, with pallid skin and a hairline that has migrated far past his ears. He has one of those faces that the eye just passes over. If someone asked me to describe his features mere minutes after seeing him, I don't think I'd be able to do it. He rides my elevator up to the fifth floor, and I follow him to his apartment, number 504, which is directly across from the elevators.

He steps inside, closing and locking the door behind him. He doesn't turn on the light. Streetlights shine in through the window, lighting his path as he places his briefcase on the plain, brown coffee table. I look around the living room, if you could call it that. There is very little furniture. A single bookcase holds a single row of books. There's no television. I briefly wonder what this man does for entertainment, but I do not need to speculate for long. He takes off his tweed jacket and carefully folds it, placing it beside the briefcase. He rolls up his stiff, starchy sleeves and approaches the window. That's when I see it.

He has a magnificent telescope, sleek black metal with many knobs and switches for adjusting clarity and scope. It sits on a tripod by the window, next to a rigid wooden chair. It is angled upward, toward the stars beyond.

I feel a pang of pity. He works late hours and comes home to a dark, empty apartment. His only friends are the stars, and I wonder if he has named them.

The Man in Tweed sits on his chair and grips the telescope, pressing his right eye to the lens. He lowers the body of the telescope until it is parallel to the ground, the wide end facing the apartment across the street. He does not move it, does not adjust it, he simply watches.

I step closer and peer out the window. Across the way, the apartment's curtains are wide open; living on the fifth floor must have falsely erased the occupant's privacy concerns. A young, blonde woman does stretches on a yoga mat in front of a large flat-screen TV.

The Man in Tweed is utterly immobile as he watches her. I cannot tell if he is even breathing.

Disgusted, I attempt to slap him, but my hand sinks through his pasty cheek. I put all my energy behind a second slap, but the result is the same. Completely unaware of my presence, the man continues to watch.

I want to run away, but I cannot leave. I cannot leave this vulnerable woman to this creep. Finally, she finishes her routine and exits the room, no longer in our line of sight.

Relieved, I wait for the Man in Tweed to put away his telescope and call it a night. Instead, he remains resolute. He doesn't shift the telescope to scan the other lit windows for another source of entertainment. He waits for the woman to return.

I step back, a heavy feeling in the pit of my stomach. I'm not much better than him. Here I am, watching from a distance, families and couples utterly unaware of my prying eyes. I tell myself that I'm different. This isn't my choice. I have no choice. That's what I tell myself.

❦

I drop down to the fourth floor.

My range on this floor is quite limited because the elevator still idles on the story above. I check on apartment 407.

Melody is alone. According to the calendar that hangs in the kitchen, her husband is at Cliff's for poker night. Melody is in the bathroom, and I can hear the splash of water.

She enters the kitchen and heads straight for the freezer, replacing one soggy icepack with another. She turns, and I gasp when I see her face. A dark purple bruise has formed on her left cheekbone. She tenderly applies the ice pack to her face and winces at the sting.

I circle her a few times. I see several older bruises on her arms, but nothing else that appears new. However, she is wearing a conservative nightgown, and I fear what might lie underneath.

A tear trickles down her cheek. She wipes it away. She turns to the iPhone dock that hangs on the wall. She dials.

"Hello. May I speak to Rachel, please?" Her voice quavers slightly.

My heart drops. "I'm right here," I say.

I can hear the hotline operator's soothing voice. "She no longer volunteers with us. I can put you in touch with one of our other helpers."

Melody's face falls. "No . . . Thank you." She ends the call. Slumping against the wall, she sinks down onto the cold, hard linoleum.

"I'm right here," I repeat. There's no answer, no indication that she can hear me.

I sit beside her, and I place my hand near her shoulder, stopping a hair-breadth away. I can almost feel her warmth. I want her to stop crying. She needs to know she's strong enough to overcome this. She's strong enough to get the help she needs.

Melody suddenly stops crying. Leaning heavily against the wall, she clambers to her feet. A resolute expression has formed on her face. Did she somehow receive my message? I would like to think so. She exits the kitchen, heading toward the bedroom. I wait, but she doesn't return.

T here are a lot of things I miss about being alive. The warmth of the sun on my face. The feeling of a cool summer breeze rustling my hair. The gentle aroma of my Mom's freshly-baked butter pecan cookies enveloping me and making me feel safe. There are a million little comforts I wasn't able or willing to appreciate during the last years of my life. I would give anything to experience just one of them again. But the comfort I miss most is sleep.

Ever since my husband's death, I've lived life frenetically, never truly stopping and never truly enjoying life's little luxuries. Although I suffered from mild to moderate insomnia, I never noticed how much I had grown to rely on sleep's brief escape.

The chance to close my eyes and reopen them hours later. The feeling of slight refreshment when I emerged from a night of dreamless freedom. Or, when my sleep was plagued with nightmares, the sensation of relief I experienced upon returning to the real world. Of course, the relief was always inevitably followed by a wash of disappointment and dread. But those few moments of reprieve made it all worthwhile.

Toward the end of my life, the despair that accompanied awakening had begun to fade into a dull desolation. I could return from slumber without wishing I had never awoken. Now, I wish I could experience that once again. I wish that this were all just a nightmare, and I'll wake up in my cold, empty apartment. Forever alone but alive. Likewise, I yearn for sleep. I wish I could escape this reality, if only for a few hours. But sleep eludes me.

Ghosts don't sleep.

I have been actively avoiding Will and my old apartment. I know he is still staying there because I occasionally see him in the hall when the elevator idles on the seventh floor. Henry Sanford, the elderly man who dwells in apartment 707, sits in his La-Z-Boy chair and listens to an old 1930s radio program every waking hour. He listens to the same one over and over on repeat. *The Shadow*. I feel as though I could recite it from memory. Accompanying him has been preferable to watching a complete stranger rifle through my personal belongings.

Why is Will still here? Why hasn't he liquidated my assets and moved on? While Thorwald Place is a nice apartment building, with deluxe facilities and in a prime location, the property taxes are astronomical. Although, from the little my husband told me about his brother, I can assume that Will may not be smart enough to come to these conclusions on his own.

My irritation morphs into anger as Will steps onto my elevator. Try as I might, I cannot avoid him when he is the one directing my afterlife. Oblivious to my presence, he taps the button for the basement. My anger mounts with every story we descend. I want him to go, to leave me alone in this hell. But he's been here for several days, and I fear I may never be rid of him. Is this my punishment? My husband's death was my fault, and now I am forced to see his face for the rest of eternity?

When we reach the basement Will exits the elevator, but he doesn't go to the fitness center, the storage room, or the parking garage. My anger tapers off and is replaced with curiosity. What's he doing? He appears to be studying the hall. He strolls up and down the corridor, peering at the papered walls, inspecting the wall sconces, and gawking at the ceiling.

My mouth drops open when he suddenly gets down on all fours and begins to crawl the length of the hall. It looks like he's scrutinizing the faded carpet. I press my lips tightly together to contain a giggle. I know that he has his addictions, but I wonder what kind of drug would induce this peculiar reaction.

My gaze is drawn to the steel door that leads to the storage units. Not unlike my last visit to the basement, I feel an overwhelming impulse to approach it.

"Don't be an idiot," I mutter.

The door seems to beckon to me.

I'm suddenly only two feet away from it, but I don't remember moving. How did that happen? I glance back at Will, but he's still flat on the floor.

I turn back to the door, and I'm closer still. What lies beyond it? I don't want to know. I don't want to see that little girl again. I enter the storage room.

My hypnosis fades away as soon as I pass through the door, yet I don't turn back. I don't leave. Instead, I look around. There isn't a living soul in sight. I glance toward the far corner for the Girl with No Eyes, but she isn't there. I release a sigh of relief. But that introduces another question. If she isn't here, then why was I compelled to enter?

The naked store mannequin grins at me, mockingly. I tear my gaze away, turning to leave.

I jump at the sight of the little girl blocking my path. She's standing between me and the exit. Her hollowed eye sockets seem to consume the light around them. Her mouth sluggishly opens into a silent scream. All the hairs on my arms stand on end.

"What are you trying to say to me?" I ask her, fighting my instinct to simply run. She's just a child. She can't possibly hurt me. Can she?

The girl cocks her head. I know she can definitely hear me. Her mouth remains open wide, a dark hole. I cannot see her teeth or tongue, just a bottomless black void.

Bit by bit, she raises her arm, until it lies in a straight line with her shoulder. Her finger extends. Points over my shoulder.

I whirl around and peer into the darkness beyond. At first, I see nothing out of the twisted ordinary I've come to expect down here. The sneering mannequin. The stacks of dilapidated cardboard boxes. A bundle of what looks like firewood presses against the chicken wire to my right, but the building has electric fireplaces, so I try not to wonder what the wood could possibly be used for. A rolled up oriental rug leans against the wire on my left.

Then, something moves. I narrow my eyes, straining to see in the darkness. A darkness that seems to gather, collecting shadows and assembling a form. It twists and writhes and combines and builds to create a silhouette. A man so tall that he must hunch so he won't hit the ceiling. A man so broad that he fills the entire corridor. He is only a silhouette, but I can make out the outline of a thick cloak and a bowler hat. I don't know how I can tell, but his back is toward me. I shiver as he deliberately turns to face me.

He has no face, no features, no discernible characteristics other than the hat and cloak. He is simply a shadow. I glance toward the girl, but she is gone.

The silhouette approaches me, leisurely, thick arms outstretched, snaking toward me. Recognition hits me. I know him. He was there the night I died.

I barrel out of there, moving as fast as I can, which doesn't feel fast enough. At the exit, I glance over my shoulder. He's pursuing me; the distance between us closes with every chilling second.

I burst through the door, back into the light of the corridor. Will is still here. He's by the door to the fitness center, scribbling in his cursed notebook.

"We need to get out of here!" I cry.

He hears nothing. He sees nothing. He does not move toward the elevator. He does not move toward safety.

Like a bullet, I shoot down to the opposite end of the hall, the furthest I can get from the steel door. I wait, the phantom of my heart pounding in my chest. The Shadow Man does not follow into the light.

Languidly, without a care in the world, Will caps his pen, tucks his notepad in the back pocket of his jeans, and calls the elevator.

August 31

Dear Diary,

Sorry for leaving you in suspense like that. My hand spasmed, and I had to find Jay to massage it for me. I'm really taking advantage of having a husband at my beck and call.

I'm convinced that this house is haunted. The more I think about it, the more I notice abnormal events that point to us having our very own Casper.

It started off subtle. But last night, things . . . escalated. I'll tell you what happened, and you can decide for yourself.

I woke up and rubbed my eyes, checking the clock. It was two in the morning. I'm usually a sound sleeper, and I rarely wake until the alarm clock radio blasts *Lady Gaga* into my ear. I sat up, looking for Lon Chaney, Jr., but he was curled up in a ball at the foot of the bed, fast asleep. It couldn't have been him who woke me.

I sat in bed for a minute before deciding I had to pee. Just before I put my foot on the ground, I heard a loud creak from the hallway. Right outside the door.

I gulped and pulled my foot back into the bed, remembering the scene where the demon yanked on the main character's exposed leg in Paranormal Activity, a movie Catalina forced me to see, and part of me has never forgiven her for it. I sat perfectly still, clutching my pillow to my chest, straining my ears. Struggling to hear any other sound.

Just as I began to relax, I heard another creak, followed by another. They seemed to be getting louder, like the entity was getting closer to the bedroom.

I whirled around and shook Jay.

"What is it? Am I snoring again?" he mumbled and rolled over.

"No!" I hissed. "There's someone, or something in the hall!"

Jay opened one eye. "Something?"

I nodded vehemently. "You need to investigate."

Again, I listened. There was another creak.

I grabbed the lamp, ripping the plug from the outlet.

Jay sat up, staring at me like I was a lunatic.

"Take this! Hurry!"

Instead of taking the lamp, Jay reached under the bed and pulled out a baseball bat. He rolled out of the bed.

Another creak resounded from the hall.

Jay was suddenly fully awake. "Stay here," he said.

I nodded.

I counted the seconds until Jay returned a torturous four minutes later. The bat was loosely grasped in his hand.

"What was it? Did you see it?" I asked earnestly.

"See it?" Jay looked at me funny. "No one was there. It must have just been the sound of the house expanding."

This confirmed my worst fears. Some part of me was hoping that there had been an intruder in the house. Burglars and serial killers are a lot easier to defeat than poltergeists. Probably. I don't actually have experience with trespassers, living or dead.

This was just the most recent of many strange occurrences in the house. Sometimes, I misplace something, like my keys or my hairbrush, and I just know that it isn't my fault. I may not be the tidiest person, which aggravates Jay to no end, but everything has its place. And I never misplace my hairbrush.

Even the cat has noticed something off in this house. Lon Chaney, Jr. sometimes gets a determined look in his eye. He spends hours stalking around the house, sniffing the air. I did some research, and ghosts are often accompanied by a sulfur smell. Maybe only Lon Chaney, Jr. has a powerful enough nose to smell it. Sometimes, I follow him on all fours, sniffing the air behind him, but I can't smell anything. Jay walked in on me doing this once, which was the last time I tried to smell a ghost.

I hadn't said anything to Jay about my suspicions, because they were just that—suspicions. But after last night, I'm more than just suspicious. I'm starting to believe.

12

Sabryna knows.

Earlier tonight, she "ate" a dinner that consisted solely of a bottle and a half of champagne. Afterward, she put her glass in the dishwasher and made her way down to the library. She's been sitting in the leather chair closest to the door for hours. Every time my elevator is called and I'm pulled away, I wonder if she'll still be there when I return. Whenever I make my way back, she still sits there, unmoving, hands clasped, eyes distant.

A few residents enter the library, and Sabryna doesn't seem to register their presence. No more is she the desperate housewife, eager for attention and friendship. No more is she the doting wife dying to please her unfaithful husband. She sits and waits, lips pursed, eyes distant, without movement, except for the occasional glance at her diamond Cartier watch.

Melody strolls in at around half past eight. She browses the shelves, not just looking at mystery novels this time but fiction and biographies. She gathers several books, but she doesn't leave. Instead, she sits on the couch across from Sabryna and reads.

Keeping one eye on the lonely socialite, I inspect Melody's reading selection. There appears to be a common denominator among all the books she chooses. Each of them features an abused wife or girlfriend who gathers the courage to escape her oppressor. Melody reads carefully, her beautiful nose crinkled in concentration as she absorbs every word.

This is progress. She needs to leave her husband before he does something she can't come back from. But this isn't the way to do it! I gave her resources on the phone. She should find a women's shelter and leave when her husband is at work.

I suppose that the books are giving her the courage she needs to make that difficult decision. While the choice should be obvious, it's clear to me that Melody loves her husband, and I understand that becoming a single mother is not a decision to be made lightly. I had hit the jackpot with a loving husband who didn't have a cruel bone in his body. But not everyone can be as fortunate as I am. Was.

Sabryna checks her watch and abruptly stands, approaching the library door. She holds it ajar and peers down the hall toward the guest suite.

A deliveryman stands at the door to the suite, jostling a large bag of takeout in one hand so he can knock with the other.

When the door finally opens, Roger steps out, wearing nothing but a bathrobe. He takes the food, tips the deliveryman, then disappears back into the room. If he had so much as glanced down the corridor, he would have seen his wife.

Sabryna pries her white-knuckled grip from the door handle, allowing it to swing closed.

Melody looks up curiously, but she doesn't say anything. Something in Sabryna's expression makes her quickly avert her gaze.

Sabryna leans against the wall, taking several deep breaths. Her face is drawn. Her carefully applied makeup does nothing to mask her anguish.

She stands there, perfectly rigid, for five, ten, twenty minutes. Then we return to her empty apartment.

B

The next morning, I'm loitering in the lobby, waiting for the elevator to drag me away, when my past and present collide. The front doors of the building swing wide open, bringing the dazzling golden light of the morning sun, a gust of cool autumn air, and a familiar face. *Catalina.*

Elias nearly trips over his feet as he rushes to greet her. He's one of many barriers against unwanted visitors in this high security building. They don't allow police officers in, but of course, psychos wielding knives slip through the cracks.

Catalina ignores Elias and scans the wide, empty lobby. I know that she's establishing her dominance with him. She shared that trick with me not long after we met. She's letting him know that she's in charge and that she alone will choose when to speak. I grin. I've missed her.

Eventually, she deigns to speak to him.

"I'm Detective Catalina Marquez." Catalina pulls a badge from her blazer pocket and waves it in front of his face. "I'm working the Rachel Drake murder case."

Detective? She must have gotten a promotion in the last two years. A goofy grin spreads across my face. She had often spoken of how hard it was to move up in the police force in Ottawa, especially as a woman *and* a person of color. But here she is, a *detective*, and she hasn't even hit thirty yet.

Elias turns pink. "Of course! Anything I can do to help? Rachel and I were quite close, and I know *everything* about *every* resident in this building." There's a hint of desperation in his tone, but I don't blame him. Catalina is a stunning woman. Her statuesque figure and striking features are both intimidating and alluring. Once it is made known that she's with law enforcement, she has both men and women alike eating from the palm of her hand. She's aware of the effect she has, but fortunately, she doesn't use it for evil. I haven't seen Catalina in person since she helped me to run away two years ago. She was the only person to believe me when I said my life was in danger. She had had the intelligence, resources, and determination to help me escape. Together, we found Thorwald Place, an apartment building safely nestled in the center of a bustling city. A place where I could be just another anonymous face in the crowd.

Disappointment weighs against my chest. I won't be able to interact with her. I won't be able to tell her my fears over rocky road ice cream like when we were in university. I won't be able to share the pathetic details of my life or tell her about Luke, my only friend in this backwards life. I won't be able to ask her about her own news. Has she gotten over her breakup with Daniel? She must have—it's been over two years. Is there someone new in her life? Is she married? I glance down at her left hand. There's no ring, but I notice that her hand is clenched into a fist. I scan Catalina from top to bottom, the initial excitement of seeing her is replaced with concern. She looks tense.

I have no doubt in my mind why she's here. She's here because I was brutally murdered in the elevator, just feet away from where she stands. She's here because she knows that despite our best efforts, he found me. She's here to catch my killer. But why isn't she in Ottawa arresting him?

"What can I do to help?" Elias asks again, his voice suddenly high pitched.

"Book me the guest suite. I'm going to be here a while."

Catalina drops her small bag in the guest suite and immediately heads to the elevator bay, tapping the button. I smile when it's my elevator that greets her. Finally, the universe does something in my favor. Catalina managed to convince Elias that he wasn't needed for her investigation, which was a relief, because he's already quite smitten with her, and I doubt she'd be able to get much done with his unwavering attention focused on her. Elias is married to his work, and sometimes, it's easy to forget that underneath that professional, attentive exterior is a red-blooded male. Catalina brings that side out of everyone, I suppose.

She boards the elevator and presses the number seven. The doors slide shut. I study her as the elevator begins its gradual ascent. She's staring down at the elevator floor, a frown marring her face. She must know this is where I died.

"I'm okay." I immediately feel guilty for the white lie. We never lied to each other. She doesn't hear me anyway.

She brushes away a stray tear with the back of her hand before stepping off the elevator. She marches up to my front door and knocks authoritatively.

I drift through the wall into my living room. Will is lingering by the front door. He seems to be debating whether or not to answer it.

I pop back into the hall, where Catalina is reaching into her pocket, retrieving the key I'd given her when I'd moved in. She doesn't have to use it because the door swings open.

Catalina lets out a strangled noise, mouth agape. She must have forgotten about the twin brother, as I had, if only for a moment.

Will extends a hand. "I'm Will. The brother-in-law," he says quickly.

"Oh." Catalina's skin is about three shades paler than usual, and she looks like she might be sick. I've never seen her so frazzled before. Not even back at the crime scene when she first saw all the blood, my husband's body limply displayed to torment me. She had remained cool, calm, and collected. But this rattles her.

"Would you like to sit down? I take it you knew my brother, Jay, then?" Will asks.

Catalina nods curtly, then walks toward the kitchen and takes a seat at the head of the table. My place. I frown at the irritation that pricks at my nerves.

She couldn't have known that.

Will pours tap water into a glass and hands it to her. Eyeing him over the rim, she takes a slow sip. Her habitual confidence is gradually returning. She seems annoyed that Will has seen her in a vulnerable state.

"I'm Detective Catalina Marquez," she says after a few moments of quiet scrutiny. "I'm investigating your sister-in-law's murder." With a jolt, I realize that her voice has changed over the last two years. Her accent is less thick, and she barely even rolls her R's. Catalina takes another sip of water. "I was one of the responding officers to your brother's . . . murder. I am very sorry for your loss. Both of them."

She's incorrect in assuming that Will and I had ever met. I frown. I'd caught a glimpse of Will at Jay's funeral, but we had never met prior to that. The days after the attack are a blur, and I still cannot remember if we have ever been formally introduced. I can't recall if I ever told Catalina about Jay's lack of a relationship with his brother.

"Thank you," Will says. He stands behind the chair opposite her, his entire body rigid. He doesn't sit down, and it's clear that he wants her to leave.

Catalina continues to watch him, taking small sips from her glass. She's a master at reading people. She always manages to glean their motives and get them to talk. She never fails.

"Are there any questions that you have for me?" Will asks.

Catalina slowly lowers the glass, allowing the tension to build. "I'm curious about why you're staying here, is all," she replies. I'm relieved that she notices this is unusual. Maybe *she* can convince him to leave.

Will is quiet, as if he's carefully selecting his words before speaking. "My parents inherited the place. I'm staying here until

I can get an apartment of my own in the city." He isn't lying—I had left everything to Jay's parents in my will. But I can tell he's only giving a half-truth. It doesn't explain his fascination with my personal belongings.

He's hiding something.

It's unclear whether or not Catalina can also tell that he's holding back. "I believe that Kae's killer could be the same person who murdered your brother. There are several startling similarities between their deaths, the first of which being the choice in murder weapon. The second being the sheer brutality of the kill."

Will flinches.

"I'm sorry," Catalina says, her eyes widening slightly. "That was insensitive. You're suffering from the loss of two loved ones." I frown. She sure is laying on the sympathy thick. Is that a cop trick? To get him to loosen up and admit something?

Again, Will doesn't tell her that he barely knew me. I also notice that Catalina is omitting the fact that she knows who killed my husband. I assume that she at least suspects that it was he who killed me. Neither of them are being truthful to each other. Frustration bubbles up inside me. I just wish I could get the full story.

"When did you get here?" Catalina asks, gesturing around the apartment.

"About five days ago." It was four days ago.

"Have you found anything in the apartment that might be of use to the police? I assume that you've had a chance to look around. Having been here for *about* five days, and all."

Will gives her a strange look. "I *have* looked around, but I haven't found anything that could lead to her killer."

"How would you know? You're not a detective," Catalina says with a little bite.

Will frowns. "No, but the detectives have already been through the apartment. They didn't find anything."

Catalina glares at him. "You wouldn't mind if I took a look around, would you?"

Will's tension leads to open hostility. "Unless you have a search warrant, I think it would be best if you left."

Catalina raises an eyebrow. She places the glass on the table and gets up to leave.

"Your cooperation would be appreciated. But it's not necessary. I'll be back." She glides from the apartment, the front door slamming shut behind her.

Will scowls even deeper now that she's gone. He stalks out of the room and I trail after him. He stops abruptly in the doorway to my office. He flips on the light and stands there, arms crossed over his broad chest.

He has done some significant redecorating. My framed landscape photos have been removed from the wall and are propped up against the desk. In their place, the wall is plastered with papers from floor to ceiling. I float through Will to take a closer look.

Newspaper clippings, loose pages, internet printouts. All about my husband's murder. All about the people from my former life. I step toward the wall. There is a class graduation photo of me beaming at the camera. Beneath it, there's a rare photo of me and Luke together, taken nine months ago. We're beaming at the camera from the top of the CN Tower. It was one of the few times that I'd let Luke convince me to leave my apartment building for something that was non-essential. He'd been so excited to show me around the city, viewing me as a tourist even though I'd technically been living here already for over a year. I look carefree in this photo. You would never know that only a few hours later, I had a debilitating panic attack when I thought I saw him on the street and that I haven't left Thorwald Place since. And I never will.

I tear my eyes away from Luke's smiling gaze. I scan the rest of the wall. Newspaper articles about my death are pinned beneath my class graduation photo. To the right are rows upon rows of photos of people. At first, I don't recognize anyone. Then I see Oliver Boyden's face, then Roger Hyland's. These are the residents of this building. There is a giant red X scrawled across Alexei Utkov's sullen photo. "Out of country" is written in block letters at the bottom of the picture.

The realization hits me just as the elevator rips me away. Will is investigating my death.

14

Sabryna lies in bed despite the early evening hour. An empty wine bottle sits on the night stand. Roger will be annoyed to see it when he returns from his tryst. Sabryna hasn't taken the news of her husband's infidelity well. She needs to get out of the apartment, see a therapist, leave her husband, and move on. But I fear she isn't strong enough for these difficult decisions. I watch her toss and turn for several minutes before I leave. While I don't have any reason to assume that the living can sense me, the last thing I want is for Sabryna to feel the disquiet of a ghost haunting her bedside.

As I drift past the living room toward the front door, something catches my eye. A slip of black fabric protrudes from under the table in the foyer. Curious, I move closer for a better look. It's a single black leather glove.

Memories of my death rush back to me. The strong hands that gripped me, fending off my feeble struggles. Strong hands wearing thick leather gloves. I peer closely at the glove, but I can see no indentation where my teeth would have broken the skin. I shake my head, pulling back. Many people own leather gloves. And I wasn't even sure of the color because I never got a look at them. Besides, why would Roger Hyland want to murder me? Unless he had mistaken me for someone else . . . With a jolt, I notice that my hair is very similar to Sabryna's—but without the $300 style and color.

I push away these dark thoughts. Why would Roger want to kill his wife when he seemed to have it all? A loving, doting wife who cooks meals for him, and a lover on the side. Just because he's willing to cheat on his wife doesn't necessarily mean he wants her out of the picture. There's a big difference between infidelity and *murder*.

I ponder this as I enter apartment 601, which I haven't visited since the day after I died. The conventional couple with the unconventional son. The last time I visited, they'd been eating dinner in an awkward, uncomfortable silence.

I read the names on a cable bill sitting on the kitchen counter. Mr. and Mrs. Charles Yu. The couple are seated in the living room watching *Jeopardy*. Charles is flipping through a men's health magazine on his tablet. His wife is crocheting what looks like an oversized sock.

I drift down the hall and enter the first bedroom on the right. The lights are off. A thick black candle sits on the nightstand. Its quivering flame casts sharp, dancing shadows. I drift farther into the room, glancing at the walls, which are plastered with obscure, dark posters of heavy metal bands. Music plays faintly, a raspy voice crooning about how he wants to slit his lover's throat. I shiver, vividly recalling how that felt.

The Yus' teenage son sits on his bed, thumbing through a thick, leather-bound book. His face is painted white, accented with scarlet eyeshadow and glossy black lips. In the darkness, the effect is even more surreal. He wears a black mesh shirt and tight leather leggings. That can't be comfortable loungewear.

I step over to his desk to look for something with his name on it. The workspace is covered in loose pages, each depicting disturbing charcoal drawings. But on the edge of the surface, I find what I'm looking for. A calculus test, dated last week, labeled "Clark Yu".

I stifle a chuckle and turn back to the bed. He doesn't look like a Clark. I wonder what kind of goth name his friends at school call him. Blood Dagger? Obsidian Fang?

Considering his C-minus on the calculus test, I want to tell him to do homework, but I know he wouldn't listen, even if he could hear me. Although, I'm interested in finding out what he's reading so intently.

I edge closer to the bed, but I can't angle myself to see the title on the cover of the book. I do see a library barcode, which indicates that he must have left this dank hole at some point to visit the outside world.

Clark's chipped, black nails turn the page, revealing a black and white ink drawing. The image depicts a demon being devoured by fiery flames. Cross-hatching creates twisted figures in the backdrop of corrupt souls thrashing in anguish, tiny mouths open in soundless screams. I'm reminded of the Girl with No Eyes, and I quickly tear my gaze away. Instead, I read the text beneath. It's written in Latin, and my knowledge of the dead language is non-existent. I only studied French literature in school, since it directly related to my career choice. Translators are typically only well-versed in one language, and they translate from that language into their native tongue.

Being Canadian and raised by French-speaking parents, fluency came naturally to me. But I never had much interest in learning additional languages, except for the basic Italian I memorized before embarking on a month-long trip with Catalina and Cindy. I suddenly wonder how Cindy is doing. Is she successful like Catalina is? How did she handle my disappearance? Did Catalina tell her I was alive, safely tucked away where he could never find me? By the same token, how did she react to the news of my death? I have no family left to speak of, except for Jay's parents, and I assume that they were the ones to notify her. I feel a pang in my chest. I hadn't seen them since Jay's funeral.

I sigh and shake my head. Catalina's arrival has made me nostalgic, unearthing memories best left forgotten. There's no point dwelling in the past, allowing myself to worry about people I will never see again.

My stomach churns at that thought, and I hurriedly return my attention to Clark. There are a few other, less ominous looking texts strewn on the bed beside him. The bright yellow cover of *Latin for Dummies* strikes a sharp contrast against the sullen shades of bedding. Another book is about Latin translation.

Clark should put this much effort into learning calculus. He's clearly smart, but his efforts are misguided. Why is he so interested in this book?

"Clark, honey? Do you want to come out and watch some TV with us?" Mrs. Yu's voice calls timidly from behind the closed door.

"Damn it, Rebecca. My name is Razor," Clark snaps.

I snicker. I was close with "Blood Dagger."

I hear Rebecca's footfalls as she leaves. Jaw clenched, "Razor" resumes his reading.

I drift back toward his desk. The illustrations are disturbing, with charcoal smudges giving them a dreamlike quality, making the images barely identifiable. This boy is obsessed with the occult, which can't be healthy. I remember seeing him once when I first moved into the building. He had seemed normal—happy even. He had been contentedly playing with his tablet in the lobby. At that time, he was wearing an innocuous red plaid shirt and blue jeans. It's only been two years, yet he has transformed completely. His bedroom, his appearance, and he clearly doesn't spend his free time playing Angry Birds anymore.

As I scan the drawings, my eye is caught by one that is set aside from the rest. I move closer, squinting in the darkness. It shows a man—a figure—in black shading against a dark background, which makes the outline difficult to discern. The picture is of a man standing flush against a wall, with his dark coat billowing around him. I follow the line of his shoulder, up to his head. He wears a bowler hat. He seems to be looking straight ahead, yet he has no face.

It's the man from the basement. The Shadow Man.

15

The elevator summons me, dragging me up to the ninth floor. Dr. Favreau steps on and taps the button for the lobby. She must have another night shift. No wonder her poor son has issues. He's always left alone in the apartment under the guise of being home-schooled. He's far too young to be left alone. I wonder if he sits with his father, watching him, praying that he'll wake up—if only for the company.

Sylvie gets off the elevator on the ground floor, nods at a passing security guard, and walks toward the exit marked "Garage."

The elevator stays on this floor. The lobby is empty. Elias isn't at his station. I peek into the library and glimpse a middle-aged couple browsing the shelves. They don't live within my range, and I don't think I've ever seen them before. They seem carefree and content, perusing the shelves and offering each other suggestions. I am glad to see that there is one marriage in this building that isn't falling apart. I'm more convinced now than ever that this is my curse. I must watch the lives of those around me as they disintegrate, unable to observe even the smallest happiness, such as the comfort of this loving couple. If only their happy home was within my elevator's range.

The couple gathers their books, the husband rolling his eyes as his wife snatches a copy of *Fifty Shades of Grey* at the last minute. Arm in arm, they leave the library.

The door gently drifts closed, leaving me alone with my thoughts once again.

I return to the lobby, but Elias is still nowhere to be seen. I don't want to drop to the basement; I have been avoiding it at all costs. I suppose I could jump up to the second floor, but there's no one of interest there, except for the medium who is out of the city until his séance planned for tomorrow night. A séance I have every intention of attending.

I peek into the guest suite. Catalina is there, sitting at the breakfast nook with Elias settled directly across from her. Papers are strewn between them.

Catalina has a determined glint in her eye. "What about her?" Catalina asks, tapping a photograph of Sabryna Hyland. "You mentioned before that Rachel was friendly with her?"

"*Friendly* is a strong word," Elias says. He seems to be glowing. It must be a side effect of Catalina's undivided attention. "I saw them talk to each other several times when Rachel first moved in."

I stiffen. I hadn't realized we'd ever had company. Just how much does Elias see? Perhaps Catalina is on the right track, questioning him first.

Elias continues, "Rachel made it clear that she wasn't looking for friendship, especially not with someone like Sabryna." He says her name in a derogatory tone.

I feel a spark of protectiveness for Sabryna. Had I really given off that impression? Of *snobbishness*? I hadn't wanted to make *any* friends in the building, and it had nothing to do with who they were. It had everything to do with who *I* was. I wonder if this is what Sabryna thought too. Guilt rises like bile in my throat, and I cannot be rid of it.

"Can you elaborate on that?" Catalina asks.

"Sabryna has her vices . . . Alcohol, to be specific. I wouldn't be surprised if she overuses prescription drugs, too." Elias' nasal voice is less comical now that I am seeing this side of him. He doesn't know what Sabryna is really going through. Although, he does know most of it. After all, he is the one who books the guest suite for Roger's lover. He is the one who looks Sabryna in the eye when he greets her every day.

"So you're saying substance abuse is the reason Rachel cut off ties with her?" Catalina says.

"Well, no. Rachel kept to herself. She never interacted with anyone in the building—at least, not to my knowledge. I was the only one she regularly spoke with."

Catalina stares at him for a moment. I can almost hear her wondering how much of what Elias says is bullshit.

"What about Sabryna's husband? Roger?" Catalina asks.

"I have never seen Rachel even look at him. Although, I've seen him look at her," Elias chortles.

What is that supposed to mean?

Catalina raises an eyebrow. "Are you saying that Roger is unfaithful?"

"No, no! Not at all! I'm just saying that he appreciated the view of the other residents in the building, especially someone who looked like Rachel."

I don't remember ever having seen Roger when I was alive. He was always working when Sabryna dropped by, unannounced. I wonder if what Elias is saying about his wandering eyes is even true, especially considering he's having an affair with a man. It doesn't escape my notice that he hasn't brought up Roger's affair.

Catalina makes a note on her paper. I peer over her shoulder and see that the note isn't about Roger but about Elias. "Creepy" is all she wrote.

I snicker.

This interview isn't about the residents in the building, or at least, that isn't the only reason Catalina is meeting with Elias. She's also getting a feel of him, trying to see if *he* is hiding anything. I cannot imagine why she's bothering with this. We already know who my killer is. Shouldn't Catalina be searching for links to him?

Then again, maybe that *is* what she's doing. This thought is chilling. I realize that he may have hired someone to kill me. And I realize that there is a strong chance that the assassin wasn't working alone. This building is very secure, but it's easy to get in with a resident's permission. Who living in this building could be an accomplice to my murder? My thoughts wander to the stray glove I saw lying in the Hylands' apartment.

"Anything else about Roger?" Catalina is starting to sound slightly annoyed. I don't blame her.

"Not that I can think of," Elias says, scratching his chin. "Just that he works a lot. He has a lot of business dinners, and I don't actually see him often, except when he's coming or going. That's about everything."

Catalina is quiet for a moment, and she jots something down in her notebook.

Elias studies her. "Why haven't you asked me about her boyfriend?"

I jolt at that. Catalina looks just as surprised. "You hadn't mentioned it," she says carefully.

"Hadn't I?" Elias asks.

Catalina's lips purse. "Rachel had a boyfriend?" This is news to me as well.

"There was a man who used to come to visit. He would stay late," Elias pauses, the air stiff with innuendo, "but leave. He never did stay the night."

He's talking about Luke. Embarrassment washes over me.

I hadn't realized that people thought we were together in that way.

Elias continues. "He stopped dropping by a few months ago."

"Do you have a name for me?"

"It will be in the visitor's log," Elias says.

"I'd like that name and a record of the times he visited," Catalina says.

Elias beams at her. "I'll get that to you immediately."

I wish I could tell Catalina that Luke wasn't my boyfriend, that he was just a friend. My inability to communicate is even harder now that my best friend is here. So close, yet just out of reach.

Catalina nods. "I suppose that's all I'll be needing from you." She closes her notebook and looks pointedly at the door.

"You know who has been acting very suspicious?" Elias doesn't wait for her answer. "That man who moved into Rachel's condo. The relative who inherited the place."

"How so?"

"Well, he has been asking all kinds of strange questions about the occupants of the building. He was asking me about Mr. and Mrs. Hyland yesterday evening. Of course, I didn't tell him *anything*."

Catalina gives him a pensive look. She opens her notebook and scrawls: "Is Will Archer investigating murder?" Well, she figured it out a lot faster than I did.

My eyes trail after Elias as he leaves the guest suite. I cannot help but feel like a powerless outsider, simply observing. Even if I develop a great insight into the case, there isn't anything I can do about it. Although, if I can somehow figure out a way to communicate with the living . . . Alexei's séance is tomorrow night. If I can contact him, I will have finally found my way to interact with the living. I won't just be a shadow of my former self, damned to observe others as they move on with their lives. I'll have a purpose again, or at least, a reason to live in this afterlife.

On that hopeful note, I am whisked away by the elevator.

An elderly resident accompanies me on my ride, which ends at the fourth floor. She leans heavily on her cane, moving forward inch by inch, wheezing forcefully. I wish I could help her, but the pain of being inconsequential is not as great anymore. I have a purpose. I *will* communicate with Alexei tomorrow night, and I *will* have my closure.

My good mood is further improved when I see that Melody is researching local women's shelters on the desktop in her husband's office. She's found one that is far from home but not so far that getting there will be difficult. This is exactly what I had told her to do. Husbands often look for their runaway wives at the closest shelters. Sadly, many women think that once they've left, the battle is over, but that's when the fight truly begins. Depending on the abuser's determination, it might take years before the woman can actually move on with her life.

Melody has found the shelter in Scarborough, which is discreet and has reasonably good security. She should be safe there. She's currently reading about the place, their programs, and how they help women to get back on their feet.

The front door unlocks. Melody startles, her eyes wide and doe-like.

"Melody?" Oliver calls out.

Melody opens the browser history with trembling fingers. The processor is maddeningly slow. She highlights each webpage she visited and selects "Remove". She minimizes the window, but not before I notice that she missed a page. The one for the Scarborough shelter.

Oliver stands in the doorway. Melody climbs to her feet, her hands cradling her swollen stomach.

"What are you doing on my computer?" Oliver asks.

Melody trembles slightly. "I was looking for a recipe for tonight."

"You mean, you haven't made dinner already? What's that smell?"

Melody's lips twist upward into a semblance of a smile. "Yes, I made dinner. But I was going to make dessert. I found a cute recipe for chocolate mousse on Pinterest." She sounds like she's reciting this, and I hope that Oliver doesn't notice.

Oliver is silent, watching her. He doesn't move. He is perfectly still.

"You're home early," Melody says.

Oliver grins broadly. I heave a sigh of relief. "I wanted to get home to my Melly and the Belly."

He approaches her and gives her a big hug. I freeze, waiting for the catch.

"We don't need dessert tonight, baby. We can have some of the leftover apple pie from last night."

Oliver drops his briefcase on the floor and leads Melody away from the computer. She still seems off-kilter, but she follows Oliver to the door. I'm a nervous wreck just watching this. I can't imagine how difficult it must be for her to actually *live* it.

Melody leaves the room. Oliver picks up his briefcase and deposits it on the chair beside him. He turns to the computer. Opens the web browser. Navigates to the history.

The URL for the women's shelter is listed at the very top. Oliver's hands tighten into fists. His jaw clenches, and his cheeks stain crimson. Suddenly, he stands ramrod straight. His entire body relaxes. He loosens his fists. He twists his lips into a devastatingly handsome grin and ambles toward the kitchen.

Melody is stirring the contents of a large, black pot that rests on the stove top.

"Dinner will only be ready in half an hour. I didn't know you'd be home so early," Melody says.

"That's all right, baby," Oliver says in a sickly sweet voice. He reaches around Melody and takes two plates from the cupboard above her.

Melody darts furtive glances toward him as he begins to set the dinner table. She gradually relaxes until she is bustling around the kitchen, putting the finishing touches on their dinner. She stirs the pot, utterly unaware of what simmers beneath.

16

'm back in the basement. Catalina has brought me here, and now she stands surveying the hall. Her actions are similar to Will's, and I chastise myself for not figuring out sooner that Will was investigating my death. She walks the length of the corridor and peers into the stairwell, the unlocked fitness center, and the storage room. Because it is so difficult (theoretically) to get into the building, there are no locks on the various facilities. There are only deadbolts on the actual apartment doors.

My eyes keep wandering down the corridor, but I remain as far from the storage unit as my range will allow. The Girl with No Eyes is eerie, with her misplaced eyes and soundless scream. Sylvie's husband is unsettling, with his sharp vibrations and powerful force field. But the Shadow Man, he is something else entirely. He doesn't look like the few ghosts I have seen before. He looks like something so dark and sinister that it has lost all of its humanity. I will do whatever it takes to avoid him.

I'm relieved when Catalina finally hops back onto my elevator, which stops on the ground floor. The doors slide open to reveal Will standing in the lobby. He hesitates but seems to think better of waiting for the next elevator. That would look suspicious, and after all, Catalina is a police officer. Although, I find it interesting that she has failed to tell anyone that she is out of her jurisdiction.

At first, I had assumed that she'd relocated to Toronto and was promoted to detective. That's how good a liar she is. But I overheard her taking a phone call with a friend last night. Apparently, she took some vacation days to investigate my death. I have to say, I can think of a million better ways to spend a vacation than investigating the murder of an agoraphobic nut job. She let it slip during the phone call that when her captain found out that she was illegally investigating my death, he suspended her. Neither her friend nor I were happy to hear about this, though her friend got to be a lot more vocal about it.

I pace the small elevator. I don't want Catalina to lose her job because she feels responsible for me. She might think that she has unfinished business here because she's the only one who knows who killed my husband and who likely killed me. But I don't want my death to ruin her life.

Catalina and Will ride the elevator in taut silence. Catalina takes the opportunity to scrutinize Will. He does his best to avoid eye contact. The elevator finally stops at the sixth floor, and Will eagerly hops off. He looks taken aback when Catalina follows.

He continues to walk at a snail's pace, surreptitiously peeking over his shoulder at her.

Catalina hides a smirk as they both stop outside the Hylands' apartment. "Oh, are you visiting a friend?" she asks sweetly. She knows that he isn't.

I believe that Catalina shares my suspicion—Will plans to question the Hylands about my death. This is likely why Catalina is here also, given that, according to Elias, Sabryna is the only person in the building I ever interacted with "socially."

Will recovers quickly and replies, "Oh—yeah—I'm visiting a friend for coffee." He moves on to the next apartment and knocks on the door.

Catalina grins. "The Yates couple lives there. They'll both be at work at this hour."

Will flushes. His eyes dart about, searching for an escape. He ducks into the stairwell.

Shaking her head, Catalina turns to apartment 604 and knocks.

The door opens to reveal a fully made-up Sabryna, who is wearing a red silk dress that suggestively hugs her curves.

Sabryna freezes in the doorway as she eyes her visitor. Her painted smile is thin. "Can I help you?"

Catalina is all business. "Yes, ma'am, you can. My name is Detective Catalina Marquez. I'm investigating the murder of Rachel Drake. I was hoping we could talk?"

Sabryna's eyes narrow. "I'm not a suspect, am I?" she asks in a sardonic tone.

"No one has been ruled out, yet, Mrs. Hyland, but I'm here because according to the concierge, you may have had a unique relationship with the victim."

Sabryna raises her eyebrows. "Unique is one way of putting it. I haven't spoken with her since a little while after she moved in. I tried to befriend her, but she would have none of it." She sounds bitter.

"The victim was a severe agoraphobe who suffered from social anxiety issues. It likely wasn't personal."

Sabryna looks genuinely shocked by this. She blushes. "Come on in."

Catalina strides into the condo. Her eyes dart back and forth, taking in the vast foyer and the living room beyond.

"Come, have a seat." Sabryna is all smiles. She's the picture of a perfect hostess.

Catalina's shrewd eyes swivel to Sabryna. Sabryna's friendly but it's so obviously insincere. Catalina reluctantly settles onto the sofa.

"You've been staying in the guest suite, haven't you?" Sabryna says between gritted teeth. "I've seen you around."

I gasp, but being dead, no one notices. No wonder Sabryna has been sizing Catalina up! She thinks that she's the competition. She believes that Catalina is the one sleeping with her husband.

"So, you're a detective, right? With which division?" Sabryna asks. It seems as if Sabryna is interrogating Catalina.

Catalina doesn't skip a beat. "I'm actually on loan. Unfortunately, the details are confidential." She can't have Sabryna looking into her credentials. Or she'll figure out that she has no right to be here, investigating a crime outside of her jurisdiction.

It is clear that Sabryna knows Catalina is lying, but she doesn't know the truth. She must think that Catalina has come here with some pathetic story to check out the wife. And to be honest, Catalina is making this delusion seem very plausible.

Sabryna stares at her for a moment. "Would you like something to drink? Coffee or tea, perhaps?" Hostility emanates from Sabryna in nearly palpable waves.

"No, thank you, I won't be long," Catalina says. It's probably a good idea to refuse any kind of beverage from this woman.

Sabryna appears to be growing tired of this charade. "I really don't know what I can tell you. I didn't know Rachel at all."

"Is it possible that your husband knew her?"

Sabryna's eyes narrow. "Roger did *not* know her. If he had, he would have mentioned it to me." Sabryna gets a faraway look in her eye. She shakes her head almost imperceptibly. "Now, if you'll excuse me, I am terribly busy, and I must get back to my . . . prior engagements."

Catalina's lips part, and her brows furrow, but she quickly composes herself. "Yes, of course. I'll be on my way. If you think of anything, please give me a call." She hands Sabryna a small, plain white card with her name and phone number handwritten neatly on it. My heart sinks. It does *not* look like a real business card.

Sabryna leads Catalina to the door and closes it firmly behind her. She collapses against the wall, tears streaming down her cheeks.

The elevator carries me away while Sabryna continues to sob silently.

I worry all day about whether or not I'll be able to attend the séance tonight. All I need is *one person* to call the elevator, *one person* to have a midnight hankering for ice cream, and I could be torn away from my *one chance* at communicating with the living. As far as I know, Alexei hasn't booked any other séances. This will be my only opportunity.

After witnessing Catalina's encounter with Sabryna, I tell myself that I cannot afford any distractions. I decide to ride the elevator, up and down, up and down as I plan for this evening.

I cannot predict how the séance will work and if Alexei, or Rasputin, will be using a spirit board. My first order of business will be to convince Alexei that I am not his client's dead wife but the spirit of the woman who died in this building nine days ago. But then, what exactly do I want to tell him? He needs to find who killed me, but I have no idea where the police are in their investigation.

Do they need help? Are they at a dead end?

Are they even still investigating my death, or have more urgent cases come up?

I go over my game plan. There are many obstacles in communicating with Alexei tonight. First, I have to pray that my elevator will stay rooted on the second floor so I can attend. Then, I have to figure out how to communicate with Alexei and tell him my name. After that, I have to hope that he will contact the police and set up another séance with them. Assuming, of course, that they believe him and don't write him off as another mental case. Too much of this is outside of my control.

But I'm getting ahead of myself. Baby steps. I don't even know if he'll be able to hear me. Or see me. Smell me? I hope he won't be able to smell me, because I haven't showered in over a week, and I'm sure the stench of decay would be overbearing. I laugh hysterically at my joke, only somewhat aware that I might be going insane.

By the time it's quarter to midnight, I'm a complete wreck. The client has yet to arrive, and if he has, he must have decided to take the stairwell up the measly single flight. I've been trapped on the fourth floor since Oliver Boyden got home late from a night out with the guys. He seems to have a lot of those. I pace the hall fretfully, then decide to enter the Boyden apartment. I might as well kill some time before the séance.

Oliver is in the kitchen rummaging through a drawer. Melody is in the living room, sitting stiffly and reading her book.

"Where is the damn bottle opener?" Oliver shouts.

Melody jumps up, her book tumbling from her grasp. She waddles into the kitchen. "Let me look," she says.

Oliver's eyes narrow. "If I can't find it, what makes you think you can?"

I cannot believe how little it takes to set him off.

Melody begins to tremble. "You're tired and stressed, from work—"

"Don't tell me I'm tired and stressed. I know I'm tired and stressed, and it isn't from work."

He lifts his hand.

She whimpers.

I am ripped away by the elevator.

17

A man and woman step into the elevator. I study them each in turn. They are both solemn, they are both silent, and they are both dressed in varying shades of brown. They look like they stepped out of a sepia-toned photograph. The woman carries a bundle, something swathed in off-white cloth, but I can't tell what it is. I'm not sure I want to know.

Alexei opens the door before they have a chance to knock.

"Welcome," he says.

"Thank you so much for fitting us in on such short notice, I'm Ben Hammstein, husband of the deceased," the man rambles.

He extends a sweaty hand, but Alexei does not shake it. Instead, he turns to the woman. "And who are you?"

"I'm Isobel's sister, Clara," she says with a scowl. "Thanks for introducing me, Ben."

"I was about to," Ben mumbles, but Clara doesn't seem to hear.

Alexei nods, then ushers them both into his darkened living room.

"It is almost midnight, so we should get started," Alexei says in a hushed tone.

He leads the couple to a round table he's recently set up in the center of the living room. Like everything else in this apartment, the table is black. There are three stools positioned around it. It's almost as if Alexei knew Ben would be bringing someone else with him. I shake my head. Alexei is a medium, not a psychic. Ben probably told him that someone would be accompanying him when they spoke over the phone earlier.

"Did you remember to bring an object that was dear to Isobel?" Alexei asks.

"Ben almost forgot, but I didn't," Clara says. She doesn't seem to notice Ben's scowl as she hands Alexei the bundle. Alexei unwraps it slowly. It is a vintage porcelain doll wearing a white lace dress which is yellowed at the fringes. The doll's eyes seem to follow me from across the room. Of course it had to be the creepiest doll since Annabelle. Alexei reverently places it on the table.

Alexei then lights a single black candle which sits at the center of the table. The flickering light dances on his tattoos, making them seem like they've come to life, coiling and contorting across his pallid skin.

"Why is everything in here black?" Clara asks.

"The shadows cannot collect where there is no light," Alexei says quietly.

Clara and Ben exchange a glance. "So . . . How does this work?" Ben asks, tugging at his tie until it nearly chokes him.

Alexei quietly returns his matchbox to his pocket. Then he says, "Have a seat."

The pair exchange another glance before planting themselves on the rigid stools. Alexei turns his back to them and approaches a large onyx-colored chest that rests against the far wall. He reaches into it and pulls out a conical-shaped crystal on a short, coiled chain.

"I have many different techniques for communicating with the dead. The technique we select will depend on the strength of the spirit. We begin with the pendulum, as it can detect most spirits," Alexei says. He dangles the chain from his long, bone-like fingers. "Do you know what question you want to ask first?"

"Qu-question?" Ben tugs his tie yet again.

Alexei stares at him.

The candle flickers, and shadows dance across his gaunt face.

Clara purses her lips. "You didn't come up with any questions, Ben?" Her attitude is grating. It's clear that she hadn't come up with any questions either.

"Ah . . . I-I just want to communicate with her. I d-don't have any specific questions, but I c-can come up with some," Ben says.

Alexei does not look impressed. He sits on his stool, towering over the timid pair.

"Hold hands."

Clara looks down at Ben's sweaty palms distastefully before taking them in hers.

Alexei closes his eyes and begins to breathe deeply. In and out. In and out. I feel the hairs stand on the back of my neck, but

I cannot tell if this is due to him or simply my fraught nerves reacting to the situation.

Alexei opens his eyes. They are ice blue. I cannot remember if they had been that striking moments ago.

"Spirits, I call to you. I give you permission to come forth to speak. Isobel Hammstein, come to us."

He holds out his hand and lets the crystal dangle on its chain. I wonder about its significance.

It is remarkably still. I am surprised that Alexei, with his lack of muscular definition, is capable of holding it so still.

Ben opens his mouth to speak, but seems to think better of it and snaps his mouth shut.

"Is there a spirit here?" Alexei asks.

"Yes," I say.

Nothing happens.

I reach out to push the pendulum, but my fingers simply glide through it, without any resistance.

"I ask again, is there a spirit here?" Alexei repeats slightly louder, as if ghosts are hard of hearing.

"YES," I say forcefully.

This time, the crystal twitches.

I focus all my energy on the crystal. I feel something—a strange tugging sensation deep in my chest.

The pendulum swings back and forth. I did it!

Clara gasps, and the couple grabs at each other. Ben begins to move backward.

"Do NOT break the circle," Alexei commands. Ben jerks back to his seat.

Just as suddenly as it began, the pendulum stops swinging. It is deathly still, which defies the laws of physics.

"Show me what 'yes' is," Alexei says.

I'm not sure I understand.

"Yes," I say.

Nothing happens.

"YES," I shout.

The pendulum swings back and forth, as before.

"Is this Isobel Hammstein?"

"No," I say.

Again, nothing happens.

"NO," I shout.

The crystal jerks from side to side.

Alexei's eyes widen, and he frowns.

"What does that mean?" Clara whispers.

"It is not Isobel," Alexei says.

Ben gasps. Clara becomes deathly pale.

I should have lied. I don't want them to stop.

"Is Isobel here?" Alexei asks.

The pendulum remains perfectly still. I glance around the room, but I'm alone.

"YES," I say. This time, it swings back and forth on the first try.

Alexei puts down the pendulum. "Do not break the circle," he repeats, his accent thicker than normal. He goes back to the chest and gropes around inside, then pulls out a Ouija board and a pointer.

He moves the candle to the edge of the table, then places the Ouija board atop the melted wax.

He carefully positions the pointer at the center of the spirit board. The porcelain doll stares at me from its perch on the edge of the table.

Ben and Clara look like they can barely contain their excitement. I am a horrible person. If I weren't stuck here, I'd be going straight to hell.

Alexei looks at the couple with an unreadable expression on his face. "If you see anything strange or out of the ordinary, close your eyes."

Ben stares at him, his mouth agape.

Clara looks affronted. "Why on earth would we do that?"

Alexei speaks solemnly. "You may have heard the expression, 'Eyes are windows into the soul.' That is not exactly true. They are actually doors. If you look directly at a spirit, you are inviting it in. And it will not be easy to evict."

Ben releases a deep breath.

"It is unlikely you will be able to see anything," Alexei adds hastily. "It is unlikely either of you have the Gift. And you are far too old to have retained your childhood innocence. You should be fine."

Ben doesn't look convinced. Clara's face is as pale as the cheeks of the porcelain doll that still sits on the table watching me.

Alexei ignores their discomfort and settles onto his stool. "Place your hands gently on the pointer." He demonstrates with his own elongated fingers. After some hesitation, Ben and Clara follow suit.

"Spirits of the other side, I call to you," Alexei's voice is strangely alluring. I feel myself drawn closer to his side.

"I give you permission to speak through us." I am pulled even closer. My energy is focused into the tiny pointer.

I have so many things I need to say, but that will have to wait. There is something far more urgent that needs to be addressed.

The pointer slides, gradually shifting toward the 4.

"Four," Clara says helpfully.

I push the slider again, as hard as I can, but it moves painstakingly slowly.

"Zero," Ben says with a frown.

I draw the pointer to the final number.

"Seven?" Clara says, brows furrowed.

Alexei looks pensive but doesn't speak. Does *he* understand?

Clearly, they need to be pushed, because I don't know how much time Melody has.

Something shifts, catching my eye. The room is nearly pitch black, but I can almost see something moving, just out of the candle's sphere of light.

I shake my head and turn back to the board.

"H," Ben and Clara chant.

Again something moves. I peer into the darkness, but I cannot see anything. But I know something is there. Watching. Waiting for its turn with the spirit board. It circles the table, just out of sight. Searching for a weakness in the circle. Feeling myself growing weaker, I push the pointer again.

"E." It is Alexei who speaks this time. But his eyes are not on the board. They are staring, affixed to the shifting cluster of shadows.

Can he see the spirit that is attempting to break the circle?

I push again, using all my energy.

"L," they say. Ben shifts on his stool, his fingers breaking contact with the pointer for a mere second.

The creature rushes to the table. It is in full sight now.

It is the spirit from the basement. The spirit that came for me during my dying moments. The Shadow Man with no face.

I expect it to reach for the pointer or for Alexei. Instead, it plunges deep inside Ben.

Ben's body goes slack, his head lolling to the side. He shudders. He slowly raises his head. His face is veiled in darkness.

Ben turns toward Clara, reaching out. He wraps his fingers around her pale, slender neck.

Eyes wide, Clara's hands clutch at her throat. Her fragile fingers try to pry away Ben's strong, unrelenting hands.

"SPIRIT BE GONE," Alexei bellows. He towers over the table and in a single breath, extinguishes the candle.

The room plunges into darkness. I am rocketed back into my elevator.

September 9

Dear Diary,

I haven't been able to sleep. The events are escalating, and it's keeping me up at night. Even my boss, Gregory, has noticed the stress I'm under. Monday, he called me into his office and asked if everything was all right at home. It was utterly humiliating. I lied and said that renovations were keeping me up late. He put a caring hand on my shoulder and gently suggested I take a few days off and go to a spa. I hesitantly agreed, but I don't have any intention of leaving the house. Not until I have my proof.

Yesterday morning, I woke to discover that the Scrabble pillows were shredded. And I mean, shredded. *Jay is convinced it was Lon*

Chaney, Jr. rebelling because I forgot to cut his claws or to feed him his Sunday night treat. But the slices in the fabric don't look like they could have been made by Chaney's tiny paws. They are thick and deep. I know that it wasn't Lon Chaney, Jr. who destroyed this memento of our marriage. It was something else—

I hear something in the hallway. It's daytime, but I still need to investigate.

I'm back. Something horrible just happened, and I decided it was time to tell Jay everything. I thought he was ready to hear the truth.

When I went out into the hall, there was no one in sight, and I thoroughly investigated the rooms. It was in the bedroom.

I saw something lying on the bed. I was overcome with dread, but I approached it, slowly. It was a dead bird. On my pillow. Its neck was twisted at an unnatural angle. It was not just any kind of bird. It was a blue jay.

Jay came into the bedroom, swore, and went to get a garbage bag. I watched from a healthy distance as he disposed of the bird, and I helped him to strip the bed.

I loaded the washing machine, poured in a considerable amount of bleach, and set the cycle to heavy. Jay watched me from the doorway, leaning against the frame, arms crossed, eyes narrowed.

That's when I thought it would be a good time to tell him my suspicions. "I think our house is haunted," I said.

Jay frowned. "Is this because of the bird? It's obvious that your cat did it."

My cat. Whenever Lon Chaney, Jr. did something wrong, he suddenly became my cat, but whenever we were snuggled up, watching a movie, it was Jay that he chose to cuddle with.

I didn't want to start a fight, so I bit my tongue. "Chaney has never killed anything before. And it isn't just the bird. It's the floorboards creaking at night. It's the torn pillows. Lon Chaney, Jr. has been acting strangely, sniffing around the house."

Jay raised an eyebrow. "You do know that all these strange occurrences can be blamed on the cat? We've just moved into a new home, and it's very possible that the previous owners had a pet. Lon Chaney, Jr. might be acting out because he can still smell it."

"Wouldn't he just pee on everything? Not put a dead blue jay on your pillow? I think it's symbolic."

"What? You think that some evil spirit is haunting our house and that it wants to kill me? And instead of doing so, it leaves cryptic messages in the form of dead birds and misplaced hairbrushes?" Jay shook his head in disbelief. He turned and walked out. He left the house, and I don't know when he's coming back.

I don't have rock-solid proof of a supernatural being inhabiting this house. Because of this, Jay won't believe me until it does something more drastic. But by then, it could be too late.

18

'm relieved to discover that I'm able return to Alexei's apartment immediately after my expulsion. The overhead lights are on, and there is no sign of the Shadow Man. He must have also been driven out of the apartment by Alexei. I am the only spirit haunting this room.

For now. I can't be sure the Shadow Man won't return, like I did.

Clara has applied a bag of frozen peas to her slim neck. Dark bruises spread across her pale, almost translucent skin. She tosses her brother-in-law a nervous glance.

"Wha-what was that?" Ben asks. His glasses are off, and he's rubbing his eyes in large, concentric circles.

Alexei paces, seemingly unable to keep still.

His eyes dart around the room, peering into the corners. "Another spirit pierced the veil between our worlds. This one was not as friendly as the last."

He thinks I'm friendly.

"But the first spirit, it was communicating with Isobel?" Clara asks in a husky voice. Straight down to business then. She is not nearly disturbed enough that her brother-in-law nearly murdered her moments ago.

"It would appear so," Alexei says. Is he being deliberately vague? Does he know I was lying? Although it appears that he cannot see me, it seemed like he had seen the Shadow Man.

"407 HEL," Ben says. "What could that mean? Isobel and I were married on April 6th, and the 7th would have been our first day of marital bliss. Maybe she was referring to that?"

Alexei stares.

Clara delves into her purse and pulls out a planner. "On April 7th, I had to go to the dry cleaners to pick up my dress for the gala I hosted, but that wasn't until the 8th."

"Was Isobel a part of that gala?" Ben asks.

"No."

Again, Alexei simply stares.

"H-E-L. Hello? Maybe she was greeting us?" Clara says.

I was trying to say HELP. Remarkable what difference a single letter makes.

"Perhaps she is with Great Aunt Helen. Although that old bag definitely isn't in heaven." Clara is distraught.

"H-E-L . . . L? My wife isn't in *hell* is she?" Ben becomes equally distraught.

This is hell.

Apparently, Alexei feels the same way, because he stands up abruptly and says, "A thousand apologies for the failure of this séance. You should be leaving now."

Ben and Clara reluctantly rise. Alexei ushers them to the front door. He opens it wide and all but shoves the couple through.

"Can we try again another time?" Clara asks.

"I am afraid that is not a possibility," Alexei says. My heart sinks.

"Will we be getting a refun—"

Alexei slams the door shut, muffling the rest of Ben's question.

He returns to the table and pauses. "Help?" he wonders aloud.

Yes. Yes! I obviously wasn't spelling "Helicopter." There are only so many possibilities! "Yes, help!" I say to him. "Apartment 407. GO!"

Alexei shakes his head. He gathers the Ouija board and deposits it back into the chest. He removes a bundle of herbs. It looks like sage. He lights a match and begins to burn the bundle. He walks around the room, waving the burning sage in front of him.

My nostrils fill with the acrid smoke, and even though I don't breathe, I feel as though I am suffocating. I soar from the room, into the hall, where the air is clear and I am myself again. I sigh. I haven't encountered sage before in my afterlife, but I suspect that I won't be able to enter Alexei's apartment again until the scent has faded.

It's a little past midnight, which is usually quiet. I go into apartment 207, but I am greeted by the sound of moaning and loud thumping. I quickly leave. That leaves apartment 201 which belongs to the concierge.

I have not entered this apartment before. The difference between this unit and the others in the building is quite startling. The coffee tables are scuffed with ringed water marks coating the glass surface. The couch has what looks like an old spaghetti stain right on the center cushion. The floor rug is threadbare and looks like it's one sweep of the vacuum away from disintegrating. It's clear that Elias doesn't have the same amount of money to throw around on luxury items as the other residents. I realize that Elias probably rents the apartment for free, as one of the perks of his position. I peek into his bedroom, but Elias isn't home. Even if he were, watching someone sleep isn't riveting entertainment.

I'm pulled up to the ninth floor, then to the basement by the insomniac gym rat. I don't want to stay in the basement, especially in the wee hours of the morning, so I hop up to the ground floor.

Catalina is in her guest suite, but she isn't sleeping. She's chugging the last dregs from her coffee pot. From the looks of it, she's been scanning through files on her computer. I lean over her shoulder, and I see that she's looking at my personal logs for my work at the crisis hotline. I'll bet she'd had no trouble hacking my password.

She must suspect that my killer was in contact with me. What better way to reach an agoraphobe in a high-security building than by telephone?

I haven't thought about my mystery phone call since before my death. Catalina needs to identify who made that call. The person knew my real name, said he was coming for me, and then later that night, I died? It can't be a coincidence. Catalina's eyes start to drift shut, but she catches herself and shakes her head. Sighing, she resumes reading the logbook. I worry about her. She needs sleep. I don't want her to get sick. I don't want her to put herself in danger. What if she finds my killer but she's too tired, too sleep-deprived to protect herself from him? I stay with her long after she finally drifts off.

19

Clark slouches in front of the bathroom mirror. I barely recognize him without his makeup, but I know that the Yus only have one child. Clark has his own bathroom, which is just off his bedroom. The sink is speckled with caked makeup. Tubes of white foundation, mascara, and eyeliner litter the countertop. I'm surprised that his parents allow him to keep his bathroom this messy. Although, from observing their interaction the other night, it's clear to me that they're too terrified of him to apply any kind of strict parenting tactics.

Clark is short and thin, nearly all bone with little muscle. He looks years younger without his makeup, much closer to his true age of fourteen. But it's his expression as he studies himself in the mirror that gives me pause. His fine facial features are twisted into an expression of revulsion and hate. He has just showered, and he is molding his hair with gel, which does more to make it look greasy than to actually manipulate the fine strands. I wonder if that is his goal.

He takes the tube of foundation and squeezes a glob onto his palm. He rubs his hands together, then applies it to his face, methodically rubbing it in until his entire visage is ghostly white. He applies dark blush to his cheekbones, highlighting them and camouflaging the remnants of his youthful baby fat. He sweeps red eyeshadow to his eyebrows and carefully blends it under his eyes. The overall effect is one of exhaustion and sleep deprivation.

Clark carefully applies thick eyeliner, creating a Cleopatra-like effect. He adds thick layers of mascara, one on top of the next. Then, he carefully stencils black lip liner around the contour of his lips, followed by a crimson shade of lipstick that he seals with a kiss against the grimy mirror.

The effect is eerie.

He resembles a 1990s Marilyn Manson, but without the flair of an artist expressing himself. He reminds me of the faint echo of a sound which has reverberated against several walls and has lost its power and magnitude.

Clark, who has now become *Razor*, leaves the bathroom and slips into thin black leggings and tall leather boots. He puts on a skin-tight, red tank top that zips down the front. He shoots himself a smirk in the full-length mirror that's nailed to the back of his bedroom door, then saunters out into the hall.

"Clar—I mean Razor!" Rebecca greets him the instant he opens the door. It's clear that she's been hovering.

"Rebecca." Clark nods civilly.

"Good morning!" she says, ignoring the obvious fact that it's the afternoon.

Clark goes into the kitchen, strides past his father without a word, and snatches a piece of toast from a plate on the counter. He bites into it, allowing the crumbs to fall onto the spotless floor. Rebecca grimaces, but she doesn't say a word.

Clark spits a mouthful of toast into the sink. "It's cold."

Rebecca's eyes widen. "Oh, well, um, I made it this morning, and it's been out a few hours, waiting . . ."

Clark interrupts her. "Whatever. I'm going out with friends. I don't know when I'll be back, so don't wait up." I can't imagine this kid having *friends*.

Charles exchanges a glance with his wife before speaking. "Now, young man, you will be back by your curfew, which is eleven o'clock."

"Whatever," Clark says again. He slams the front door behind him.

I am forced to ride the elevator down with this sullen teenager. He spends the entire descent taking selfies, pouting for the camera and rearranging his hair to make sure it is the perfect level of messy yet chic. I roll my eyes.

Clark flips Elias off as he exits the elevator. Elias tenses but doesn't react. His eyes follow Clark as the boy saunters across the lobby.

Elias' usual smile is nowhere to be seen, and he wears a guarded expression. Clark shoves through the double doors without giving him a second glance.

I drift into the guest suite. Once again, I find Catalina poring over her files. She has thin dark circles under her eyes, which are the only indication that she didn't get enough sleep. Her hair is pulled back in a ponytail that is so tight, it stretches the skin on her forehead. The TV is set to the news station with the volume down low. The broadcaster is discussing local events. A music festival I cannot go to that I *wouldn't* have gone to even if I were still alive.

Years ago, Jay and I took a road trip to go to that same music festival. I smile at the thought. We got there early, set up our tent, and then hardly ever left it the entire weekend.

I tear my gaze away from the television and move closer to Catalina. She's currently scrutinizing a file on Sabryna. There are many questions scrawled across the page. Questions about Sabryna's hostility, her "friendship" with me, her relationship with her husband. Lost in thought, Catalina taps her pen against the desk. She seems to come to a decision about something. I wish I could ask her what she's thinking.

Catalina leaves the suite and goes straight to my elevator, riding it up to the seventh floor. She doesn't hesitate before knocking on my apartment door.

Will swings it open almost immediately. My husband's face wears a wary expression.

"Let's cut to the chase," Catalina says. "I know why you're here."

Will looks guarded. "I'm not sure what you mean. My brother's wife just died . . ."

"I know you're investigating your sister-in-law's death. And I know that you think that her killer might be the same person who killed your brother. Am I right?"

Will freezes. He looks Catalina up and down, then nods silently. He gestures for her to enter the apartment, closing the door behind her.

"What gave me away?" he finally asks.

"I've been talking to people, different residents from around the building, and they've mentioned that you've been asking them similar questions. It didn't take me too long to figure out what you're up to. I am a detective after all."

At that, Will produces a small smile.

"So, I've been thinking, it might be beneficial if we join forces, combine our investigations. Two heads are better than one, and all that crap."

Will studies her. "Are police officers allowed to do that? Consult with the public?"

Catalina stares down at her hands for a few moments before looking Will straight in the eye. "Well, technically I am out of my jurisdiction, as I may have mentioned before."

From Will's expression, I can tell that she had definitely *not* mentioned that before.

"The local police didn't actually invite me. I came here on my own. I knew your brother and his wife, and I was one of the investigating officers assigned to his murder."

Why is she downplaying our friendship? She doesn't mention that we were roommates for three years or that we went to university together. She doesn't mention how we met in an intro to psych course because I tripped over her backpack that she'd rudely left strewn across the aisle in Science Hall 302. She doesn't mention that not only had I tripped, but I'd fallen down the aisle's steps, smacking my head hard on the cement floor. She doesn't mention that I was knocked unconscious, and she was the one to call 911. She doesn't mention that she spent the afternoon in the emergency room with me, apologizing over and over while I pretended to suffer from memory problems. She doesn't mention her role after Jay's death—that she was my only support, the only person I could trust. Why doesn't she mention any of this?

"I need to show you something." Will leads her out of the living room, down the short hallway, to the door to my—his—office, which is shut. He hesitates, then gestures that she should enter ahead of him.

The look on Catalina's face is priceless. Her eyes bulge, and her breath catches. Will's collage on the wall has grown, and it now looks like a patchwork quilt of newspaper clippings, scraps of paper with notes, and colorful strings linking different people together. It's clear that he's spent hours—days even—on this project.

Catalina schools her expression and steps closer, inspecting the images plastered to the wall. Sabryna's beaming face. Dr. Sylvie Favreau's somber expression—a professional photo printed from the hospital website. A candid picture of Clark smoking in the parking garage. Elias hovering by the elevator bay. Roger returning from a late-night tryst.

"These are the residents of the building," Catalina says, but it sounds like a question.

Will sighs, rubbing a hand over the day-old stubble that sprinkles across his jawline. "Yes. I believe someone in this building killed Kae."

20

The elevator's poor timing is slowly driving me mad. It takes me to the second floor where Alexei steps on. He violently stabs the "four" button with his index finger. Relief washes over me. He's figured out my message. My excitement is tinged with worry. I hope that Melody is all right. There were no ambulances last night, so I don't think that Oliver has seriously hurt her. Although, I can't know that for certain.

Alexei mutters under his breath during the two-flight climb. On the fourth floor, I struggle to keep up with his long strides as he glides down the hall. He stops at apartment 407.

He seems to fight an internal battle before finally tapping the shiny brass knocker three times.

Melody appears in the doorway. I dart around Alexei so I can get a better look at her. She's standing on two legs and she seems to be fully intact. I sigh with relief.

"Hi, can I help you?"

To my dismay, I spot a bruise under her right eye which is slightly swollen.

Alexei scowls, his eyes lingering on her bruise.

"Honey, who is it?" Oliver's voice comes from the other room.

Melody looks at Alexei expectantly.

"I am Alexei Utkov, your neighbor from downstairs."

Melody looks confused. "How can I help you?" she asks again.

Oliver appears in the doorway behind her. His eyes widen in unadulterated excitement.

"*Rasputin?* You live in my building?" Oliver sounds like a child in a candy store. "What are you waiting for, Melly? Invite the man in!"

Alexei's ashen skin colors slightly, giving a rosy hue to his otherwise deathly complexion. He enters the apartment, furtively scanning his surroundings, taking in the tidy apartment with the homey touches.

"Have a seat!" Oliver exclaims. "Would you like something to drink? Melly, get the man something to drink!"

"A glass of water would be fine," Alexei says. Absorbing his surroundings, he perches on the edge of the sofa. This apartment is the polar opposite of his own, with its warm colors and soft, inviting furniture.

Melody hurries into the kitchen, and I hear the water running.

"I can't believe you're here. I've seen every episode of your show. I had no idea that you lived in the building. Are you new to the area?" Oliver is speaking very fast. It looks like Luke has a rival for biggest Rasputin fan. Oliver's reaction would endear me to him, if I didn't know firsthand that he beats his pregnant wife.

Alexei shakes his head. "No. I have lived here for years."

"Oh." Oliver loses his steam. He picks at a cuticle with his thumbnail. He seems to be at a loss for what to say. I see the moment when he realizes that he doesn't know why Alexei is in his apartment. It's unlikely that Alexei popped in for a visit with complete strangers.

"Do you know my wife, Melody?" Oliver asks.

"No, we just now met for the first time."

Oliver seems very puzzled, but he doesn't want to be rude and ask his guest why he is here. I chuckle. He probably doesn't want Alexei to realize he has the wrong apartment and leave.

"So, you know more about me than I know about you," Alexei says, his tone friendlier than I thought him capable. "What do you do?"

Oliver grasps onto this topic like a lifeline. "I'm a software engineer."

"Ah, so the next time I have problems with Wi-Fi, I will know who to call."

Oliver bristles at this assumption. Before he can correct him, Melody returns from the kitchen and places a glass of ice cold water on a coaster in front of Alexei. She takes a seat opposite the men. She leans back slightly and places a hand on her watermelon baby.

"When are you expecting?" Alexei asks.

"In about two months. December fourteenth. We've got the nursery all set up, but we still have to finish baby-proofing the apartment." Melody glows with excitement, and a little smile dances upon her lips.

"I said I'd get around to it, you don't have to go around telling everyone," Oliver snaps.

Melody's face falls. Her gaze meets the floor, which is no easy feat given the size of her stomach.

Alexei glances between them, but he doesn't say anything.

"So, what brings you here?" Oliver finally asks. The novelty of having a minor celebrity in his house is finally waning.

"I held a séance last night."

Melody gasps loudly. "Here?"

"Melody, let the man finish," Oliver says. "Well, was it in this building?"

Alexei nods.

"And . . ."

"I was meant to reach the deceased wife of a man, my client, but I contacted someone else instead. I believe it may have been that woman who was killed in the elevator."

Well, he's intuitive after all.

"That still doesn't explain why you're *here*," Oliver says.

"During the séance . . . we were interrupted." Alexei doesn't say by whom or by what, which is good, because Melody is looking a little green around the gills. "The only message that came through was '407 H-E-L.' I am not sure what that means, and I thought that it could be an apartment number."

"407 could represent a million things," Oliver says reasonably. "It could be a date, a—a . . ." He can't even think of anything else.

"Of course, those were my thoughts exactly," Alexei says. "But I thought I would be remiss not to check out apartment 407 and see for myself."

"But what do you think the H-E-L represents?" Oliver asks thoughtfully.

"Could be anything," Alexei says nonchalantly. Again, he glances over at Melody. At her downcast expression. At her bruised face.

Melody's face lights up, and I know that she knows what the H-E-L stands for. She hides her expression before Oliver notices. "You said that you communicated with the woman who died in the elevator? The one who lived on the seventh floor?"

Alexei nods. "Rachel Drake. I was wondering if you knew her. That could explain why she wanted me to come here."

Melody opens her mouth to speak, but Oliver interjects, "We didn't know her. Apparently, she was a shut-in—no friends or family—and she spent all her time in her apartment. Ever since her husband was murdered. That's what they've been saying on the news anyway."

They've been talking about my past on the news? Why is this the first I'm hearing of it? I begin to pace the stretch of living room beside the couch. Of course, this makes sense. A brutally murdered white woman living in a wealthy apartment building in downtown Toronto. *Of course* there would be significant news coverage.

I'd only caught a glimpse days ago. But it's still disconcerting to realize that the world knows my secrets, and that all the secrecy, the lies, the safety I built up during my life has been torn down after my death.

Oliver continues. "So none of us knew her. She didn't talk to *anybody*." His tone is very final.

"Of course. It was just one possibility." Alexei stands. "Well, thank you for your hospitality. I should get going. I have a series of appointments to attend to today, and I do not want to be late."

What? He can't leave now. Not when he's so close.

Melody struggles to her feet. "It was a pleasure to meet you, Mr. Utkov. If you ever want to visit again, feel free to drop by."

Alexei glances at her bruise, then averts his gaze. "Thank you for your open invitation. I really must be going."

Oliver cuts in, leading Alexei to the door. Melody places her hand to her chest and walks in the opposite direction, toward the open window. She gazes out at the muggy, pollution-ridden street.

"Rachel . . ." she breathes.

She knows.

21

ittle Etienne Favreau sits quietly in his bedroom, reading in the subdued light of a lamp that's shaped like a rocket ship. He was alone; Sylvie has just gotten home from a shift at the hospital. He's spent all day by himself at home, doing homework and reading. I'm surprised and a little indignant that Sylvie doesn't hire someone to take care of her son. I spend whatever time I can watching over him, whenever the elevator allows me, though, I know that there would be nothing I could do if he were in danger. Earlier today, I got to spend almost an hour with him, and I took the time to study the shelf beside his desk. He has thirty-seven well-worn books, and I can tell that he's read many of them several times. They're all in French, and they're all far beyond what I would have thought a nine-year-old's reading level would be.

I haven't visited Raymond in the third bedroom since that first time I saw him. I find it odd that Sylvie doesn't have a nurse on call to look after her husband. Fleetingly, I wonder if she expects Etienne to care for his invalid father. That's ridiculous. He's too young to take care of himself, let alone someone else. Although, here he is, in his impeccably tidy bedroom, reading the original version of *The Three Musketeers* by Alexandre Dumas. Despite the exciting content of the book, his face remains impassive. His eyes skim the pages without a spark of passion or curiosity.

He cocks his head to the side when he hears the front door open. He uses a scrap of paper in lieu of a bookmark and turns off his rocket ship lamp. He hurries to the front door, where Sylvie is carrying take out.

"*Bonjour, maman,*" he says. I have yet to hear him speak any English. This worries me. Toronto is a primarily Anglophone city, and this might serve to isolate him further. He's home-schooled, which will only worsen matters.

"*Allo, mon petit cheri.*" Sylvie plants a kiss on his forehead. She continues in French, "Go set the table. I picked up some food on my way home from the hospital. I hope you feel like chicken fingers!"

Etienne produces a small smile, takes the bags from his mother, and races out of the room. The sounds of cutlery jingling and tiny feet scurrying over linoleum carries from the kitchen.

Sylvie goes straight to the third bedroom. I notice for the first time that the door is mounted with a lock. Is this to keep Etienne out? But why would she want to do that? Does Etienne even know that his father is in there?

That's a chilling thought. Sylvie has told everyone that Raymond is dead. Does Etienne believe this too? What does she plan to do when—if—Raymond wakes up? Tell everyone that he miraculously returned from beyond the grave? I have a sinking feeling that she must not expect him to wake up at all.

Sylvie closes the door tightly behind her. She retrieves a vial of medicine from the cabinet on the far wall. She changes the old IV bag for a fresh one. She bustles about, as if this is a familiar routine and there is nothing strange about it. She takes his blood pressure with an arm pump, and carefully records the results in a log book. His blood pressure is very low.

I glance around the room, but Raymond's ghost isn't here. I wonder where he could have gone. Is it possible that, like me, he has a specific range that he's restricted to? Considering that he is technically still alive, I think that this is highly likely. He's probably linked to his body, just like I am to my death spot. But still, I wonder if his prison is spherically shaped, like mine, and if so, how large its diameter is. If I can somehow figure out how other ghosts live, what their restrictions are, maybe then I can find a way to escape my invisible cage. Maybe I can find out how to move on. The Girl with No Eyes is certainly not able to communicate with me, what with her physical abnormalities. The Shadow Man is someone I am actively avoiding, and if I come across him again, I will run in the opposite direction not stop to chat about geometry. Perhaps if I can find Raymond again, I can attempt to communicate and get answers to some of these burning questions.

I turn back to Sylvie who is tapping the bubbles out of a particularly long and lethal-looking needle. I had a fear of needles when I was alive, and I shudder as she pumps the fluid into her husband's IV bag. She puts the needle on a tray on the table and tosses the empty vial toward the garbage can. It misses and rolls across the floor.

The vial continues to roll until it stops near my feet. The dim light of the heart monitor illuminates the tube, creating an unearthly aura around it. I bend over and read the label.

"*Pentobarbital.*" I stand up abruptly. I may not have a medical degree, but I spent the better part of my career translating medical documents. I picked up quite a bit, including the names and uses of the more common drugs.

Why would Sylvie be giving her husband pentobarbital? This is a drug used in hospitals in extreme cases of brain trauma, when swelling in the brain has to be reduced before surgery. It keeps the patient unconscious to mitigate the risk of further brain damage.

Sylvie doesn't make a move to retrieve the empty vial. She lingers at Raymond's bedside, studying his face while wearing a peculiar expression on her own. It isn't one of love or worry. It's something else.

Just as she had the first time I visited this room, she leans forward to whisper something in her husband's ear. This time, I'm ready, and I lurch forward so I can hear.

"This is what you deserve." She reaches out to brush a strand of stringy hair from his forehead. "Your punishment is far from over."

"*Maman! Maman! Je meurs de faim!*" Etienne calls from the kitchen.

"*Un moment!*" She rises and approaches the door without a second glance at her husband. She flips off the light as she leaves the room. A click of the lock, and she is gone.

All the pieces of the puzzle slide into place, revealing a picture I'm not sure I ever wanted to see. The reason why nobody knows her husband is still alive. The reason why she keeps the bedroom door locked. The reason why Raymond's blood pressure is so dangerously low.

Raymond isn't sick. He may never have been sick. He isn't in some inexplicable coma caused by brain damage that is somehow the side effect of a heart attack.

Raymond's coma isn't natural. It's induced. By his own wife.

September 26

Dear Diary,

Jay finally believes me. After last night, how could he not?

We went out to dinner and a movie last night, which was a much-needed outing for the two of us. It's been tense since the bird incident, and Jay has been quieter than usual. The movie was boring, some action flick featuring Arnold Schwarzenegger struggling to speak and shoot bad guys at the same time. There was a hair in my dinner, but I ate it anyway.

We were pulling into the driveway when it happened. A shadow moved behind the bedroom window, and the curtain shifted. We've been having a cold spell, so the windows were closed. I naturally assumed it was Lon Chaney, Jr. until the shadow returned. It looked like the outline of a tall man, peering down at us through the sheers.

I shrieked, reaching for Jay's arm. He looked up and gasped in shock. He could see it too.

"Stay here," he said, and raced into the house.

I waited for less than a minute.

"Fuck that," I muttered, unbuckling my seat belt. My false bravado vanished as I approached the house. Jay had left the front door ajar. I flipped on the light in the hall and peered inside. Nothing seemed to be out of place.

I pushed aside my fears and began to climb the stairs, tension mounting with every step. I didn't hear anything. There was no movement at all from above. When I got to the top, I could see Jay standing in the bedroom. He was staring out the window.

"Jay?" I hissed.

He turned around and frowned. "There's no one up here," he said.

"Are you going to check the rest of the house?" My voice was beginning to sound hysterical. "He could still be in the house!"

Jay hesitated. "All right. Stay here. Keep the door closed until I get back."

Of course, he didn't find anything. But this time was different. This time we actually saw something in the house. And—more importantly—it wasn't just me who experienced it.

Of course, we called the police, but there wasn't anything they could do. They did a full sweep of the building and found nothing out of the ordinary. There was no evidence of a break-in, and nothing was missing.

I wanted to tell the police officer that my grandmother's sapphire earrings were missing, but that had happened weeks ago and couldn't possibly be related.

Jay is finally acknowledging that something is wrong. This morning, he called to get the locks replaced. I didn't have the heart to tell him that locks won't protect us from a poltergeist. He seemed so determined.

I'm "working from home" today until the contractor comes to change the locks. Until then, I sit here on the bay window seat, writing in this journal. It's overcast outside, but it doesn't look like it will rain.

Almost everything that's been happening can be rationally explained. However, recently I've noticed dark changes in Jay's attitude and personality. It's as if something is deteriorating inside him.

The other night, for example, I woke to an empty bed.

"Jay?" I remembered that he was working the night shift and wouldn't be back for another couple of hours.

I wasn't sure what woke me. I got out of bed and went downstairs to the kitchen. I poured myself a glass of ice cold water, then kicked the fridge door shut behind me. As I left the kitchen, Lon Chaney, Jr. bolted past me and darted up the stairs, his tail fluffed to maximum volume.

The little hairs on my arms stood on end, following Lon Chaney's lead. Slowly, I turned to see what had spooked him. Someone was in the living room. I shrieked, dropping my glass, which shattered into a thousand pieces, the shards scattering across the hardwood floor.

"Kaela?" It was Jay.

"What are you doing here, in the dark?" I asked, flipping on the light switch.

Jay rubbed his eyes from the sudden brightness.

"I could ask you the same question," he said. Touché. "I just got home. We were having a slow night, and Roy said he'd cover for me."

"Roy who? Is that the vet tech who accidentally let all the dogs out last week?" I said.

Jay smiled. "Who let the dogs out?"

I shook my head. "That wasn't funny then, and it isn't funny now."

Jay grinned and came toward me before stopping suddenly. "You're bleeding!"

I looked down and noticed I was standing in the shattered glass. Blood welled between my toes. It looked bad, but I didn't feel anything.

Jay scooped me up and brought me back into the kitchen. He plopped me down on the counter. He opened a drawer and started rummaging around in it.

I rolled my eyes. "Second drawer on the left."

Jay shot me a sheepish grin and opened the drawer, retrieving the first aid kit. He inspected my foot with laser-like focus.

"Doesn't this hurt?"

I was surprised that it still didn't. "A little," I lied.

Jay carefully cleaned the area and began to wrap it with gauze.

"You're good at this. You should be a doctor or something," I teased.

"Or something," Jay said, after a moment of silence.

He carried me up to bed and went downstairs to clean up the glass. I was asleep moments after my head hit the pillow.

The following morning, Lon Chaney, Jr. tracked blood into the room. He jumped onto the lily-white duvet, smearing blood all over it. I shrieked, which made him race out of the room, trailing even more blood behind him.

I shook Jay awake.

"What is it?" He already sounded irritable.

"Did you forget to clean up the glass last night?" I asked, equally if not more irritable.

Jay opened his eyes and stared at me. "I guess I forgot."

"You forgot? Where did you go last night then?"

Jay looked at a loss for a moment. "I don't remember," he said finally.

I softened my voice. "We need to do something. Chaney is bleeding."

"Too bad you don't have a veterinarian on hand," Jay said. He hopped out of bed and followed the bloody paw prints from the room.

Not only is Jay having mood swings, but he's getting forgetful too. I did research online, and I discovered that both are among the more sinister indications of a haunting. Prolonged exposure to a dark spirit has adverse effects on the human mind. Some symptoms include memory loss, mood swings, irritability.

The final result is insanity.

22

The Woman with No Past sits in shadows, consumed by the ghosts that haunt her present. The curtains are tightly drawn, an effective barricade against any smidgen of light from the outside world. Her eyes are downcast, gazing at the thin gold band that hangs loosely at the knuckle of her ring finger.

If I speak, will she hear me?

Before I can gather the courage or the words, she stands and wanders into the kitchen. Robotically, she opens the cupboards and drawers, taking down plates and glasses, bowls and cutlery. She brings everything into the dining area, where she sets the table for three. In my heart, I know that she isn't expecting company. Once she finishes, she sits at the head of the table. Her back is ramrod straight. She doesn't move. She doesn't go to get food to put on her plate. She simply sits and gazes straight ahead. Her face is nearly expressionless but for a hint of melancholy. I look around nervously, but no spirits join her for her meal.

I tentatively take the seat opposite her, watching her face for any sign of awareness, but her eyes are vacant. She doesn't see me. She doesn't sense me.

I stare at her poorly fitted wedding band. She's lost someone, just as I did. But she's gone mad. Is it because of the isolation? Could this have been me, had I not had Luke as a friend to tether me to the world outside? Not for the first time, I realize how lucky I was to have a friend like Luke. He was patient with me, understanding of my neuroses, and despite the fact that he wanted more, he never pushed me. At least, not until the last time I saw him.

At that moment, music trickles in. I realize with a start that it's coming from the living room. Soft piano chords. A haunting melody. A familiar melody. It's the same music the Woman with No Past danced to nights ago. Her lips curve into a small smile. The song begins to quicken, reaching a rapid staccato before tapering off, fading into sheer silence. She rises and clears the table.

⁕

The Man in Tweed wears a different suit today. It is still tweed. It is still brown. But it's a marginally darker shade that makes his dull eyes look even duller.

I gather the courage necessary to follow him into his apartment. I secretly hope that the elevator will pull me away, but at the same time, morbid curiosity overwhelms me. He leaves his briefcase on the table and goes into the bedroom, where he shuffles around for a bit. He eventually settles down in front of the large living room window. He does not waste any more time. He quickly focuses his telescope onto the woman across the way.

She is in her bedroom with the curtains shamelessly spread open wide. She's wearing a flimsy bathrobe and has her hair bundled up in a fluffy pink towel. She is studiously applying eye makeup. It's clear that she has big plans for tonight, and I hope that the Man in Tweed won't be getting a show.

I glance back at him. He continues to stare, never blinking, hardly breathing. Repulsed, I leave.

I was upset when I discovered that Alexei didn't act upon the information I gave him. Without much effort, he managed to figure out that I was steering him toward apartment 407 and that I was asking for help. He did go and meet Melody and Oliver, and while he was there, he clearly noticed that something was off. But instead of calling the police or asking someone for advice, he simply went about the rest of his life, seemingly disinterested in the fact that Melody might be in real danger.

At least, I don't think he's taken any action. Alexei hasn't been around the last two days since the séance. I've noticed that he tends to leave his apartment late at night. This morning, he received a phone call, and I discovered that he's been holding séances off-site. At first I was pissed off, thinking he was avoiding me.

But then, I remembered the Shadow Man and the impression he made on Alexei. He's not unwilling to communicate with *me*, he's terrified of this creature—and for good reason. I shudder when I think of what might have happened if the Shadow Man had had just a few more seconds of contact with Ben before Alexei banished him. I might have had company in this afterlife.

A heaviness weighs against my chest. Having another ghost around wouldn't be so bad. The Girl with No Eyes and Raymond aren't exactly sparkling conversationalists. I can't help but feel as if I lost my chance for a friend, for some form of companionship. I've never felt so alone, not even when I was alive, tucked away in my self-inflicted isolation. I jolt back, a queasy feeling in my stomach. Am I disappointed that Clara didn't die?

Instead of ruminating over these disturbing thoughts and what they could mean for my sanity, I drop down to the fourth floor to check on Melody. I cannot access much of her apartment, but fortunately, she is in the living room, within my line of sight. Oliver is nowhere to be seen.

She sits by the window, gazing out, a book in her hands. She's trying to read, but I can see that her mind is racing a mile a minute. She is lost in her thoughts, thinking about her own life, not of the imaginary one depicted in the book.

"Rachel, are you there?"

I freeze. Can she sense me? Or is she calling out to me because of what Alexei told her?

"I'm here," I say.

Melody doesn't turn toward my voice. She barely moves at all. She cocks her head slightly, as if she's listening for the distant whisper of spirits from another realm.

I reach out and try to touch her arm. As usual, it simply glides through.

Melody remains perfectly still for several moments before continuing to speak. "I'm leaving him tomorrow. Tomorrow night he's going out of town for a few days, visiting family in Vermont. After he leaves, I'm gone."

I want to cheer, but Melody seems so torn, so forlorn. This is the most difficult decision of her life, but it just might end up saving it.

"I'm not going to take much with me, just my grandmother's ring and my baby blanket. Some pictures," she sobs gently.

"You're doing the right thing," I say. "You and your child will be safe and *happy*."

Melody stops crying. I wonder if she *can* hear me, or at the very least, sense the intent of my words. She places a hand on her stomach, and I notice that her baby is kicking. I open my mouth to speak again, to provide additional comfort and support, but I am torn away by the elevator.

23

The following morning, my spirits rise with the sun. Melody is finally going to escape. She didn't need me after all, and Alexei's apparent indifference won't matter one bit. She'll be safe. Both she and her son.

Will hops into the elevator and rides it up to the sixth floor. I somehow know where he's headed before he even steps off. Visibly holding his breath, he knocks on the Hylands' door.

Sabryna answers almost immediately. Her perfectly painted eyes perk up, and she leans forward subconsciously.

"How can *I* help *you*?" she asks in a sultry voice.

I laugh at the look on Will's face. Catalina had warned him that Sabryna was exceedingly hostile, but it's clear to me that she's only antagonistic toward those she believes are sleeping with her husband. And nobody can be unfriendly toward someone who looks like Will. A memory of Jay appears, unbidden, and I push it away.

"I'm Rachel's brother-in-law. Well, I was . . . before her death," he says. I grimace. Considering he's been speaking with many people in the building, shouldn't he have developed a better routine by now? Although, Sabryna's blouse has a plunging neckline, and it would be hard for any straight man to focus on a specific task with those two distractions ogling up at him.

"Is that right? It's a horrible tragedy, what happened to her." Sabryna is appropriately somber. "I wasn't aware that she was married."

"My brother died a couple of years ago."

"My condolences," Sabryna says automatically.

"I'm actually hoping to speak with anyone who knew Rachel. Just to get a sense of what happened to her in the years following my brother's death. Hopefully, I can shed some light on where she's been and what she's been doing."

Sabryna eyes him. "Rachel and I were friends. Close friends. But, unfortunately, I'm just going out to run some errands now. But if you come back tonight, around seven, I can *definitely* help you get closure."

We were friends? I feel indignant. She's playing up our relationship so she can see Will again. While I'm glad to see that she doesn't plan to drink herself into a stupor tonight when her husband doesn't come home, her attention would be better suited elsewhere. I'm suddenly surprised to discover that I feel protective of Will. Despite the fact that Jay hadn't interacted with his brother for years before his death, I have started to notice striking similarities between them. They're both stubborn and driven. Jay worked long hours at the clinic, and Will has spent nearly every waking minute investigating my death. They're both charming—to varying degrees. Jay's charm was often laid on thick, but Will's is more subtle. He's more awkward, but occasionally the charm shines through. Clearly, Will cared more for his brother than Jay ever knew. I wonder if Jay's death was the tipping point, causing Will to overcome his addictions and turn his life around. I still don't know what Will actually does— in the real world—when he isn't conducting amateur murder investigations. I realize that I don't actually know much about him at all. It's obvious to me now that Jay's few words about his brother hadn't captured the full story.

"All right, that sounds great. I'll see you at seven," Will says. I do notice a major difference between Jay and Will. Jay was aware of his good looks, but Will, it seems, is completely unaware of Sabryna's intentions for him. Tonight should be interesting.

Sabryna watches him as he leaves. Her eyes are filled with emotion, but I can't quite read them. Is that pain? Or longing? Or something in between?

Will returns to my elevator, takes it to the ground floor, and enters the guest suite. Catalina has her nose buried in a file.

She looks up. "What did I tell you? A vile woman."

"Actually, she was quite pleasant with me."

Catalina deliberately puts down her file. "Then why are you back so fast? Shouldn't you be questioning her?"

"She's busy now. She has errands to run. She told me to come back tonight, at seven."

"For a trophy wife, she sure has a lot of errands," Catalina says. I'm a little surprised by the snark in her words. I've noticed that she's grown hard and a little bitter. Is it because of my death, because of the nature of her job, or because of something else that has happened in the last two years? "Will her husband be there tonight?"

"She didn't say."

Catalina looks thoughtful. "It might be better if her husband isn't there. You can likely get more information out of her that way."

"What do you mean?" Will seems genuinely confused.

Catalina conceals a smile with her hand. "Nothing. Just be subtle in your questioning. We don't want her to know she's a suspect."

Sabryna's a suspect?

I tuck away this tidbit of information for further contemplation.

Catalina drops a file into a brown legal box. It looks like she is packing everything up.

Will notices this too. "Are you going somewhere?"

Catalina laughs. "No, of course not. You'd be lost without me. I'm taking these boxes up to your apartment so that all our files and materials can be kept together. So we can get a full picture of both crimes and see how and if they tie into each other."

"Right, that makes sense." Will approaches the table and begins to help her. "Did you have any luck with the Toronto Distress Line?"

Catalina shakes her head. "They require a warrant if I want them to release the records of any of her callers. Apparently, the local PD did request them but only for the last two weeks before her death. For all we know, her killer could have called her before that."

That would mean that the police know about my anonymous caller. The one who called hours before my death. The one who killed me.

"How did you find out that the detectives on the case got a warrant?" Will asks.

"I may be out of my jurisdiction, but I'm not totally useless. I phoned the call center and acted like I already knew about the warrant, and I was just confirming it. There was one man I spoke with—Luke Brennan—who was friends with Kae. According to the building's visitor's log, he used to visit Kae quite frequently up until a few months ago. I'm meeting him for coffee tomorrow to try to pick his brain about her death."

Will nods thoughtfully. "Maybe he'll give you some information about that suspicious man who called on the night of her murder."

So, they're looking into my mystery caller after all. That's good. It might have been him. If we—they—can link him to the caller, then that might be enough evidence to at least convince the police to investigate him.

Catalina drops the final file into the box and looks around the room. "I think we have everything."

"If not, I know where to find you," Will says. He is so much like his brother in that instant, with that spark of humor in his eyes, that I feel like I've been punched in the stomach. That's another similarity between them, I note numbly. They both have a goofy sense of humor.

Had.

Catalina is also affected. She looks away, turning toward the box. She lifts it, grunting from its weight.

"I'll take that," Will says, reaching for the box.

Catalina raises an eyebrow. "Alert the media, there's a gentleman in the building. I can carry it myself." She stomps past him toward the exit.

Will seems dazed, but he quickly darts ahead of her to open the door, holding it while she walks through. Still a gentleman, but slightly less important than he probably would have liked.

They ride my elevator up to the seventh floor, where they step off. I move to join them, but the elevator continues its journey, oblivious to my wants and desires.

24

A petite, red-headed woman dressed all in white steps into the elevator as it idles on the ninth floor. Despite her size, she nearly fills it with her presence. She stabs the button for the ground floor with a long, dagger-like fingernail.

I've never noticed her before. She must live outside of my range. She's quite beautiful but in the way that money buys, with plastic surgery and expensive cosmetics, salon-colored hair and press-on nails. She gets off on the ground floor and heads straight for the parking garage. I travel through the wall at the back of the guest suite to cut her off, curious to see what kind of car she drives.

I'm guessing it'll be a BMW.

Clark and two other teenagers are loitering by one of the cement pillars. Clark is smoking something that isn't a cigarette. He leans against the column, jutting his hip out in a model's pose. He's wearing bloodred pants and a baggy, black T-shirt that has been torn intentionally. It looks like something with rather large claws has attacked him. I shudder at the sight, but I can see that there is no blood, no scars on the pale skin that's exposed underneath. It's just an effect.

To his left, there is a young girl, approximately the same age, who is sitting cross-legged on the ground at his feet. She's focused on a sketchbook, where she is drawing something with an HB pencil. She's dressed with an equal amount of deliberation. She wears pale blue jeans that are torn open into wide, gaping holes which reveal her knobby knees. She wears a lacy black tank top. A tangle of silver necklaces and chains are wrapped around her scrawny neck, creating the illusion of strangulation. Her hair is platinum blond but with the layers underneath dyed dark violet. She wears only eye makeup—thick black eyeliner and broad brush strokes of purple eyeshadow. It makes the rest of her face look sallow. A little blush and lip stain would have made her look prettier, healthier. But instead, the purple eyeshadow looks like the severe bruising of the malnourished, under rested, or the dead.

With a smile, I realize that I would likely fit in with these two, with my blood-soaked sweater and ashen complexion. If only they could see me. If only anyone could see me.

I push away the hysteria that fights to break through the surface, instead focusing my attention on the third kid. He sticks out like a sore thumb. He's dressed more clean-cut, with untorn, relatively well-maintained blue jeans and a plain green T-shirt. His hair is a mess of tawny curls, and it looks like he hasn't attempted to run a brush through it since last Christmas. He sits awkwardly on the ground facing the other two. He scrunches his nose as he flips through a graphic novel. I catch glimpses of red splashes throughout the pages.

The redhead from the elevator steps through the door and walks briskly to her car, unaware that she has company. I glance up at the security cameras, something I must have done thousands of times when I was alive—at least, when I wasn't housebound. The three teens are carefully positioned so that they are hidden from the door to the building. They're also out of sight of the video cameras. I scowl. If a group of teenagers could figure out how to evade the cameras, maybe my killer was able to elude them as well. Will is convinced that my killer is someone in the building, but this assumption may be based on faulty logic. My killer may have entered—and left—Thorwald Place undetected.

Clark takes a drag from his joint and passes it down to the girl. Without looking up, she takes it. She continues to draw in silence.

"I'm just so fucking bored," Clark says.

"Did you finish reading that book you found?" the girl asks. She hands the joint back up to him and continues to sketch, the sound of tiny scratches on the page reverberating throughout the garage.

"What book?" the other boy asks.

The girl stops sketching and glances up. She exchanges a meaningful look with Clark.

"Razor found a book on eBay. It's really old and authentic-looking. It's all about the afterlife, dark spirits, and the devil and stuff," the girl says. I wonder what "and stuff" refers to.

"It's written entirely in Latin, so of course, I've been learning Latin," Clark says. "But it's a dead language, and there are a lot more words than I thought there would be."

The boy puts down his graphic novel. "So, is that why you invited me to hang out with you? Because you want my help reading a *book*?"

Clark scowls. "It's not just any book, Noel. It's a *Book of Shadows*, a book of spells, a book about demons and ghosts and other monsters in the world. Aren't you interested in finding out what else is out there? It's all that Rayna and I ever want to talk about."

Noel frowns slightly and picks at a piece of dirt on his sneaker. "That does sound interesting . . ."

Rayna pipes in. "Come on, we've been friends since we could barely talk. Sure, we haven't hung out in a while, but I think it would be fun if we brought the old gang back together."

She glances up at Clark, an enigmatic look that Noel doesn't notice.

Noel seems torn. "You know I don't speak Latin, right? With it being a dead language and all, I never really saw a need to learn it."

"But you're *super* smart," Rayna says in a saccharine voice. "You could learn it *so* fast, and I think it would be, like, a fun activity for all of us to do together. Like when we used to read the *Berenstain Bears* books together. It'll be *exactly* like that but much, much better."

Noel looks at Clark, and I see a dozen emotions flash across his face, including one of adoration, love even, before he settles on nonchalance. "Fine," he says casually.

I look up to see Clark smirking before taking another drag.

"I'll help you with the book. I'll go to the library tomorrow after school and find some resources for learning Latin," Noel says, tearing his gaze away from Clark.

"No need, I have a few on me right now," Clark says. How convenient.

He pulls a few books on Latin vocabulary and conjugation out of his spiky backpack.

Noel smiles slightly at the sight of *Latin for Dummies*, but he's smart enough not to say anything.

"There are a few good websites too, but I haven't been able to check them out because my parents monitor my internet usage like fucking hawks," Clark says.

"And I would have researched it, but then I remembered that you *love* learning, and that this would be, like, the *perfect* opportunity to hang out with you again," Rayna says. She sure is laying it on thick. Noel is oblivious to her insincerity and laps it up like an eager puppy.

"Do you have the book that you want translated in there too?" Noel asks.

Clark glowers at him. "No. That book is ancient. I'm not going to lug it back and forth to school."

Noel flushes. "Of course. That would be . . . stupid."

"We'll show you the book later," Rayna says. "You're going to love it. The pages are old and they smell like something curled up and died in them. And it's filled with such gorgeous pictures of demons and innocents being tortured in hell . . ." she trails off dreamily.

Curious, I step closer to her and peek at her sketchbook. Her illustration is that of a devil's face, with horns and a forked tongue. Vivid eyes, with cat-like pupils that slice across the page.

It looks like this demon might step off the page and join us from the world of her imagination.

I tear my eyes away.

Rayna adds some finishing touches to her drawing. "Satan is my muse," she whispers.

Clark snickers. He slouches, leaning heavily against the cement pillar. He never takes his eyes off of Noel, who flips through the books in childish wonder.

September 30

Dear Diary,

Finally, I have something to write about that isn't related to the ghost that's haunting my house. I should be relieved, but the story I have to tell isn't particularly uplifting.

My boss, Gregory Copeland, used to hit on me a lot before—and after—I got engaged. He's mostly laid off since I got married, although, I sometimes get a strange vibe from him. He sits too close to me during briefings, and his eyes often stray below my neckline. I've taken to dressing conservatively for work, wearing outfits that even nuns would probably consider prudish. Tonight, I had to work late to wrap up the translation of a document for a law firm we contract with *from time to time. Lara is our only other medical translator, and she's been on sick leave for a couple of weeks, so I was the only person who could do this. I didn't mind. I would be paid overtime, and that money could go toward renovating the house.*

Or exorcising it.

I was chugging down my fourth cup of coffee (of the evening) when I got an eerie feeling, like I was being watched. I glanced out the glass door of my office. Gregory was in the hall, looking in my general direction. It was quarter to nine. I'd thought he'd gone home hours earlier. I slouched low in my seat, hoping to avoid detection, but there was no use. He'd already spotted me.

He strolled over and planted himself in the doorway, staring at me with a look of exaggerated surprise. "You're here late!"

I gave him a tight smile. "Just finishing up the Robertson file. The deadline is tomorrow." He already knew both of these things.

I turned away from him and pointedly stared at my computer screen. He didn't take the hint and instead he entered my office.

"How are the renovations going? Have you finished the kitchen cupboards yet?"

Had I told him about that? "No. We've put renos on hold for a couple of weeks." I didn't mention that it was because I want to move. Whatever's haunting us is haunting the house. I don't want to pour more money into it when there's a strong likelihood that we'll have to uproot ourselves. I hope to do that—just as soon as Jay admits there's something wrong. Just as soon as he admits that there's an evil presence in our home.

In the meantime, Jay isn't exactly happy that we're living with a gutted kitchen. He's a bit of a food snob, and he's cranky without his gourmet meals. Me, all I know how to use in the kitchen is the coffee percolator and the ice cube tray.

"That's too bad," Gregory said in a tone that hinted that he didn't think it was too bad. He leaned against my desk.

I fastidiously stared at the computer screen. The man couldn't take a hint if I stapled it to his forehead.

"Well, have a good night! I'll see you tomorrow," I chirped.

He didn't budge. If anything, he seemed to get closer.

"I really need to get this done so I can get home to my husband," I said pointedly.

Gregory pushed away from my desk, and I tried to hide my sigh of relief. But he didn't leave. Instead, he walked around my desk, until he was standing behind me.

I opened my mouth. I didn't know what to say that wouldn't get me fired, so I closed it immediately.

Gregory leaned over and made a show of looking at my computer screen. I could feel his hot breath on my neck. "That looks good," he said huskily.

Suddenly, his hand was on my shoulder.

I jerked away, slamming against the side of my desk, hard.

"Ow!"

"Are you all right?"

"Yes—no—I'm married," I gasped, clutching my spleen.

"You don't have to be."

He actually said that.

It took all my willpower not to slap him across his arrogant face. "Yes, yes I do have to be. I'm not interested in you. Do I have to go to HR about this?"

I immediately regretted bringing up HR when a shadow crossed his face. His lips formed a grim line. Time slowed to a stop, and I thought he might hit me. Instead, he spun around and strode to the door.

I was feeling both victorious and sick to my stomach when he hesitated in the doorway. Without turning around, he said, "You'll change your mind soon enough."

He sounded so sure of himself. So convinced that he was speaking the truth. So determined. A wave of dread washed over me.

I packed up my desk and took my work home with me. But I never did shake the feeling that I was being watched.

25

Will arrives at the Hylands' apartment promptly at seven. Sabryna greets him. She's slightly out of breath, and there's a rosy tinge to her cheeks. I notice that she's changed her clothes yet again. This time, she's wearing a snug red dress that rides up her thighs as she walks.

I assume this is for Will's benefit.

"Come on in," she purrs.

Will doesn't seem to notice that anything is out of the ordinary. He follows her into the dimly-lit apartment.

"Sit down." Sabryna gestures toward the sofa. "Would you like something to drink? A glass of red?"

"Ah, sure," Will says as he settles onto the seat.

Carrying two glasses of wine that are filled to the brim, Sabryna returns to the room with a little extra sway in her hips that nearly causes a spill. She hands Will a glass, and he murmurs a thank you.

"How long have you been living in the building?" Will asks.

"Nineteen years. My husband and I moved in a year after we married. It's a wonderful place, despite that creepy little concierge. He wasn't working here when we moved in, or I definitely would have insisted we find another condo. Do you know Elias Strickland?" Sabryna leans toward Will and places a palm on his arm.

"We've met. He's not the most pleasant man," Will says. His eyes are glued to her hand which remains on his arm. "But I'm here to talk about Rachel Drake."

Sabryna leans backward slightly, and Will releases a small breath of relief. "Right. Rachel. What do you want to know?"

"Anything. Everything. I have the impression that she didn't get out much. It seems like you're the only person in this building who claims to have actually known her, aside from the concierge, of course."

"Right," Sabryna says again.

Will waits expectantly.

"She moved in almost two years ago. I tried to befriend her, but she made it difficult. She rarely left her apartment, and, well, she never allowed me into her apartment." That much is true. "To be honest, I hadn't seen her in months."

"Earlier you mentioned that you were quite close." Will sounds more confused than accusing.

Sabryna flushes slightly. "Yes, well . . . I was the only person in the building who knew her at all."

"How can you know that for sure?" Will asks. "If you didn't see her that often, it's possible that she made friends with other residents of the building."

Sabryna looks pensive. "That's an excellent point." She doesn't offer anything else.

A small frown dances on the corners of Will's lips. "Is there anything else you would like to mention? Have you noticed any suspicious behavior in the building? Any new faces?"

Sabryna remains silent. "Not that I can think of," she says unconvincingly.

"Well, then, I suppose I should be going." Will begins to get up.

Sabryna grabs his arm with a carefully manicured hand. "No! I mean, no, don't leave. Finish your drink first."

Will looks down at his large wine glass, which is still full. I half expect him to chug it, but instead, he takes a small sip.

"So, how are you enjoying Toronto?" Sabryna asks.

Will is finally clueing in on the real reason why Sabryna invited him over. He shifts uncomfortably, glancing at her wedding band. "It's a nice city. I haven't gotten to see much of it, what with the investigation and all."

Sabryna nods knowingly. "Don't work too hard. Toronto has a wonderful nightlife, and you should get out. Have fun while you're still young."

Will smiles tersely. "I'll do that. As soon as I find Rachel's killer."

"Ooh, a man with a mission. I like that."

I scoff. I can't believe she just said that.

Apparently, neither can Will. He takes an especially deep sip of his wine, coughing when it goes down the wrong pipe.

Sabryna scoots closer to him on the sofa until their thighs are almost touching. Normally, I would leave at a time like this, but it's clear that Will is looking for a way out. If only I could provide it for him.

"So . . . Where are you from originally?" Sabryna continues.

Will is trying very hard to maintain eye contact, but his eyes keep straying lower. "I—um—I'm from BC, my family is in Vancouver."

Sabryna leans across Will and places her wine glass on the coffee table. She brushes up against him and shifts even closer.

"Has anyone had the chance to properly welcome you to Toronto?"

Will is speechless. Without warning, she lurches forward and kisses him. Will launches himself backward.

"I—um—I really need to stay focused on the case. I can't—um—" Will stammers.

Just then, the front door bursts open. Roger stands in the foyer, briefcase in hand.

Will's eyes are giant saucers. Sabryna is practically on top of him, her red, silk dress has ridden up so high that I catch a glimpse of lace.

Roger glares at the two of them. His eyes drift toward the lipstick smears on Will's lips.

"WHAT THE HELL IS GOING ON HERE?" he shouts. "Get the HELL off my wife!"

Technically, *she's* on *him*, but nobody hears me when I point that out. In several quick strides, Roger is on them. He tosses Sabryna to the side and picks Will up by the collar, which is no mean feat considering the man is almost two hundred pounds. But Roger is built like a line-backer, and he easily tosses Will across the room.

"No, Roger! What are you doing?" Sabryna screams.

Will gets up off the Persian rug and eyeballs the distance between himself and the open door. It's over twelve feet. Roger rushes toward him, swings his arm, and punches Will square across the jaw.

"If I ever see your face again, I'll be sure to break it," Roger says.

I'm not entirely convinced he didn't already break it. Blood streams out of Will's nose, down his face, staining the expensive rug and mingling with the spilled red wine. He clambers to his feet and jogs out the open doorway.

Roger relaxes the instant Will is out of sight. He turns to Sabryna. "I'm fine with your sleeping around, but not here. Not with someone from the building. Not under *my* roof."

Sabryna looks up at him from her position on the sofa. "Don't you care? I was with someone else!"

I feel the tug of my elevator, but I resist it. I can't leave yet. I have to make sure Sabryna is safe. I move toward the doorway to avoid hitting the invisible barrier as it moves. I sense the elevator stop. It must be on the floor above or below this one, since I wasn't ripped back. I take several steps forward and feel the new location of the invisible wall. I tuck away this new information for later. So long as I stay within my self-contained prison when the elevator moves, I won't be torn away.

I turn back to Roger, who's staring at his wife with an unreadable expression on his face.

"If we had a prenup, I would've left you years ago. But since I hadn't had the foresight to prepare one, I'm stuck with you. And you're stuck with me. Deal with it. All you have to do is pretend to be happy. If you try to divorce me, I'll make sure you end up with nothing. And right now, it looks better to the Senior

Partners if they think I'm happily married to a wonderfully devoted woman."

Roger leaves the room, and I hear water running in the bathroom. Sabryna remains on the couch, completely devastated. She grabs a tissue and blots away her tears, leaving behind murky, gray streaks that trail down her beautiful face. Quivering, she stands, adjusts her dress, and picks up the two wine glasses. She takes them to the kitchen, and I hear the quiet clinking as she loads the dishwasher.

I had thought something seemed fishy about her invitation. It was strange that she had instructed Will to come over so late, just when her husband was expected home. She was dressed to impress, and she had practically jumped Will when the clock turned seven fifteen. Had all this charade been to get a rise out of Roger? To make her husband realize that he loved and missed her? If so, her plan had backfired miserably. Roger just openly admitted to her that he didn't care if she was faithful and that their marriage would be over if he didn't want to risk losing half of their marital assets. What a piece of work.

⚬⚬⚬⚬⚬

I pop up to my apartment, where I find Will in the kitchen. Catalina is using one of my best hand towels to staunch the flow of blood, which seems to be lessening.

"Why is there lipstick on your face?" she asks.

I don't know how she can see it under all the blood.

"Sabryna jumped me. Then her husband came home and sucker-punched me," Will explains, his voice nasal and stifled under the hand towel.

Catalina raises an eyebrow. "She *jumped* you? I'm sure that's what happened."

Will nods, then winces from the pain. "She *did*. I think she might have timed it that way. Like she wanted to make her husband jealous."

Catalina snickers.

"It's not funny."

"It's a little funny. And it looks like it worked. If she had all this planned, I doubt she had anything to do with Kae's murder. She would have been more concerned with hiding the truth about Kae's death and would not have had the time to come up with a villainous plan to deceive her husband."

Catalina steps closer. She carefully pulls Will's hand from his face. She inspects the damage closely. "It might be broken."

"Ow," Will complains as she pokes his nose tenderly.

"Don't be a baby," she says with a faint smile. "Hold this." She hands him the hand towel and starts to leave the room.

"Where are you going?" Will's voice is muffled.

"To get my car keys. I'm taking you to the hospital."

"The *hospital*?" Will doesn't like the sound of that.

"Your nose is probably broken. Unless you want to end up looking like Owen Wilson, we'd better get you there quickly. Although, your face is almost too pretty. It could use a couple of imperfections." She turns around and grabs the keys from the hook near the door.

Will stands in the kitchen, staring after her, a little bit of pink coloring his bloodstained cheeks.

"You coming or what?" she calls out.

Smiling, Will trails after her.

26

Oliver notices Melody's odd behavior. It's a little after midnight, and she must be exhausted, but she hurries around the bedroom, packing the suitcase for his trip to visit family in Vermont. She rolls his shirts with shaky fingers and positions everything in an obsessive-compulsive row that would make me run for my money. Oliver is watching her from his seat on the chaise longue.

"Don't get up to help," I say. "She's only seven months pregnant."

"What's wrong, baby? Are you worried you're going to miss me?" Oliver asks. Of course he assumes this is the reason why she's nervous. I'm glad he doesn't suspect the truth. Although, he *had* seen the webpage in his browser history. Why didn't he confront Melody about it? What is he waiting for?

Melody startles at the sound of his voice, but she quickly recovers. "I will, but you're only gone a week, right? You're coming back next Tuesday?"

Oliver gives her a condescending look. "I'll be back next Monday afternoon."

Melody stops what she's doing. "Oh. I guess I misheard you."

"Of course you did." I want to slap him in the face.

I can't wait for Melody to be out of this hellhole, even if that means I'll never see her again. Maybe when she escapes this prison, I'll be released, too. One can hope.

Melody finishes packing the suitcase and zips it shut. Oliver gets up and pulls it off the bed, wheeling it down the hall and leaving it in the entranceway. Melody follows, wringing her hands nervously. I've never seen her do this before, no matter how anxious her husband makes her. It is bizarre that she is more frightened now—in the face of escaping it all.

The telephone rings, and Melody nearly jumps through the roof. Oliver shoots her a strange look. He pulls his cell from his back pocket and answers.

"I'll be right down." To Melody, he says, "The taxi is here."

"Already?" Melody squeaks.

Oliver frowns slightly. "You don't want me to miss my flight, do you? It's leaving at 3 a.m. I'd better get going."

"Yeah, you don't want to miss your flight," Melody says. Her eyes well with tears.

Oliver's expression softens. "Don't worry. The time will fly, and I'll be back before you know it. Just don't cause too much mischief while I'm away."

He leans over and gives her a soft kiss on the cheek, followed by a bear hug. He lingers, his hand running circles on her upper back.

"I'm going to miss my Melly and the Belly," he whispers.

There is pounding at the front door. Oliver spins around and whips it open.

An extremely peeved Elias stands in the doorway. "Mr. Boyden, sir, I cannot hold the taxi for much longer. If you want to catch your flight, which I carefully booked for you, *in first class*, I suggest you leave now."

Oliver clenches his jaw. "I'm saying goodbye to my emotionally fragile, pregnant wife."

Elias looks chastised.

Oliver turns back to Melody apologetically. "Goodbye, Melly. I'll call you first thing in the morning."

Melody nods wordlessly. Oliver follows Elias out the door, and they head to the elevator. I stay in the hall, watching as they board the other elevator, which Elias had ridden up to this floor. I'm relieved that I have more time with Melody.

I return to the apartment, where Melody is pacing the large living room. She glances up at the clock on the mantle, which reads quarter to one.

Why Oliver chose to take a flight in the middle of the night is beyond me, but he'd been complaining about having to stay late to tie up last-minute loose ends at work, so I suspect that he didn't have much choice in the matter. Melody is exhausted, and I hope that she will make it to the shelter intact. The streets of downtown Toronto aren't particularly safe after midnight. I hope she isn't fleeing one monster just so she can fall into the clutches of another.

Melody goes into the closet and retrieves a small black suitcase which has a vibrant green ribbon tied to the handle. She plops it on the bed and begins to load it with basic necessities. Clothes. Toothbrush. She lovingly places her grandmother's ring and her baby blanket between bundles of clothes. She knows that she doesn't have to—and shouldn't—bring mementos from her past life with her to her new one. But I understand how hard it can be to let go of the past. I'd kept a few things from my past life when I moved to Toronto. My engagement ring, my favorite mug, Jay's comfiest sweater, my diary. The latter I've barely touched since moving to Thorwald Place. I don't know why I'd taken it with me. I suppose I wasn't ready to let those memories go. And I doubt I am now.

My attention is drawn back to Melody as she removes a letter that is taped to the underside of her dresser drawer. She carefully places it on her husband's pillow. "Oliver" is written in block letters on the envelope.

A goodbye letter. That isn't a good idea, as there's no telling how Oliver will react to it. I feel a chill in the air.

Oblivious to my fears, Melody continues to pack her bag. Her movements are even more erratic, more staccato than earlier. She resembles a marionette on lurching strings.

She returns to the living room and stops abruptly at the bookshelf. She stares at the photographs of herself and Oliver for an excruciating length of time. She takes down two of the frames and carries them with her to the bedroom. I'm about to follow her, but my eye is caught by the sight of something moving in the foyer.

The doorknob jiggles, then turns. The door swings wide open. Oliver stands in the doorway, slightly out of breath. He looks at the table in the foyer, then glances around the living room.

"Baby? Have you seen my passport?" Oliver calls out.

I hear a clatter from the bedroom. Oliver dashes toward the sound. I follow in hot pursuit.

Melody hovers by the bed, her eyes as round as saucers. A shattered picture frame lies at her bare feet. Oliver stands in the doorway, his mouth agape. His eyes dart from Melody to the half-filled suitcase on their bed.

"What is this?"

Melody opens her mouth, but no words come out.

"Should I rephrase the question? Why are you packing a suitcase, Melody?" Oliver's voice is perfectly calm.

Melody's tongue darts out, moistening her lips. "I—I—I was going to surprise you. I wanted to see if I could get a ticket to Vermont. To surprise you."

"The doctor said you shouldn't be flying because of the baby. That's why you weren't coming with me in the first place. That's why you were staying behind."

Melody shakes her head fitfully. "I went back to the doctor since then. He said it would be okay. I'm fine for traveling until the final month of the pregnancy."

Oliver twists his lips into a striking grin. "Well, that's wonderful news then."

Melody wipes a loose tendril of hair from her sweaty forehead with a shaky hand.

Oliver strides toward the bed and seizes the envelope she left on his pillow. "And what's this?"

"No! Don't read that. That's just a note I wrote for you when you—we—get back. Just a little letter. It was supposed to be a surprise." Melody is beginning to sound desperate, frantic, terrified.

Oliver tosses her a disparaging glance and slides the folded paper from its pristine white sleeve. He reads the letter in rigid silence. His hands begin to shake.

"Were you going to run away, Melody?"

Melody shakes her head, but it's futile. There's no disputing the hard evidence he holds in his hands.

"Do you think I'm stupid?" Oliver spits, crumpling the hand-written letter in his fist.

Melody shakes her head again. She takes a step backward, bare foot, crunching in the broken glass from the frame. She whimpers, then takes another step.

"In what twisted. Backwards. Fucked-up world would you think that taking my son away from me is a good idea?" Each word is like a bullet piercing flesh.

Without pause, he lunges forward, grabbing Melody by the arm. She stiffens, then tries to pull free from his steel grasp. Oliver still seems collected, calm, and in control of his actions. There is a hard gleam in his eye, however, something I have never there seen before. Something cold. Something inhuman. A shadow shifts in the corner of the room. I glance over to it and notice the darkness swelling—growing and taking form.

I feel the familiar tugging of the elevator. I am torn away just as Oliver raises a closed fist.

27

No! Back in the elevator, I spin around. It's empty. Seconds tick by as it traitorously descends. Third floor. Second floor. Lobby. Basement. The doors slide open noiselessly. No one is in the corridor.

I wait ten seconds, fifteen. Twenty. The doors stay open. This has happened before. Why does this happen? Is it programming in the elevator? If so, shouldn't it happen *more* often? It always seems to happen at the same time—around one in the morning. A chill travels down my spine. I died in this elevator at around one in the morning. When the elevator was at the basement level. Does the elevator make these regular nocturnal visits because of me? Am *I* making the elevator move?

Pushing down the fear that wells up inside me, I edge toward the open doors. One. Two. Three. I thrust my head into the hall, quickly assessing its dingy walls. There is no one there.

I am both relieved and terrified by this. If no living person called the elevator, this supports the theory that the elevator is here because of me.

I shake my head. None of this is important right now. What *is* important is that Melody is in danger. I return to the elevator. Never have I needed to move this elevator more than right this moment. I stare at the buttons on the panel. I could try to go to the fourth floor—but I would be powerless to help Melody. I need to get to the second floor. I haven't been able to communicate with Alexei except for when he's holding a séance, but if there's the slightest chance he can hear me—and understand my message—I need to try.

I take a deep breath, which of course does nothing to calm my nerves. I don't need oxygen anymore. I press the number two. Nothing happens.

I begin to breathe slowly, returning to my coping technique that I haven't needed in a long time. I breathe in and out through pursed lips. In and out. In and out. Despite not having any need for oxygen, the old familiarity of the breathing exercise calms me, allowing me to focus my attention. In and out. In and out. I feel my focus center. My determination culminates at a single point. I press the number two.

Nothing. Frustration wells up. I stab at the button again. Again. Still, it doesn't light up. Still, the elevator doors remain open, taunting me. Why won't they shut?

I scream and punch through the wall, lurching through it. I have never felt so helpless in my entire life. Not when my husband was murdered. Not even when *I* was murdered. At least then I could do *something*. I could fight back, although that did me little good. Now, I am useless, a wisp of air, nothing more than a shift of shadows or a chill up the back of someone's neck.

I dash out of the elevator, down the hallway, and into the fitness center. It's empty. No one is exercising at this hour. I dart into the basement level parking garage, but it's also empty.

I hop up to the lobby, my last hope. The guest suite is empty. The library and party area are empty. The parking garage up here is empty. I yowl in frustration. I know that I probably wouldn't have been able to communicate anyway, unless by some fluke Alexei was around. This leaves only one last option.

I drop back down to the basement corridor. I glance around at the dark expanse that is a feeble imitation of what it once was. A mere echo of how it appears to the living. The elevator doors are closed now. I give the elevator no more than a passing glance. Instead, I approach the storage room. I notice that the one time I do not feel the inexplicable magnetic pull to the door is the one time I willingly enter.

There is a palpable temperature drop the moment I step through the door. Again, I wonder if this sensation is psychological. I normally do not sense temperature changes, as noted when Rosanne in 304 nearly burnt the building to the ground when baking cookies last week. But here I am, shivering in the cold, desolate basement. Then I realize. If I can sense a chill, then it must be on this side of the veil.

I wade through the darkness, my eyes growing accustomed to the faint glow of the exit sign. This red realm seems otherworldly, filled with unwanted relics of the past. I peer into the shadows, searching for a sign of the Shadow Man. But he is composed of shadows, so I imagine he can coalesce in any corner, at any time. This doesn't stop me from treading forward slowly, studying the darkness, searching for the faceless figure.

The thick scent of blood and decay circles me before I see her. The Girl with No Eyes has taken her habitual position in the far corner. Again, she stares into it, her back facing me. I wonder about her story. How did she lose her eyes? Why does her mouth open in a soundless scream? I'm terrified of her, but I need her.

Her dress may be old-fashioned, but it also seems timeless. Given the cyclical nature of fashion, I can't tell when she died based on its style alone. Five years ago? Twenty? Fifty? If it were recent, I should have heard about it. I should have heard something on the news about a little girl whose eyes were brutally ripped out. What would happen to me if I were stuck here for decades? Will I, too, become unable to communicate with even the dead? Will I, too, become a shell of my former self, driven mad by isolation?

Regardless of the mystery that shrouds the Girl with No Eyes, she has been dead longer than I have. She has had more time to grow used to the limitations of our condition. I wonder if she knows how to communicate with the living, or how to interact with inanimate objects. To have an influence. To press a damn elevator button.

I turn away from the little girl, combing the shadows for any sign of movement. Any thickening of the darkness. Relieved that nothing had formed behind my back, I turn back to the little girl.

She stands closer to me now, a hair's breadth away. Her saucer-like eye sockets stare up at me, vacant and black. My blood goes cold. I resist the temptation to retreat. She hasn't done anything to hurt me. Last time she *warned* me about the

Shadow Man. She's an ally until she does something to prove otherwise.

I look at her unflinchingly. Her face is young, much younger than I had thought before. She cannot be older than six or seven. At least, that was her age when she died. Now, she could be older than me. She continues to stare, and I stare back. I realize I can see *into* her eyes. See the dark chasms where her eyes once were. The walls are scratched and scarred, as if by an irregularly shaped instrument. My nostrils fill with the same cloying stench of her, and a wave of nausea washes over me. I stare into the redness, the moist glow of the wounds, the jagged edges of sliced nerves that never healed.

The Girl with No Eyes continues to gaze up at me, neck craned at an extreme, inhuman angle. She doesn't say anything, but I can tell she knows I am there. She can sense me, as I can her.

Even without eyes, she is aware.

"Hello." My voice betrays me with only the slightest quaver.

She does not move. She does not react to the sound of my voice.

"My name is Rachel."

She remains perfectly still, deathly still. Then, she jerks her head from side to side, viciously, violently. Her voice is hoarse and low. "No, it's not."

How does she know that? I lick my lips. "My name is Kae."

She doesn't move.

"I need your help."

She slowly and gradually tilts her head further to the side, as if she's listening. I take this as a good sign. An indication that I'm getting through to her.

"A woman on the fourth floor is in grave danger. She might die. Her husband is going to kill her, and I—we—need to help her." I try to mask the panic in my voice. I have been gone for so long. I might already be too late.

"A friend?" the girl croaks.

"Yes! She's a friend." I resist the urge to fist-pump the air. I'm actually getting through. After almost two weeks of being unheard and unnoticed, *finally* someone can hear my voice.

"A new friend to play with?" she whispers.

What? She must have misunderstood. "No. She's in *danger*. She might die. We need to help her!"

"She might die, she might die," she adopts a singsong tone, her voice growing stronger, bouncing off the desolate walls.

Is she mocking me? "We have to help her," I repeat, but it's useless.

"She might die, she might die. I will have a new friend," the little girl is perfectly still. The only thing that moves is her mouth, and her voice seems disjointed, disconnected from the rest of her body.

She's insane. She *wants* an innocent person to die so she will have company? How twisted is this? My thoughts shift. What would it be like to have another person here, someone to talk to other than this deranged lunatic? If Melody died, I wouldn't be completely alone anymore.

I shake away these dark thoughts.

"She will die. But on the *fourth floor*. You can't travel that far, can you?" I try to reason with the child.

The girl's lips curl into an exaggerated frown. Her lips twist further and further, stretching downward. It is so grotesque, but I cannot tear my eyes away.

She whirls around and drifts back to her corner, her head still twisted at an irregular angle. Unnerved, I flee the storage room. The large analog clock on the wall of the fitness center reads 1:30. I have been gone for a half hour. Anything could have happened during this time. I feel the familiar tug of the elevator. I eagerly embrace it, returning of my own volition.

The elevator slowly creeps to the ground floor where it stops. The doors slide open to reveal a man, dressed in a black suit, carrying a black leather briefcase. His hair is disheveled and his eyes are bleary—likely from a late night at the office, staring at a computer screen. He strides into the elevator and efficiently punches the button for the ninth floor.

No! That's not within the range of Melody's apartment. But I know what I have to do.

The moment the elevator hits the third floor, I jump up to the fourth and lunge toward Melody's apartment. I enter the living room which is empty. I push against the invisible dome wall, which spreads farther as the elevator approaches the fourth floor.

The door to the bathroom is ajar. Water is running. I push forward, advancing until I am at the edge of my maximum range. Oliver stands at the sink. He wears the same clothes as earlier, but his tie is loosened, and his sleeves are rolled up past his elbows. He's washing his hands which are stained red. Crimson tendrils curl down the white, porcelain sink, swirling down the drain. Oliver wears an unreadable expression, his lips thin and his eyes narrow. Already my range is diminishing, and I jump backward, trying to stay within my range so I am not torn back to the elevator. I try to see into the bedroom, the last place I saw Melody, but the door is closed, as if sealing her fate.

October 10

Dear Diary,

Lon Chaney, Jr. is missing.

It took me longer than it should have to notice his absence. Tuesday night, I went to put food in his bowl, and I discovered that he hadn't touched his breakfast. I searched the house, frantically scouring every nook and cranny, checking any spot that he could have squeezed his tiny body into—in case he had gotten stuck.

When it was clear that he wasn't locked in a cupboard or hiding between the sofa cushions, I realized that he must have gotten outside. Lon Chaney, Jr. is an indoor cat, but like most indoor cats, he yearns to be free of his domestic prison. He only occasionally attempts to escape, and it's usually half-heartedly, which makes me think it's more for show than out of an actual desire to explore. Lately, he has been so indifferent to open doors, which, of course, may have been part of his cunning strategy. He slipped through the cracks and now he's been missing for almost two days. At first, I wondered if he had escaped the house, knowing that there's something sinister residing in it. Now, I'm not sure he was so lucky.

I prowled the streets that night, armed with a high-powered flashlight, calling out his name and peering into shrubs and under cars. I received some strange looks from the neighbors. Their concern was likely exacerbated by my stupid choice in name for the cat. It was a full moon that night, and they may have thought I was searching for the actual Wolfman.

I didn't find him, though a few stray cats responded to my calls. I gave them treats and then sent them on their way. When Jay got home from his late shift, he immediately accompanied me on my hunt, and he comforted me when our search yielded nothing.

Today, Jay had to go in to work, so I recruited Cindy and Catalina to help me make flyers and post them around the neighborhood. The strangest thing happened, and now I think that they, too, are beginning to suspect something is wrong with my house.

Catalina stood in my finally renovated kitchen, talking on the phone, trying to recruit friends and acquaintances for the search party she'd assembled. So far, it was just her and Cindy helping me.

"Where's your sister?" I asked Catalina as she finished leaving her sibling a message on her voicemail.

"No clue."

I was disappointed, but two helpers were better than none.

Cindy burst through the door, holding several rolls of packing tape she had gone out to pick up at the dollar store.

She dropped the bag unceremoniously on the new marble countertop.

"I have the supplies. Don't worry, if Lon Chaney, Jr. is anywhere in a three-mile radius, we'll find him."

Catalina avoided my eyes. Lon Chaney, Jr. was old, and I knew that she had her doubts about our finding him.

I gulped, and tears welled in my eyes.

Catalina noticed my expression and immediately took charge. "All right. The first forty-eight hours are critical in any missing persons case."

"He's been missing for two days already," I said.

Catalina barely faltered. "Well, the real cut off is at seventy-two hours. We will find Lon Chaney, Jr. And we will bring him home." She turned to me. "Go grab the rest of the flyers. We're heading out in T-minus ten minutes." Catalina grabbed my paper map and began to mark out our route with a red pen.

I nodded, grateful that she was my rock. I told myself to get a grip and went to the printer to pick up the last stack of flyers. I had insisted on printing in color, because black and white doesn't capture the vivacity of Lon Chaney, Jr.'s green eyes or the depths of his russet cloak.

The wireless printer was still printing, which was strange because I had sent another print job over half an hour earlier, when Cindy had gone out to get additional supplies. Flyers were still pouring out of the printer, but they were different. Something was wrong with them.

I inched toward the printouts. I tenderly lifted the top sheet from the pile. The flyer was almost the same. "MISSING" was written in block letters at the top. A full-color photo of Lon Chaney, Jr. was in the middle with his stats and my contact information below. The modest reward for his safe return was listed below that. But the color photo was what drew my eye. A smear of red ink slashed across his throat.

I yelped and dropped the sheet.

The printer suddenly stopped as Cindy and Catalina rushed into the room.

"What's wrong?" Cindy asked. She followed my gaze to the stack of papers. All the new flyers had this horrible deformity.

Catalina bent over and picked up a sheet. "Looks like we broke the printer with all these flyers," she said humorlessly.

I didn't laugh and neither did Cindy. My eyes traced the red smear which sliced across Lon Chaney, Jr.'s tawny coat. Without another word, Catalina crumpled the sheet and tossed it into the wastepaper basket. I caught Cindy glancing around the room with an unreadable expression on her face. She stopped when she realized I was staring. She blushed and looked away. We collected the unmarred flyers in silence and went out to post them.

I don't know if that was an omen or a threat, but I know now more than ever that whatever is haunting our house had something to do with Lon Chaney, Jr.'s disappearance. I still hang on to that shred of hope that he escaped before the entity got to him. I can only hope that the mutilated image was a threat—not a promise.

28

right sunlight beams through the spotless windows of apartment 407. No one is home. The place is tidy and seemingly untouched, bearing no hint of the horrors it saw last night. I triple check the closets, confirming that Melody's suitcase is definitely gone. Does this mean that she escaped? Did Oliver let her take her meager belongings and leave? Or did Oliver use the suitcase to . . . transport her body?

There was a lot of blood in the sink last night. Maybe it was Oliver's. Maybe he cut himself picking up the glass from the broken frame. Maybe Melody cut herself on the broken frame, and Oliver, being a loving, kind, considerate husband, cleaned it up.

I do another lap around the apartment, but everything seems to be in place. Oliver is out, and I am alone.

Or am I?

"Melody?" I call out. My voice sounds shaky and high-pitched. "Are you here?"

The air is tranquil, oblivious to the anxiety radiating from me. I pass through the living room into the bedroom and try again.

"Melody? Are you here?" I still hear nothing. I stand directly in the spot where I last saw her cowering in fear as her husband raised his arm to strike.

"Melody?" There is no change in temperature like when the Girl with No Eyes is around. I don't feel any different, like when I first saw Raymond Favreau, and I was drawn toward the obscure stain on the ceiling. I tentatively sniff the air. Nothing.

If Oliver killed Melody, she isn't here. At least, she isn't here now. I don't always see the Girl with No Eyes in the storage room. Raymond's spirit isn't always in the third bedroom of Sylvie's condo.

I wonder what factors can affect a ghost's presence. Location seems to be a significant variable. Time of death? That might be the case. I seem to always be around, always drifting from place to place, fully conscious of what is happening around me.

But maybe other ghosts drift in and out of consciousness, based on variables that I cannot even begin to fathom. Or maybe ghosts are always there, in the periphery, but invisible, until they choose to be seen.

That's assuming they have control over their actions—over where they go and what they do. Both the Girl with No Eyes and Raymond don't seem to be sane. But that begs another question—am I?

I linger in Melody's apartment, unwilling to give up my search until the elevator forces me to. It drags me away, first to the seventh floor and then to the lobby. I watch Elias at his station as he makes frenzied phone calls. I can always tell when he's stressed. He develops a thin sheen of sweat on his upper lip, one that he tries to wipe surreptitiously with the back of his sleeve. Right now, he's trying to book a first-class train trip across the country for the stingy couple in apartment 803.

My attention is drawn away by movement in my peripheral vision. I stare. Luke is here. I hurry toward him, wearing a silly grin on my face. But then I remember. He can't see me. My smile fades as I study him. I hadn't thought I'd ever see him again. His face is drawn, his lips are curved into a frown—an expression I've never seen on his face before. His eyes are outlined with red rims that rival the rich color of his hair. He runs a hand through it, which is longer than when I saw him last.

I'm torn back to the last time I saw him. Luke and I were on my couch, watching a movie. I can't remember what movie it was now other than that it was some comedy with Will Ferrell. Luke had brought more than enough popcorn for us to share. I remember catching myself running my fingers through his soft hair.

"You need a haircut," I'd said with a laugh. His breath caught, and he looked down at me with piercing green eyes. Before I knew what was happening, he leaned forward and our lips grazed. I jerked away from him, sending the popcorn flying. Disappointment was written plainly on his face. Disappointment and hurt. I couldn't meet his eyes after that, and he left shortly after the movie ended. That was over four months ago. That was the last time I let him come to my apartment. The last time I ever saw him.

I force my thoughts to the present and find myself staring down at my wedding band. It is forever fused to my ring finger. Jay may be gone, but he certainly isn't forgotten.

I wasn't ready—I may never be ready—to move on, but Luke made it just a little harder to remain floating in my stagnant pool of grief.

Luke signs in as a guest with Elias at the desk. If Elias recognizes him as who he'd once said was my "boyfriend," he doesn't give any indication. I reluctantly follow Luke toward the guest suite.

Catalina answers the door on the first knock. "You must be Mr. Brennan."

"Call me Luke," he says with a small smile that doesn't quite reach his eyes.

He follows Catalina into the guest suite, and I notice that he's holding a tray with two cups of coffee. He offers one to Catalina, who accepts greedily. Catalina leads him to the breakfast nook where they sit across from each other at the little round table. She studies him for several moments.

"I take it you were close to K—Rachel?" Catalina asks gently.

Luke nods. He doesn't lift his eyes from his coffee. "We were good friends."

"Friends? Nothing more?"

Luke raises his gaze to meet hers. "Just friends," he says firmly.

"The concierge seemed to think you were her boyfriend."

Luke's eye twitches. "Well, he was mistaken."

Catalina studies him for a moment. "You mentioned on the phone that you hadn't seen her in a few months."

"Four months. But we chatted on the phone regularly. But not nearly as often as I would have liked." I feel a pang of guilt at that comment. I'd been pushing him away, and not answering all his calls had been a part of it. Now, I would give anything to be able to talk to him again.

"When was the last time you talked to her?"

"The night she . . . died." Luke runs a hand through his hair. "She was stressed out. I should have come over. If I'd been here—" He cuts off, but the implication is clear. He is racked with guilt over my death. But what happened isn't his fault. I wish I could tell him that.

"Do you have any idea what could have made her want to run?"

Luke takes a shaky breath and shakes his head. He looks so distressed.

My stomach twists. "Rachel was always afraid. Afraid of someone—or something—from her past. She never told me anything, but I could tell. There was a hollow emptiness where her past was concerned, and no matter what I did or what I said, she wouldn't open up about it." Guilt weighs down on me. Seeing his distress—not just from my death but from the lies I told during my life—is almost too much to bear.

Catalina also looks upset. She's finally allowing some emotion to crack through her hard police officer veneer.

"Rachel had been through a lot. She wanted to move on with her life. She was afraid of lingering too long and letting the past—what happened to her—define her."

Luke shakes his head, letting out a humorless laugh. "It seemed to me like that's exactly what she did."

A sharp knock at the front door makes both of them jump.

Catalina glances over her shoulder. "Stay here," she instructs Luke.

She goes to the door and peers out the peephole. She tenses, holding her breath. She doesn't answer it.

I drift through the wall.

A troll-like man with wispy gray hair stands on the other side. I instantly recognize him as one of the detectives who worked my case in the days after my death. I haven't seen him in over a week. Does this mean there's been a break in my case?

"Detective Cherry!" Elias hangs up the phone and jumps out from behind the desk, hurrying toward the man. "To what do I owe this pleasure?" He oozes with insincerity and curiosity.

"Mr. Strickland. It has been brought to my attention that Officer Catalina Marquez is staying on the premises, in the guest suite. Is this correct?" He knocks on the door again, and I wonder why Catalina hasn't answered.

Elias frowns. "*Detective* Marquez is staying in the guest suite."

"Detective, huh?" Cherry chuckles. "Marquez is no detective. And she isn't within her jurisdiction. Did she neglect to tell you that?"

Elias' jaw drops. "She had a badge, and she said that she was investigating Ms. Drake's death."

"So, she was impersonating a detective?"

Shit.

He pounds on the door harder.

Catalina opens the door mid-knock, a pleasant smile plastered on her face. "Detective Cherry! What are you doing here?"

"*Officer* Marquez, I see you're still looking into the murder of your friend."

"Yes, I am," she says curtly. Her eyes dart out into the hall, landing on Elias, who hovers behind the detective. I wish they didn't have the audience. Elias will feel obliged to tell everyone in the building that Catalina isn't who she claims to be. No one is going to trust her anymore. This will put a damper on her investigation, if it doesn't snuff it out completely.

"I spoke with your Captain," Cherry begins.

Catalina blanches, but her face remains impassive.

"He told me about your investigation. How you were looking into a powerful man in Ottawa for the murder of your friend. How you were using . . . unorthodox means of investigation . . ." He trails off, observing Catalina. "How long is your suspension?"

She was investigating him? My stomach churns as I consider how dangerous that must have been for her. What he's proven to be capable of . . . As Detective Cherry said, he's a powerful man, and he would have had the means to ensure that she stop investigating him.

That must be why Catalina was suspended. Although, she must not have found anything incriminating—no evidence pointing to him as a suspect for my murder—or she wouldn't have needed to come here.

Detective Cherry is still speaking. "What I mean to say is, we have this investigation under control. We don't need an outsider coming here, undermining our authority. And I've heard that you've been posing as a local detective." He is surprisingly diplomatic.

Catalina is not. "I haven't undermined your case. Not at all. I never actually said that this is my jurisdiction. I never actually told anyone that this is my case. Some people chose to read between the lines." She shrugs.

Detective Cherry's eyes narrow. "As I said, we are handling this investigation. You're no longer welcome here."

"Oh, so have you made an arrest?"

Somehow, the detective's eyes narrow even further. "No."

"Do you have any tangible leads?"

His jaw clenches, and he doesn't respond.

"I didn't think so." Catalina is smug. "You let me continue doing what I'm doing here, and *when* I catch the killer, I'll let you take credit for it."

Detective Cherry bristles. I'm not sure that Catalina's approach with him is the best for her career *or* my investigation.

Catalina suddenly seems to realize that she shouldn't poke the beast. "Just give me five days. Five days is all I need."

"If you're not gone within *three* days, I am contacting your Captain. You're already suspended, so you'll likely lose your job. If you can't respect jurisdiction and authority, you have no right being in this profession."

Catalina licks her lips nervously. The detective, satisfied that he has finally gotten through to her, turns and addresses Elias.

"Mr. Strickland. If *Officer* Marquez here hasn't vacated the guest suite in seventy-two hours, you are to kick her out and contact me immediately." He hands the concierge an embossed business card.

Elias nods and glances back at Catalina with renewed interest. She frowns and slams the door in his face.

Luke, who was standing out of sight, steps forward. He looks uncomfortable.

Catalina turns to him. "Is there a chance you didn't hear all of that?"

"I should be going . . ."

Catalina studies him for a moment, then looks away. "I understand."

Luke starts to leave, but he hesitates at the door. "There is one strange thing I noticed near the time of Rachel's . . . death," he fumbles over the word. "One of the last calls she received was from a domestic abuse case. A woman who was being beaten by her husband."

Catalina nods. "That's in her personal logs, and in the transcripts which I . . . got access to."

Luke runs a hand through his tousled hair. "I shouldn't have done this, it's against the rules. But I traced that call. It was made from someone in this building. Her name is Melody Boyden."

29

The German in 607 is yelling on his phone again. His long face flames with anger, and he waves his arms emphatically, nearly flinging the phone across the room. I really wish I could understand what he's saying. He's throwing out a lot of *nein*s, but other than that, I haven't a clue.

His apartment is very sparse, with chrome furniture and abstract paintings that adorn the steel gray walls. There are warm shades of orange, which add a splash of color and warmth to the otherwise sterile room.

I approach the balcony, but I quickly reach my barrier several feet away from the door. Suddenly claustrophobic, I spin around and rush to apartment 604, where my range is broader, where I can reach the window and the outside world. I don't even look for Sabryna or Roger. I simply rush through the apartment and I burst out on the balcony.

My claustrophobia immediately subsides as I take in the vast night. The sky is clear, providing an unobstructed view of the full moon. I could almost see the stars in the sky if it weren't for all the light pollution. My thoughts turn to the Man in Tweed and his telescope. How could I have initially misinterpreted his hobby? You can't see the stars in the city, and even so, living on the fifth floor, he wouldn't be able to see much of the sky, what with the tall buildings facing him.

I peer across the street, in the direction of the apartment of the woman he is so infatuated with. The lights are on, and she is energetically bouncing around the apartment, half-dressed, clearly getting ready to go out on the town. I make a mental note to avoid the Man in Tweed's apartment tonight. This is definitely going to rile him up. I look into the apartments above and below, before realizing that this makes me no better than the Man in Tweed. It's possible that we're both just curious and lonely, watching those we care about from afar, while they are unaware of our presence or even our existence.

I turn my gaze back to the woman across the way. She has donned a flattering mauve dress, which is neither too conservative nor too revealing. She applies hairspray liberally to the twisted, elaborate bun that sits on the top of her head. She leans back and then calls out toward the hall. She adjusts her necklace while examining her appearance in the long oval mirror. Satisfied, she rushes to the front door and swings it open.

A man stands framed in the doorway. He wears a casual black suit and holds a modest bouquet of flowers. She accepts them and obligatorily sniffs them. She gestures for him to come in and points toward the living room while she heads to the kitchen.

The man doesn't sit, but instead, he walks toward the window and looks out.

My breath catches.

It's the Man in Tweed.

He looks different, almost handsome. He isn't wearing tweed, so now his moniker is no longer appropriate. His hair is neatly combed, and he holds himself with a newfound confidence that was missing when he was alone in his dark apartment, sitting at the window, watching the world outside.

How does he know her? How long has he known her? Did he know who she was before he started watching her from his window? Or did he decide to meet her *after* he began observing her, after he discovered he liked what he saw?

The woman returns to the living room with the flowers in a vase, which she sets on the glass coffee table. She speaks with the man coyly, her entire body language flirtatious. She twirls a loose tendril of hair around a finger and laughs at something he says.

I have so many questions and no way to get answers. I cannot simply hop across the street into that apartment to listen to their conversation. The fact that he knows this woman, that he's in her life, makes his spying even creepier—and possibly dangerous.

I need answers, and I might know where to find them. I drop down to the fifth floor, straight into the Man in Tweed's apartment.

I look around. As usual, the apartment is impeccably tidy. Not a single paper is left out. The books on his shelf are all lined carefully in a row, pulled out so the spines are even with one another, no matter the size of the book. I suppose this gives me some insight into his personality. All the books are spy thrillers, mostly Tom Clancy novels with a few Lee Childs thrown in.

Unfortunately, my range is significantly limited since the elevator is still on the sixth floor. However, I can see into his office, which looks unused. His briefcase rests on the chair, and aside from a closed MacBook, his desk is clutter-free. There are two bookcases along the eastern wall, and all these books are just as carefully positioned as the recreational reading in the other room. I try to get closer to read the spines, but they are out of my range. So is the master bedroom.

I sigh and return to the living room. I have no idea who this man is or what he does for a living. He works someplace that requires a suit but no fashion sense. Maybe he's an accountant.

I hop back up to the sixth floor and return to the balcony. The lights are out in the woman's apartment. They've clearly left, gone wherever their date might lead. Despite my aversion to his nighttime activities, I'm going to have to spend more time watching this man, so I can get a sense of who he is—and more importantly—what his intentions are for the woman across the way.

I hop up to the seventh floor to my old apartment. I go straight to the office. Again, my mobility is limited, but I can see the wall where Will set up the names and apartment numbers of all the residents in the building. The slot for 504 is empty, however, which speaks volumes. Many of the other residents have entire dossiers, and this one doesn't even have a name. I wonder what obstacles Will and Catalina encountered when trying to speak with this man. Why didn't Elias provide his name when Catalina was debriefing him? Is it possible that even Elias doesn't know who he is?

I look around the apartment, but Will is nowhere to be found. Is he off chasing a lead? Will's been here for over a week, and I have never seen him taking any downtime. He stays up most of the night, flipping through files and adding scraps of paper and newspaper clippings to his serial-killer wall. He is driven to find his brother's murderer, which is understandable. But if he doesn't slow down, he'll burn out, and he won't have the mental capacity or the strength to find my killer.

I approach the desk. It's littered with loose pages, many of them pulled from my carefully organized filing cabinets. I grumble, but I don't really blame him. It's not like I'll be using them ever again. On the desk beside an old Tim Horton's coffee cup, there's a bottle of prescription pills. I squint in the darkness, but I can't make out the name it's prescribed to. I inch closer. *Tramadol.* A narcotic.

Is Will revisiting old vices to numb the pain? Or had he never quit in the first place?

⁂

Tired of my musings and irritated by the invisible barrier that is so much smaller on the seventh floor, I float back down to the sixth. Despite the hour, Clark is out. His parents are asleep in their beds, likely unaware that their son isn't occupying his. I know that he's troubled, but they need to set down some ground rules and force him to abide by them.

With a teen like that, if you give him an inch, he'll take a mile. He needs to be reprimanded, grounded, or even have his allowance taken away until he learns respect and tries to pick up his grades.

I laugh, realizing how old I sound. I'm not even thirty, and I sound like a grumpy grandma. The laughter is quickly replaced by remorse. I'll never be a grandma or even a mother. I'll never have children, and I'll never have the chance to decide how to raise them. Although, this might be a good thing. Watching my children from beyond the veil and being unable to communicate with them would have been the ultimate hell. These thoughts ruin any sense of hope I had for the night, and I succumb to the dark places inside my head.

Like an addict seeking out her drug, I go to the Hyland apartment. Sabryna is alone, sitting by candlelight, writing in cursive on a sheet of paper. I try to read it, but the lines are erratic. Her pen scratches against paper in wide, jilting letters that are impossible to read by the poor light.

Instead, I study her face. She wears no makeup and looks years older than I initially thought her to be. Her hair is flat, without any product or moisturizer, and I can see that gray roots are beginning to sprout. She wears silk pajamas and a thin bathrobe. Her long, bright red nails strike a vivid contrast to the rest of her dull, muted appearance.

Again, I try to read what she is writing with such focus. But she finishes, quickly signing what now appears to be a letter. She places it in an already addressed and stamped envelope. She leaves the room, then the apartment.

She takes my elevator down to the lobby, where she places the envelope in the slot for the concierge to mail. What is so important that it needs to be mailed in the middle of the night? Elias won't collect the mail to send off until morning. Considering

Sabryna's ordinarily meticulously crafted appearance, I'm shocked that she would risk being seen like this by one of the other residents.

I trail after her, back to her apartment, where she crawls into bed, alone. She turns out the light and lies in the dark.

30

The elevator is silent. Both Catalina and Will are lost in their own thoughts as they ride down to the fourth floor. I wonder if Catalina has mentioned Detective Cherry's threat. The ultimatum will throw a wet blanket on their investigation, especially since Catalina will no longer have an acceptable explanation for hanging around the building. If Elias even lets her back in the building once she's kicked out.

The elevator doors slide open, and Catalina leads the way down the hall to apartment 407. The Boyden apartment.

Yesterday, when Detective Cherry arrived and disrupted everything, Catalina was meeting with Luke. Despite the fact that he knew that she wasn't investigating in an official capacity,

Luke gave her the name of the second-to-last caller I spoke with that night. I hope that he doesn't get in trouble over this. The call center values confidentiality over everything else. If they find out that he gave up this information without a warrant . . . That volunteer job means the world to him. I'd hate to see my death hurt him any more than it already has.

Before knocking, Catalina turns to Will. "Remember what I said earlier. If this is a domestic abuse situation, we *cannot* let the husband know that we suspect anything. That means we are just completing a simple interview, and we *cannot* let anything slip."

Oliver takes his time coming to the door. I breeze past him, delving deeper into the apartment. I explore as far as my range will allow, but Melody is nowhere to be seen—alive or dead.

"Hello," Oliver says pleasantly. "How can I help you?" He speaks directly to Catalina, ignoring Will entirely.

Will clenches his jaw. "Hi, this is Will again, remember me? I dropped by about a week ago. I'm looking into the murder of my sister-in-law, Rachel Drake."

Oliver tears his eyes from Catalina's cleavage to shoot Will a glance. Catalina scowls at Will. Clearly, subtlety is not in his vocabulary. He's already put Oliver on edge.

"Right, Will. Nice to see you again," Oliver says.

"I'm Catalina, a friend of the family." It's interesting that she's already changing her story. She's no longer claiming to be a detective on the case, which is good, because she can't get in trouble for saying she was my friend. Especially since it's true. Does that mean she's planning on sticking around, despite Detective Cherry's ultimatum? I don't think I can lose someone else, not so soon after my death. I genuinely hope she stays, if only for my own selfish reasons.

"I'm so sorry for your loss," Oliver tells Catalina. Will frowns, but Oliver remains oblivious.

"Would you like to come in?" Oliver asks Catalina.

She produces a tight smile and nods. Will barely makes it through the door before it swings shut.

"Please, have a seat. Would you like anything to drink?" Oliver is so hospitable. I'm surprised that he has these basic hosting skills when it was clear that in the past, Melody was the one responsible for these behaviors.

"Oh, no thank you," Catalina replies.

Oliver sits down beside her.

"No, thanks, I don't want anything to drink either," Will says. Catalina shoots him a look. Oliver glances over at him, but he either doesn't pick up on the sarcasm or he chooses to ignore it.

"May I ask where your wife is?" Catalina asks.

Oliver's face transforms into one of a grieving man. "Melody isn't here. She won't be back either."

Catalina leans forward. "Where is she?"

"She cheated on me. A few nights ago, she admitted to me that her child, the one she carries in her womb, isn't mine." His eyes are filled with anguish. "I threw her out of the house, and I haven't heard from her since."

Could this be true? I shake my head. I can't imagine Melody cheating on her husband. Not just because she loved him, but because she was *terrified* of him. Is Oliver lying to protect his pride? Or is it because he did something . . . something he can't take back? Something that will have him thrown into prison for twenty-five to life if anyone ever found out?

"That's terrible!" Catalina says, her brows furrowed. Will looks skeptical, which is a good sign. If he doesn't believe Oliver's story, he will investigate it. He will figure out the truth, whether Melody is safe at a women's shelter, or if Oliver killed her.

"Don't believe him, no matter what he says." Will doesn't hear me. Nevertheless, I hope that what I said has burrowed its way into his subconscious.

"Unborn child? Is that Shane?" Catalina asks. She must have read his name in my handwritten notes after Melody's call to the hotline.

Oliver nods. "Yes, that's the name we came up with. Together. Before I knew the truth."

"I know that this must be very painful for you," Catalina says. "But do you have a forwarding address? Somewhere she can be reached?"

Oliver sighs and buries his face in his hands. He holds that position for five long seconds before raising his head, a single tear trailing down his cheek. "I believe she said that she's going to Vermont with the father of her child."

Vermont? That's where *he* was supposed to be going that same night. This can't be a coincidence. He couldn't come up with the name of another state?

"I see," Catalina says. I can't tell if she's buying what Oliver is selling. She's a good actress, and I know that she would see the merit in allowing Oliver to believe that she's fooled.

"Thank you for your time, Mr. Boyden," Catalina says. She stands to leave, and Will instantly mirrors her.

Oliver looks up at them through reddened eyes. "Do you have any other questions? I want to help."

Catalina smiles. "No, you've done more than enough."

"If you have any other questions, don't think twice about stopping by. I might be able to help." Oliver seems reluctant to let his company leave. For the first time, I wonder if this isn't for show, if he's truly mourning Melody. I know he was capable of hurting her—I saw it with my own two eyes. But murder? There must be a logical explanation for what happened that night, one that doesn't result in bloodshed.

"Of course," Catalina says. "We can see ourselves out." She nods to Will, who follows her.

Oliver remains sitting, his face still wearing a mask of pure anguish. As soon as the door closes, he stands, and all indication of emotion slips away. His face is nearly expressionless, marred with just a hint of suspicion. Shock punches me in the gut. I can't believe I almost fell for his act. He leaves the living room and crosses the hall. Where is he going? I'm pulled away before I find out.

Will and Catalina return to my apartment in thoughtful silence. They enter the office where they take seats on opposite sides of my desk. I look at the desk, with its strewn paperwork, but the bottle of pills is gone.

"Well? What do you think?" Will finally asks.

"I'm not sure. We know for certain he was beating his wife. Kae made notes about it in her log." Catalina picks up a pen and begins to twirl it between her fingers. I wonder if she even realizes that she's doing it.

"But?"

"But he seems to be genuinely missing his wife. I can't tell if he's being sincere or not," Catalina admits. I'm disappointed. I thought that she of all people would be able to see through his façade.

But Will doesn't seem so sure. "I don't know. I mean, when we first got to the apartment, all he could do was stare at your breasts. That doesn't look like a man who misses his wife to me."

"Excuse me?"

Will raises an eyebrow. "Don't tell me you didn't notice. When he opened the door, all he could do was stare at you, and he barely even acknowledged my presence."

"Are you jealous?" Catalina asks. "I'm sure he would have looked at you too, if you had been wearing a shirt with a low-enough neckline."

"I'm just saying that his wife left him a few days ago. He shouldn't be straying."

"A man with principles. I like it," Catalina says.

Will shakes his head, a small smile tugging at his lips. "I don't know how we can reach Melody Boyden. Does she have any family or friends that we can contact to ask about her baby's father?"

Catalina looks down at her file. "No family. They died when she was eleven. She used to have a very big presence on social media, and she had a lot of friends and contacts until she got married a year and a half ago. Then she kind of faded away. She likely became completely tied up with the man she married. I've seen it happen a million times before."

Either that or Oliver didn't approve of her spending time with them. That seems more likely. Will and Catalina need to figure out what Oliver is truly like. They know he's abusive, but they don't know the true extent of his violent temper. This frustrates me to no end.

Catalina twirls her pen, again and again. "I say we give it another few days and then I go to talk to him—alone," she suggests.

"Why alone? I'm not sure I'm comfortable leaving you alone with a pregnant-wife beater and potential murderer," Will says bluntly.

"I can handle myself. Oliver is much more likely to open up if he's alone with me. I can make him relax, and he might let something slip about Kae. It's worth a shot."

It suddenly dawns on me that Catalina and Will did not go to talk to Melody just because she was one of the last people to speak to me before my murder. Oliver has demonstrated more than once that he has trouble reigning in his rage. If he caught Melody on the phone that night and figured out that she was talking to the crisis hotline, he would have been furious. If he somehow found out who I was—that I was living in his building—then *he* might have been the one who killed me.

31

ate that night, the Man in Tweed returns home from work and follows his evening ritual to the letter. He places his briefcase on the chair in the office. He removes his blazer, folds it meticulously, and places it beside the briefcase. He rolls up his shirt sleeves. But tonight, he doesn't go to the window. He doesn't set up his telescope and prepare for an evening of voyeurism.

I rush to the window. The woman across the way is sitting and reading by lamplight. She appears to be intact and unharmed. I breathe a sigh of relief and return to the foyer. The Man in Tweed has left some mail on the tiny utilitarian stand by the front door. I stoop over and attempt to read the letters in the poor light. The top envelope is addressed to a "John Smith."

Is that his name? His *real* name? It's a credit card bill. The bank must have his real name.

"John Smith" is a common name. Extremely common. The Man in Tweed even looks like a "John Smith." But I just can't shake the nagging thought that "John Smith" isn't his *real* name, just like "Rachel Drake" wasn't mine.

"John Smith" returns from the bedroom in a different shirt. He picks up the tweed jacket and puts it back on. He leaves the apartment in the same manner he did this morning, but this time, he doesn't take his briefcase with him.

I want to stay and watch out the window, to see if he goes to the woman across the way, but I am wrenched away as he directs my elevator downward.

He gets off on the ground floor. Elias doesn't seem to be surprised to see him. He mumbles a "good evening" as the Man in Tweed strides across the lobby and out the front door. Elias checks the large, ornate clock that hangs on the lobby wall. It reads quarter past eleven. I suspect that Elias has grown used to the Man in Tweed's comings and goings and the exact minute at which each occurs. Given the Man in Tweed's highly impeccable appearance and apartment, I'll bet he has a regular routine, one which Elias likely has memorized.

Elias locks up his desk and heads over to the elevator bay. I trail after him instead of passively waiting for the summons of my death spot. The elevator rises, but it doesn't stop on the second floor, where Elias' apartment is. It continues upward to the fifth floor. My curiosity is piqued. Who is Elias visiting at this hour? He crosses the hall and stops at apartment 504.

That's the Man in Tweed's apartment. What is he doing here? He knows that he isn't home.

Elias pulls a large keyring from his pocket, muffling the sound of the keys jingling with his closed hand. There must be several dozen keys on the ring. What does he need so many keys for? He glances up and down the corridor. No one is around. He flips through the keys and selects one. He inserts it in the lock and turns it with a loud click.

The Man in Tweed has requested some kind of service. That must be it. I know that Elias offers a turndown service for residents of the building. To the best of my knowledge, no one has ever accepted this offer. At least, that's what Elias told me when I moved into the building. He seemed to be pushing this "perk" on me. But I didn't want to give him—or anyone else— permission to enter my apartment, so I politely declined.

Again, Elias looks down both stretches of the hallway. Satisfied that no one is in sight, he opens the door and slips inside. The apartment is dark, but he doesn't reach for the light. Instead, he produces a flashlight from his back pocket. He retrieves a pair of white latex gloves from another pocket and expertly slips them on. He scans the foyer with the dim beam of his flashlight. The light catches upon the stack of mail. He approaches it and lifts the bundle, flipping through each item. I peer over his shoulder. Every envelope is addressed to "John Smith."

Elias places the pile in exactly the same order and position that he found it. I am equally impressed and disturbed. This clearly isn't his first rodeo.

He creeps into the living room. Like me, he focuses on the bookcase first, but unlike me, he can interact with the objects. He pulls a few books down and flips through them, before carefully returning them to the shelves. I'm not sure what he's looking for.

He goes to the office next where he opens the drawers which are empty. This office is just for show.

The Man in Tweed's briefcase rests on a chair. Elias tests it, but it's locked and requires a five-number code. He rolls the lock a few times—testing—but to no avail. Again, I'm impressed when Elias returns the tumblers back to the exact same numbers that they initially were resting on. He's making sure that he doesn't leave a trace. With the Man in Tweed's apparent obsessive-compulsive tendencies, this is probably a good thing. He would undoubtedly notice even the tiniest of changes in his barren apartment.

I finally learn the nature of the books on the shelves in the office. They are books on a variety of topics: bird watching, job interviews, cooking vegan, varnishing furniture. Books on basic economics and politics, biology and law, Russian language and Japanese pop culture. There doesn't seem to be any rhyme or reason to the subjects of the books he owns. I still have no idea what his profession is. Based on these books alone, I would believe that he's a jack-of-all-trades. I do notice one book on star-gazing, and I wonder if that's what inspired him to buy the telescope. Maybe when he realized that he couldn't see the stars in the city, he decided to use it for other purposes. Despite this possible explanation, I don't see signs of any other hobbies in the apartment. It's incredibly sparse, with no woodworking tools, no tap shoes, and certainly no musical instruments. Why would he buy a book on how to play the guitar when he didn't even own one?

Elias also seems very interested in the books. He spends what feels like hours flipping through them. A scrap of paper slides out of a book about Greek architecture. Elias examines it for a moment. Before I can see what it says, he slips it back into the book, which he returns to the shelf. This is frustrating.

The second bedroom is empty. And I mean completely empty. It doesn't have any furniture, no pictures on the walls, no rug on the floor. Elias quickly closes that door, but I find that it tells a story in itself. This apartment didn't come cheap. Why would John Smith buy an apartment with three bedrooms when he only needed two? Is it because of the location? Because it's across the way from that mysterious woman he is so infatuated with?

Elias also seems to become exasperated by the lack of answers. I follow him into the master suite, where the furniture is sparse and utilitarian. The bed is neatly made, military style. Other than a lamp and a digital clock on the nightstand, the room is bare.

Elias slides open the top drawer of the night table. It's completely empty. So is the bottom drawer. Shouldn't he have something in them? Tissues, a book, *something* to indicate that this room is lived in?

The dresser drawers contain rows of clothes neatly folded and stacked precisely. A dozen tweed suits hang in the walk-in closet. But I notice that there are other clothes as well. The suit he wore last night. A tan khaki coverall. A tacky blue and pink Hawaiian shirt. A formal black tuxedo. What kind of man makes use of such eclectic styles of clothing? And yet all he ever seems to wear is tweed.

Elias also finds the contents of the closet interesting. He takes out a small digital camera and snaps a few pictures. Is he investigating John Smith? If so, why? Does he suspect that John Smith isn't who he appears to be? That he has multiple personas, as I discovered when he visited the woman across the way last night?

I'm not sure what's more disconcerting—Elias's snooping or what I'm learning about the Man in Tweed.

A thump resounds from the hallway. Elias startles, then peeks out of the closet and into the master bedroom, where he has a clear line of sight into the hall beyond. The Man in Tweed is home early.

Elias is surprisingly calm as he surveys his surroundings. He spots the row of pants in the back of the closet and dives into it, rearranging the hangers until they envelop him completely. He has all but disappeared.

Not worried that I might be caught snooping, I stroll into the hallway and see the Man in Tweed placing something in his briefcase, which he rapidly snaps shut, clicking the lock. Again, I was too slow to catch a glimpse. To see if it holds the answers to all the questions tonight has raised. To see if it holds his identity, his truth.

The Man in Tweed enters the bedroom, where he finally flips on a light. However, the dull glow of the bedside lamp does little to brighten the surroundings.

He removes his clothes, meticulously folding each item as he takes it off. He places everything on the wooden straight-back chair that sits in the corner. John Smith is much leaner than I had initially believed. His tweed suits and loose shirts hide ripples of muscle underneath. I count six abs. He looks like he works out regularly, but I've never seen him go down to the fitness center. Being connected to the elevator, I know everyone's daily routine. Perhaps he has a membership at another gym, one with a more impressive weight room.

He turns around to place his folded shirt on the chair. The length of his back is covered in long, raised scars. They're thick and gnarled, and they span across his muscular frame. They almost shine silver in the dim light. I turn away before he takes off his pants.

Giving the Man No Longer in Tweed some privacy, I pop into the closet. Elias is still tucked away out of sight. I wait an appropriate amount of time before returning to the bedroom. The light is out, and I see a dark form on the bed. I step closer. The Man in Tweed lies on top of the bedspread, naked. I suppose that's one way to keep the sheets clean.

His eyes are closed, his breath even. Is he asleep already? I'm curious to see if Elias escapes unnoticed, so I stay, carefully averting my eyes from the figure lying on the bed.

The minutes tick by slowly. John Smith never moves. He doesn't snore. He doesn't twitch. I would worry that he's dead if I didn't believe I'd see his spirit leaving his body.

Eventually, after nearly half an hour has passed, Elias emerges from the closet. He moves painstakingly slow, his eyes glued to the form on the bed. He tiptoes down the hall. He steps on a loose floorboard, which lets out a thunderous creak. Elias freezes, his cheeks turn as white as a ghost. He glances over his shoulder, but the Man in Tweed is undisturbed. Elias turns and moves even more slowly as he sneaks toward the exit. I release the breath I was holding when he slips out the door and closes it quietly behind him. He removes his gloves and tucks them into his back pocket. He retrieves the keyring and locks the door.

I hover nearby as I watch him. I'm not entirely sure of *what* he was looking for. It is clear that both he, Will, and Catalina don't know who the Man in Tweed is. It seems like Elias was looking for some indication of the man's identity. I wonder if Elias is some kind of amateur investigator.

He returns the keys to his pocket with a flourish. Like a cat, he slinks down the corridor toward the pair of elevators, a Cheshire grin on his face. Elias has a glow that I've never seen on him before. He's happy, confident, at home in his skin, which is a new look for him.

I speculate about the reason for this abrupt change in mood as we descend. He clearly didn't find what he was looking for before his visit was interrupted. Like the Man in Tweed when he visited the woman across the way, Elias has had a complete change in demeanor. Whenever he is around residents of the building, he appears nervous, eager to please, *smaller*. Now, he stands tall, and I notice that he isn't all that unattractive. What is the reason for the persona he depicts to the world? Is it intentional? He may have a social anxiety disorder, which causes him to become nervous and jittery around others. But I think this is more than that. This is a complete transformation in his attitude and personality. Why would he pretend to be an inconsequential, perpetually-anxious man when in reality he is anything but? And why is he investigating the Man in Tweed?

October 17

Dear Diary,

We finally found Lon Chaney, Jr.

I searched the streets in the days following his disappearance, with the help of Catalina and Cindy. I took a couple of days off work for the search, hoping that Chaney would show up on my doorstep in the middle of the day, covered in mud and little bits of whatever places his adventures led him. No such luck.

Gregory called me into his office today. He knew that I had used sick days for something other than sickness. I told him that my cat was missing, which he seemed to have thought was a euphemism for marriage troubles. Again, he asked me about the state of my renovations. Again, I wondered just how he knew so much about my private life. He didn't do anything inappropriate—this time. However, I still get the impression that he thinks that wedding contracts have an expiration date.

I still haven't told Jay about Gregory and his creepiness. Jay's been distant lately. His forgetfulness is only getting worse. He often zones out on entire conversations. He hardly sleeps. Sometimes, I wake in the night to find him standing at the foot of the bed, gazing out the window.

Watching. Waiting. But for what?

When I came home today, the freshly cut flowers I put out just yesterday morning were dead. I'd left them in the middle of the kitchen table and added fresh water last night. Whatever darkness that's lingering in this house isn't just affecting Jay. It's affecting everything. I can feel myself being affected most of all. The fear. The paranoia. The heavy weight of dread pressing down on my chest during every waking—and sleeping—hour.

And now, there are house flies everywhere. They buzz around my ears as I get ready for work in the morning. They swarm our food when Jay and I try to eat together. The last three nights, we've eaten out, unable to stomach the filthy hordes.

I made a dozen fly traps and put them out, but the flies are multiplying faster than I can catch them. I scoured the entire house this weekend, searching for whatever was attracting them and disinfecting everything as I went. I could find no scraps of meat, no forgotten food or anything else that could be their lure.

Jay found me on all fours, washing the living room floor Sunday night when he got off his shift.

"I called the exterminator. They moved up their appointment to first thing tomorrow morning," he said.

I stopped scrubbing and wiped away a tendril of hair that had worked itself free from my ponytail. "There are a lot of flies. And they're everywhere, not limited to any one room." I glanced around. "But I think there might be more in the living room than in the rest of the house."

Jay looked around the room which was shrouded with the stench of bleach. I knew I had ruined the hardwood floors, but Jay didn't say anything.

We were going to replace them anyway.

I followed Jay's gaze to the fireplace. It was functional, but we had yet to use it, even though the nights were starting to get colder.

I climbed to my feet and approached it.

"Wait," Jay said.

I turned the bronze knob and opened the glass door. A swarm of flies flew out of the darkened pit.

"Stop," Jay said. He put a hand on my shoulder.

I shrugged him away and pulled aside the metal mesh screen. I could hear the buzzing of more flies lying in wait.

"At least let me get a flashlight."

I ignored him.

The fireplace was empty. Just a few unburnt logs rested decoratively at the bottom.

I looked upward. The hum grew louder. There was something lodged in the flue.

I couldn't see into the inky blackness, but that didn't stop me. I reached upward. I felt something. Something stiff. Something cold.

It fell from its place wedged in the chimney, brushing my face as it landed with a sickly thud.

Flies erupted from it like a plume cloud.

I coughed, finally snapping out of my trance.

Chaney was swarmed with maggots. His entire body writhed and convulsed from the sheer number of them. His eyes were gone, replaced with cavernous pits that were infested with tiny larvae, feasting on him from the outside in.

"No, no, no," I sobbed, jerking away.

I fell into Jay's arms, and this time, I didn't push him away. I closed my eyes tightly and wept against his strong shoulders.

After several minutes, I stopped crying and looked up at him. I needed him to understand.

"All of these things that have been happening . . . the flowers, the flies . . . Chaney . . . it can't be a coincidence."

Jay continued to hold me, stroking my hair, but saying nothing.

I studied his face. "Do you finally believe me? Do you finally believe that our house is . . . haunted?"

Jay caught my gaze, then quickly looked away. He never responded.

32

ife goes on. Dr. Sylvie Favreau is in the kitchen, preparing breakfast for her son. She slaves over the stove, cooking French toast, which is fancy for a weekday. As usual, Etienne sits at the kitchen table, waiting patiently. They discuss their daily lives as if nothing peculiar lies behind the door to the third bedroom.

Catalina knocks on the door—she is the reason I am on this floor. I hope I am here long enough to solve just one mystery in my afterlife. It may be too late to help Melody, but if I learn why Raymond is kept in a coma, perhaps I can move on?

Sylvie seems surprised to find a stranger at her door.

"Hello. How can I help you?"

Catalina smiles warmly. "Good morning, I'm Catalina Marquez. I am—was—a friend of Rachel Drake's." Again, I notice that Catalina is no longer pretending to be here on official business.

Sylvie's smile is strained. "I knew Rachel well. Why don't you come in?" She ushers Catalina into the kitchen. "Do you like French toast? Or as my people call it, toast?"

I roll my eyes at the joke that Catalina expertly ignores. Instead, she practically drools at the sight of the homemade breakfast. She's been living off stale McDonald's muffins for the past week.

"I love French toast. It isn't too much bother, is it?" I can tell that Catalina is praying that Sylvie doesn't change her mind.

"No, not at all. I always make too much. I'm used to cooking for three, but since my husband passed . . ." Sylvie trails off before turning back to the stove.

Etienne looks up at his mother with expressionless eyes, but he doesn't say anything. Does he know about his father? Catalina doesn't notice anything out of the ordinary. She takes a seat across from Etienne.

"Etienne, why don't you set another place at the table?" Sylvie asks in French.

Etienne nods mutely and scurries to the counter. He grabs a stool and clambers on top of it, reaching to the highest cupboard for the dishware.

He places a plate in front of Catalina, and then sets the cutlery out carefully, in the style of a formal dinner party.

Catalina hides a smile. "Hi, Etienne," she says in English. "I'm Catalina. I'm a friend of someone who used to live in this building."

Etienne stares at her blankly before returning to his seat.

"Etienne, say 'hello' to our guest. Don't be rude," Sylvie says, in English this time.

"Hello," Etienne says in a small voice, his eyes never leaving his empty plate. I'm relieved to learn he does speak English, though he has a slight accent.

"Hello, Etienne." To Sylvie, Catalina says, "Your son is very well behaved. And he's very good at setting the table. Better than I was at his age. Better than I am now!"

Etienne's ears turn pink.

"Yes, yes, Etienne's very well behaved. He's nothing like other children his age—tiny brats who spend all their time playing video games and watching TV. His father used to let him do those things, and Etienne started to act out because of it. But since Raymond... Well, Etienne has been much more obedient." Sylvie's lips are pursed, and she pokes at the French toast with her prongs. I can't believe she's talking about her husband like this in front of Etienne. I'm seeing a new side to her, and I'm not sure I like it. There's no kindness in her voice when she refers to her husband.

There's no pain or remorse or grief. No guilt.

Etienne becomes even more still, even smaller, if that were even possible. I watch him carefully, wondering again if he knows that his father is in the other room.

Catalina seems unaware of the thin threads of tension between mother and son. Sylvie serves breakfast, and they all dig in.

"Wow, this is delicious! You could be a chef if you weren't busy saving lives," Catalina says.

"In another life," Sylvie says. "Etienne, how's breakfast?"

"*Merci, maman*," Etienne replies automatically. I frown.

Satisfied with this robotic answer, Sylvie turns to her guest. "So, what is it that brings you to my door? You must know that I was Rachel's physician."

"Yes, I found note of that in her files. She was very organized." Catalina takes another bite of the French toast. "I'm actually looking into her death." Catalina is hyper-casual. She gives Sylvie a side-ways glance.

Is she investigating *Sylvie* for my death? I nervously glance toward the door to the third bedroom. Maybe the idea isn't *that* absurd. But my killer was definitely male. I can still feel the strong hands that grabbed me from behind. Sylvie's delicate surgeon's fingers wouldn't have felt like that. Unless they're stronger than they look . . . I shake aside the tendrils of paranoia that snake over me, threatening to suffocate an already dead woman.

"Looking into it? Do you mean you're investigating her death?" Sylvie looks interested, not at all frightened or worried. This could be an indication that she's innocent, but then again, she casually invites strangers into the apartment when her supposedly dead husband is held hostage in the guest bedroom.

"Yes, I'm investigating her death. *Informally*."

"Well, I'd love to answer your questions," Sylvie says. She looks pointedly at Etienne, and Catalina nods understandingly. "But I have to leave for work in twenty minutes. Perhaps we can continue this conversation at another time?"

"Of course," Catalina says. I scowl. If she hadn't spent so much time yammering about the delicious breakfast, she might have gotten some information from Sylvie.

They spend the next five minutes discussing the Toronto weather, the architecture of the building, and me. I heave a sigh of relief when the elevator sweeps me away, and I don't have to hear any more of their mundane chatter.

I ride up and down the elevator as the early risers and hard workers head out to the outside world. A place where I can't go. How I wish I could. I wish I had left this place when I had the chance.

Now I'm trapped here for eternity.

Hours after Catalina met Sylvie, the elevator stops on the fourth floor, and Oliver Boyden steps on. It's the middle of a workday, but he isn't at work. I inspect his face. He doesn't look sick. He has a pink glow to his cheeks and a skip in his step that makes me want to slap him with supernatural strength. Unfortunately, my supernatural strength is non-existent. I wish that I were a poltergeist so I could haunt him.

Why hasn't he caught another flight to Vermont? What's keeping him here? Guilt? Unfinished . . . business?

He loads several boxes into the elevator, which takes him down to the ground floor. He unloads them and heads into the garbage room.

What's in the boxes? My stomach churns when I see a tuft of green fabric peek from the top of one box. God, please don't let it be *Melody* in these boxes.

Oliver tosses one box into the dumpster. Then another. He lifts the third, but its bottom breaks, and its contents tumble onto the concrete. Women's clothes. Jewelry. Picture frames. Swearing, Oliver grabs a couple of shirts and swings them into the dumpster.

Alexei stands in the doorway, a box of recycling held forgotten in his spider-like fingers. He looks at Oliver with a strange expression on his already strange face.

"What are you doing?"

Oliver jumps. Then he laughs, emitting charisma through the roof. "I'm just doing some spring cleaning."

It's October.

Alexei doesn't let him off the hook that easily. "Are those your wife's belongings?"

Oliver suddenly looks downtrodden. "Yes, these are Melody's."

Alexei waits for further explanation.

I can almost hear the wheels turning in Oliver's head. "She left me. For another man. The father of her child." At least he's sticking to the same story he told Catalina and Will.

"She left you, and she did not take her things with her?" Alexei's expression is unreadable.

Oliver stares, a hard glint forming in his chocolate brown eyes. "She took what she wanted and left the rest for me to clean up. Typical woman."

Oliver bends over and picks up a picture frame. It has a crack down the center of its glass pane, right across Melody's broken smile. It looks like one of the picture frames that Melody had packed in her suitcase. Is it the same one? Try as I might, I just can't remember.

Oliver stares at the picture, working up a single tear that crawls down his face. That's a neat trick. I wish I could cry on demand like that.

It would be a much more useful, less dangerous skill for an agoraphobic translator than a narcissistic wife-killer.

Alexei approaches Oliver stiffly and picks some of the clothes up off the ground. "Not that I care about the needy," he begins, "but you could have donated this to a charity, like a women's shelter."

Oliver's eyes flash. He looks like he could snap, like he could kill. Then, suddenly, the anger is gone. It evaporates into thin air. He smiles up at Alexei. "You're right, but I can't bear the thought of a woman walking around Toronto wearing Melody's clothes. Looking like her, smelling like her. I'd rather die."

<hr />

The Man in Tweed follows his regular evening ritual. He settles onto his chair at the telescope by the northern window. His hands grip the cold black metal. He releases a tiny sigh of disappointment when he discovers that the windows are dark in the apartment across the way. He sits and waits for her to return.

I jump when there's a sharp knock on the front door. I look to the Man in Tweed. His normally impassive face looks wary. He clearly isn't expecting anyone.

He approaches the door quickly; his cat-like tread is nearly silent across the hardwood floor. Instead of immediately opening the door, he peers through the peephole. He steps back, stunned by the face that greets him.

Another harsh rap on the door cuts through the silence. The Man in Tweed doesn't move to answer it. He doesn't move at all. He stands frozen, muscles tense, face taut.

The doorknob suddenly turns. I can tell from the expression on his face that he hadn't realized he'd left it unlocked. He slips behind the door as it opens.

A petite figure steps inside. "John? Are you here?"

My breath catches. It's the woman from across the way. How did she find him?

"Why are you here?" he asks quietly. His voice is deeper than I had expected it would be.

The woman jumps, spinning around. The Man in Tweed closes the door behind her, plunging them into near darkness. Neither of them make a move to turn on the light. Neither of them move at all. They stare for several moments, without speaking. The woman's lip is trembling slightly, the only indication that she is frightened. The Man in Tweed is as unreadable as ever.

Eventually, the woman speaks.

"If you're wondering how I found you, you should know that your telescope has a reflective lens." She produces a faint smile as she gestures toward the window, where the telescope stands on display. "I first noticed it a few weeks ago, right around the time when I met you. All it took was a few questions, and I quickly found out who lives here. A nameless man who fit your description."

John Smith doesn't respond. He doesn't move. He just stares. Only the tension in his body gives away that he's less than pleased that she's found him.

The woman continues. "I know who you are. I know *what* you are."

John watches her, eyes narrowed, his brows furrowed in confusion. "Then why are you here?"

"Because I don't care." She reaches up and pulls him toward her, sealing her words with a kiss.

33

atalina never did settle into the guest suite. Despite the mahogany wood dresser and the large wardrobe that leaned against the far wall, she kept all her clothes and other belongings in her duffel bag. When it came time to leave, she didn't need to pack anything except for her toothbrush.

Catalina's time in this ten-story building has come to an end. Elias stands in the doorway, hands on his hips, glowering at her as if she's a slug unworthy of being squished by his shoe. It's incredible how much his opinion of her has changed after one brief conversation with Detective Cherry. Catalina isn't quite past her deadline to leave, and Elias *could* have waited until a reasonable waking hour to kick her out. But to his surprise and obvious disappointment, Catalina was already awake when he pounded on the door. He gives her a cold smile.

Catalina nods, slings her bag over her shoulder, and tosses the room key to Elias, who fumbles. The key drops onto the ground at his feet.

Elias' scowl deepens as his cheeks flame bright red. "Do you need me to show you the exit?"

Catalina's expression is deadpan, but I can tell she's amused. "Yes, please."

Elias doesn't seem to realize she's toying with him. He spins on his heel and leads the way across the lobby. Catalina doesn't follow. Instead, she presses the button to call the elevator. My elevator greets her with a gentle chime. Elias stops in his tracks, shoulders stiffening. Catalina punches the button for the seventh floor quickly, and the doors slide shut before Elias can reach her.

Catalina taps her fingers on the hand rail as the elevator lazily climbs. What is she planning? With the high security in this building, she won't be able to stay for long, not without Elias or the security guards catching up with her and throwing her out.

At the seventh floor, Catalina all but runs to my apartment. She pounds on the door impatiently. I glance back warily. Elias can't be far behind. Eventually, Will appears, wearing nothing but a pair of sweatpants. He rubs the sleep from his eyes in adorable confusion. A knife stabs my heart. Jay rubbed his face the exact same way. I tear my eyes away.

"Morning," Will mumbles.

Catalina seems to suddenly forget the reason she came. She stares at his chest for a full ten seconds before responding.

"Hi, Will. Um, I'm sorry, I didn't realize how early it is. Uh, Elias found out I'm not supposed to be investigating Kae's death, and I was kicked out of the guest suite. I probably don't have long before security comes to escort me out."

Will's eyes land on her duffel bag. "Come in."

Catalina steps into my apartment, and he closes the door behind her. She smiles when he peeks through the peephole. "As much as I appreciate your concern, I probably should get going anyway. I don't want to draw any more attention from the local PD."

Will turns around and studies Catalina's face. "Does this mean you're giving up on the investigation?"

"No! No, not at all."

"How are you going to investigate if you're not allowed in the building?"

"You'll be my eyes and ears. And muscle," Catalina's eyes linger on his chest again before returning to his face. "I'll get a room at a nearby hotel."

"That's ridiculous. You can stay here," Will says. "Elias can't tell me who I can and can't have as a house guest."

Catalina examines Will's face. "Are you sure that's a good idea? Alienating the man who knows most about what goes on in this building might not be our best plan of action."

Will shakes his head. "Elias doesn't know nearly as much as he lets on."

A loud banging erupts at the front door. Will jumps, but Catalina looks like she was expecting it.

"Wait here." She marches to the front door and swings it open.

"Good morning!" she says in a sing-song voice. Elias looks stunned. The two security guards that flank him seem unimpressed.

Elias opens and closes his mouth several times. He reminds me of a fish on dry land. "You—what—you—" He stops and takes a moment to compose himself. "You're not supposed to be here."

Catalina smiles broadly. "I'm staying as a house guest of one of the residents. That isn't against the rules, is it?" Will appears in the doorway behind Catalina.

Elias' eyes flit between Will and his "house guest." "No, of course not," he says through gritted teeth.

"Well, in that case, is there anything else I can help you with?" Catalina's voice has the slightest edge.

"You're not supposed to be investigating the murder anymore!" Elias says.

Catalina twists her features into a look of exaggerated confusion. "I'm not investigating anything." She puts an arm around Will's waist. Will's eyes widen in response. "I'm staying here as a guest." Catalina puts a lot of innuendo into the word.

Elias blinks.

"You're not going to kick out a guest of a resident, are you?" Catalina asks loudly. Only now do I realize that Elias' loud knocking has drawn a small crowd. Among the onlookers is Mrs. Duval from 705. She stands in her doorway, watching with extreme interest.

"No," Elias says reluctantly.

"Is there anything else I can help you with?" Catalina repeats, her tone ever so pleasant now that she's won.

"That. Will. Be. All." Elias marches back to the elevator, the security guards trailing after him.

Catalina slams the door shut and spins around, a victorious grin brightening her entire face. "That was fun!"

Will leans against the wall, arms folded across his broad chest. "I guess that means you rethought my offer?"

Catalina strides past Will, snatching up her duffel bag on the way. "I call dibs on the bed," she calls over her shoulder.

Without a murmur of protest, Will collapses on the couch and immediately falls asleep.

That evening, I follow Catalina to Sylvie's apartment. She plans to ask the doctor more questions about me. The elevator pulls me away before they even have the chance to move past pleasantries and into the nitty gritty of my life and death. I don't know why I feel so betrayed by my elevator. I should have been expecting it.

Now I'm on the sixth floor. Sabryna lies on the settee in her living room, drinking champagne straight from the bottle and watching *The Real Housewives of Orange County*. As usual, Roger isn't around. I wonder if his lover has already booked a night in the guest suite now that Catalina has moved out.

I sigh and hover closer to Sabryna. I suppose if we both have to be alone, we might as well both be alone together. I look down at her. She's wearing a full mask of makeup, despite the fact that I haven't seen her leave the building in all the time I've been a ghost. Why won't she leave? What's keeping her here? With a jolt, I realize that someone might have wondered the same thing about me. If they'd cared enough.

I suddenly realize that Sabryna's self-pity is contagious. I flee the apartment without glancing back.

I drift into apartment 601. Clark is in his bedroom with the boy and girl from the parking garage, Noel and Rayna. Clark's parents aren't around, and I'm surprised to see that the liquor cabinet has yet to be raided.

Noel sits on the floor with the ancient book that Clark says he found on eBay. He has a notebook filled with scrawled notes. Rayna lounges on the bed, lying on her stomach with her sketchbook in front of her. She wears a contented smile as she sketches with broad, violent strokes. Clark sits on his desk chair, feet propped up on the desk, which is littered with his own drawings and notes. There isn't a piece of homework in sight.

Noel stops reading and pushes his glasses up his shiny nose. He stands and stretches.

Clark's eyes snap over to him. "Anything?"

Noel's cheeks turn pink from the undivided attention. "I'm getting there. I think I've almost found it. I have some relevant information that might be of use."

With almost inhuman speed, Clark is off his chair and snatching the papers from Noel's clammy hands. His eyes hungrily consume the words on the page.

I lean over his shoulder, trying to read it, but Clark rapidly finishes and tosses the sheet to the ground. "It's not enough."

Noel nods silently. Not enough for what? What are they looking for?

Clark returns to his perch on his chair. Noel studies him curiously. He looks like he wants to say something, but he doesn't.

Clark isn't looking at Noel, but he seems to sense his penetrating gaze. "Spit it out," he snaps.

Noel bites his lip, carefully selecting his words. "I'm just curious about your, um, fascination with this book."

Clark's dead gaze swivels back to Noel. "That book might hold the answers to everything."

Noel frowns slightly. "I noticed those pictures you draw— all the pictures you draw—they always look the same. They always

Helen Power

look like the same figure, with the same hat and coat. Who is he?"

Rayna stops drawing, finally interested in the conversation. She sits up and looks at Clark. They exchange glances, just like they did in the parking garage. Again, I wish I could read their minds, know what they're thinking, *understand* the context of what is happening.

Clark tears his eyes away from Rayna. He stares at the drawings which he has pinned to the wall. "You want to know who he is?"

Noel nods.

"He's the Devil with No Face." Clark stands and tears down one of his illustrations. He examines it closer before tossing it to the floor at Noel's feet.

He interprets Noel's silence as an invitation to continue.

"A long time ago, when I was a little kid, he used to visit me. He would come to my bedroom while the world slept. I would sneak out of the apartment and meet our friend—another child—a girl. We would play in the corridors, in the stairwell, in the basement. Those were the only times I felt free. But then, the girl got scared. She said she didn't want to come play. She didn't want to see him anymore. She said he sometimes got inside her, made her do horrible things. One night, she decided to make it stop. The maintenance man had left his toolbox in the storage unit in the basement. The girl took out a screwdriver and carved out her eyes."

Noel's mouth falls open.

Clark savors this reaction before continuing, "Of course, she was no surgeon. She cut too far, too deep into her skull. She bled out in minutes. All I could do was watch in horror as my only human friend died in my arms. After that, I couldn't see the Devil with No Face anymore. He hasn't come to me since." Clark sounds melancholy, as if the Shadow Man's sudden disappearance is the worst part of the story. Rayna gazes up at him, mesmerized by a story she's clearly heard before.

"What kind of games can you play with a ghost?" Noel says.

"Games?" Clark asks, in a daze.

"You said that you used to play with him. What did you play?"

Clark doesn't answer. Instead, he retrieves the sketch from the ground and lovingly pins it back onto his wall. He runs his hand along the picture, smoothing the wrinkles but smearing the charcoal, making the dark figure even more obscured, even more surreal.

The elevator pulls me away, and I'm left with the sight of Clark's wistful expression imprinted on my memory. I ponder this new revelation as I ride the elevator first up to the ninth floor to pick up a family of four and then back down to the lobby. Now I finally know the story behind the Girl with No Eyes. The Shadow Man had gotten inside her, just like it had gotten inside Ben during Alexei's séance. What was it that Alexei had said during the séance? *Eyes are doors to the soul* . . . The girl did what she could to protect herself from the Shadow Man, and she died because of it.

Alexei had also said something about the innocence of childhood. Is this why Clark and the Girl with No Eyes could see the Shadow Man? And when Clark lost his innocence after his only living friend died, he could no longer see the Shadow Man.

That much made sense, but playing games with that evil ghost? I can hardly imagine the Shadow Man playing tag or hide-and-go-seek. What did they do that was horrible enough to convince a seven-year-old that self-mutilation was her only escape?

October 23

Dear Diary,

I'm waiting for my death.

    I stayed late at work tonight, feeling the pressure of a midnight deadline for a powerful client. Instead of hovering like he usually does, Gregory took off early. He seemed to have gotten the hint that I had no intention of leaving my husband. Gregory had been awfully quiet since I spurned his most recent advances, but I knew that he wouldn't be so easily discouraged. He had something brewing, something planned, and I knew I wouldn't like it. I just had no idea how much I wouldn't like it. When I found out that I would have to stay later than usual, I left a message on Jay's voicemail because I couldn't reach him.

He didn't call me back. I assumed he was upset. At dinner last night, we had fought over the escalating incidents around the house, and I couldn't bear to face him tonight. When he didn't pick up, I left a trite message. I miss the days when I could slam the receiver in an act of passive aggression. Instead, I pressed the "end" button extra hard.

When I got home, the house was dark and the air was stagnant.

"Jay? You home?" I called out, dropping my purse onto the kitchen counter. I walked toward the fridge where Jay had neatly pinned his schedule under a magnet from Italy and another from Barbados, the only two exotic places I've ever traveled to. He was supposed to be off this evening.

I bristled with irritation and stomped toward the stairs. I flipped on the light, but nothing happened. The power was out.

"Jay?" I called louder. I clomped up the stairs, secretly hoping he was asleep so I would wake him.

I slipped on something wet, and slammed to the ground, my hands barely quick enough to break my fall. I fumbled to my feet, wiping my sticky hands on my cashmere sweater. As my eyes adjusted to the darkness, I peered down at the mess on the floor before me. Dark, slick liquid coated the hardwood stairs, as if someone had taken a giant paintbrush and painted a large stroke upward. Puzzled, I followed the path up the stairs. It led to the master bedroom.

My irritation slipped away, replaced with dread. I didn't want to go in.

"Jay?" I whispered. I stepped closer to the room, which was blanketed in darkness.

A figure lay on the bed, propped up, arms open wide. Unmoving. I shivered in the cool breeze that stole through the open window.

"Jay?" I raised my voice slightly.

The figure didn't move.

I stood there in silence, shivering as my eyes gradually adjusted to the dim light that crept past the curtain.

Lying in the middle of the bed, fully dressed, Jay was propped up at an uncomfortable angle. His face was expressionless. His eyes gazed at nothing. I tried to turn on the light in this room, but it didn't work either.

Was he having another episode?

I stepped toward him, arm outstretched. My hand trembled as I shook his shoulder. "Jay?"

His skin felt cool to the touch. The gentle movement tipped him over, completely revealing his face in the moonlight. His eyes were vacant, his mouth slightly opened. His clothes were soaked in the same dark liquid that had tripped me on the stairs. Blood.

"Jay!" I shook him violently. His body convulsed limply like a rag doll.

I heard a creak in the hall, followed by a quiet thump.

I jerked back. I stared at the empty doorway. There was another thump. I jerked out of my trance and darted into the closet. I tried to close the door, but it was stuck. Something was on the floor jamming the door. My diary.

Now, I'm hiding in the bedroom closet, writing by the faint moonlight.

I'm not alone.

I know he's out there. Waiting for me. Taunting me. I shouldn't have trusted him. How could I have been so blind? The signs were all there—his obsessiveness, his assertiveness, his knowledge of details of my personal life, tidbits of information I'd never willingly share with him.

It was never a ghost that haunted me. It was something much more malevolent.

I hear another sound coming from the room beyond my hiding place. I wonder what new torment he has planned for me.

But I don't care. The worst has already happened.

My husband is dead.

34

"I see you've settled in nicely," Will says, a smile on his lips. He stands in the doorway to my old bedroom, which Catalina commandeered yesterday. Her duffel bag sits on the chair by the window.

Other than that, my room remains untouched, still bearing the remnants of my life.

"Yes, I have, thank you. The bed is really comfortable. How are you faring on that lumpy couch?" Catalina asks.

That's unfair. My couch is not lumpy. The cushions just haven't been rotated since my death.

"It's great. I repositioned the lumps so they fit *around* my body, cocooning me. It's really quite comfortable," Will replies.

Catalina smiles and leaves the bedroom, brushing past Will to get to the hallway.

Will's eyes idle on her as she passes, then he follows her into the office.

Catalina strides toward the desk and retrieves a piece of paper, which she hands to Will. "These are the notes from my interview with the Monroes. They didn't know Kae. They didn't know who could have killed her. They didn't know anything."

"So, we're out of leads," Will translates.

Catalina has found a pen, and she is twirling it between her fingers. "Not necessarily. We still haven't managed to interview *everyone* in the building. There's a chance that someone else knew her. Someone else might have the information we need."

Will sighs and slumps into the chair. "We're grasping at straws. We need a tangible lead. I still think that we need to question Oliver Boyden again. He is the only person we've met who has a strong motive."

Catalina smiles.

"What?" Will asks.

Catalina shakes her head. "You just sound a lot like a cop."

Will shrugs. "I adapt easily to every situation."

Catalina twirls her pen again. "Melody called the crisis hotline *once*. How would Oliver have known that it was Kae who was on the phone? That she was living in the same building? And he found out so quickly that he killed her that same night? That seems a little coincidental, don't you think?"

"Why are you defending him?"

Catalina's eyebrows shoot through the roof. "I'm not *defending* anybody. I understand that you want to hang onto that lead, our *only* lead, but I just don't think it's *leading* anywhere."

"He's a computer engineer. Maybe he hacked the computer at the crisis hotline. Maybe—"

"Within *one hour*? He found out who Kae was and got to her—killed her—all in *one hour*?"

Will sighs again. "I just think there's something off about him. I got the impression he was lying about Melody and about how she left him. And he definitely would have had reason to hurt her . . . And Kae."

Catalina nods slowly. "I see your point. We shouldn't wipe him off the board completely. I'm just worried we'll get tunnel vision. He isn't our only lead."

"Kae's former boss," Will says.

"Yes, Gregory Copeland."

Him.

My chest tightens. They're talking about him. I haven't heard his name in so long. It's been so long since I've allowed myself to think it. To remember. I feel lightheaded. If I were able to interact with the world, this would be the point where I would have to sit down.

"Kae thought that Copeland was the man who stalked her and killed her husband. She had a strong argument, but no proof. Nobody believed her because of his status. His relationship to the mayor. His money. Kae was so terrified that he would seek revenge—that he would try to claim his prize—that she ran away, came here, and locked herself up for two years! We can't ignore the high likelihood that he's responsible for her death. That he hired someone to kill her, if he didn't do it himself!"

"Now who's getting tunnel-vision?"

Catalina looks affronted. "I don't have tunnel-vision. I'm just following the facts from the previous case—"

"Even if there's no indication that Copeland was responsible for her death?"

"Even if, and that's a big *if,* Copeland didn't kill Kae, there's no doubt in my mind that he killed your brother. Or have you forgotten about him? He's the one you're supposed to be avenging!"

Will flinches, as if he's been slapped. "I want justice for *both* of their deaths."

"Why? You didn't even know Kae."

"We met once," Will interjects. "At Jay's funeral. And I'm not doing it for her. I'm doing it for my brother. He would have wanted her killer to be brought to justice, just as much as he would have wanted his own killer found. I don't see why these two goals have to be conflicting."

Catalina rubs her face with her hands. "I'm sorry. That was way out of line. I'm just used to investigating crimes with an entire precinct to back me up. With physical evidence and forensic experts feeding me the pieces to the puzzle. I just feel like we're getting nowhere fast in this case, and if we wait too long, the trail will go cold, and we'll never catch the killer. Or killers."

Will takes a tentative step forward and places a hand on her shoulder. "It's all right. This is hard for both of us." He's quiet for a moment. "I know you and Kae were closer than you let on."

Catalina looks up at Will, and I see that her eyes are wet.

"How well did you know her?" Will asks.

"I was one of her bridesmaids."

Will sucks in a breath but doesn't say anything. He wasn't even invited to the wedding, but it seems that he would do anything to find his brother's killer.

Catalina's phone rings.

"Hello?" She immediately perks up. She grabs a piece of paper and the pen she was twirling frantically moments ago and quickly jots down some information. She leans back, eyes wide.

"Yes, um, thank you for this information. I owe you one." She ends the call.

"What is it?" Will asks impatiently.

Catalina's face is as white as a sheet. "That was Christine."

"Who?"

She shakes her head. "Uh—my contact from the precinct."

"And?"

"Luke Brennan has been arrested for Kae's murder."

35

uke? Arrested for my murder? This isn't possible.

Will doesn't look surprised, but of course, he doesn't know Luke. Neither of them do.

"Did they say what kind of evidence they have?"

Catalina shakes her head. "She said the evidence is 'compelling.' But they always say that. I'm heading down to the precinct now. Maybe I can get more information from my contact, assuming I can steer clear of Detective Cherry."

She ducks into the bedroom and grabs her bag. She stops at the door, turning to face Will. "It looks like we were both wrong," she says before leaving.

Luke can't be my killer. It's not possible.

Luke had been nowhere near Thorwald Place that night. He'd wanted to come over to comfort me, but I'd turned him down. There's no doubt in my mind that I shouldn't have. I should have let him come over. I would still be alive. Either that, or Luke would be dead too. It's a chilling thought.

How can the police think that this is logical? If Luke *had* come to my building that night, he wouldn't have gone to the basement, he would have come up to my apartment. Don't the police see this critical flaw in their line of thinking? What kind of evidence do they have? Is it circumstantial, or did they actually find physical proof that he's the killer?

I follow Catalina as she crosses the lobby. Elias gives her the stink eye from his perch at his station. I slam into the invisible barrier.

No! I can't go with her to the police station. I can't go to see what evidence they have or to see how the police have been treating Luke. This is all a mistake, some ridiculous cosmic screwup that I need to fix!

I pound against the invisible barrier, slamming against it with my fists, using all my strength. It doesn't move. It doesn't make a sound. It just remains, resolute.

A weight crushes my chest. Luke was my only friend. He was the only person I trusted in this city, the only person I allowed into my apartment. We watched Netflix and ate chips and M&Ms, throwing food at the screen whenever Louis said something creepy about his cat during one of our *Suits* marathons.

Luke can't be my killer. He had hot pink pepper spray. He couldn't hurt a fly. He was always so kind. So attentive. Not just to me, but to all the people who volunteered at the crisis hotline. While he mostly works behind the scenes, he has many repeat callers, people who ask for him because of his kind and understanding personality. His sweetness and genuineness.

Then I realize.

My panic attack subsides as quickly as it came. Luke isn't my killer. He was framed.

36

atalina is gone for the rest of the day. Will took off shortly after she left. Every time the elevator passes the seventh floor, I pop into my apartment. Every time, I find it empty. I wonder if Will has gone to meet Catalina at the police station. Maybe he still believes Melody's husband is the killer, and he's looking into him instead. Either way, the suspense is killing me.

Sylvie is having important guests over for a late dinner tonight. She's wearing a white apron over her blue silk dress when the door swings open to reveal the man and woman who'd come up in my elevator.

"Come in, come in," Sylvie chirps. She takes their coats and hangs them on wooden hangers in the front closet.

"Dinner will be ready shortly. We're having chicken sauté and cream of broccoli soup."

The guests make the appropriate yummy noises and follow her into the dining room, where they take seats at the table. It's set with a delicate lace tablecloth and fine silverware, which only reinforces my assumption that this is a special occasion. Etienne enters the dining room wearing a tiny navy suit with a perfectly dimpled tie. He looks so adorable, despite his somber disposition.

"Well, hello! You must be Etienne!" the woman proclaims. "I'm Eloise."

Etienne is silent.

"I'm Sherman, Director of Clinical Services." The man has a stilted British accent, which sounds slightly phony. He presents his hand to the tiny boy. Etienne stares, then takes it and gives it a gentle shake. Eloise giggles, a sound that's unsettling coming from a woman of her age and grace.

Sylvie serves the dinner shortly after. I can almost see the waves of exquisite flavor wafting from the platters. I cannot smell anything from the real world, which is a good thing, I suppose, given that that would only add to my torment.

The couple makes small talk with Sylvie while Etienne quietly eats his dinner. They talk about work and about the charities that Eloise is involved with. Sylvie is clearly trying to make a good impression, and I wonder if she's up for a promotion of some sort at the hospital. They never mention it, which I suppose would be tactless.

"I was so sorry to hear about your late husband," Eloise says. "Sherman tells me he was quite the golfer."

Sylvie hesitates, holding a dainty forkful of chicken inches from her lips. "Thank you, Eloise. It was quite tragic."

Sherman turns to Etienne. "How are you dealing with the loss of your father?"

Etienne peers up at him. "He's not gone."

Sherman coughs and gives Sylvie a questioning look.

Sylvie's eyes harden, but her voice is soft. "Etienne is having a hard time dealing with his father's . . . passing," she says.

Etienne frowns, finally displaying something other than despondence. "He's not gone," he repeats.

"Etienne, that's enough," Sylvie says.

Eloise's cheeks flush, and she exchanges a look with her husband. The room is quiet save for the sound of Sylvie's knife scratching against her plate as she methodically slices the rest of her meat. The sharp sound cuts through the silence, causing both guests to flinch involuntarily.

They sit uneasily, utensils in hand, unwilling or unable to continue eating.

"He visits me. He watches me sleep." Etienne's voice is quiet, but every word resonates across the room.

Eloise gasps, her fork dropping to her plate with a clatter. Sherman glances at Sylvie.

Sylvie shoots Etienne a glare, but that doesn't deter him.

"He stands at the foot of my bed until I wake up." Etienne's big brown eyes are unblinking. He gazes up at the couple in earnest. "If I don't wake up, he does this."

Etienne stands up and lifts his pant cuffs. His lower legs are covered in tiny scratches, little raised marks that face all directions. Some are old, but some are very new, no more than a few days old.

Eloise gasps.

"He's in the bedroom now," Etienne says.

Eloise glances nervously toward the hall. Sherman is rigid. His white knuckles clutch his cloth napkin.

"He's always in there. Waiting."

"Etienne." Sylvie's tone is a warning.

Etienne looks at her, then quickly drops his pant legs and returns to his seat. His previous determination is gone, and he is once again a meek boy, afraid to utter a single syllable out of line.

Sherman clears his throat. Appetite forgotten, he stares down at his plate. Eloise is looking green, and her eyes keep darting down the hallway, as if she expects Raymond's ghost to manifest in the shadows.

Sylvie notices their hesitation. She puts down her knife and fork, fires a look of derision at Etienne, and says, "If you're done with dinner, I'll bring out the dessert."

Eloise clutches at Sherman's hand under the table. Sherman takes the hint. "Dessert would be lovely, but I'm afraid my wife isn't feeling well. We should be heading back home. It's getting quite late."

The clock on the credenza reads only seven thirty.

Sylvie's smile is strained. She stares at them before replying, "Of course. Perhaps we can reschedule for another time."

Sherman nods and says something vague about having his assistant set something up, but his next few months were already booked solid. Eloise's eyes are still riveted to the hallway. I wonder if she can see something I can't. I wonder if she senses the presence of a spirit in this apartment. If so, is it Raymond she senses or me?

Sylvie ushers them to the front door. Sherman is very apologetic for cutting the evening short. Eloise looks as though she would rather run out of there than endure any more niceties.

Sylvie shuts the door behind them and returns to the dining room, where Etienne remains at his place at the table, eyes cast downward submissively.

"Etienne."

Etienne tears his eyes away from his half-eaten dinner.

"Go to the Quiet Room."

Etienne slides off his chair and enters the hall. I go to follow, but I am summoned by the elevator.

Eloise and Sherman are riding down to the lobby.

"That boy is clearly troubled," Sherman says. His eyes search his wife's face with concern.

Eloise makes a non-committal sound. She wears her shawl wrapped tightly around her, as if there's a chill that she cannot shake.

37

atalina shows up at my apartment late tonight, bearing little news from the police station. She hadn't been able to get in to talk with Luke because he's only speaking to his lawyer. He hasn't made an official statement yet, but he's expected to give one soon.

Will and Catalina sit at the kitchen counter. Catalina takes a bite from a burger she picked up at the new Five Guys location across the street from the police precinct. Will ate hours ago, and he sits across from her, hiding a grin as he watches her scarf down her meal in an extremely unladylike manner.

"The evidence is undeniable," Catalina admits.

"What proof do they have?"

Will is on the edge of his seat, literally. Instead of replying immediately, Catalina scoops up a dollop of ketchup with a French fry and pops it into her mouth. She chews slowly before swallowing, as if savoring his anticipation. I want to smack her.

"That threatening phone call that Kae received the night of her death? Turns out it was made from Luke's cell phone. He tried to delete the record from the system, but nothing on the Internet can ever truly be erased. It explains why he didn't tell me about it when I interviewed him. He was trying to cover it up."

Luke called me that night? He was the one who threatened me, terrified me? But why? That doesn't make sense. He's being framed for my murder. I'm sure of this now more than ever. Somehow, Gregory found out where I was, observed me, learned the identity of my only friend in this city, and framed him for my death. In his eyes, it's the ultimate punishment. But how can I communicate this knowledge to Catalina and Will?

Catalina is still talking. "Apparently, they were pretty close friends. The theory is that Luke wanted to be more than that, but Kae shut him down. They're saying that that's enough motive for him to want to kill her."

There's a hint of truth to her theory, but it's distorted with lies. Luke had wanted more, but he doesn't have a mean bone in his body. He would never have hurt me. He isn't like Gregory—arrogant and self-important. He's sweet and thoughtful and self-deprecating. He wouldn't have killed me for such a stupid reason. He wouldn't have killed me, period.

"Do you think he did it?" Will asks.

Catalina considers this for a moment. "I don't know," she finally answers. "When I met him, he seemed genuinely upset about her death. More so than a casual acquaintance would be, which was why I suspected he wanted something more. He also seemed willing to do whatever it took to help me find Kae's killer. But then again, murderers often try to insert themselves into the investigation, either to mislead, or out of a sense of sick satisfaction."

"She didn't know Luke from before Jay's death, did she?"

Catalina shakes her head.

Will sighs and cradles his head in his hands. "So, he couldn't have killed Jay."

Catalina puts her burger down and places a hand on his arm. "This isn't necessarily the end of this investigation. There's a good chance that Luke made the phone call but had nothing to do with her death."

Good. Now they're seeing the possibility that Luke is innocent. Which, of course, he is. A psychopathic murderer wouldn't come over in the middle of the night to binge-watch *How I Met Your Mother* reruns when I was suffering from insomnia. His favorite character was Lily. Lily! A psychopath's favorite character would definitely be Barney.

Will and Catalina exchange a loaded look. Catalina pulls her hand away from his arm and continues eating.

"We need to come up with a game plan," Catalina says between fries. "What are we going to do next?"

Will watches her thoughtfully. "I still think that Oliver might have something to do with her death."

Catalina looks at him with tired eyes, but this time, she doesn't argue.

"I want to talk to him again to see if I can get anything else out of him," Will continues, "It might be better if I go alone, 'cause otherwise, I won't have his undivided attention."

A small smile flashes over Catalina's face, but then it's gone. "I should go back to the police station tomorrow anyway. See if I can charm any more information from the cops working the case. I might also drop by Luke's workplace. See if I can get any info from his coworkers."

"I'll come with you for that," Will says quickly.

I roll my eyes. It sounds like he doesn't want to spend an entire day apart from her. Is that bitterness I'm feeling?

"Well, I'm off to bed," Catalina says, tossing her wrappers in the garbage can. She hesitates. "I can take the couch tonight."

Will shakes his head vehemently. "No, you take the bed. I'm getting used to the couch. I've given all the lumps first names, and we've gotten really close. If we switched sleeping arrangements now, they would get confused, and that wouldn't be good for either of us."

Catalina rolls her eyes and leaves.

⁕

Alexei paces his apartment. He takes four long strides across the carpet before he spins around and continues in the opposite direction. He grips something tightly in his hand—a piece of green fabric—but I can't get a good look because of his frenetic movements. Outside, a crescent moon emanates cerulean light into this black room.

He halts abruptly and tosses the cloth onto a chair. I step closer to inspect it. It's a light green cotton shirt. I speculate over its strange shape before identifying it as a maternity top. This shirt must have belonged to Melody. Alexei grabs his coat from the front closet and leaves the apartment.

Why does Alexei have one of Melody's shirts? Did he return to the garbage room after Oliver left? He must have gone through the boxes, searching for clues to her disappearance. This is a good sign. It means that *someone* has noticed that Melody is gone. *Someone* cares. Although, out of everyone in the building, Alexei is the last person I would want to suspect something. To this point, he has barely acted on his suspicions. I fear that his ambition and self-inflated ego will keep him from ever finding the truth. However, the fact that this mystery has kept him up at night, pacing his apartment, is a good sign.

I drift out into the corridor, but Alexei isn't there. I drop down to the lobby just in time to see him leaving the building. So, he isn't going up to the Boyden apartment to confront Oliver. It's late, so maybe he'll take action in the morning. I haven't lost all hope. Not quite yet, anyway.

Quickly reaching my barrier in the lobby, I jump back up to the second floor where my range is broader. I return to Alexei's apartment and stare at the faded green shirt that is strewn across the armchair.

I had thought that my story was unique, but it seems as if everyone in this building has a strangely tragic story, one wrought with mystery and misery. Melody was abused and may have been killed by her husband. Sabryna is alone, despite being married to a rich, successful man. Sylvie and little Etienne have a dysfunctional family dynamic, and Sylvie has taken her controlling nature to an extreme with what she has done to her husband. The Man in Tweed is an enigma, one that I'm not entirely convinced I want to understand. The Woman with No Past clearly has one, but she has hidden it away, tucked it behind a closed door that she refuses to open, even though insanity has found its way through the cracks. Will and Catalina are haunted by memories of the past, and they are driven to find my killer— no matter what the cost.

Even Elias is hiding something. The fact that he snuck into the Man in Tweed's apartment is suspicious, especially since he came prepared with a flashlight and gloves and his entire demeanor changed, as if he was finally coming into his element. I need to know more about Elias, who he is, and why he is investigating John Smith.

Elias lives in apartment 201, which is within my current range. In the past, I have been totally disinterested in Elias' life, but now, I need to know more about him. His apartment is dark and quiet. I quickly check the master bedroom and see that Elias isn't tucked away in bed, despite the late hour. He has no social life to speak of, so where is he?

His apartment appears average. Despite the upscale building, his furniture has an inherent cheapness to it. Nothing is in serious disrepair, but quality appears to be lacking. It looks like Elias purchased items he didn't want to furnish a three-bedroom apartment he didn't need.

The kitchen is spotless, in keeping with his nature— he's an impeccable creature who despises disorder with every fiber of his being. I return to the master bedroom. It's tidy as well, with the thin bedspread smoothed evenly over the mattress. The nightstand is bare except for a lamp and a single book. What kind of book does Elias read before bed? I press closer, reaching the edge of my enclosure.

It's a black, leather bound book with gold embossed letters on the front. It looks familiar. I strain closer still. "Kaela D. Archer."

I jerk back. My vision swims. The air is sucked from my lungs. I'm trapped in a tidal pool, the undertow pulling me down, dragging me toward the dark depths of the vast ocean floor.

Why does Elias have my diary?

October 30

Dear Diary,

I begin this entry writing as Kaela D. Archer, but that will not be my name for much longer.

The ceremony was beautiful, even though he was there. Catalina said I shouldn't go—that it could be dangerous and that Jay's killer might make an appearance. I told her that I had to lay my husband to rest, and that he wouldn't dare attack me in broad daylight, in front of dozens of witnesses. Catalina reluctantly agreed, but she still wore her sidearm and stayed by my side for the entire funeral.

The week after Jay's death is a blur. I only remember bits and pieces. I'm told I hid in that closet for hours before I was found. I don't *even remember who found me, just that I fought with all my might, terrified of leaving the safety of that closet. It took three officers to drag me from it. They tried to hide the sight of Jay's body on the bed, exposed in full daylight, but I still saw him.*

The sight haunts me when I close my eyes and torments my every waking moment. I see his blanched skin that has taken on a bluish hue. I see his arms spread wide, limply draped across the bed. I see his eyes, still open, still blue, but clouded, unfocused, gazing at nothing. Those eyes will never look at me again.

I cannot believe how stupid I have been. All this time, I thought I was haunted by a ghost. The soft footsteps in the hall. The dead bird on the pillow. The vandalism. Lon Chaney, Jr.'s death. It wasn't a ghost but a stalker. After this revelation, it didn't take long to figure out who it was. But he is powerful, affluent, and influential. I have no proof, just the weight of the fear in the pit of my stomach and the iron certainty that I am right.

The other mourners have long left, but I still sit at the gravestone, writing in this diary. This will be my last entry. Catalina is patiently waiting in her car. When I'm finished here, she will lead me away from this place to begin a new life. I'm not safe here. The police did not believe me when I told them who killed Jay, and I don't blame them. But they should have investigated. They may have found the proof they needed.

Catalina helped me to set up papers, to change my name and never look back. But I will always look back. To my life. To who I was and what I was. Even my new name, Rachel A. Drake, an anagram of Kaela D. Archer, is a constant reminder.

I cannot believe that I was so foolish as to think that all our troubles were caused by a ghost. But now I know.

Ghosts do exist, and I am one of them.

38

The Woman with No Past seems to have a past after all. After being deposited on the eighth floor this morning, I was drawn to her apartment, desperate to uncover her secrets. There are too many mysteries in this building, and I'm relieved that I've finally uncovered the answer to at least one of them.

I found her in the third bedroom, which I have never had the opportunity to explore. It lies just out of my range, and the door has never been open before now. I crane my neck to peer around the woman's skeletal figure. The walls are painted a color that makes them look like they were coated with Pepto-Bismol. A delicate birch bark bed rests against the far wall. A gauzy curtain drapes around it, creating an ethereal feel of femininity and nostalgia. A wooden chest lies open at the foot of the bed. It is overflowing with toys, teddy bears, dolls. A small table is set up in the corner with a miniature floral tea pot at its center. Tea cups are placed in front of each empty seat, like a tea party for ghosts.

This is a little girl's bedroom.

The Woman with No Past lingers in the room, not venturing farther than a few steps past the threshold. She stands there, perfectly still, never moving, barely breathing, before she finally turns and leaves, closing the door firmly behind her.

She enters the empty bedroom, the one with nothing but a wooden rocking chair, and I trail after her. She approaches the closet and swings it open. I had expected it to be empty, but it contains a single cardboard box. The woman retrieves it and sets it in the middle of the barren room. Devastatingly slow, she lifts the folds, revealing what lies inside.

At the top of the box, there are photographs—glossy pictures of herself with a handsome man and a bright, exuberant young girl. Some of the pictures are well worn and slightly faded. These are the pictures that had once been in the frames on the piano. Perhaps she removed them after something horrible happened. I won't have to speculate for much longer.

There is a picture of the Woman with No Past, who looks much younger and full of life, grinning ear to ear as she pushes a three-year-old on a swing. The handsome man sits at the grand piano with the little girl atop his knee, the two of them giggling as they play a duet. The woman flips past several newspaper clippings. One of them is an obituary for the handsome man. It's dated ten years ago. She slides this article under the stack of photos before I can get a closer look. Next, she gazes at a picture of the little girl blowing out five candles on a birthday cake. There is another photo of the little girl when she's slightly older. She strikes a pose in front of the fireplace, wearing a red and white gingham dress.

I know this girl. I recognize the dress, the braids, if not her face. I look up at the mother. Her expression is devoid of emotion, but she is cradling the picture with utmost care. Does she know that her daughter is still here, that she hasn't moved on? Does she know that her little girl haunts the basement?

⟨oᴅᴇᴇᴇᴇᴏ⟩

This morning, I barely catch a glimpse of Catalina before she heads out to the police station. I can only hope that I get good news about Luke. He is undoubtedly innocent. Elias has my journal, the gateway into my past. That is proof that he has not only been inside the Man in Tweed's apartment, but he's been inside mine as well. At first, I had thought he was investigating the Man in Tweed, trying to figure out who he is. If that were the case, then why would he have gone into *my* apartment, and taken *my* diary?

There's more to the story, but I'm missing some of the pieces to the puzzle. My gut is telling me that Elias is not a killer, and my brain is telling me that there isn't a single logical reason why he would want to kill me. He seems to take great pride in his job, and keeping the residents safe and comfortable is a major part of it.

Would he jeopardize his career by killing someone in the building? I never suspected that he had any ill will toward me, and he has been talking about my death with many residents and police officers, never giving away any sign of contempt. If anything, he seems to have *liked* me.

But after seeing his apartment, his measly belongings and cheap furniture, I know that Elias might be desperate for money. It can't be cheap to live in this area, even if he has discounted rent or lives here for free because of his job. But would he be desperate enough to work for him? Would he be desperate enough to *kill*?

After five in the evening, Will rides the elevator to the fourth floor. Before knocking on the door to Oliver's condo, Will glances up and down the hall. He pulls the prescription pill bottle out of his pocket and dry swallows a couple of capsules. I watch him warily as he tucks the bottle out of sight. He sighs, then knocks on the door.

Oliver lets him into the apartment reluctantly, looking past Will into the empty corridor.

"Where's your friend?" Oliver asks after offering Will a seat.

Will bristles immediately, but he manages to remain civil.

"Unfortunately, Catalina couldn't make it. I would like to speak with you about Rachel."

Oliver already looks irritated. "The dead woman? Again? I already told you—I didn't know her. Why don't you go interrogate Rasputin? Apparently, he's been communicating with her ghost."

This comment stops Will in his tracks. "Rasputin?"

"You claim to be investigating her murder, and you don't even know we have a minor-celebrity in our midst? Amateur."

Will frowns. "I know all the residents in this building. But you said that Rasputin—Alexei—has been communicating with Rachel? How do you know that?"

Oliver shrugs. "He came to visit one day and told me so himself. It's all a bunch of bullshit if you ask me. The woman was afraid of her own shadow. I really doubt she'd communicate with the likes of him." Oliver gestures toward the door. "I guess I've helped you as much as I can."

Will shakes his head adamantly. "We're not done here."

"Are you thick? I already told you, I never knew the dead woman."

"Right, but I have reason to believe that your wife did."

"Melody didn't have ties to anyone in this building."

"Are you sure? Melody was a stay-at-home wife, and Rachel worked from home. It's perfectly plausible that they might have met in the building and become friends."

"Melody told me everything. She never mentioned Rachel, so I know that she didn't know her." Oliver's eye develops a noticeable twitch.

"Melody obviously didn't tell you everything. She didn't tell you that she was sleeping with another man or that she was having his baby. She didn't tell you that she was planning on leaving you for him . . ." Will is baiting him. Antagonizing a man who is willing to beat a pregnant woman? This isn't going to end well. His nose hasn't quite healed from his last altercation with someone in this building.

Oliver's hands clench tightly into fists. I wait for the swing to come, for Will to have his lights knocked out for a second time in a week, but Oliver manages to recover. I don't know if I'm disappointed or relieved. I can only hope that someday, that temper will be his downfall.

"My wife did not know Rachel Drake," Oliver says firmly. "Have you been interrogating everyone else in this building so closely? This is bordering on harassment. I should call security and have you thrown out."

Will doesn't seem afraid. "You should call security. Maybe you can explain to them where your wife is."

"Get the hell out."

39

The Man in Tweed and the Woman Across the Way lie intertwined in his bed, demonstrating that he does in fact know that bedsheets are meant to be used. He strokes her long blonde hair with surprising tenderness.

She notices his scars but doesn't ask, even though I can tell she wants to. Instead, she looks up at him and says, "Who hired you?"

John tenses and doesn't answer. He continues to caress her hair in silence.

She doesn't ask again, but instead she gazes up at him with sincere brown eyes. "I need to know," she whispers.

John looks away. "Caroline, once I tell you, you'll know. You won't be able to forget."

Caroline nods. "My stepmother. I knew it."

John studies her face with concern. Caroline doesn't seem upset but resigned.

"How much?" she asks.

Again, he tenses. Again, he doesn't answer immediately.

"How much was my life, my share of the inheritance, worth to her?"

John's jaw clenches. "Four million."

Caroline lets out a low whistle, then pulls away from him to get a better look at his face. "That's a lot of money."

His eyes narrow. "It is," he admits.

"You could buy a lot with that. That measly telescope you have in the other room? You could buy a whole observatory with that kind of cash."

John shakes his head. "All I need is right here in front of me."

Caroline's smile slips away. "Did you have any other . . . jobs while in this building?"

John looks down at her. "The woman in the elevator?" he asks.

I freeze. Could he have been hired to kill me?

Caroline nods and waits expectantly.

John shakes his head. "I had nothing to do with that."

The ghost of my heart pounds in my chest. If Gregory was going to have someone kill me, who better to hire than a professional hitman? But John says that he didn't kill me. He's been truthful with Caroline about everything else—the good and the bad. He doesn't seem to have spared her any details about his previous contracts. I'd been present when he told her all about an Iranian businessman he took out in Calgary several months ago. I'd felt queasy at the specifics, but Caroline had seemed to be understanding, forgiving.

So, why would he pretend not to have killed me if he had? Caroline didn't know me from a hole in the wall. We hadn't been friends, not even acquaintances, so it wasn't like he was sparing her the pain. Besides, how careless would he have to be to linger at the scene of the crime for weeks afterward? John Smith is a killer, but I don't think he's mine.

John's features remain taut, but a sliver of emotion breaks through. "You know that your stepmother won't just . . . stop. She'll hire someone else."

Caroline's face falls. "I know."

"I can't let that happen."

"I know."

⟨◦⟩◦◦◦◦◦◦⟨◦⟩

Catalina is pissed. She slams the door to my apartment as she enters. A grim expression sullies her fine features. She stalks into my office, where she finds Will poring over the files he has spread out over my desk.

Will glances up. "Did you learn anything from your police contact?"

She's suddenly strangely still. "Yes, I learned something very interesting."

Will waits expectantly.

Catalina doesn't say anything else. She crosses her arms and glares at him.

Will shifts slightly in his seat. "Well . . . What was it?"

"I couldn't get any information on Luke Brennan. Or Kae's case," Catalina says. "But I did learn something very, very interesting."

"You said that already," Will says with a smile.

"Why didn't you mention that you spent four years in prison?"

Will's smile is immediately wiped from his face. "I didn't think it was relevant."

"Not *relevant*?"

"Not relevant to the case."

"Of course it's relevant! I'm investigating a crime with a *criminal*," she snaps. "Do you know what this could do to my reputation and my career?"

Will's cheeks redden. "You don't know what you're talking about," Will says quietly.

"Oh, I don't? Officer Rodriguez gave me the highlights. I called the Vancouver PD to confirm."

Will's jaw clenches. He gets up to leave, but Catalina cuts off his escape.

"When you were eighteen, you were convicted of dangerous driving, causing death. You got away unscathed, but your passenger wasn't so lucky."

Will freezes, standing inches away from Catalina. "Let me go," he whispers.

Catalina ignores him. "The real kicker is, what were you doing in the car with your brother's girlfriend? No wonder he didn't want anything to do with you after you got out of prison."

"Let me go."

"You don't have to go anywhere. *I'm* leaving." Catalina tears into my bedroom to get her bag and leaves without another word.

40

Jay once told me that something horrible happened between him and his brother in high school. It's why he broke off all contact with Will and never even invited him to our wedding. No matter how many times I asked, how nicely I pleaded, or how desperately I begged, Jay wouldn't say what his brother did to deserve this treatment. Now, I know, and I'm not sure what I should make of it.

It's because of his brother that Jay moved across the country for college. He joined a fraternity, started going by the name of "Jay" because of his obsession with the Toronto Blue Jays. His given name was Mick Jagger. His parents were huge fans of the Rolling Stones, and they thought it would be perfectly natural to name their firstborn after the group's lead singer. The only time Jay ever spoke about his brother was when he was bemoaning his name, wondering why Will was blessed with a normal one. I told him that I understood his pain, because I was named Kaela with an "e" instead of Kayla with a "y," which was a pain whenever I had to get someone to spell it. Jay said it wasn't the same thing.

Fortunately, he had his name legally changed months before the wedding so that our wedding license wouldn't reveal his real name. Our wedding invitations lyrically read "Jay and Kae" so that everyone would be forced to notice our cute couple name. I smile at the fond memory.

I suddenly realize that I've been reflecting on my former life—my life with my husband—without succumbing to the pain and anguish that typically accompanies opening that door. Does this mean I'm ready to move on?

ⓒⲇⲻⲉⲉⲉⲟ

"I don't think we should be doing this," Noel says. He wipes his clammy hands against his wrinkled plaid shirt.

Clark ignores him and shoves open the door to the storage room. Instead of turning on the light, he takes a lighter from his back pocket and flips it. Guided by the flickering flame, he presses onward, venturing deeper into the abyss.

I glance around nervously. There's no sign of the Girl with No Eyes or the Shadow Man, but that doesn't mean they aren't here. Watching. Waiting.

I'm not sure what Clark and his friends plan to do tonight, but I have a feeling that this won't end well.

Noel trails behind Clark and Rayna, looking increasingly uncomfortable the further they go. Clark suddenly stops and raises his head into the air. He takes a deep breath.

"This is the spot," he whispers.

Rayna grins wickedly and drops the large bag she's been carrying onto the hard concrete. She leans toward Clark and plants a sloppy kiss on his lips.

Noel's face falls, and he quickly looks away. "I'm not exactly sure what we're going to be doing here."

Rayna pulls away from Clark, a triumphant look on her face. Clark seems unaffected by what just happened. He watches as Rayna reaches into her bag and pulls out several large, black candles, which she dumps onto the ground unceremoniously. She pulls out the *Book of Shadows* as well as the notebook in which Noel carefully transcribed the translations. She rummages around inside before finding a piece of white chalk. She scuttles across the ground like a spider, reaching the center of the corridor. She begins to draw.

Anticipation builds with every stroke of white on gray.

I turn back to Noel who wrings his hands nervously, his unease mirroring my own. They're planning to perform one of the rituals in that book. But translation can be a tricky business, which is something I can attest to. There are many nuances that can easily be lost. Noel is inexperienced and will undoubtedly have misinterpreted significant portions of the text. I just know he did.

Rayna finishes drawing and stands up, wiping her chalky hands on her short, black skirt, leaving behind ghastly hand prints. Shuddering, I look down at her work.

It's a pentagram. Clark places a candle at each point and begins to light them.

"I don't think we should do this, I mean, we don't have all the things needed for the séance," Noel says.

Great. I'm an honorary guest of another séance. Maybe I should put the fear of God into them so they won't attempt anything like this again. I grin, imagining their horrified faces if they were able to see my spirit. My mangled corpse, head lolling from my near decapitation. Blood soaked through my sweater. My eyes staring at them vacantly from beyond the veil.

I blink. These thoughts are disturbing and unnecessary, and I shove them away.

Clark looks up at Noel as he lights the final candle. "Sit down at that point." He gestures to the one farthest from him. Rayna doesn't need instruction, and she plops down gracelessly in her own position.

Noel hesitates.

"Don't chicken out on us now," Rayna says, rolling her eyes.

Noel gulps and brushes aside a wayward lock of hair. He sits in his designated spot, so they are all equidistant from one another. To demonstrate his worthiness, he reaches for the book and opens it.

"No," Clark says suddenly. He grabs the book from Noel's grasp and flips to another page. "We're going to be doing something different."

Noel is aghast. "But that's the page that I translated."

Clark smiles thinly. "And you did an *excellent* job at it. Your work helped me to figure out a few other pages. Ones with more interesting information."

"Wait—what? I don't understand."

"We're not going to communicate with the dead. There's been a small change in plans. We're going to summon a demon."

Noel's eyes widen like saucers. "No! That's not a good idea. That's too dangerous—"

"It's dangerous, but not if we do it right. And I read the ritual, so we'll do it right. It won't be able to escape the pentagram unless we let it," Clark says.

"You want to contact that demon that used to visit you when you were a kid?" Noel asks.

"Yes. The Devil with No Face."

I shiver at the name.

"Even if you can summon him, you won't be able to *see* him. Not anymore. You're too old. I read other pages in that book too. Apparently, only children can sense those from the other side. Ghosts, spirits . . . demons. Kids can sense them, see them. Talk to them. But once they lose their innocence, they lose that ability forever. We're too old."

"Not necessarily," Clark says with a Cheshire grin.

"Razor found something in the book that can help us get past that little issue," Rayna adds.

Noel's curiosity seems to overcome his fear. He looks over at Clark expectantly.

Clark reaches into the bag once again and pulls out a vial of thick red liquid.

"What is that?" Noel asks warily.

"The Blood of an Innocent."

"What?"

Clark smiles again. "Rayna stole it from the kid's ward at the hospital where her dad works. It's blood from a baby. Doesn't get much more innocent than that."

Noel blanches. "Blood from a *baby*? Oh God, you're not going to *drink* that, are you?"

Clark laughs. "Of course not! That's disgusting. Besides, I wouldn't want my *stomach* to be able to sense the demon."

Rayna seems emotionally detached as she observes Noel's reaction to this new information.

"If you idiots are done yapping, maybe we should get started? It's almost midnight." Despite her words, Rayna sounds slightly bored. It's a powerful persona she puts on, and I can't tell if it's an act or if she genuinely is this blasé.

Clark turns to her. "I'll read from the book. When it's time . . . you know what to do."

His words chill me to the core. Noel is already glancing toward the exit, desperate to leave.

Clark seems to read his mind. "If you leave during the ritual, the demon will be able to escape the circle. Do you want that?"

Noel shakes his head vigorously.

"Good. Now, close your eyes and focus."

Noel obeys reluctantly. Clark tosses Rayna a meaningful look. She nods and slips a hand into the duffel bag. She pulls something out, and I catch a glimpse of silver before she hides it under her skirt in one quick movement.

Clark uncorks the vial of blood. He pours it onto both hands. The liquid is dense and glistening crimson. He smears it over his eyes, rubbing it and spreading it until he has painted thick circles around them. He pours some into his ears. He then takes the remainder of the blood and dribbles it over his lips.

"What are you doing?" Noel's voice has gone hoarse.

Clark smiles, and tiny dark rivulets drip down his chin. "So I can see him, hear him, and speak with him. Close your eyes."

Noel closes his eyes again. His hands are fists, clenched tightly at his sides.

"Get out of here!" I tell Noel. I try to shove him, to push him toward the door, but he's just as unreachable as every other human in this world.

"We call to you, dark spirits of the unknown."

The air is suddenly still. Clark's voice lacks the usual echoic sound of beings from the other side. It sounds loud and clear, like it could travel across the miles unobstructed. His voice is alluring, making me want to come closer, but I remain in place, between Clark and Noel.

"Spirits, come forth. We wish to make an offering."

Chords of gentle music tickle my ears. I tear my eyes away from Clark's morbid visage, but I do not see the source of the music.

The Girl with No Eyes appears behind Rayna. She faces Clark and stands perfectly motionless. I look down at the chalk pentagram. The spirits are supposed to be *inside* the pentagram. Something has gone terribly, terribly wrong.

Raymond appears farther down the corridor. He shakes with his habitual intense vibration, but other than that, he doesn't move. He, too, is staring at Clark, captivated by his words. My eyes are drawn back to Clark's face. He looks at the Girl with No Eyes, his mouth open in surprise and recognition. He spots Raymond, too, and a small smile forms on his glistening lips. He turns and looks at me. *He sees me.*

He continues to scan the room, but then his lips curl into a distorted frown. He wanted the Shadow Man to come.

"Demon, come forth. I have a sacrifice here for you."

A sacrifice? What does he mean by "sacrifice"?

Shadows shift and gather in the corner, just beyond Raymond's shuddering outline. The Devil with No Face takes form and slithers toward the circle.

Clark grins, a grotesque vision, blood staining his teeth and dripping from his eyes, weeping into his white foundation. He nods to Rayna. "It's time," he breathes.

She retrieves the item that was tucked under her skirt. A dagger, sharp and gleaming in the candlelight. She turns to Noel.

Noel's eyes are clamped tightly shut, his lips thinly pursed. He rocks back and forth and hums gently, as if to soothe himself. He's utterly oblivious to what is about to happen.

Rayna smirks, then hands Clark the dagger.

"Noel," Clark says gently.

Noel jolts at the sound of his name.

"Noel, you can open your eyes now."

Noel pries one eye open and focuses directly on the Shadow Man. A whimper escapes his trembling lips.

Clark's lips curve upward with pleasure. "You can see him, can't you, Noel?"

Noel's entire body shakes with fear. His mouth opens and closes wordlessly.

Clark speaks. "I offer Noel to you . . . as a vessel."

Noel's eyes widen as the Shadow Man saunters toward him. The silhouette of the demon's head tilts up and down, as if he's appraising this meager offering.

In a lightning-quick movement, Clark grabs Noel's hand to slash it with the blade. Noel snaps out of his stupor. He jerks back, grabbing the dagger from Clark's tenuous grasp. He turns it back onto him and cuts him deep in the arm.

Clark yowls in pain, drawing backward. Rayna growls and lunges toward Noel, claws outstretched. She knocks the knife from his hand, and it clatters across the floor. Noel shoves Rayna away, and she falls, tipping over a candle which extinguishes.

The music strengthens, the piano culminating in sudden staccato.

Clark climbs to his feet and launches himself at Noel. Noel swings and punches him in the face. Clark falls to the ground with a sickening thud.

Noel stands in the center of the room, panting from both fear and exertion. His eyes are wild, roving around the room, taking in the monsters that surround him. He spots the *Book of Shadows* on the floor several feet away. He launches toward it.

I can barely hear my own thoughts over the music which is now thundering across the basement walls.

The Shadow Man shifts and expands, gathering more darkness from the corner near Rayna's hunched form. He absorbs this darkness and uses it to propel himself forward, lunging toward Noel.

Noel jerks back, but doesn't lose his grip on the book.

"Demon be gone!" he bellows.

The music cuts off mid-note. Silence engulfs us. I spin around, scanning the shadows, but the Shadow Man is gone. Raymond has disappeared. The Girl with No Eyes gazes at Clark's immobile form, crumpled on the ground, unconscious, before drifting away to her corner, no longer interested.

Rayna lies panting on the ground beside Clark.

"You bastard," she spits at Noel.

Noel shakes his head. Still grasping the *Book of Shadows* tightly between bloodied fingers, he leaves.

41

Clark barely managed to contain his blind rage. He'd regained consciousness not long after Noel left. Furious with Rayna for letting him leave with the book, Clark spat at her, then tore out of the basement, leaving Rayna to clean up the remnants of chalk and blood.

Once locked in his bedroom, Clark let the monster out. He screamed and growled, tearing his drawings of the Shadow Man from the walls.

He threw books. Overturned furniture.

His parents were awoken by his thunderous howls. Wide-eyed, they'd cowered in their bedroom, wise enough to ride out the storm from in there.

I hope Noel destroys the book before Clark and Rayna get their claws back into it. I fear what will happen if Clark has another chance at his sinister ritual.

I'm summoned to the sixth floor.

Sabryna's sitting on the couch in her living room. She wears a thin, cream, silk nightgown. Her face is scrubbed clean, revealing lines which betray her true age. Her long, flaxen hair flows in gentle waves past her shoulders. The door opens, and Roger strides in.

He hums a bothersome tune and doesn't even glance at his wife on the sofa. His eyes scan right past her as he removes his coat and black leather gloves.

"Roger," she says in a low voice.

"What?" He seems surprised to see her there, as if he genuinely hadn't noticed her sitting there before.

Sabryna stands before him, a determined expression on her face. "Who are you fucking? What's her name?"

Roger falters for a moment but quickly catches himself. "You wouldn't know *her*. She isn't from your generation."

In two quick strides, Sabryna is before him and slaps him, hard, across the face. The sound resonates across the room. Roger's head snaps back. He lets out a breath of surprise.

He turns toward her, and I see a pink mark already forming on his cheek. "You bitch."

Sabryna raises her hand and strikes him again.

A thick veil of rage passes across Roger's face. He swings and hits her. She flies across the room and slams into the cabinet, the framed photograph of them from their wedding clatters to the ground with a crash.

Sabryna climbs to her feet.

She releases a guttural war cry and grabs onto his shirt. Several buttons fly through the air, clattering across the hardwood floor.

With little effort, Roger grabs her wrists and pulls her hands away. He shoves her back to the ground, where this time, she stays. He looks down, his expression twisted into a look of absolute disgust. Without another word, he disappears into the hall, slamming the door to the bathroom behind him.

I gaze down at Sabryna. She sits on the cold floor, panting. Her flimsy nightgown has ridden up her thighs. Tears streak her ashen cheeks. She looks so vulnerable. So exposed.

Something behind her catches my eye. Something shifts in the corner, beside the cream-colored sofa. The shadows mingle and morph and merge.

Suddenly, Sabryna rises. She straightens her silk nightgown, smoothing the wrinkles that had formed at her hip.

She goes out onto the balcony and looks up at the stars. Despite her rapidly forming goosebumps, she doesn't rub her arms together. She doesn't acknowledge the cold. She climbs onto the iron railing.

She never looks down as she plummets to the ground.

42

A few days after I first moved into the building, I was startled by a gentle knock at the front door.

My heart raced in my chest as I tiptoed toward the door. I peered through the peephole. A beautiful blonde woman stood in the corridor. She was fashionably dressed, her hair perfectly styled, her makeup impeccably applied, and her flawlessly manicured hands were holding a basket of muffins.

"Hi, I'm Sabryna. Sabryna with a Y," the charismatic woman greeted me with a stunning smile.

"Wouldn't it be Sabrinay then?" I asked.

The woman stared at me, unblinking, her polished facade flickering slightly from confusion.

Too late, I realized that I had forgotten to crack a smile, ruining the execution of my joke. I felt regret, regret that I couldn't befriend this charming woman. I declined her offer to go for coffee and shut the door, both on her and on any friendship we could have had. Maybe if I hadn't been so afraid, maybe if I'd let her in, maybe things would have ended a little differently. For both of us.

At first, I hear nothing, not even the thud of her body as it hits pavement. Silence. Then, screams. I rush to the balcony and stare down at the street below. Sabryna lies motionless on the road. A vision of white on a black canvas. Her arms spread out toward the heavens. She looks like an angel.

The police arrive in less than ten minutes. They break down the door. Roger is still in the shower when they enter. His cries of outrage transform into sobs of horror as they tell him. I am pulled up and down, up and down as the police come and go, bringing their officers and detectives, medical examiners and forensic investigators.

The rest of the night, I am unable to rest, unable to forget the sight of Sabryna's lifeless corpse. I should have seen it coming. I should have recognized the signs of her depression, the clues that her loveless marriage and isolation were eating away at her soul.

But even if I had seen the warning signs, what could I have done?

43

The haze that blanketed me following Sabryna's death begins to lift the following morning. I start to pay closer attention to what is going on around me. The building is in an uproar. Police officers have flooded the premises, and it seems like a third of the residents have forgotten their jobs and responsibilities and are loitering in the lobby, gossiping. They're much more interested in Sabryna's suicide than they were in my brutal murder. I try not to take this too personally.

Catalina enters the lobby. She glances at Elias, who's engaged in a dynamic conversation with a pair of police officers. She easily evades his attention and slips into the crowd, listening to the hushed conversations. She expertly inserts herself into a discussion between two women. She casually brings up my name. Is she curious to see if there might be a connection between my murder and Sabryna's death?

Will, who had been loitering in the lobby for several hours, spots her immediately. He wades through the crowd, veering straight toward her.

He interrupts the woman she's chatting with. "We need to talk."

Catalina's face tightens, but she doesn't look nearly as angry as she was the last time they spoke. "Not now," she hisses.

"Then when?"

Catalina scans his face. She seems to see something in his haggard features because she nods in consent. She pulls him into the empty library.

"Make it quick," she snaps. "I have a murder to solve."

"You were right, I should have mentioned my past. But what you were told isn't true."

"Which part? The reckless driving? You were caught running a red light two minutes from the crash. The fact that you were with your brother's girlfriend, that you *killed* your brother's girlfriend?"

"None of it."

Catalina's eyebrows shoot through the roof. "Oh, so they just caught the wrong guy then."

"Yes." Will sighs and runs a hand through his unkempt hair. "That night, Jay had been drinking. A lot. He wasn't always the studious, hard-working guy that you knew. In high school, he was a jock. He was popular, and he partied a lot, and he made some bad choices. But that night, he went too far. He knew he shouldn't get behind the wheel of the car, but he did anyway.

His girlfriend was just as drunk, and she didn't even have her seatbelt on. After the crash, Jay panicked and called me. I came, and I saw how drunk he was. I saw Chloe's body thrown from the car, lying on the sidewalk. She was dead on impact. I knew then that Jay would go to prison for a long time for impaired driving, maybe even murder. I thought the police would go easy on me because I was sober. I hadn't realized that Jay was photographed at a traffic light, speeding through a red light in the freezing rain. I didn't realize that I would be arrested for dangerous driving causing death, because of the weather that night. I didn't realize I would have to take a deal so I would only get a four-year sentence instead of the maximum of fourteen."

I stare at Will, incredulous.

"You really expect me to believe this?" Catalina says.

"Think about it! You said you got the highlights from Officer Rodriguez. Didn't he tell you that I didn't have a scratch on me?"

Doubt creeps into Catalina's expression. "He did say that."

"Not a single scratch. Not even from the air bags deploying. Doesn't that seem strange? The police didn't notice, either, because they were incompetent or because they just didn't care." Will is slightly out of breath, and his blue eyes search Catalina's face.

My stomach churns. I'm sure it's possible that he could have walked away unscathed while his passenger died. Especially if Jay's girlfriend hadn't been wearing a seat belt. This isn't concrete proof of anything.

Catalina studies Will, her expression inscrutable. I know that look. I used to joke that she's like a walking lie detector. She always seems to be able to tell when someone's lying to her. She stares at him for what feels like an eternity. Will shifts his weight from one foot to the other. Desperation is etched on his features. Catalina finally speaks.

"You were protecting your brother?"

"Yes, I was," Will says quickly, the words tumbling over each other in his rush to speak them. "And what did I get in return? Four years in prison. A family that all but disowned me. I get out of prison, and my brother wants nothing to do with me because I remind him of that night. I couldn't get a job because I was an ex-con. Jay gave me money, but . . ." He hesitates, then the rest spills out. "I had a problem with gambling and drinking. I blew through the money too fast. I made bad investments. I found out later that Jay hadn't given me the cash out of the kindness of his heart. It was hush money." Will spits out the last few words.

My heart pounds in my chest. He's lying. He has to be. Jay hated his brother, and now I know why. Will killed Jay's girlfriend. He had to have. Though, a thought niggles in the back of my mind. Why hadn't Jay ever mentioned her to me? Why hadn't he told me about Will's incarceration? He didn't mention either, not once in our time together. Had it been because he was hiding something?

Catalina places a hand on Will's arm. He stares down at it for a few moments.

"I believe you're telling the truth," she says in a low voice. She pauses before adding, "Jay was lucky to have you for a brother."

Will finally looks up at her, pain ingrained in his crystal blue eyes. "He didn't think so."

"Well, I know so." She doesn't remove her hand.

Will still doesn't look convinced.

"And what you're doing now, trying to find his killer, find his wife's killer, that's much more than any sibling could ask for. Heck, if I were murdered, Rosa would probably cry for a week, get a massage, then move on. Finding justice for me probably wouldn't ever cross her mind."

Will produces a small smile. "You have a sister?"

Catalina nods. She thinks for a moment. "For what it's worth, I think what you did was very brave. Illegal—and stupid. But brave."

I've always thought that Catalina was the best judge of character. In freshman year, it was Catalina who warned me that my boyfriend Brady was no good, and he cheated on me with a girl on the track team only a week later. Catalina was the one who told me to give the seemingly standoffish Cindy a chance when we met in sophomore year, and she quickly became one of my closest friends. Catalina even warned me that she'd thought my boss was creepy, and he—I shake my head, forcing my thoughts back to the present. How could she be so wrong about Will?

She has to be wrong.

Will and Catalina are standing very close to one another, which Will only now seems to notice. He glances down at her lips.

"You do realize you just confessed all this to a cop?" she says, inching forward.

Will looks at her in surprise.

"I'm afraid I'm going to have to take you down to the precinct. I can get you on a whole slew of charges. Aiding and abetting a criminal. Perjury."

"Are you going to cuff me?"

Catalina smiles slowly. "I'm thinking about it."

Will grins wickedly and leans in for a kiss.

I want to leave, but I can't look away. I want the elevator to summon me, but for once, it's dormant. I want to scream, but no one will hear me.

44

Jay once told me once that he was different when he was younger. He was wilder, less disciplined. But he left that life behind when he moved to Ontario for university. He told me he made mistakes and did things he wasn't proud of, and while I pushed him to elaborate, I understood when he wasn't able to tell me more. I knew he would find the words to tell me when he was ready, but he never had the chance. Could this be the mistake he was referring to?

I shake my head. I have to consider the source. A former drug addict who just might be taking up where he left off. I think of the painkillers Will has been taking. Does he have a prescription? If he had bought them on the black market, they wouldn't be in a prescription pill bottle, would they? Can I believe anything that comes out of that junkie's mouth?

I return to my familiar breathing technique to center my focus and calm me. I don't believe a word that Will has said. I can't. But why does Catalina? She should be a better judge of character than that. I can't stop the niggling feeling at the back of my mind. Will's story does explain a few things. It explains why Jay never told me the circumstances surrounding his falling out with his brother. It would explain why Jay was always overly nervous on the roads when there was heavy rainfall. Considering how my parents died, I was always grateful that he was a careful driver.

I need answers, but I have no way of getting them. I can't ask Jay about that night. I can't ask him why he never told me about his brother and his dead girlfriend. I'll never have the chance to ask him. Jay loved me, and I have to believe that he would have told me the truth when the time was right.

No, I don't believe a word of what Will said. Jay isn't responsible for what happened that night, Will is. I believe this with all my heart. But why do I have this knot in the pit of my stomach?

Rebecca anxiously hovers outside her son's bedroom door. I slip past her into Clark's bedroom. The lights are off, and Clark is hidden under a bundle of blankets on the bed. The black drapes are pulled tightly shut. Not even a sliver of sunshine dares to trespass into this sickroom.

According to his parents, who speak in hushed tones in the hall, Clark hasn't been feeling well the last two days. He was fine immediately after the ritual, but quickly fell ill soon after.

Clark is no longer the same raging lunatic. He lies in bed, his eyes open, staring vacantly up at the ceiling. Despite the lack of makeup, his face is deathly white and coated in a fine sheen of perspiration. His damp hair clings to his forehead. He shivers incessantly. I know his illness is genuine and not made up to avoid school because he allowed his mother to come into the room to bring him soup and crackers.

I scan the room, which is much tidier than when I was last in it. Rebecca must have straightened up. Clark's torn sketches are stacked neatly on the desk. His books are placed alphabetically on the shelf.

I'm about to leave when I notice a bizarre smell. I pause and sniff the air gently. It's something rancid veiled in a sickly sweet scent of apples. I glance back at Clark, but he remains immobile. His eyes are closed now, like he's finally resting. I cannot get out of there fast enough.

45

Sometimes, when I need to think, when I need to escape, I visit the German's apartment. It's cold and sleek, and there's something about its quiet tranquility that allows me to collect my thoughts. I feel at peace. Of course, that's when the proprietor isn't there. The German is anything but calm and soothing, with his guttural yells and foreign fury. Fortunately, he's usually gone, likely at work, yelling at his underlings in person.

I'm in his apartment, basking in silence when I feel the strangest tugging sensation. I wait for the inevitable summons of the elevator, but it never comes. The sensation fades. I look around and see that I'm still standing in the middle of the German's living room. It pulls again, stronger this time. I leave the apartment and enter my elevator. It doesn't move. It wasn't called to another floor.

Again, something invisible, yet powerful, pulls at me. I grit my teeth and fight it with all my strength. I somehow manage to remain firmly planted in my elevator. It feels different from when my elevator moves but oddly similar. When my death spot shifts, it feels as though I am being sucked back to it. This, on the other hand, feels as though the world around me is disappearing, and I have to do my best not to tumble into an empty abyss.

The invisible force is persistent, and I nearly lose my hold on this reality. I have nothing to grab on to, nothing to anchor myself here, nothing but sheer will and the desire to survive. But I am not strong enough. Darkness engulfs me.

I open my eyes to near blackness. Before me, Alexei sits at his small oval table. The room is lit only by a single candle which reveals the dark letters of the Ouija board. Alexei stares at it fixedly. There is no one else in the room but him.

He must have summoned me away from the prison of my elevator. Is this my chance for escape? Am I finally free from the confines of the invisible barrier? I attempt to move away from the table, but I am transfixed by the sight of the flame and the letters on the Ouija board. My legs become leaden. I cannot move. I suppose it doesn't matter. If I could leave the building— leave my prison—where would I even go?

Alexei's pale blue eyes lift from the board and penetrate through my bones. He is looking through me, not at me, but I know he knows I'm here.

I see that he has forgone the pendulum which he started with last time, and instead, he has gotten straight to business. I glance around. I'm comforted to discover that the Shadow Man is not in sight. But the walls are so dark, the shadows are so thick, I might not see him even if he were two feet away from me.

"Are you Rachel?" Alexei asks in a voice that's surprisingly uninhibited by the journey across the veil.

I shift the pointer toward *Yes*. It's easier now than during the first séance. I must be getting stronger. But I still cannot control my elevator.

It must be because I am invited here or because the spirit board has a magic of its own.

Alexei sucks in a breath, but other than that, he doesn't move. "Did you send me to apartment 407 last time?"

Yes.

"Were you spelling out help?"

Yes. Could his questions be any more indirect? I don't know how much time we have together, before the Shadow Man comes, and the suspense is killing me. Pun intended.

Alexei leans back slightly. He seems to come to an internal decision, and he leans forward once again. "Is Melody dead?"

I hesitate, then slide the pointer to the point in between *Yes* and *No*. *Maybe*, I think.

"You are unsure." He understands my meaning. "Have you seen her?"

No.

Alexei seems to become frustrated with these one word answers. Well, welcome to the club. I'm just glad to be heard.

"Did Oliver hurt her?"

Yes. I slide the pointer so quickly it nearly loses contact with Alexei's extended fingers.

"Do you think Oliver killed her?"

Again, I hesitate. *Yes*. I answer.

Alexei's jaw clenches, and he doesn't ask another question immediately. Lost in thought, he stares at the spirit board with a look of absolute determination etched across his face.

"Are you . . . trapped in this building?"

I suppose that's a diplomatic way of asking if I'm haunting it. I slide the pointer back to *Yes*.

"Who killed you?" he asks. I don't answer. He needs to ask simple, yes or no questions. My energy is already draining from communicating with the spirit board. I don't want to waste strength spelling out "I have no fucking clue".

Alexei intuits the reason for my lack of a response. "Do you know who killed you?"

No.

The police think it's Luke, but I know better. But who could it have been? Catalina is already looking into Copeland, my prime suspect. There's no rationale in pointing Alexei in that direction. There isn't much he can do about it. Then I remember.

I turn my attention toward the Ouija board. This is going to be more complex than a simple yes or no answer.

"E . . . L . . . I . . . A . . . S" Alexei reads aloud as I struggle to push the pointer from letter to letter.

"Elias Strickland? The concierge?" he asks.

Yes.

"Did Elias kill you?" he asks.

I consider the question. All I know is that he has secrets, and he has my diary. I slide the pointer to the space in between *Yes* and *No*.

Maybe.

Alexei looks stunned. He gives a curt nod.

"*Beware the darkness that lurks in shadows,*" Alexei says.

What? I look down at the Ouija board, unsure of how to respond.

Alexei suddenly seems to realize that he doesn't need to use his usual, vaguely ominous performance language with me. I'm already a believer.

"There is a . . . an entity that resides in this building. I'm sure you've encountered it."

I slide the pointer to *Yes*.

Again Alexei seems lost in thought. I give the pointer an impatient wiggle.

Alexei seems to get my message loud and clear. He smiles grimly. "The man who walks in shadow is not of this world. He was never human. He was *created* by humans."

A chill tickles the back of my neck.

"He is a manifestation of all the dark urges, the wicked desires and cruel impulses of those who inhabit this building. He thrives on the pain, the fear, the hate, the evil that lives in every one of us. Those emotions strengthen him, fortify his form, giving him essence . . . and power."

I absorb these haunting words. With all the events I've observed these last few weeks, I can understand why the Shadow Man has such strength. There is no end to the pain, the fear, the hate, or even the evil I've witnessed within these walls.

"When he gains enough power, he acquires the ability to possess those with the darkest compulsions. That is what happened during the last séance I held here. Mr. Hammstein must have harbored ill will toward his sister-in-law, and the Shadow compelled him to act upon it. You were here. You saw what happened."

Again, I slide the pointer to *Yes*.

"I know he can do that to the living—but I do not know what influence he holds over the dead."

There is a sudden chill in the air. I rub my arms against my body, which of course does nothing to warm me. Alexei's words ring through my head. The Shadow Man isn't just dangerous to the living. He's dangerous to me. I must avoid him at all costs.

Alexei doesn't say anything else. Instead, he stares thought-fully down at the Ouija board. The light of the flame dances on the sharp edges of his face, creating an almost demonic effect. Shivering, I pry my eyes away.

An inky silhouette stands beside me. I attempt to jolt backward, but the board still has its hold on me. I look to Alexei for help, but his eyes remain glued to the spirit board, lost in deep contemplation, utterly unaware that his words may have summoned the very monster of which he spoke.

Cowering, I gaze up at the Shadow Man as he towers above me. Even at this proximity, he appears to be nothing more than shadow. Featureless, a smooth, black void. Yet, somehow, I know he is watching me. Studying me. Sizing me up.

In a single, fluid movement he cocks his head toward the table. Lightning quick, the pointer is wrenched from Alexei's fingertips, and it flashes across the Ouija board, barely hesitating on each letter before moving on to the next.

Hello Kaela.

The Shadow Man knows my name. My *real* name.

Realization dawns on me. Not only has the Shadow Man been gorging on the horrors I have witnessed since my death, but when I was alive, I myself must have been a font of pain and fear. The Shadow Man had been siphoning those emotions from me over the last two years, exacerbating my fears, intensifying my anxiety and paranoia. And, in turn, I'd been adding fuel to his fire.

But what does he want with me now that I am dead? Does he also feed off the hatred, the anxiety, and the fear of the souls trapped in this building? Is there no reprieve?

He reaches toward me, obsidian fingers extended. Ice-hot tendrils emanate from him, snaking around my immobile body, caressing my skin and making me tremble. He moves closer. Closer.

"I banish you, spirit!" comes Alexei's thunderous roar.

I am jolted back into the elevator. I am alone, but I still cannot shake the cold that has cut deep into my soul.

46

The Man in Tweed wears black today. He enters the lobby with a black-clad Caroline clinging to his arm. His face is stoic, hers is drawn. Dried tears line her cheeks.

As they ride the elevator up, John regularly darts glances down at Caroline, but her eyes remain downcast. I follow them into his apartment. Several books are stacked neatly on the coffee table. There's a blanket draped on the arm of the couch. The condo is still stark, but it looks lived in, which it hadn't before Caroline first came over.

Caroline disentwines from him and wanders toward the window. The sun shines bright, striking a sharp contrast with her dark clothes and pale cheeks.

John moves toward her and places a reassuring hand on her shoulder. "We didn't have a choice."

She looks up at him through bleary eyes. "Didn't we?"

John looks uneasy.

"We could have just run away together."

John shakes his head. "That wasn't an option. Your stepmother would have hired people to track you down. She wanted that money. We would have had to spend the rest of our lives looking over our shoulders. That was not an option."

"But how am I any better than her? Now I get her inheritance, and it's like I planned it that way all along!"

Silent, John watches her.

"I don't want the money, I don't want any of it. I just want things to go back the way they were."

"That's not an option either," he says quietly.

Caroline studies the floor. The guilt of her stepmother's death—of what they must have done—has taken a physical toll on her. She looks thinner, paler, almost gaunt. I feel a twinge of sympathy. Just a twinge. After all, she condoned the murder of her own stepmother. Remorse won't change that.

I look to John. Regret is etched into his entire demeanor. Caroline may not be quite innocent of this, but John is one hundred percent guilty. I watch him as he watches Caroline. Does he truly feel guilt, remorse? I doubt he could, given his profession. If he was capable of ordinary human feelings, he wouldn't be able to do his job. But the way he looks at Caroline makes me think I might be wrong.

He suddenly grabs her arms. "We can still run away. We can take the money and leave this place. Start somewhere else. Build new identities. We can be whoever we want to be."

A flicker of hope crosses her face, but she shakes her head. "I don't want the money. I can't take the money."

John shrugs. "So, we'll donate it all to charity. We can run away together and build new lives from scratch. I've done it before. We don't need money to do that."

Caroline meets his unwavering gaze. She finally allows herself to smile, then she kisses him.

◌◌◌

"No, go away," Clark mumbles. The thermometer clacks against his bottom teeth.

Sylvie shushes him. She removes the thermometer and squints in the dim light to check its reading.

"He doesn't have a fever either," she tells Rebecca, who hovers in the doorway with her husband.

"You don't have any idea what's wrong with him, do you?" Charles says sharply.

Sylvie's eyes narrow. "I am a cardiac surgeon. Not a pediatrician. I told you to take him to the hospital." Her cold eyes survey the frail form that lies huddled before her.

Clark has gotten worse. He's the ghost of his former self. His pallid skin is gaunt and brittle, his lips are dried and cracking, oozing puss and blood. But his eyes are the worst—blank and cloudy. He told his mother that he can't see anything, not even light. Despite this, his parents keep the room cloaked in darkness, as if they fear that the sunshine will turn him to ash.

Sylvie's tone turns gentle but firm. "You need to take him to the hospital. They can run tests for specific pathogens. I can't test for anything off-site."

"Pathogens? Like a virus?" Rebecca's eyes widen.

Sylvie tells them that his illness isn't like anything she's ever encountered before. No rash, no fever, which rules out most common illnesses. She isn't even sure that this is something he caught. It could even be a slow acting disease that has been brewing beneath the surface for months or years. But again, she reminds them that she isn't a pediatrician.

This isn't her specialty.

I can't help but wonder if this illness was caused by the ritual. The timing can't be a coincidence. During the ceremony, he smeared the blood of an innocent on his eyes, ears, and lips, and now he is blind, his ears are producing a sickly yellow crust, and his lips are cracking. Maybe the blood was contaminated. I try to tell the family, but they can't hear me, and Clark lost his ability to see me when he washed away the last remnants of blood that caked under his eyelids.

Sylvie spends an hour examining Clark and speaking with the Yus before finally convincing them to take their son to the hospital. Clark is despondent as his father carefully unwraps him from his cocoon of blankets, lifting him like he is made of glass and one wrong move might cause him to shatter. He carries his son's listless body to the door.

At the threshold, Clark jerks to awareness. He shrieks, shrill, sharp noises that cut through the afterlife with shocking clarity. His entire body convulses, and his arms and legs thrash against his father, knocking himself free.

He falls to the ground with a sickening thump. He ceases his squealing and scrambles back to his bed on all fours before burrowing under the blankets like a savage rodent. Charles leans against the doorway, breathing heavily, blood welling in the deep scratch on his cheek. Frozen in fear, Rebecca gapes at her son. Sylvie checks her watch, then turns to leave.

Sylvie is pensive as we ride the elevator up to her apartment. I would say that I'm perturbed by her lack of concern for young Clark's well-being, but I'm growing accustomed to the lack of empathy that resonates among many of the residents of this building.

I go ahead of her and enter the apartment. A strangled, inhuman noise greets me. Etienne is hovering in the hall, outside the third bedroom. I rush to him. He isn't the one making the sound, but he can hear it too. His ear is pressed against the locked door, his eyes squeezed shut.

I cross through the door and into the bedroom, unimpeded by any deadbolt. Raymond is in the bed, but rather than lying immobile, he is thrashing his arms and choking on the intubation tube.

Sylvie tears into the room soon after I arrive. Eyes hard and calculating, she approaches the cabinet and loads a syringe with a crystal white fluid. She grabs his arm and wrenches it back to the bed, expertly injecting the sedative.

Etienne stands in the doorway, his eyes wide. His father catches his eye, drool and bile dribbling down his chin as his thrashes begin to weaken. He looks up at his wife, a questioning, pained expression on his face, before his eyelids flutter and eventually shut.

Sylvie leans against the cabinet, panting from the exertion. Despite Raymond's muscle atrophy, he is still strong enough to leave a few bruises on his wife's slight arms. She catches her breath, then returns the syringe to the tray, sealing the cabinet tightly behind her. She turns to Etienne, who trembles in the doorway.

She stares at him silently for a moment. What is she going to say? What possible explanation could she have for what she's doing to his father?

The silence stretches before Etienne finally breaks it.

"What are you doing to *Papa*?"

Sylvie's demeanor changes. She's suddenly frantic, desperate even. She steps toward her son. "*Papa* wanted to leave and take you away with him. I couldn't let that happen. You understand that, don't you?"

Etienne's eyes dart back and forth from his mother to his incapacitated father. He doesn't respond.

"You understand, don't you? He needed to be punished."

"When will his punishment be over?" Etienne asks.

"When I say it is."

"But—"

"Are you questioning my judgment?" Sylvie's previous desperation is replaced with a sudden stillness.

Etienne gulps and shakes his head quickly.

"No dinner for you tonight," she says. "Go to the Quiet Room."

Etienne blanches, but nods. He turns to leave. I follow him as he crosses the hall, approaching a door I hadn't noticed before. Sylvie remains in the third bedroom with her husband.

Etienne raises his hand to open the door, but he hesitates. He turns and looks up at me, gazing straight into my soul.

"Please help *Papa*."

He can see me. He can *see* me.

"I—I will."

Satisfied with my answer, my promise, he turns, and I am drawn away before I can see what horrors lie beyond that closed door.

47

pace the length of the Hylands' living room. Roger is in the bedroom, flipping through his and Sabryna's wedding photo album. It's one of those books that are professionally developed by the photographer, with inspirational, romantic quotes on alternating pages. But it's not the album that catches my attention. It's the tears streaking Roger's stubbled face. He has spent more time at home the last three days than he did in the weeks since I died.

I know he hasn't seen his lover. He hasn't gone to work. He's barely left the apartment. It's a shame that it took Sabryna's death—her suicide—for him to realize how much he truly cared.

I haven't seen Sabryna since her death, and I have to assume that she is either tied to her death spot on the pavement or she moved on shortly after her suicide. I hope it's the latter. I wouldn't wish this fate on my worst enemy. But I can't think about that right now. I'm plagued by Etienne's haunting plea for help. I couldn't help Melody, and I couldn't help Sabryna, but I *have* to help Etienne. I need to save him and his father, but I'm not sure how. I still can't interact with any physical objects on the other side, no matter how hard I try.

The Ouija board was the only exception to this rule, but of course, Alexei keeps it locked away in his onyx chest when he isn't using it.

I can't communicate with Raymond. I think it may be because a fragile thread is still holding his soul to his body when he's in a coma, and that makes him unable to communicate with either side. If I could get Raymond's soul back into his body, would he awaken? Of course not, because he would still be in an induced coma. The drugs would still be pumping through his veins, clouding his mind and body. There has to be *something* I can do.

I *can* communicate with Etienne, which is more than I had been able to do before. Maybe I can help him, like I helped callers on the crisis hotline. I can give him guidance and emotional support and provide him with the tools he needs to survive. But Sylvie has Etienne so afraid, so diffident and well-behaved. Will he be able to stand up to her?

There's a loud rap at the front door. At first, Roger doesn't seem to notice it, but it grows louder, more persistent. He finally puts down the photo album and goes to answer it. Detective Cherry towers in the doorway, flanked by two uniformed officers.

"Roger Hyland, you're under arrest for the murder of Sabryna Hyland." Detective Cherry gestures to the officer on his right, who takes out a set of handcuffs.

"You have the right to remain silent. Anything you say can and will be used against you in a court of law . . ."

"This is ridiculous!" Roger says. "I didn't kill her!"

Detective Cherry ignores his protests and leads him from the apartment. I follow as they board my elevator.

"I didn't kill her," Roger repeats as we begin our descent to the lobby. The two officers exchange incredulous looks. Detective Cherry remains apathetic.

"I'm a lawyer!" Roger tries a different tactic. "This is police misconduct. I will sue your asses—"

"I'd watch what you say, Mr. Hyland." The detective's tone is a warning.

Roger opens his mouth, then closes it again. He seems to think better of provoking the police.

They step off the elevator in strained silence. Roger is resolute.

A chill fills the lobby, creeping up my spine and tickling the hairs on the back of my neck.

Sabryna appears behind me. She watches as Roger is led from the building. I stare at her.

Sabryna notices me for the first time.

"Hello Rachel," she says in a pleasant voice.

I open and close my mouth a few times before finding the right words. "Sabryna, I'm so sorry. I wish I could have done something to help, but I couldn't. I couldn't communicate with you at all—"

Sabryna raises an elegant hand to silence me. "There's nothing you could have done." She seems to suddenly understand the implication of my words. "Have you been watching me since your death?"

"You and other residents." I shrug. "I've been tied to the elevator and its adjacent apartments."

Sabryna nods as if this makes perfect sense, even though I had a hard time grasping the concept at first.

"Your husband . . . I'm so sorry, Sabryna."

"For what?" Sabryna looks genuinely confused.

"Your husband was just arrested for your murder," I say gently. She witnessed it, but I'm not sure if it has registered yet. I'm not sure she truly understands what's happening around her. She wasn't exactly stable when she was alive, and death can be a shocking life experience, especially when it's your own.

"I know," Sabryna says. She gazes off toward the door, where her husband stood moments ago. "That's how I planned it."

I'm sure I heard her wrong. "Excuse me? What do you mean?"

Sabryna throws me a serene smile. "They say that the best revenge is a life well lived. I say it's a life well ended."

A new type of chill creeps down my spine. She planned this? She framed her husband for her own death?

I shake my head. "It won't work. The police will figure it out."

Sabryna gives me another serene smile. "Oh, Rachel, no they won't. I had his DNA under my fingernails, fresh bruises on my back from him pushing me. I wrote a letter to a trusted friend, saying that I feared my husband would kill me. I invited that poor boy Will over, and Roger punched him, demonstrating he's prone to violence. All that is more than enough to send him to prison for life."

I'm speechless.

Sabryna's head jerks to the side. She stares at something down the corridor.

"Do you see that light?" she murmurs, awe tingeing her tone.

I follow her gaze, but I see nothing there.

Without another glance in my direction, she floats down the hall and fades into the shadows.

48

"T he case is closed," Catalina tells Will the following morning. She's clearly exhausted, only having gotten in during
the pre-dawn hours. She caught a few hours of sleep
before rousing a groggy Will, who slept on the couch, his long
limbs spilling onto the floor.

Will sits up abruptly, eyes still unfocused and sleepy before
he gets his first cup of coffee. "What?"

"Luke confessed."

The floor nearly falls out from under me.

"He *confessed*?" Will asks.

The police must have coerced a confession out of him. It will
never hold up in court. It can't.

Will trails after Catalina into my office, where she has booted up her laptop. She produces a flash drive from her back pocket and slides it into the laptop's USB port.

A video plays on the screen. It's a color video, but the image seems monotonous. It lacks vitality. Luke sits at the end of a steel table. A large mirror is mounted on the wall behind him, reflecting the back of his head and his slumped shoulders. Catalina skips ahead through the film. The video is long, filmed over the course of several hours. No wonder he confessed. He was likely exhausted and hungry, and it looks like his lawyer wasn't present.

I lean closer, studying his face on the grainy screen. He has massive purple circles under his eyes, which are dull, lacking their usual spark of wit and charm. What did they do to him?

"Yes, I killed her." Luke sounds remote. My stomach drops.

"Why did you kill her?" A voice asks from off camera.

"It was an accident."

"Slitting a woman's throat is hardly an accident."

"I just wanted to scare her. Make her realize that she needed me. But when I had the knife in my hands, I . . . couldn't stop."

I don't move. I stare at the screen, at Luke, at my friend. This isn't possible.

"Why don't you take me through that night? Step by step. Tell me everything that happened."

"Rachel and I are good friends. Best friends. We have been ever since she joined the crisis hotline. When she first started, we spent a lot of time together. We had a connection. I knew she had a past, and I thought that eventually she would open up to me about it. She wore a wedding ring, but there was no husband. She was passionate about volunteering for the crisis hotline, so I thought that maybe he'd been abusive. That she'd fled from him. I thought time would heal her, that being there for her when she needed me would help her to move on."

Luke sighs. "But she didn't get better. She was getting worse. She stopped leaving her apartment building altogether. One night, we were watching movies in her apartment, and I misread her signals. I tried to kiss her. She never invited me back again. She didn't give me a chance to explain. I never had the chance to tell her I love her. And she needs me. She needs me, but she just doesn't realize it." Luke is insistent, hysteria bubbling through the surface.

My heart clenches at his use of the present tense.

The voice is unaffected by his outburst. "Tell us about that night."

Luke takes a deep breath. "Well, Rachel was working the shift from eight to midnight. I called her around seven thirty, but she didn't answer. She used to always answer my calls, no matter what time of day or night, but she was only answering one out of every three." Luke licks his lips, which are chapped and bleeding. "So, I blocked my number and made a call to the hotline. It was just to spook her. She had no one else, and I knew she would turn to me. She needed me. She trusted me."

I stiffen at his words. I *had* turned to him. I *had* trusted him.

"You see, Rachel had a secret past, one that she wouldn't even open up to me about. One time, when I was at her place, she fell asleep on the couch during a movie. I went into her office to check my email on her laptop. I found her diary. From before. She'd written all about the horrible things that happened to her. So, that night when I called, I used her real name, so she'd fear the worst. Honestly, I don't even remember exactly what I said anymore. All that matters is it didn't work. She didn't invite me over to protect her. So, I knew I had to step up my game." Luke trails off, staring into the distance, past the camera.

"Then what?" the voice prompts.

Luke jolts, as if torn out of a reverie. "I went to her building. I had swiped her access card the last time I visited her. She never left her apartment, so I don't think she ever noticed it was missing. I took it in case she needed me or there was an emergency. I didn't think I would have to use it."

"How did you get past security?"

"The video cameras in the garage have spotty coverage. It was easy to get in without being spotted by any of them. I cut the power to the building. I knew I had only a few minutes before the backup generators kicked in. I turned the camera in the ground-level garage ever so slightly so that I could sneak back out, unseen. Then I slipped down the stairwell to wait for Rachel, since I knew she would be going down to the fitness center. Because she'd told me on the phone that she was going to work out to get rid of her nervous energy after that scary call." Luke pauses, frowning, as if he can't believe what happened next.

"I even wore a ski mask, so she wouldn't recognize me. Then the elevator door opened. I saw her standing there with her back to me. I just wanted to scare her so she'd run into my arms later. But when I grabbed her, she fought back. She was stronger than I thought she would be. I took out my knife—just to show it to her, just to scare her—but then I saw her bag. I shouldn't have called her. I shouldn't have used her real name. I knew she was a runner, and it all became clear to me. She wasn't going to the fitness center. She was leaving. Leaving Toronto. Leaving *me*."

His voice breaks.

He swallows. "I couldn't think straight. I was so upset. Then a darkness crept inside me. Took control. I just couldn't help myself."

Luke trails off, staring at something beyond the range of the camera.

"We need you to say it," the disembodied voice says.

Luke's voice is flat, emotionless. "I held the knife, and the glint of metal caught my attention. I saw my eyes in its reflection. I wanted to, no, I needed to know what it felt like to be used. How its sharpened blade would slide through smooth, soft flesh."

"That's enough." The voice finally sounds rattled.

"But don't you need me to say it?" Luke asks. He no longer looks impassive, defeated. He looks angry—though, if it's at himself or the police officers, I'm not certain. "I took the knife. I held her against me with my left hand and cut her throat with the blade. It slid through her flesh without resistance, like wading through warm water. It didn't take much effort to slice her open ear to ear. She didn't even have the chance to scream. The walls were painted red within moments, a geyser of scarlet erupting from—"

Catalina slams the laptop shut.

Luke admitted to everything. He isn't innocent. He wasn't framed. He *killed* me. A heavy weight stomps on my chest, and I immediately recognize the signs of a panic attack. I take a few steps back, struggling to calm down. I squeeze my eyes shut, trying to be rid of the sight, but Luke's image is burned into my retinas. The pressure on my chest grows heavier, unbearable, and I plunge into darkness.

49

wake in the elevator. My steel tomb. The air is stock-still and deathly silent. The elevator does not move but stays dormant, waiting for the call of the living to awaken it. The digital display tells me that I am no longer on the seventh floor but on the ninth. How did I come to be here?

Still suffering from the aching remnants of my panic attack, I tentatively step off the elevator into the corridor. No one is in sight. Whoever called the elevator here did so at least a few minutes ago. This means I must have lost at least that much time of consciousness.

I allow myself to drift into the apartment across the hall. Approaching the window, I am greeted by an indigo sky. The sun has long disappeared and was eagerly replaced by a crescent moon.

Where did the day go? When I was alive I would sometimes lose consciousness to my panic attacks, and an unconscious woman is a vulnerable woman. No matter what happened, I would always try to remember to keep breathing, so I wouldn't be put at greater risk. But now that I'm dead, I don't need to breathe. So what happened?

I'm interrupted from my frenzied thoughts by the sound of a gentle click. I spin around and see the front door slide open slowly, revealing a dark silhouette in the doorway. It slips in, shutting the door behind it.

A man stands in the foyer, head cocked to the side, listening to the silence. He finally steps into the living room, where the moon brings his identity to light. Elias.

I don't even feel shocked at this revelation. Too much has happened in too short a time, and nothing can surprise me anymore. Numbness has sunk deep into my bones. It is much more tolerable than the sharp pain of betrayal. I push aside these thoughts. I have to. The only way I have survived these last two years is by forgetting. Forgetting Jay. Forgetting the horrors of the weeks leading up to his death. And now, I must forget my own death if I am to survive.

Elias slinks past me, down the hallway. I glance around. This apartment belongs to Samira Narang, another resident I've only gotten to know in death. The apartment is tastefully decorated. There are no extravagant flourishes, no unnecessary expenditures so frequently spotted in this building. I haven't spent much time watching Samira. In her mid-twenties, she typically spends her days at work and her nights out with friends.

The few evenings she's at home she spends sipping wine and reading Jane Austen novels while curled up on her sofa. She's one of the few normal people in this building, yet she's rarely around for me to benefit from her sanity.

Elias pauses at the end of the hall, just outside the master bedroom. He slides the door open a crack and slithers through the gap without the slightest sound. Samira sleeps nestled deep under the covers of her four-poster bed. She looks serene with her long lashes fanning her face and her arms hugging a soft pink pillow to her chest. She is beautiful, with smooth skin and long, silky black hair. Elias slips closer, watching her sleep.

He takes out his phone and snaps a few pictures of her. I frown. Why is he investigating her as he did the Man in Tweed? Who is this woman, and why is Elias so interested in her?

I expect him to leave now that he sees that Samira isn't out on the town but at home, asleep. He cannot investigate anything with her there. What if she wakes up? But he stays at the foot of the bed, watching her as her chest rises and falls.

A trickle of uncertainty filters through my numbness. What is he doing?

He stands like this, for one heartbeat, then ten. Finally, he moves. He doesn't head for the door, like I thought he would. Instead, he turns toward her dresser. He slides the top drawer open. A gloved hand slips inside, feeling around before pulling something out. There is a flash of purple lace before he tucks it into his pocket. A knot twists in my stomach.

Elias starts to close the drawer but seems to decide against it. A strange expression on his face, he leaves it open. Won't Samira notice that in the morning? Unless that's his intent. For her to notice something off in her apartment.

After one last prolonged stare at Samira, Elias leaves the apartment, carefully locking the front door behind him.

I almost don't notice, but someone ducks into the stairwell as Elias approaches the elevator bay. Someone may have seen Elias. Someone may have seen what he was doing. But why didn't they stay? Why didn't they confront him? I push forward to investigate, remembering too late that the stairwell is out of my range.

I'm drawn back to Elias as he boards my elevator and returns to his own living quarters. He goes straight to the second bedroom which I have yet to explore. My last trip was cut short when I discovered my diary in his bedroom.

I stop dead in my tracks, the realization sinking in. My diary. He wasn't investigating my death. I'd been a fool. He is just a voyeur who enjoys sneaking into apartments and touching things, taking things that don't belong to him. I shudder as I think back to my own life. Since I rarely left my own apartment, the only way he could have gotten his hands on my diary would have been when I was asleep. I imagine him watching me, taking pictures of me as I slept, like he did just now with Samira.

I gather my strength and follow him into the second bedroom. Nothing could have prepared me for this. Elias has wallpapered the room with photographs. A table rests against the wall, and it's covered with various tchotchkes and clothes. Are these things that Elias stole from the female residents? Elias has a key to every apartment in the building in case of fire or flooding or some other kind of emergency. I was reluctant to give him a key at first, but it is the law. I step toward the wall and peer at the photographs. Many of the pictures are of residents as they sleep, but some are candid pictures, snapshots taken in the lobby or library. None of the subjects seem to be aware of the camera. None of them pose or acknowledge its presence. I see several photographs of Sabryna, in bed, arm stretched out to the empty place beside her. Those lonely nights when Roger was with his lover, it seems that Sabryna wasn't as alone as she had thought. There are several pictures of Melody in the library, the red-haired woman and the starchy woman, both I've seen around the building several times. There are also pictures of me. Many more than I had feared. They are mostly of me sleeping, which confirms my darkest suspicions. Even when I thought I was safe, I wasn't.

I wait for the crushing weight to return to my lungs, for the hyperventilation and accompanying fear and dread, but it doesn't come. I may have relied on Elias for my safety, but I never truly trusted him. This betrayal doesn't cut as deep as Luke's. Instead of the crushing weight I'd felt when learning of Luke's dark side, I feel a new sensation. It burns me from the inside out. Rage.

Elias leaves the room and returns with my journal. He perches on the chair nearest to his shrine and opens my diary to a page in the middle. A small smile forms as his eyes dart across the page. He is engrossed by the words that I wrote at the worst time of my life.

The rage I feel is all too real now. It burns through the numbness, the detachment, and sets a white-hot fire to my incorporeal body. Elias sits there, calmly reading my innermost thoughts and emotions, totally indifferent to the fact that I am dead. He is totally unaware that he's invading the privacy of a ghost. I smile. He won't be unaware for much longer.

My vision darkens around me. It's similar to a panic attack, but this time, I don't fight it. I embrace it. Rage consumes my heart. Its scope spreads like wildfire. Flames trail down my limbs and extend beyond. I cannot contain it any longer.

I open my arms and my fury is set free, leaping and licking toward Elias' hunched form. The pictures on the wall beside him sway, and several fall, floating like dead leaves to a forest floor.

His head snaps up. Visible goosebumps form along his sleeveless arms, and he runs his hands up and down them. Suddenly wary, he glances around the room. He exhales deeply, and his breath condenses. I am disappointed that my flames have turned to ice instead of scalding him, but hopefully, they will chill him to the core.

With this thought, my fire is depleted, leaving me hollow. Elias continues to peer around the dim room, which has already returned to its previous balmy temperature. Disgusted by my weak display of power, I return to my elevator.

50

The following afternoon, I find myself idling on the sixth
floor, so I decide to drop in on the Yus. I expect to find them
hovering over Clark's sickbed or perhaps gone altogether,
having taken him to the hospital as Sylvie had insisted.

I find neither of the above. Clark isn't in bed, but he sits
on the couch, fully dressed in jeans and a T-shirt, watching a
Jeopardy rerun with his parents while nursing a bowl of soup.
He looks much better than before. His hair is neatly combed
and uncharacteristically parted to the side in a straight line.
While he is still gaunt and frail, there is new life in his eyes as
he attempts to provide questions to Alex Trebek's complex
answers. Whatever illness that had plagued him earlier is all

but gone. Not only has he made a remarkable recovery, but he's interacting with his family in a civil manner. Maybe the near-death experience caused a drastic turnaround. Or maybe he's still feeling under the weather and is relying on his parents' care to bring him back to full health.

Either way, I hope that this is a permanent change for Clark. I pray that he doesn't ask Noel for the *Book of Shadows* and that he won't make further attempts to contact the Devil with No Face. I hope that he's learned his lesson, though, I know that might be wishful thinking.

For once, the elevator allows me to stay and witness a family's peaceful gathering. I sit and watch television with Rebecca, Charles, and Clark, imagining that they're my own family. I play pretend that they can see me, and that I belong.

A short while after the show ends, Clark rises and approaches the baby grand piano that stands near the balcony door. I've never seen him play before. His parents look pleasantly surprised.

Clark settles onto the bench, closes his eyes, and begins to play by heart. I move closer to him, entranced. I've never seen him play before, and he's surprisingly good. The song is a slow, haunting melody. His fingers creep across the keys, gradually picking up the pace. The strains of music are achingly familiar, but I cannot place where I've heard them before. Clark smiles as his fingers dance with remarkable agility for a boy who was just on his deathbed. The song begins to staccato.

Now I remember. It's the same music that I sometimes hear trickling through the corridors at night. The song that the Woman with No Past danced to with her imaginary partner. The song that flooded through the basement the night Clark held his ritual. How does Clark know how to play this song? On that note, I am whisked away, the last few bars of the melody echoing through my mind long after I leave.

⁓⟡⟡⟡⟡⟡⟡⟡⁓

"Now what?" Catalina asks Will. That's the million-dollar question. Last night, both Will and Catalina slept like the dead for almost ten hours. I guess now that my killer has been caught, they can finally rest. But why can't I?

My killer has not only been caught, but he has confessed to the crime, thus ensuring a twenty-five years to life sentence in prison. Why am I still here? Shouldn't I have moved on, now that I've found *closure*? I hope my soul isn't waiting until Jay's killer is caught. If so, I'll never move on. I'm hyper-vigilant about finding my door, following that light, but nothing out of the ordinary has appeared to me since last night when I barely frightened Elias. Sabryna managed to move on so effortlessly after her death, and I can't help but envy her. However, I'm fairly certain I don't want to go to the same place she went.

"I'm not sure," Will replies.

Catalina looks up at him casually before returning her attention to the pages before her. They're both sitting in my office, which still has all the notes from my murder investigation strewn about. Notes that are no longer needed . . . now that my killer has been caught. Catalina seems to choose her next words carefully. "Luke killed Kae."

Will glances at her. "I am aware of that."

"What I'm saying is, he didn't know Kae when she was Kaela. He only knew her as Rachel. He didn't know your brother. He couldn't have killed Jay."

Will's face hardens. He leans back in his chair and crosses his arms across his chest. "I am aware of that, too."

"I'm sorry we didn't find his killer."

Will shrugs, seemingly indifferent. "Well, we can't get them all."

"Still . . ."

"What?"

She gestures toward the wall, the boxes of files, and the desk. "It seems like I'm no longer needed here."

Will studies her for a moment. "I wouldn't say that," Will says softly.

Catalina looks at him, and their eyes lock. "What would you say?"

The corner of his lip turns upwards into a crooked half-smile. "I say that your business here isn't over."

In two quick strides, they collide, lips bridging, arms clinging. With a swipe of his arm, Will clears the desk and sits her on it, their lip-lock never breaking. Catalina pulls Will's shirt over his head, ruffling his hair.

I tear out of the room. I wish they had given me some warning signs, so I could have rushed out of there faster. Noises carry out of the office, so I am banished from my own apartment. I stand in the corridor, contemplating what to do.

I go into apartment 707, where Henry Sanford is once again listening to the same old radio show on repeat. Ominous music plays from his record player, filtering through the darkened apartment. A sinister cackle comes from the brass gramophone.

"Who knows what evil lurks in the hearts of men?"

I do.

I know the secrecy, the darkness, the evil everyone harbors inside. What they all keep locked away, behind closed doors.

51

sit in darkness, waiting for the sun to rise, and with it, the residents of this building. I'm back in my old apartment, which looks the same but feels different from this side of the veil. The edges are shadowy and distant, and the place is littered with Will and Catalina's papers and files. They have begun to pack them up in boxes, likely to be placed into storage and never to be viewed again. I can't help but feel resentful. They get to move on with their lives, but I'm trapped here. My only fond memories of the apartment are contaminated with the presence of the man who killed me. Luke is another name I must banish from my mind. Like these files, that name and memories of him will be tucked away forever. I refuse to ever retrieve them.

Catalina pads in barefoot, wearing nothing but one of Will's button-up shirts. She looks around the room, then sighs, collapsing onto the couch. She must be having a hard time sleeping despite the fact that my murder was solved, but she should no longer be plagued with guilt about my death. I wasn't killed by my stalker from years ago. I had unknowingly invited that new horror into my life—a horror that had nothing to do with my life before.

Catalina grimaces and reaches down under the couch cushion. She pulls out a book that was wedged in between the pillows. The gold letter label "Kaela D. Archer" glimmers in the faint light.

How did my diary get back into my apartment? Did Elias return it? I summoned a ghostly wind that terrified him. Did he know that it was done by me? Is that why he returned the book? I snicker. If Elias suspects that the building is haunted, this might make my afterlife marginally less painful.

Catalina opens the book to the first page and begins to read. She is sobbing by the time she reaches the end of the last entry.

"Are you all right?" A voice calls from the hall.

Catalina tucks the book away before Will enters the living room. She nods, quickly wiping away an errant tear.

Will watches her silently for a moment before taking her hand and leading her back into the bedroom.

I'm relieved when the elevator summons me, steering me down to the third floor. I immediately drop down to Alexei's apartment. I'm not sure how far he's progressed in investigating Melody's disappearance. This is the first time I've seen him since he last summoned me. He sits at the kitchen table, phone pressed to his ear.

"Yes, of course. I can be ready to leave by the end of the week." Alexei's pallid cheeks are uncharacteristically pink.

Curious, I step closer, peering over his shoulder at his laptop screen. He's researching flights to Vegas for Thursday. He must have gotten his own show after all.

My chest tightens. Alexei is the only adult in the building I can communicate with. When he leaves, I'll have lost my connection to the other side. I won't be able to communicate at all. It will be like I was never here. Etienne can see me, can hear me, but he's too frightened to talk to me. Too terrified of his mother.

And I don't know how long I have with him before he grows older, loses that touch of innocence, and with it, his ability to sense those on the other side.

Alexei ends his call and struts into the living room. He stops, hesitating, picking something up off the couch. It's the green tunic that he had retrieved from the garbage room.

Melody's shirt.

Tension flashes across his gaunt features before he tosses the shirt aside and stalks into the master bedroom. A realization suddenly strikes me. Alexei is the only person who has noticed Melody's disappearance. He's the only person who *cared* enough to realize that Oliver's story doesn't make sense and that Melody may no longer be alive.

When he leaves, who will continue the search for her? Who will find out if Oliver killed his wife and bring the monster to justice?

Caroline enters the building, pulling a small, brown suitcase on wheels. She brushes past Elias who attempts to intercept her.

My elevator receives her when she presses the button, and she rides up to the fifth floor.

She inserts a key into the lock on the Man in Tweed's apartment door. She doesn't need to turn it, because the door swings open.

She steps into the doorway.

"John?" she calls out.

Silence greets her.

She enters, glancing around. Her entire body tenses. The apartment is nearly empty. The furniture, the books, everything is gone. All that remains is the telescope that rests in its place by the window.

Caroline drifts farther into the room. The walls glisten white. Caroline touches one with a hesitant hand. It comes back with the remnants of not-quite dry paint on her fingertips. All trace of John Smith, the Man in Tweed, is gone.

Her footsteps echo as she wanders from room to room. Her face is drawn. Her hands are clenched into fists.

In the bedroom, where the bed once stood, there is a single sheet of paper.

She unfolds it with trembling fingers.

Her eyes rove across the page. I drift toward her, but I'm hindered by my invisible wall.

The paper crumples between her fingers. She falls to the ground. Silent sobs rack her body.

52

This is the first time I have seen the Woman with No Past venture from her domestic prison. She dons the same faded midnight blue dress as she did weeks ago. She has painted her face in the same broad strokes. Dark slashes cutting across her cheekbones, and the rouge of her lips almost glows in the harsh fluorescent lighting.

She rides the elevator down to the basement. The phantom of my heart skips a beat. Does she know of the Girl with No Eyes? Does she know that her daughter is down there? She must have known where her baby died, where her body was found, so why is this the first time she's visiting her? The temperature in the basement is frosty, but still, I venture from the elevator, following the Woman with No Past down the derelict corridor. She does not hesitate before pushing open the door at the end of the hall.

The Woman with No Past treads down the aisle, her footsteps making no sound on the cold concrete. She slowly approaches the corner her daughter usually haunts. The little girl isn't there. Instead, another figure stands cloaked in shadows.

I inch closer, peering through the dense darkness, wishing the emergency lights provided better lighting, something more substantial than this faint luminescence that drenches the world in crimson. The figure is short and slender. I sigh with relief when I see that it isn't the Shadow Man. It's Clark.

The Woman with No Past approaches him. Her painted grin masks her true expression. Melancholic chords of music coast through the stale air. The beginning of the same song as before. The same song as always. I look around, but as usual, there is no obvious source of the sound. The melody prompts the Woman with No Past to twirl and dance. Her ethereal body sways to the haunting rhythm.

Clark emerges from the shadows, and I get a closer look at him. Something is wrong. He has two faces. One superimposed upon the other. Under the expressionless features of a young boy, there is the face of an older man who is at least twice his age. This man is smiling in adoration at the woman who dances before him.

I don't understand what is happening. Is there a ghost *inside* Clark? The pieces of the puzzle suddenly fall into place, but something is still missing. The ritual he held, his debilitating illness, his sudden recovery. Realization dawns on me. In the demonic ritual Clark held with his friends, he'd been intending to offer up Noel as a vessel for the Shadow Man. But the ritual was interrupted. Instead of cutting Noel, Clark broke his own skin, the last step in the ritual that opened him up to a possession. His illness these past few days has been his body fighting off the possession . . . before he finally succumbed. But it isn't the Shadow Man inside him—I saw him at Alexei's séance.

Like the ghost in Clark, my eyes are transfixed by the Woman with No Past as she dances. Her limbs bend and twirl to the music, moving faster and faster as the tempo quickens. She twirls like a ballerina, her arms dipping and weaving in the darkness. I don't even notice we have company until a voice cuts through my trance.

"Mommy?" The Girl with No Eyes asks. Her head is twisted toward the Woman with No Past, her eye sockets directed at the figure in front of her. Not for the first time, I wonder if she isn't as blind as she appears to be.

The Woman with No Past's movements stop abruptly, her arms suspended in the frigid air. Her head tilts downward to face the little girl.

The Woman with No Past says nothing, but she arches her body toward the child. She extends a hand, not quite touching her, but stroking the air alongside her dead daughter's face.

Clark steps closer, and the girl's head jerks toward him.

"Daddy?" she whispers.

The man inside Clark angles his head in confirmation. Of course, I recognize him now. He's the man from the photographs the Woman with No Past had so lovingly gazed upon days ago. Photos of her husband playing the grand piano that sits unused in her apartment. His spirit never left the confines of this building after death. *He* is the source of the music that's been seeping through the building late at night. It all finally clicks into place. The spirit possessing Clark is the Woman with No Past's late husband. The father of the Girl with No Eyes.

"It's time," the Woman with No Past whispers, her voice hoarse from lack of use. She settles onto the cold cement ground, lying down, her dress fanned out around her. Her husband lies beside her. They both close their eyes at the same time. Almost instantly, the spirit steps out of Clark's body. He approaches his daughter. He extends a hand, which the Girl with No Eyes takes in hers.

They wait for what feels like hours—but could have been only minutes—before it is clear that the Woman with No Past has stopped breathing. A little while later, her spirit sits up, rising out of her body.

She smiles, a genuine expression that reaches her eyes and brings life to them. She wears the same dress, but it's far more vibrant, no longer fraying, its color a deep, royal blue. Her face is clean of the gaudy makeup, and her cheeks are flushed. She looks far more alive in death than she did at the end of her life.

She gazes down at her daughter, who has also changed. Large brown eyes peer up at her mother in adoration. She has reverted back to the sweet little girl from the photographs. She reaches out with her free hand and gently grasps her mother's.

Together, they smile. Together, they walk down the corridor. Together, they vanish into darkness, the final chords of the music fading with them.

53

The following morning, I ride up and down, up and down the elevator with the rush of worker bees, buzzing off to their hives to make honey. I don't mind as much as usual. I have a lot to think about.

Clark awoke shortly after the husband's spirit left his body. Brows furrowed in confusion, he'd gazed down at the woman lying beside him. He'd slowly climbed to his feet, swaying unsteadily. He'd hurried back to his apartment without contacting anyone about the dead body.

I saw him again this morning as he got ready for school, and he looked healthy. His face was unpainted, rosy with energy, and it seemed to reflect a renewed outlook on life. I can only hope that this lasts and that he doesn't resume his obsession with demons after the novelty of being alive has worn off.

This morning, an ambulance was called when an elderly resident entered the storage center to retrieve her Christmas decorations far earlier than the season warranted. Police surveyed the scene before the coroner took the Woman with No Past's body away. There were no obvious signs of foul play, and I suspect that the coroner will deem her death to be of natural causes. She was ready to go.

The Woman with No Past, her husband, and their daughter disappeared and left behind no trace other than a sense of calm, which had been previously lacking in the storage room. The way they left reminded me of Sabryna's walk into the light, and I know that they're in a better place. Together. I considered trying to follow them to the Afterlife, but then, I thought of Etienne. And Melody. I'm not quite done with this world yet.

It's been days since Etienne asked me for help, but I haven't been able to do anything. As usual, he ignores me when his mother is present, and my elevator never idles within range when she's at work. I think Sylvie has been taking fewer shifts and maybe even skipping work entirely since her husband began to awaken days ago. She must have realized how close she'd cut it, and she isn't willing to risk another incident. This is yet another obstacle I have to contend with if I'm hoping to reunite Etienne with his father.

Waking Raymond is just the first step. After he awakes, he'll be confused and weak, and he might not be able to reach safety before Sylvie returns home and injects him with another sedative. My best option is to convince Etienne to seek outside help—help from the *living*. He needs to find an authority figure and tell them what's happening. They'll take care of the rest. This won't be easy.

Clark was about his age when he stopped seeing the Shadow Man. What if Etienne stops seeing me right when it matters most?

The elevator rests on the second floor. I get off, meandering toward Alexei's apartment. I just need one more séance with him before he leaves.

Alexei's apartment is a mess, filled with half-packed boxes and items of clothing lying in heaps on the floor. Eclectic, supernatural-looking items are draped around the living room. If Alexei plans to make his deadline for departure by the end of this week, he had better develop a more effective packing system.

Elias is in the second bedroom with him, dumping books into boxes. This isn't part of his job description, and I suspect he agreed to help so he can snoop through Alexei's belongings. Or maybe he needs extra cash. I think it's probably a little bit of both.

Elias stifles a sigh as he seals up a box with far more packing tape than the job requires. He shoots a look at Alexei.

"A lot of changes going on in the building lately."

It's obvious that Alexei doesn't want to engage Elias in conversation, but he takes the bait. "What do you mean?"

Elias shrugs in a way that's anything but nonchalant. "Ms. Drake dies, and her brother-in-law moves in. The strange man in 504 moves out. The tragedy with the Hylands. Then Mrs. Boyden disappears . . ." Elias glances at Alexei, who doesn't say anything. "And, of course, you're leaving."

I hover a few feet away from Alexei, holding my figurative breath.

Alexei doesn't look up from his box. "Melody Boyden?" he asks in a strange voice.

"Oh, you know her?" Elias asks.

Where is this conversation going?

"Yes. Her husband is a fan of mine." Alexei seems to be moving items back and forth on the dresser and not actually packing them into the box.

Elias watches him silently. His eyes are shrewd, and he loses his usual pretense of bumbling nervousness.

Alexei continues. "She did not *disappear*. Oliver says that she left him."

Elias scoffs.

Alexei hesitates, then says, "Actually, I saw them earlier today."

"Who?"

Alexei scowls. "Who do you think? Melody and Oliver."

He saw Melody? *Alive?*

Elias looks equally surprised. "She came back?"

Alexei nods. "I just saw them for a few minutes. She was begging him to take her back. Oliver accepted her apology, and she has moved back in for a trial run."

Melody is alive! Alexei has seen her! I should be thrilled, but disappointment envelops me like a shroud. She came back. She shouldn't have come back. It isn't uncommon for battered women to return to their oppressors. Oliver was Melody's entire life for so long, and many women experience a sort of Stockholm Syndrome with their abusers. But I'd thought Melody was different. Stronger. I try to embrace the sense of relief that she is still alive, still safe. At least, for now.

"So, she's here in the building? Now?" Elias has a glint in his eye. If I hadn't known who and what he is, I would have shrugged it off as an innocent crush. Or maybe genuine eagerness to see an old friend. But there's nothing about Elias that's innocent or genuine.

Alexei nods. "Like I said, it is a trial run. There is a good chance that Oliver will kick her out, especially after what she did. Though, he did mention having to pull an all-nighter at work tonight, so it looks like their first night back together will be spent apart."

I'm beyond confused. Is it possible that Melody's child really does belong to another man? Had there been some truth to Oliver's lies? Something doesn't sit right with me. Oliver kept Melody under lock and key. How could she have had the time to have an extramarital affair? Unless it was with someone else in the building. But I've been spending a lot of time observing my fellow residents since my death, and there definitely aren't many eligible bachelors.

I shrug away the uncertainty. Whether or not Melody has been having an affair is not the problem. The problem is that she's still in grave danger for as long as she stays in this building, with Oliver.

Alexei and Elias are quiet for a while, though, I notice that neither of them is effectively packing anything.

Alexei shoots him a sidelong glance as he painstakingly labels a box. "I suppose you know all the residents of this building pretty well?"

"Better than they know themselves!" Elias retorts.

"Did you know Rachel Drake? The woman who died in the elevator?"

Is Alexei finally questioning Elias about my death? He had held that séance a week ago, and I had begun to think he had forgotten. It doesn't even matter anymore. Luke murdered me, this I know for certain. The weight returns to my chest, and I quickly shake away any thought of that betrayal.

Elias scowls. "As I said, I know everyone in the building."

Alexei watches him closely, noticing his change in demeanor. "How well did you know Rachel?"

"I knew her pretty well. Considering she was a shut-in. Why do you ask?"

Alexei shrugs. "She visited me during a séance."

Elias gapes at him. "Her ghost visited you, too?"

Alexei suddenly looks interested. "She was summoned to my séance. The real question is: *Why is she visiting you?*"

Now it's Elias' turn to shrug and look ambivalent, but I can see the vein dancing in his temple. He's much more troubled than he lets on.

Alexei continues. "I was wondering why she has not been able to move on, considering her alleged killer is behind bars."

"*Alleged* killer?"

Alexei shrugs again, and returns to slowly penning out the word "Books" on his current box.

Elias doesn't resume packing. He allows his timid expression to evaporate now that Alexei isn't watching him. He gives Alexei a cold, calculated look. "Her killer confessed to her crime. I'd say that it's an open-and-shut case."

Alexei grunts noncommittally.

Elias seems dissatisfied. "A woman was murdered. If you actually think they put the wrong person behind bars, you should say something. Others in this building could be at risk!"

Alexei looks him straight in the eye.

"It is a good thing I am moving, then."

54

atalina doesn't seem to be in a rush to get back to her old life. It's been days since Luke's confession, and she hasn't made any move to leave. I'm worried about her. Her suspension from the police force can't last forever. She might lose her job because of me. My stomach turns at the thought.

Right now, she's sprawled on the couch, eating a likely very-expired vanilla yogurt from the fridge.

"Are you trying to poison yourself?" Will grabs the yogurt from her hand.

"Give that back," she protests and swats at him.

"I would, but I'd prefer to have my girlfriend among the living," Will says.

Catalina freezes. "*Girlfriend?*"

Will rolls his eyes. "You know what I mean."

She gazes up at him. "Nope. I don't actually. Please explain."

Will shifts, suddenly uncomfortable on his perch on the bony arm of the couch. He looks down at her.

"Catalina Marquez, will you be my girlfriend?" he asks extravagantly.

Catalina's eyes widen, and she draws her hands to her gaping mouth comically. "Who, me?" She bats her eyelashes. "I thought you'd never ask!"

Will grins and sidles closer, slipping onto the couch beside her. He stops in his tracks, wincing. He sticks a hand behind the couch cushion and feels around.

He pulls out my diary.

"So, you felt it too?" Catalina is suddenly serious.

Will stares at her. "Did you put that there?"

"No, I found it there yesterday morning. I was pretty sure it wasn't there before. This couch reminds me of the Princess and the Pea, every molecule of lint can be felt through its fabric."

Will chuckles, then his gaze darkens when he realizes what he holds in his hands. "How did it get there then?"

"Maybe it was Kae's ghost." Catalina laughs abruptly. "She was really obsessed with ghosts . . . Near the end."

"Did you read it?" Will suddenly looks queasy.

Catalina nods. "All of it."

Will doesn't seem to be able to tear his eyes away from the diary. "Did she . . . describe Jay's . . ."

Concern pinches Catalina's brow. "She mentions your brother's death, finding his body, the funeral. That's how the diary ends. She didn't keep up writing after she left Ottawa."

"Were there any clues? Any mention of Copeland, or anything that could be used as evidence?"

"No, I'm so sorry." Catalina reaches out and places a hand on his knee. "She did talk about Copeland and his general creepiness, but there's nothing concrete. She mostly talked about her wedding, and then about how she thought her house was haunted. She was obsessed with the strange noises she'd heard at night, how her cat was behaving, and how she thought that Jay was becoming possessed. She thought these were all signs of a haunting." Catalina laughs humorlessly. "I guess she didn't recognize they could all be considered signs of a stalker. Even her cat's death."

Will frowns at the diary.

Catalina gently takes it from him. She cradles his head in her hands, drawing his gaze toward her.

"We can't dwell on the past forever," she says. "I think it's time to start looking forward. To the future."

55

The night is quiet. The air is tranquil. But not everyone is asleep.

Long after midnight, Elias slips from his apartment. He's dressed in black from head to toe. There's no doubt in my mind where he is heading.

I study him as my elevator brings him to the fourth floor. His eyes have a strange glint in them, and his lips are pressed into a thin smile.

He exits the elevator and creeps to the Boyden apartment. I pop into the apartment ahead of him. I've been waiting for this chance all day, ever since Alexei's confession this morning. I peer around the living room, but there's no sign of Melody. Of course there isn't. She would be in bed.

I hurry to the bedroom. The curtains are wide open on the large window overlooking the king-sized bed. Streetlights reveal a figure curled up on top of the covers. One figure. Not two.

Oliver rolls over, eyes open, and I feel as though he is staring right at me. But he can't see me. He sighs, plumps his pillow, and closes his eyes.

I race from room to room and confirm my suspicions. Melody isn't here.

The quietest of clicks sound from the front hall. Elias has unlocked the door. Realization dawns on me. Elias is here to see Melody because Alexei had told him that she is back and Oliver would be working tonight. Instead of Melody, he'll find Oliver. Oliver who isn't working late tonight. Oliver who isn't fast asleep. Oliver, whose eyes are wide open, staring at the bedroom door.

I know I should feel dread, anticipation, or something, but instead, I just feel cold. These two deserve whatever they do to each other.

Elias slips into the bedroom. His flashlight is off, but he grips it in his gloved hand.

"What are you doing here?" Oliver's voice is a low growl.

Elias jumps back, slamming into the wall. I suppose none of his victims have ever woken up during one of his many nocturnal visits.

In less than a second, Oliver is out of bed and has Elias by the throat.

"I asked you a question. What. Are. You. Doing. Here?"

Elias opens his mouth as if to respond, but instead, he swings the arm with the flashlight, driving it straight into Oliver's head with a deafening crack.

Oliver collapses to the ground.

Breathing heavily, Elias nudges him with his toe. Oliver rolls over. His eyes are still open, but they're staring at nothing.

Without hesitation, Elias crouches and feels for a pulse. Based on his cursing and the eerie lack of focus in Oliver's eyes, I assume that there was none.

Elias leaves the room. I remain.

I'm transfixed by Oliver's lifeless eyes. I know I should feel something. Guilt? At what? I couldn't have done anything to help him. Satisfaction? Maybe, especially if he murdered Melody. Especially if he murdered Melody and then coerced Alexei into covering for him.

Sweet Melody.

Now I'll never know what happened to her.

I frown down at Oliver's body. Where is his ghost? I've seen the spirit leave the body with the Woman with No Past, and that had been almost instantaneous. I move away from his body and glance toward the hall. I don't think that I want to be here when his spirit shows up.

I'm about to leave when Elias returns, his gloved hands clutching a plastic shower curtain. He lays it out on the floor beside Oliver and rolls him onto it. There's a dark pool on the hardwood floor where his head has been. That's twice in as many weeks that blood has stained this bedroom.

Elias grunts as he lifts the body over his shoulder and lumbers out of the room. He can't seriously be disposing of the body *now?*

He steps out into the empty corridor. I don't know if I should hope that someone might step out into the hallway. If they did, there is no doubt in my mind that Elias wouldn't hesitate to kill them. He didn't hesitate with Oliver. Although, he may not have struck him to kill.

My elevator door opens and Elias boards with his precious cargo. He presses the lobby, then seems to think better of it and presses 2.

On this floor, he hurries into his apartment, clearly straining under Oliver's weight. He carries the corpse into the bathroom and dumps it into the shower.

"This isn't a long-term solution," I say. "The body will start to smell. And so will you, if you can't shower." I can't help but see the humor in this. Elias will get caught, I'm sure of it.

Elias stares down at the body. His hands are shaking. His right eye has developed the most peculiar twitch. He's finally losing his cool resolve. I, too, look down into the bathtub. Oliver's blood-stained face presses against the translucent plastic shower curtain. His eyes are glassy. His mouth is twisted open in a silent scream. This was a horrible way for him to go, but I can't help but wonder if it's the same way Melody died. Did he crack her over the head? Did she die in the exact same spot as he did? This wasn't what I wanted when I recruited Alexei to find justice for Melody. I thought Oliver would be arrested, locked away in a cell with no window for the rest of his days. This isn't what I wanted.

But it will do.

56

T he following morning is deadly quiet.

There are no sirens, no police, no crime scene investigators. I know that Oliver's body has yet to be found. I pace
the lobby, my eyes glued to Elias as he hovers at his station. His
hair is combed, his suit is neatly pressed. The only sign of strain
is in his eyes. They flash back and forth, taking in everything,
shrewdly observing and calculating. He knows that he's fucked
up. It's just a matter of time before he is caught.

Unless, of course, he's already disposed of the body. I highly
doubt it. I somehow know it's still in his shower, waiting to
be taken care of. I'm watching Elias make phone calls as I am
summoned to the ninth floor.

The doors slide open, and I'm greeted by a pair of innocent green eyes. Etienne.

"*Maman* has gone to work," he murmurs. He gazes up at me expectantly.

I reach out to take his hand before I remember that I cannot touch him. Instead, I nod and follow him back to his apartment. How did he know to summon the elevator? Evidently, he's more observant than he lets on.

Once we're inside, Etienne locks the deadbolt behind us.

"Etienne," I say in a gentle voice. I don't want to frighten him. "Etienne, you need to call the police."

Etienne's eyes widen, then he shakes his head furiously. "I can't."

"Etienne, what your mother is doing is wrong. She's hurting your father. You need to call the police and an ambulance."

Etienne's eyes fill with tears, but he shakes his head adamantly. "I can't. I just want *Papa* back. He'll know what to do."

I suspected this was what he would say, but I had to try. The police are much better equipped to handle this situation than a nine-year-old boy.

Without another word, Etienne heads into the kitchen, takes the stool and reaches the top cupboard. He finds a key and then leads me to the third bedroom, which he promptly unlocks.

It's almost as though he doesn't need me. He's clearly been planning this for a while.

Etienne goes to his father's bedside and places a tiny hand on Raymond's arm. How often does Etienne do this? How often does he sneak into his father's room when his mother is at work? I glance around, but Raymond's ghost isn't here. I consider this for a moment. Does that mean he's back in his body, albeit temporarily? Or is he elsewhere in the building, haunting other rooms or corridors?

"Do you know how to wake him?" Etienne's voice is barely a whisper.

"Yes," I say, resigned. If he won't call the police now, maybe he will when his father wakes and is choking on his intubation tube. I bring Etienne to the medicine cabinet, which he unlocks with another hidden key.

"This is the medicine that your mother uses to keep him unconscious." I point to the vials of pentobarbital. I scan the labels of the other vials, and I'm disappointed to see that Sylvie doesn't have anything that can reverse the drug's effects. But she does have saline.

I instruct Etienne on how to dump the contents of the first vial of pentobarbital and replace it with saline. He continues this process with the next three vials, until the front row of containers is completely innocuous. No matter which vial Sylvie selects, she'll be giving her husband a solution of salt water, which will allow for the pentobarbital to leave his system.

I explain to Etienne what to do when his father begins to wake, which will likely be sometime in the middle of the night. He nods studiously, as if committing my words to memory. After I finish, he returns to his father's bedside. He strokes his father's matted hair and whispers assurances into his ear.

57

lexei is leaving tomorrow.

My last permanent connection to the real world will soon be gone. I pace his apartment restlessly as the movers load boxes onto a dolly. They trek up and down the hall with all of the medium's worldly possessions. One of the movers must have been sensitive to my presence because I noticed the little hairs on his arms would rise every time I came near. He feigned a headache and was quickly replaced by another mover who was just as oblivious to my being there as everyone else. I know the fact that someone was sensitive to me should give me some comfort, but he's long gone, and I don't know when another like him will come.

Now, I stand in this cavernous living room. The black walls and furniture had made the room seem much smaller, but now that it's nearly empty, I understand that that was just an illusion. Alexei supervises as two men count to three, then lift his sofa, pivoting it toward the open front door. He curses at another mover when he nearly knocks over an antique vase which is apparently "irreplaceable."

I had had high hopes for Alexei, but he never followed through with anything. He didn't look into my death. He didn't really look into Melody's disappearance. I still don't understand how Oliver coerced him into lying to Elias. I won't wonder for much longer. With his back to the front door, Alexei takes inventory of the remaining boxes.

His long, spider-like fingers reach into his jean pocket and pull out his cell phone. He dials a number and waits as it rings. He reaches voicemail.

"Oliver, it is Alexei."

Why is he calling Oliver? Is this his chance? Is he going to finally tell Oliver his suspicions? Tell him that he's going to the police and that he knows that Melody never went to "Vermont" to be with the father of her unborn child? None of this matters anymore because Oliver is dead. Yet still, I need to know what happened to Melody. Did she suffer? Is she finally at peace? These are questions a simple phone message won't answer.

"I am just about all packed up," Alexei says. "I am having most of my boxes shipped. I will depart to Vegas first thing in the morning."

There's a long pause, and I think that Alexei is ready to hang up. "I just wanted to thank you for reaching out to your contact. This show will be perfect for me—a new beginning, so to speak."

My blood runs cold.

"I hope you recognize that I owe you nothing. We are even. My silence is your repayment. This is the last you will hear from me, and I do not expect to hear from you either. Ever."

A chill races down my spine, followed by a fierce heat. Alexei had a price. A job in exchange for his silence. The flames of rage lick up inside my soul. Melody is dead, and the one person who noticed her disappearance has been paid to keep quiet. The vase quivers, then topples to the ground, shattering into thousands of "irreplaceable" pieces. Alexei stares right at me. He finally sees.

58

I sit in my kitchen and pretend that I am still alive. I imagine that I have a pot of tea brewing on the stove and that I'll get up any minute to pour myself a steaming hot cup, which I'll enjoy while gazing out the window at the silent street below. It's a quarter past midnight, and the street is quiet despite the busy neighborhood.

Alexei departed shortly after my outburst in his apartment. He left the movers to finish, found Elias, and demanded he find him a hotel nearby. I didn't try to stop him. I didn't try to communicate with him, either, because I knew it would be pointless. Alexei is a waste of clean air, and I'm glad that he's no longer living in my final resting place.

A chime sounds from Catalina's laptop. I peer into the living room, where Catalina has fallen asleep on the couch. Will didn't wake her when he came in to ask her to come to the bedroom with him. He stood watching her, then retrieved my folded afghan from the ottoman and put it over her gently before he went to bed.

The chime sounds again, a little louder this time, rousing her from her slumber. She looks around warily before a smile crosses her face as she takes in the blanket draped over her. She sits up, stretching, her hand rubbing her back as she grimaces. A flicker of concern crosses her features as her eyes skim the laptop screen. Her breath catches.

Curious, I rise to see what kind of email she could have received in the middle of the night when she's suspended from her job. I peer over her shoulder. "Sorry this is so late, but it took me a while to dig it up . . ."

I don't get to read more, as a loud creak sounds from my bedroom. Catalina tenses, closes the laptop, and lies back down. I frown down at her.

I'm so singularly focused on Catalina that I barely notice Will creeping through the living room toward the front door. He slips out into the hall. I turn to Catalina, who's still lying on the couch, frozen, but her eyes are wide open. I move closer to her, but the elevator pulls me away.

Will exits the elevator on the second floor and makes his way to apartment 201. Elias's apartment. His knock is so quiet that I don't expect Elias to hear it, but he does and opens the door. I dart in ahead of him, peeking into the bathroom. His roommate is still there.

I return to the foyer in time to hear Elias greet Will.

"Mr. Archer, what can I do for you at this late hour?" Elias pretends not to be ruffled, but he's tense, his hand gripping the doorknob with white-knuckled fingers. I notice he's fully dressed. Had he intended to deal with the corpse decomposing in his shower tonight?

"May I come in for a minute, Elias?" Will asks.

I can tell Elias wants to say no, but instead, he nods and holds the door open.

"Ask to use the washroom," I say to Will. I immediately regret it. Elias would kill him, there isn't a doubt in my mind. He has nothing left to lose. Fortunately, Will doesn't seem to hear my suggestion.

Instead, he scans the sparsely decorated foyer. He turns to face Elias, who has closed the door behind him.

"There's something about you . . ." Will begins, "that I just couldn't quite place my finger on when we first met. There's just something off about you. Then, a week ago, I saw you sneaking out of Samira Narang's apartment. I wasn't sure exactly what I saw, so I snuck into the stairwell before you could notice me."

It was Will whom I'd spotted that night. I turn to Elias to see his reaction. The short, stout man stands rigid in the doorway. His jaw is clenched, but his face is otherwise neutral.

Will continues. "I racked my brain for possible reasons why you were in her apartment. You weren't having an affair, because, well, look at you. She's out of your league."

Elias takes a step closer, but Will doesn't seem to notice.

"Then, suddenly, Rachel's diary appears. I had searched her entire apartment for that thing. I looked on her bookshelves, I went through all her boxes and filing cabinets. I even checked for secret compartments in her furniture. I all but tore the place apart. And then, suddenly, the diary appears under a couch cushion? Did you honestly think I wouldn't notice when it magically reappeared?" Will raises an eyebrow.

Elias shrugs. "I'm not sure what you're implying."

"Oh, I'm sorry. I thought I was being perfectly clear. Let me rephrase. I know you sneak into apartments when women are asleep. I know you took Rachel's diary. I know you returned it. What I would like to know is if you read it."

I blink. Why would he care if Elias read my diary?

Elias looks like he can't decide if he's surprised or aggravated. "Didn't you come here to investigate Rachel's death? I'm not sure if you missed the headline, but her killer has already been caught. You should leave well enough alone and go back to your former life."

Will's patience seems to be wearing thin. "I need to know—did you read the diary?"

Elias licks his lips. "I never saw the damn thing."

In two quick steps, Will is on him. He grabs the collar of Elias' shirt with balled fists and slams him against the wall.

"Did you read the diary?" he repeats, fury painted across his face. Before, Will was so much like Jay, but now, there is barely any resemblance.

Elias' cheeks redden, but he doesn't fight back. "Yes."

"What was in it?"

"Nothing of interest," Elias wheezes. "It should have been called *Diary of a Mad White Woman*. She was delusional. She was convinced that there was a ghost in her house. That her cat had supernatural powers. That her husband wasn't her—" Elias gasps.

A cold glint flashes across Will's eyes. He lets go of Elias, who drops back to the ground, gasping for air. When he's breathing normally, he looks up at Will, his expression a mix of terror and fascination. "You—*you* were the ghost haunting their house."

What?

Will sighs. At first, he looks disappointed, but then a grim smile stretches across his face.

In one quick movement, Elias grabs the dish that holds the keys from the little table in the foyer and swings it around, but Will easily deflects it.

It falls to the floor where it shatters.

"Really?" Will smirks. He swings and punches Elias, who crumples to the ground. Will grabs the flashlight from the hall table. He is about to crack open Elias' skull—a shocking parallel to last night's events—when the door bursts open.

"Don't move!" Catalina shouts.

Will stops, arm hanging mid-air. He stares at Catalina who holds a gun pointed at his chest.

"Oh, thank God you're here!" he says. "Elias just attacked me! I caught him sneaking into an apartment the other day, and I came here to confront him—"

"Save the lies, Will." Catalina's expression is hard, but her eyes are screaming. "I knew you were acting strange after I found the diary. You were so worried when I said I read all of it. And then, I found this." She reaches into her pocket with one hand, the other one still training the gun on Will's chest.

She retrieves a bottle of pills and tosses them at Will.

He catches the bottle but doesn't move his gaze from Catalina's.

"This prescription bottle doesn't have your name on it. You've been stealing or buying black-market narcotics."

Will shrugs. "I'm an addict, you got me there."

Catalina nods slowly. "I got an email right before you snuck out tonight. The police report from the crash. You told me that Jay had been driving, that you took the fall for him."

Will wears a contemplative look on his face, but he doesn't say anything.

"It couldn't have been Jay. The police questioned him, and he had a rock solid alibi. He was out of the province visiting universities with your father the night you killed his girlfriend."

Will grimaces. "It was an accident."

"You're under arrest."

"For what? For wanting what I couldn't have? For wanting something that belonged to my brother?" Will laughs. "I've already done the time. And then some."

"No," Catalina says. Her voice trembles ever so slightly. "You're under arrest for the murder of your brother."

The planet seems to shift on its axis. My eyes lose focus, and I struggle to breathe. *Will* murdered Jay? The implications of this revelation crash over me all at once. I've spent the last two years hiding from a man that had nothing to do with my husband's death. I uprooted my entire life, said goodbye to lifelong friends, hid myself away for two entire years. And now, the real monster has been living in my home, sleeping with my *best friend,* and I had no idea.

Will's eyebrows rise. "That's a wild accusation."

Catalina continues. "I heard you sneak out tonight, so I followed you. I heard everything through the door."

"Everything?"

"Everything."

"It isn't polite to eavesdrop," Will says, his tone shifting playfully. "And whatever you read in the diary or think you heard through the door, it's nothing but wild theories based on the ramblings of a crazy woman who thought her house was haunted."

Catalina's hands shake almost imperceptibly.

Will steps toward her, arms extended in a non-threatening manner.

"Step back!"

Will smiles. He takes another step.

Catalina cocks her gun, pointing it at his head.

Will stops moving. He hovers several feet away from her, and runs a hand through his hair.

"Why did you kill him?"

"He deserved it," he replies. "He was not the Mr. Nice Guy everyone thought he was."

"But you are? I'm sure you had good reason to do what you did. Help me understand, Will."

Relief washes over me as I realize what Catalina is doing. It's police procedure 101. She is trying to establish rapport with him, to distract him so she can find an opening to overpower and arrest him.

He hesitates. I can tell he wants to believe that he can bring Catalina onto his side.

"I needed money—a lot of it. I asked Jay, but he flat out refused me. He basically said he didn't give a fuck. I knew he'd just gotten married, although, I wasn't even invited to the wedding. He didn't want me anywhere near his new bride. So, I paid them little late night visits. His wife—your best friend—freaked out, convinced that there was a poltergeist in their home. Jay figured out the truth pretty quickly. He gave me some cash and told me to get lost."

"That must have been painful for you."

Will startles, then smiles.

"It was, but it's not that easy to get rid of me. I started dropping by the house more often and began moving things, making noises. It was quite amusing because his whiny wife would freak out over the smallest things. One day, I accidentally ran into her. She thought I was him. She had no idea that I wasn't the man that she vowed to spend the rest of her life with." He chuckles. "How horrible is that? Then, of course, she assumed that Jay was behaving strangely and might be possessed because he didn't remember some of the conversations he supposedly had with her."

Will takes an almost imperceptible step forward. Catalina doesn't seem to notice. Her eyes are hard, and her hands are gripping the gun so tightly, I'm worried she'll accidentally pull the trigger. No, not worried. I'm hoping she will.

Will's tone changes. He's no longer pleading with her. He's taunting her. "Then I started having . . . fun. I mean, I got Jay's marriage disintegrating mere *months* after they exchanged vows. Neither of them were sleeping well, and, well, let's just say his wife wasn't as good in bed as you are." Will winks.

The floor nearly falls out from under me. This can't be true. I would have noticed. I should have noticed. Will looks and acts a lot like Jay but enough that even *I* couldn't distinguish between them? My stomach roils with nausea.

Catalina looks like she's going to be physically ill. Will takes another step forward, and still, she doesn't stop him.

"But when Jay found out how far I had taken things, he went ballistic. He screamed and raved, told me he was going to go to the police. Get me arrested. I couldn't go back to prison. I explained this to Jay, but he just laughed in my face. He seemed to think I *deserved* whatever I had coming to me! His own brother! He called me names, he accused me of being a murderer." Will shakes his head in disbelief.

"So, you killed him," Catalina says quietly.

Will's eyes flash in amusement. "Is that a question?"

Elias lets out a groan. Catalina glances down at him which is all that Will needs. He lunges across the short distance left between them, knocking the gun from Catalina's hand and slamming her to the ground. She gasps, the breath knocked out of her. Will climbs on top of her. His strong hands grip her throat and tighten. Catalina tries to kick him off, but he's too strong, too heavy, too determined.

Elias is still only half-conscious. Catalina's gun lies on the ground a few feet from her grasp.

"I suppose I would have had to kill you anyway. You read the diary. You found my pills. You were looking into my past. I knew you'd figure it out eventually." Will is barely even out of breath as he tightens his grip around her neck.

Catalina twists her head and spots the gun lying on the ground. She reaches out, fingers clawing toward it. It's just a few inches away from her outstretched hand.

My attention is grabbed by movement just beyond Will's hunched form. The shadows are twisting and joining. They contort and build to create a large, hulking form. The Shadow Man.

I remember what Alexei said—that I should avoid this entity at all costs. Panic rises, and the need to escape overwhelms me. I take a step back, the weight of fear crushing my chest and suffocating me. The Shadow Man cocks his head, seeming to leer at me from his position only three feet away. He ignores Catalina and Will and slides toward me. *I* am who he's come for tonight. Pressure builds inside me. The need to run has never been stronger.

Catalina lets out a rasping cough, tearing my focus back to her. Her face is turning blue, and her feeble hands slap weakly against Will's powerful chest.

I push aside all feelings of fear, of pain, of inadequacy, even as the Shadow Man closes in on me. I take a deep breath. In. And out. I look at the gun and focus intently. I think of Catalina, of how she was there for me when Jay died. I think of how selfless and brave she is. How in control she was when Lon Chaney, Jr. ate the Scrabble tiles. Whenever I tell that story, I usually focus on Jay—because that's when I first met him. But Catalina is the one who sat with me in the emergency room. She's the one who clutched my hand, saying that everything would be all right. She switched around her shifts at the precinct when Lon Chaney, Jr. went missing.

When Jay died, she searched for his killer, and when justice wasn't an option, she risked her job to make sure I would be safe. And she put her job on the line—her life even—to come to Thorwald Place to solve my murder. In the corner of my eye, the Shadow Man slithers closer. I ignore him. I pour all my determination, all my strength, all my power, all my love into one absolute movement.

The flames erupt from inside my soul, burning outward and reaching toward the gun. I give a push, a ripple of fire, and the gun slides across the floor, straight into Catalina's open hand.

She grips it tightly, raises her arm, and presses the barrel against Will's temple. His eyes burn with delirious rage, but before she has to shoot him, he releases her from his viselike grip and stumbles backward.

The Shadow Man is closer than ever before. He studies me. I can sense the disappointment oozing from him. My flames burn harder. Flames fueled by love, not hate or fear or pain. He lets out a growl of frustration. He jerks backward, his body disintegrating. His collected shadows tear apart, falling back into the darkest corners. He no longer has power here. He no longer has power over me.

He's gone for now, but certainly not for good.

59

feel lighter now. Drifting down the hall in Elias' apartment, I pass clusters of policemen as they hunt for evidence. They pull apart his secret bedroom, photographing the walls plastered with the faces of the unsuspecting.

Not only did Catalina stop Will last night, but she also called in reinforcements who have brought Elias to justice. I couldn't tell if the police were more excited when they found his shrine filled with pictures and mementos or the corpse rotting in the shower. Elias won't be working as a concierge ever again. He will be put away for a long time, trapped in a place where the locks aren't so easy to ignore.

Catalina told the police everything.

She told them how Will haunted my house, nearly drove me insane, and ultimately killed my husband. She told them that he came here to search for the evidence implicating him in his own brother's murder. Catalina seemed resolute. Afterward, she returned to my apartment. She packed up her belongings. Before leaving, she returned to the couch and retrieved my diary. Clutching it to her heart, she left, closing the door on the past.

Bystanders gather in the lobby. They aren't sure which is more exciting, Will's arrest for a past murder or Elias' unexpected perversions. All the residents are enthusiastic, hoping that he had selected them for his clandestine midnight visits. I want to slap them in their keen faces, tell them that this isn't a privilege but a violation.

Oliver's murder is already all over the news. He was a prominent software engineer. The media is painting him as a hero—but they have no idea who he truly was. What he did.

My elevator rises to the ninth floor, bringing Samira Narang back up to her apartment. She is visibly shaken. Someone must have told her that she was one of Elias' favorites. What would have happened if she had been a light sleeper? If she had opened her eyes while Elias was there? Would she have faced the same fate as Oliver?

I leave her to her privacy; she has been violated enough. Instead, I enter apartment 907. A lunch bag and a Batman backpack are placed by the front door. I move farther into the apartment. Etienne stands at the stove, cooking scrambled eggs. Behind him, Raymond sits in a wheelchair at the kitchen table. He is gaunt—his cheekbones are razor sharp, and his skin hangs limply on his atrophied arms. He was only in a coma for five months, but the effect on his body will take longer to recover from. His eyes seem cloudy, as though the fog from the pentobarbital has yet to leave his system, though, there's a small smile dancing upon his lips as he watches his son stir the eggs with a large wooden spoon.

There is a spark in Etienne's eye and a color to his cheeks that was absent when he was under his mother's care. Etienne brings the frying pan to the kitchen table, piling a heap of eggs onto the plate in front of his father. I'm glad to see that our plan worked, that Raymond is awake, but I can't help but wonder what happened to Sylvie. I doubt she left of her own accord. I suspect the police may have paid another, quieter visit to remove this particularly unique breed of monster from her home.

"Where is your mother, Etienne?" I ask.

He doesn't answer me.

"Etienne?" I repeat.

He doesn't react. I know he isn't ignoring me, but instead, he has grown up, lost his innocence, and he can no longer sense me. I don't know how to feel about this, but it doesn't matter. I won't be here much longer.

I hear a sound from the third bedroom, and I drift over. The door stands open, revealing the darkened room beyond the doorway. The hospital bed remains in place; the IV bag and heart monitor are untouched.

Something catches my eye in the corner of the room. On the ceiling. The stain that had once mesmerized Raymond's spirit is still there. It's much smaller, about the size of a quarter, but it's still pulsating. Shifting.

Growing.

I resist the urge to move closer. I turn to leave. Then I realize. The hospital bed isn't empty. It has an occupant. A slender woman, with blonde hair and pallid skin, is hooked up to the tubes and wires.

Etienne appears in the doorway, his hands clasped tightly on the handles of his father's wheelchair.

"When will her punishment be over?" Etienne repeats the question he asked his mother over a week ago.

"When we say it is," Raymond responds. A shadow of doubt crosses Etienne's face before he gives his father a tentative smile and closes the door.

60

stare at the closed door. How will Raymond explain away his miraculous return from the dead? What will he tell people who ask about Sylvie's whereabouts? How long does he think he can get away with this? There are too many questions for him to answer.

He won't get away with it. He can't.

Despite the horror of knowing what Etienne and his father have done, my body is even lighter now. I feel like a dandelion blowing in the wind. Like a single gust of air would send me into the heavens. Is this what Sabryna felt when her husband was arrested for her murder? Is this how the Woman with No Past and her family felt when it was their time to move on? My elevator brings me to the lobby, where a small crowd of residents has gathered, gossiping about everything that has happened these last few weeks. I float past them. There is nothing left for me here.

I feel a tug on my soul. It's different from the call of the elevator or the summon of a séance. It's gentle but persistent. Light coalesces at the far end of the corridor, just past the guest suite. It shifts and expands, calling to me. Whispering my name. My *real* name.

I'm no longer afraid of the outside, afraid of the unknown. Nothing can hurt me anymore. My time here is over, and I'm yearning to see what comes next. I'm almost ready to move on. There's just one thing holding me back.

I step forward.

The light radiates heat like the sun. I close my eyes, basking in its warmth. Still, I hesitate, glancing back. A woman stands by my elevator—her hand placed gently on its closed doors. She wears a dark coat with the hood pulled tightly over her head, framing her angelic face.

I catch a glimpse of a distended belly and familiar wide-set eyes, and hope fills my soul. She gazes through the crowd, and her eyes lock on mine. I can hear her whisper over the gentle hum of the crowd. "Rachel."

My breath catches as she glides toward me. Her brows furrow in confusion, then understanding, then happiness.

"Melody," I gasp. "You can see me?" My eyes linger on her pregnant belly. The blood of an innocent. Her baby's blood courses through her veins. I shake my head, already having my answer. "You're alive," I say instead, with a smile.

She smiles back.

"There was so much blood." I remember the sight of Oliver cleaning up in the bathroom. It feels like a lifetime ago.

Melody nods, her smile fading only slightly. "I could have died that night. When I finally awoke, he was asleep on the bed beside me. I got up, careful not to wake him. I left the apartment with nothing but the shoes on my feet. I went to the hospital, then the shelter farthest from my home. Like you told me."

Warmth washes over me. I smile at her.

"Thank you, Rachel," Melody says. "For watching over me."

The tug becomes more insistent. My attention is drawn back toward the long corridor. The glimmering light.

She gives me a final, contented smile before slipping through the crowd toward the exit. The knowledge that I played a small part in her escape fills me with peace. I watch Melody step into the sunshine, ready to embark on the first chapter of her new life.

The tug grows more demanding. I turn back toward the corridor. The light has grown larger and brighter and warmer than it was moments ago. A cool summer breeze caresses me and rustles my hair. The aroma of freshly-baked butter pecan cookies envelops me. I finally feel safe. Loved.

A silhouette steps into the light. I slowly drift toward him, savoring every moment. An arm extends, a hand beckons. I'm greeted with a familiar smile, tousled hair, sparkling eyes.

I take his hand and join him in the light.

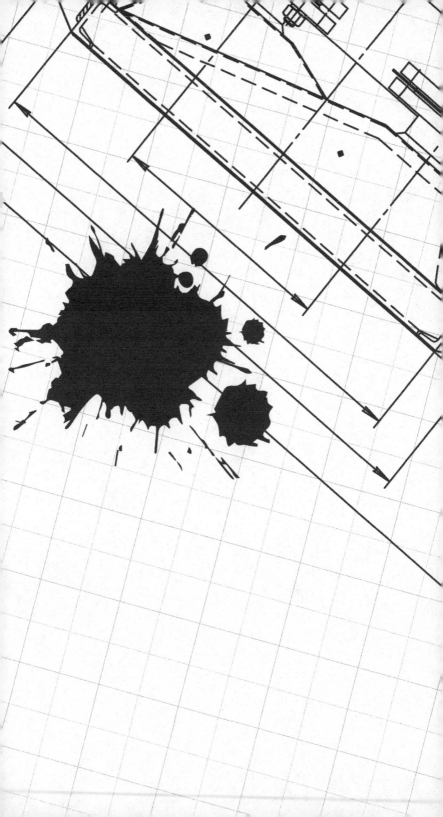

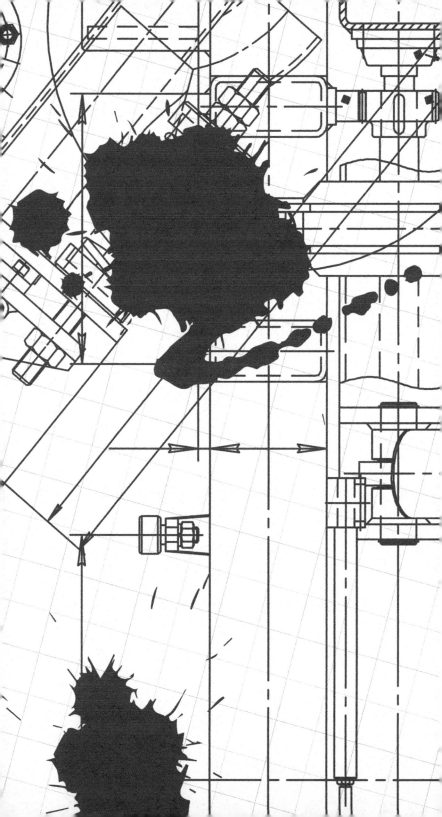

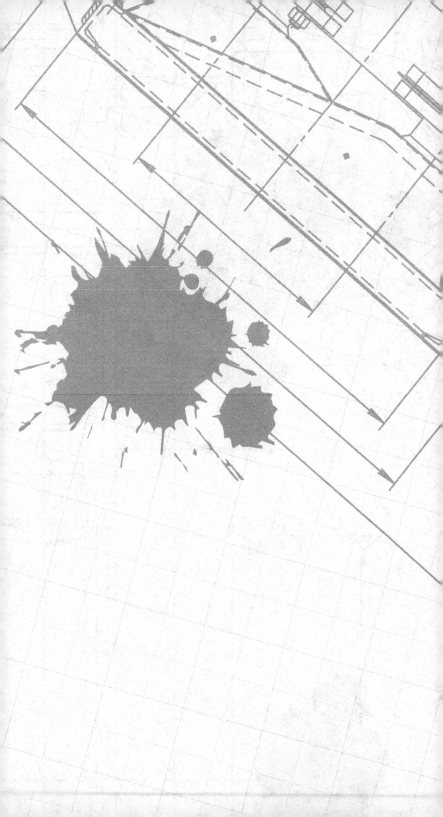

For Further Discussion

1. What did you like best about this story?

2. What are the feelings this story evokes in you?

3. Which one of the characters do you identify with? Why?

4. Did any of the characters remind you of anyone you know?

5. Do you believe in ghosts?

6. Share your favorite quote from this book. Why did this quote stand out?

7. The novel seems to suggest that all too often we don't know our neighbors. Do you agree? Do you consider this a problem?

8. Which ideas do you think Helen Power, the author of this book, wanted to address with this novel?

9. If you could ask Helen Power one question, what would it be?

10. If you were making a movie of this novel, who would you cast?

Acknowledgments

There are so many people that I want to thank for their part—big or small—in bringing *The Ghosts of Thorwald Place* from a creepy dream that I once had into a full-fledged nightmare.

First of all, thank you to my incredibly talented editor, Helga Schier. Your passion for the project, dedication, and expert guidance has transformed this novel into the best it could be. It was a privilege to work with you.

Maryann Appel designed the stunning and ethereal cover for this book. Thank you for creating a cover that has captured the essence of Thorwald Place and the twisted stories that happen behind its doors.

I want to thank the entire CamCat team for their enthusiasm and hard work. Without them, this book would never have been published.

Thank you to my mom for her unwavering support and for fostering my love of reading and writing from an early age. She's always the first to devour my stories, and she never fails to ask the difficult questions, like "Why did this character do that?" or "Where did I go wrong that made you so twisted?" Thank you also to my dad, who's not a reader, but said he'd read this manuscript and instead accidentally read a different one of mine that my mom had saved on her computer. Now that this one is published, hopefully he won't make that mistake again.

To my good friends Grace Snudden, Amanda Wiley, and my lovely sister, Alexandra—thank you for beta-reading an early draft of the story and giving me your invaluable advice and thoughts!

The creators of National Novel Writing Month have created the absolutely perfect circumstances for a challenge-oriented, goal-driven person like me to write this novel (and another new one every year!) Thank you to everyone who's worked to keep NaNoWriMo the beast that it is—from the authors who give pep talks to whoever manages the social media and comes up with writing prompts. The dinner party scene with Sylvie and Etienne was inspired by a Twitter prompt (write an awkward dinner party), and it's one of my favorite parts of the novel.

To the founders of #PitMad on Twitter—thank you for providing an awesome mechanism for newbie authors to interact directly with publishers and agents. It's through this innovative program that *The Ghosts of Thorwald Place* found a home to haunt with CamCat Books.

Thank you to my close friends and writing buddies— Amanda Wheatley, Tori Levang—for letting me bug you non-stop about my writing every single November (and often in the months in between).

To my friend Lauren—who was the first person outside of my family that I told my story idea to. Thank you for giving me the courage to write it by saying "I would read that!" Now you have to.

To my writing group and fellow writer friends in Windsor— Alison, Sebastien, Celia, Cindy, Lexie—I miss you guys! Thank you for providing the perfect outlet to rant about our writing projects over drinks and soggy burgers.

I'd also like to give a shout out to my Uncle Alek for being my biggest cheerleader (minus the pompoms), and for dedicating a special spot on your coffee table for my stories. To my Aunt Antoinette: Thank you for your support all these years. I hope you found this story "Kool."

To my Instagram and Twitter friends—thanks for following and supporting me through this process as I posted about it nonstop. To those who followed me before I began this journey—thanks for sticking with me while I shifted from posting incessantly about my reading to posting incessantly about my reading *and* writing.

And, last but not least, thank you to you, the reader who made it all the way through the acknowledgments, for giving this genre-blending ghost story a chance.

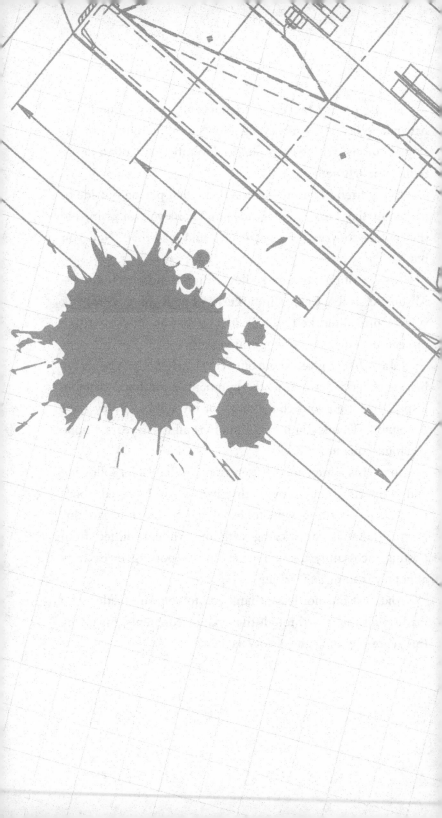

About the Author

H elen Power's very first story featured a vampire that liked to stab unsuspecting princesses with needles, despite having a perfectly functional set of fangs. Even though she was only seven when she wrote this story, this massive plot hole has haunted her to this day. Since then, she has had several short story publications, including ones in *Suspense Magazine*, *Hinnom Magazine*, and Dark Helix Press's Canada 150 anthology, *Futuristic Canada*. Her stories range from comedy to horror, with just a hint of dystopia in between. *The Ghosts of Thorwald Place*, a supernatural thriller, is her first novel.

She's an academic librarian living in Saskatoon, Canada. Her education is all over the map. She has degrees in forensic science, environmental studies, and library science collecting dust in the corner of her closet. This eclectic background has helped with both her job and with her writing, though she rarely has to conduct criminal investigations in her role at the library.

She is an avid reader of all genres and publishes book reviews weekly. In her spare time, she haunts deserted cemeteries, loses her heart to dashing thieves, and cracks tough cases, all from the comfort of her reading nook.

If you've enjoyed

Helen Power's *The Ghosts of Thorwald Place*,

you'll enjoy

Michael Bradley's *Dead Air.*

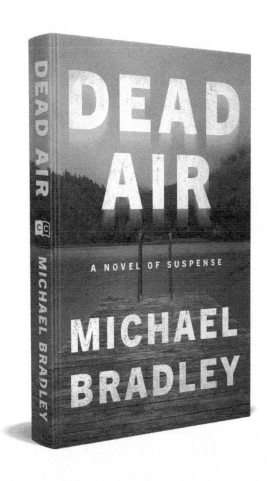

Chapter One

She'd been found out. There was no other explanation.

On any other night, Kaitlyn Ashe would relish the breathtaking view of the Philadelphia cityscape. The twinkle of white streetlights, red, yellow, and green traffic lights, and the white and red hues from car lights on the streets below looked like a swirling star field, constantly changing as if at the whim of a fickle god. From the twentieth-floor broadcast studio, she could look down upon Center City, could see as far east as the Walt Whitman Bridge and across the Delaware River to the distant lights of Camden, New Jersey. Yes, every other night, this view was mesmerizing. But not tonight. Tonight, Kaitlyn Ashe trembled at the thought that someone out there knew her, knew her secret, and was making damn sure she didn't forget it. The past had come a step closer each time another letter arrived. Her fingers tightened their grasp on the latest, a crumpled paper creased with crisscrossed lines and folds. It was a cliché. The mysterious correspondences consisted of letters and phrases torn from newspapers and magazines, crudely pasted onto plain paper. Always the same message, always the same signature.

Behind her, music played softly. She turned away from the window and moved around the L-shaped counter in the middle of the room to slide onto the tall stool behind the control console. Kaitlyn leaned forward, glancing at the needles on the VU meters that jumped and pulsed to the music's beat. She touched one of the ten slider controls and adjusted the volume to remove some mild distortion.

Kaitlyn watched the onscreen clock count down to the end of the current song. Fifteen seconds to go. She slid the headphones over her ears and drew the broadcast microphone to her mouth. She tapped the green button on the console and pushed the leftmost slider upward.

Kaitlyn leaned into the microphone. "Taking things back to 2005 with Lifehouse on WPLX. That was 'You and Me,' going out to Jamie from Kristin, Tiffany from Steve, and to Tommy—Jackie still loves you." She glanced again at the clock in the upper corner of the computer screen. "It's ten past ten. I'm Kaitlyn Ashe with Love Songs at Ten. 888-555-WPLX is the number to get your dedication in tonight. I've got Adele lined up, as well as John Legend on the way next."

Her fingers darted over the control console, tapping buttons and moving sliders. Kaitlyn took the headphones off. As a commercial for Ambrosia—her favorite seafood restaurant in downtown Philadelphia—played, she stared at the crinkled letter that rested beside the console. She read it once again beneath the dim studio lights. Her eyes focused on the name at the bottom. The Shallows. She shivered. Who knew? And how much did they know?

Kaitlyn slipped a green Bic lighter from her pocket, lit the edge of the letter, and pinched the corner as the flames swept up the paper. She'd stolen the lighter from Kevin O'Neill's desk. She knew the midday DJ would never miss it. He had half a dozen more where that one came from.

She dropped the paper into the empty wastebasket, and watched the fire dwindle into nothingness, leaving behind blackened flakes. A faint trace of smoke hung in the air, then dissipated quickly. She wrung her hands and sighed. There'd be another waiting in her station mailbox tomorrow, just like the four others that she'd received, one each day this week. She was certain of it.

The flash of green lights caught her eye, and she looked down at the studio telephone. All four lines were lit up. She hesitated for a moment, then tapped the first line. "WPLX, do you have a dedication?"

"Yeah, I'd like to dedicate my weekend to kissing your body from head to toe." The smoky voice echoed through the darkened studio.

Kaitlyn laughed, and felt her face become warm with embarrassment. "Brad!"

"How goes it, babe? Having a good night?"

She forced a smile, trying to sound upbeat, just as she'd learned in her voice-over classes. "It's not too bad."

"What's wrong?"

She cursed under her breath. She never could hide things from Brad. "I got another letter today."

The line was silent for a moment. "Same message?"

She glanced at the computer, then back at the phone. "Yeah. Exactly the same."

"You should call the police."

It was the same suggestion he had made a month ago, when the letters started arriving on a weekly basis. With this week's sudden volley of letters, he had taken to repeating his advice nightly. Kaitlyn had shrugged it off as just some crank. "You get those in this business," she'd told him.

"Still no idea who sends these letters? Or what they are about?"

She hesitated for a second before replying. "No idea," she lied.

"You need to tell someone. If not the police, at least tell Scott."

Kaitlyn frowned at his remark. The last thing she wanted to do was tell her program director Scott Mackay about the letters. His overly protective nature would mean police involvement for certain. "I can't tell Scott. He'd place an armed guard on the studio door."

Brad laughed. "Would that be so bad?"

"There's no point. It's probably some infatuated teenager." She knew how ridiculous the words sounded even as they escaped her lips. No teenage listener would know about the Shallows.

"Do me a favor—watch yourself tonight when you go home."

CamCat
Books

CamCatBooks   @CamCatBooks   @CamCat_Books